BORN SINNER

SE 7 EN SINNERS

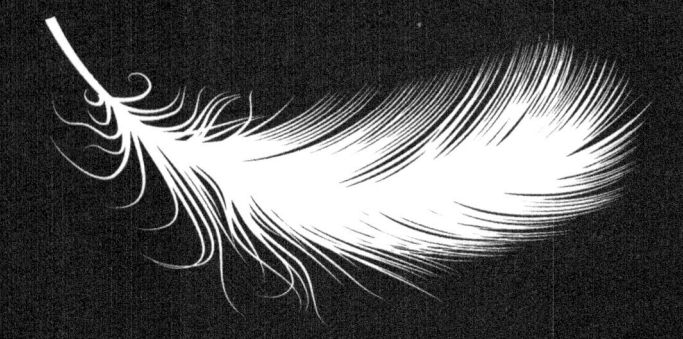

S.L. JENNINGS

Born Sinner
Copyright © 2016 by S.L. Jennings.

ISBN-13: 978-1536961119
ISBN-10: 1536961116

All rights reserved. Without limiting the rights under copyright reserved above, no part of this publication may be reproduced, stored in or introduced into retrieval system, or transmitted, in any form, or by any means (electronic, mechanical, photocopying, recording, or otherwise) without the prior written permission of both the copyright owner and the above publisher of this book.

This is a work of fiction. Names, characters, places, brands, media, and incidents are either the products of the author's imagination or are used fictitiously. The author acknowledges the trademarked status and trademark owners of various products referenced in this work of fiction, which have been used without permission. The publication/use of these trademarks is not authorized, associated with, or sponsored by the trademark owners.

ISBN-13: 978-1536961119
ISBN-10: 1536961116

Editor: Tracey Buckalew
Proofreader: Kara Hildebrand
Cover Designer: Hang Le
Photographer: Tess Farnsworth
Model: Tyson Holley
Creative: Maud Artistry
Formatting: Champagne Formats

BORN SINNER

PROLOGUE

I DIDN'T CRY THE FIRST TIME IT HAPPENED. I SHOULD have, but I didn't.

He hadn't deserved my tears.

That's what I've held onto every day since—even when I didn't believe it.

He was a mean boy that always did bad things to me. He looked under my skirt while pretending to pick up a pencil. He cornered me on my way to the girl's bathroom. He drew lewd pictures and stuffed them in my backpack for me to find.

He'd wanted to hurt me. He deserved what he got.

I didn't cry when he'd lured me from the playground, threatening to punch me if I didn't go.

I didn't cry when he'd tried to unbutton my shirt.

I didn't cry when he'd put my hand down the front of his jeans.

And I didn't cry when I'd said the words.

The words that had sent him walking out into the street into oncoming traffic, just as a yellow school bus raced by.

"Turn around. Walk."

I should've known then I was doomed. A good girl would've cried.

ONE

I T'S COLD TONIGHT, BUT NOT JUST ANY KIND OF COLD. The kind of cold that seeps into your pores and leaves a dusting of frost on your bones. The kind that chills your blood, making it congeal in your stiffening veins.

I've walked the same route to work every night, saying silent prayers for safety. Dope dealers and prostitutes scurry from the flickering harshness of broken streetlights like cockroaches, dodging undercover cops and the prying eyes of passersby. No one speaks to each other unless they want something, and even then, they settle for swift words in clipped tones. I'm invisible here. No one wants anything from me. And even if they did, I have nothing to give.

"Watch it, bitch," an asshole in an ugly green parka barks as he nearly mows me down, his gravelly voice loud enough to drown out the hip-hop music blaring from my ear buds.

It's begun to snow and, instead of focusing on his steps, he's resorted to walking through anyone who stands between him and the warm, dry shelter where his next drink is waiting.

"*Excuse* you," I sneer, glaring back at him from over my shoulder.

"Yeah, fuck you," he spits, casting his middle finger to the heavens.

I feel it inside of me. The heat of his hatred. The blackness of his soul. His eyes are empty, glazed depths of sorrow and poison. His yellowed, clammy skin is merely a vehicle for the chemical waste wrapped around weakening bones.

I find the whispers flooding my mind before I can resist them, the voices so distinct that I can no longer hear J. Cole's lyrical diatribe rattling my skull. I should fight them, but I don't. I don't want to. Not this time. I've been fighting pricks like this my entire life. At some point, you learn to fight back.

Electric synapses fire with the command, and my lips part to utter a single word.

"*Fall.*"

He doesn't even see the patch of ice before the heel of his scuffed boot skates across it. Arms flail violently as he tries to regain his balance, but it's too late. He's airborne—suspended in time like the feather-light snowflakes swirling around us. And before a single scream is ripped from his throat, he hits the piss-stained sidewalk with a deafening crack.

I exhale through the taste of metal in my mouth and keep walking, leaving pain and chaos in my wake. I turn up the music as loud as it'll go to drown out the desperate cries for help.

I never said I fought fair.

"You're here early," Lily smiles as I enter the dingy corner store where we work. Beautiful, blonde and bright, she's much too angelic to be working in a dump like this.

I peel off my fingerless knit gloves and rub my palms together before stowing the ear buds in my coat pocket. Eduardo, the store manager and the owner's nephew, is too cheap to turn up the heat. "Bored, and Sister had a date. Thought you could use the company. Busy tonight?"

Lily's sky blue eyes scan the shelves and racks of chips and six packs. "Not really. But I'm glad you came in." She smiles again. She's always smiling. Always ridiculously optimistic. And while that would annoy the crap out of me with anyone else, I genuinely enjoy her sunny disposition. It's a welcomed change from the doom and gloom of our little slice of purgatory outside.

I step around the counter that's halfway encased by bulletproof glass. Eduardo was also too cheap to spring for one that at least touched the ceiling, but some protection is better than none. "You here by yourself?" I frown. Even with the added security of cameras and an alarm system, working the night shift at any establishment in this part of town isn't safe. Especially for someone like her.

"Logan is stocking in the back. I'm fine, really. You worry too much."

I shake my head, wishing she worried more. Lily doesn't know the horrors I've seen—the horrors I've created. To her, I'm just a troubled girl with a dark past who she wants to love and nurture. But in reality, I'm a troubled girl with a dark past whose thoughts and words are weapons. And while Lily is one of the only people I can call a friend, she can't know about me. No one can. Or else I'll end up just like my mother.

I stash my coat and bag under the counter and slip on the ugly maroon vest we're forced to wear. It's not doing me any favors over my black sweater and ripped, faded jeans, but somehow Lily still looks svelte and glamorous in it. I'm clueless about what she's doing working in a rotted out neighborhood on the south side of Chicago—she looks like she comes from money, even though she swears she's not. Something about her won't let me believe that.

There's a stain that poverty leaves on everything it touches. It coats your palms when you're cold. It bleeds onto your lips when you're hungry. It paints your skin when you're sick. You can try to scrub it away, but the result is always the same. You're one of society's forsaken.

Lily has never worn that stain. I would have recognized it if she had.

A bell jingles from the doorway, startling us both. I nearly gasp audibly when I see who it is.

"God, not this guy again," Logan bristles behind us, holding a cardboard box full of Pop Tarts. Lily and I didn't even hear him approach.

"What?" My voice is barely a whisper. The wind has been knocked out of me.

"That dude gives me the creeps." Logan shakes his head, sending muddy brown curls dancing across his forehead. He drops the box and moves in closer, whispering, "I seriously think we should tell Eduardo about him. He comes in every night and buys the same exact thing…especially when *you're* working." He points his gaze at me.

"So? Maybe he works the night shift too?" I shrug.

"The night shift at a slaughterhouse. He could be a rapist or serial killer. You really want someone like that stalking you?"

I roll my eyes. "He's not stalking me, Logan."

"You don't know that, Eden. He gives me a bad vibe."

"Well, I think it's cute. Romantic, even," Lily chimes in, reaching up to ruffle Logan's shaggy brown hair. I wish I could have warned her not to do that. His greasy mop probably hasn't been washed in weeks.

"Whatever. The fucker is trouble. Just *look* at him."

And as if some biological instinct hooks itself within muscle and bone, transforming me into a lust-strung marionette, I can do nothing but.

The first time he came in nearly six weeks ago, he'd scared me. It was after three in the morning, and I hadn't heard the door chime. At least I don't think I did. I'd been engrossed in a new paperback and my Kendrick Lamar playlist, and didn't notice him until he'd been standing silently before me. No sound of footfalls or the rasp of his breath. He'd just stood there, watching me, waiting for me to notice him. I'd nearly shrieked and fallen off my stool.

The next night I was stunned once again by his presence, but this time, the flavor of my curiosity was something different altogether. I actually let myself *look* at him, while silently praying that he couldn't see *me*.

He was tall and built like someone who trained religiously. I thought maybe he played for the Bears or maybe even the

Bulls, but the way he moved was almost too lithe and graceful to pin him as an athlete. However, there was something uniquely feral about it. And his face…hard and menacing, yet unquestionably pretty. Almost like he knew he was gorgeous, but didn't want to be. Still, even the dark scruff on his chiseled jaw seemed precise and elegant.

When he approached the register, I tried not to stare at him, but I wanted to see his eyes. I needed to know what darkness lurked behind this massive beast of a man. But he wouldn't look at me. He simply slid his Arizona Iced Tea and pack of mints across the counter and waited for me to ring him up. He never said a word.

I couldn't breathe. The air had been sucked right out of the room. I felt lightheaded and my fingers began to shake violently. The whispers began to snake their way into my skull, urging me to say the words. *Look at me. Look at me.* But my tongue had turned to lead that not even my mind's compulsion could move.

I was grateful. I had a feeling his gaze could turn me to stone.

He came in every day after, buying only his canned iced tea and wintergreen mints. Sometimes it was at the start of my shift—sometimes toward the end. He never spoke, never met my eyes. I'd watch him from across the store and mentally record his movements and the way his dark clothes seemed to stretch around his body like a designer glove. Something about him was dangerous—not in the criminal way—but in the way that made my senses hum with anticipation and fear every time I heard the door chime. The way that made me afraid of myself.

Tonight is different though. He's dressed in similar clothing, and he goes straight to the back for tea and mints. And he doesn't meet my eyes. That's nothing new. But there's something else…something is off. I can feel it in the way the air seems to pulse with excitement around his frame.

It's 10:40 p.m., and I'm not scheduled until 11. How would he have known I had come in almost half an hour early? I look to Logan, whose dark eyes are trained on the mysterious stranger/my would-be stalker.

The man approaches the register with unhurried steps, although I can tell that tension grips his shoulders like a vise. I make a move to the counter to ring him up like I do every night, but before I can take a full step forward, Lily darts into my path, beating me to it.

"I've got it," she smiles sweetly. "Still my drawer, and I don't want to mess up tonight's count."

Right. Although, that's never mattered before.

A voice echoes in my head, but I shut it down before I can make out the words.

Lily rings up the items swiftly without her usual friendly chatter. But just before the man can escape our intense scrutiny, she plasters on a smile and asks him, "Will there be anything else?"

I hold my breath as he slowly lifts his chin to face her, giving me a full view of the man who's haunted my daydreams every day for the past six weeks.

Gray. His eyes are gray, but the most stunning shade I've ever seen. As if they were plucked from the crying heavens, coated in stardust and cast in steel. His eyelashes are thick and dark, much like the hair that layers his chin and surrounds full, sensual lips. A marled charcoal beanie sits atop his head, allowing just the tips of his hair to tease me.

He's too beautiful to be cold, but I know, without a doubt, he's frozen solid to the core. Still, every cell in my body is engulfed in flames just by his proximity. I'm almost certain I could melt the bulletproof glass just by squeezing my thighs together.

He squints for one quick fraction of a second, and before I can even decipher the inflection, he turns and stalks out the store. I'm speechless…scared. But not of him. I'm scared of the way my body burns for this complete stranger who has never even spoken to me.

"I told you…*totally* psycho," Logan proclaims after a long stretch of uncomfortable silence. "He's probably that guy that called and asked for your schedule earlier today, Eden."

I hear him. I just don't want to. "What did you say?"

"Yeah. Eduardo answered. Some guy wanted to know what your hours were."

I frown. "You sure he was asking about me?" I've never been the topic of interest. And I've worked damn hard to keep it that way.

"Pretty sure. He asked for the girl with the silver hair, tatts and a nose ring. You're the only one around here that fits that description. We didn't tell him anything, of course. But still… someone was looking for you."

I touch short, black polished nails to my dove gray locks reflexively. To the outside world, it's a fashion statement. But the truth is, my once jet-black hair started losing its pigment years ago. It was just a few strands at first. But then almost overnight, I had the mane of an 80-year-old.

I turn away from his questioning glare and pick up the box of Pop Tarts, if only to fight the urge to wring my hands. "I'm going to restock these," I murmur, stepping from behind the counter.

"Hey, Logan, why don't you take off a little early? I can stick around to keep Eden company," I hear Lily say as I stuff strawberry pastries onto wire racks.

"You sure? What if that guy comes back? Maybe I should stick around just in case…"

"No, no. Us girls can take care of ourselves, I promise. And if he comes back, we have Eduardo's taser behind the counter."

I don't have to look up to know that Logan's face is screwed in uncertainty. He wants to go; it's Friday night. But he also wants to be a decent human being. At least that's what he wants Lily to believe.

"Well…ok. If you think you two will be alright." The promise of a cheap beer and a joint win out over chivalry. I could make him stay if I really wanted to, but I won't. I don't like being in his head. I don't like the bitter taste of his blood on my tongue.

"We will. Go and have a good time."

I take my time shelving junk food and barely lift my head when he bids us goodnight. I want to like Logan, but his soul is murky, his thoughts impure. I don't know what they are specifically, but I can feel the intensity of them. Lust. Indulgence. Aggression. He wants to be a good guy, but this city has poisoned his heart and compromised his morals. He is merely a prisoner of this man-made Hell.

"You feeling ok?"

I swallow a shriek and grip my chest in surprise as I lurch forward. "Shit, Lily! I didn't even hear you. Are you trying to kill me?"

"Not today," she chuckles. "Sorry. Almost done?"

"Yeah. Two minutes." I squat down to arrange the last of the processed treats, careful not to touch the grimy floor.

"Ok. Come up front when you're done. Something I want to—"

Her head whips to the glass double doors, but from my crouched position, I don't see anything. "What is it?"

"Nothing." But she doesn't look my way. "Hey, do me a favor and run to the back for more potato chips. Do it now."

I glance over at the chip display. "It's fully stocked. I think Logan beat me to it."

She doesn't acknowledge my words. Instead, she moves swiftly to the front of the store. But before she can make it, the door chimes. Someone's here.

The voice is deep, the accent Russian. There's a second set of footsteps following the first. Then a third. A cold dread sweeps through the store, a bone-chilling sensation that makes me shiver from my spot on the dingy linoleum. I slowly force myself to my knees, hoping to get a view of the entrance. I've only had a couple run-ins with the Russian Mafia, and this can go only one of two ways: they respectfully pay for their stuff and leave, or they cause a ruckus, emboldened with vodka and recent violence, and get grabby with Lily.

I look to my friend--she looks as cool and calm as if a doting grandma was eyeing her from the doorway. "Anything I can help you gentlemen with?"

The first one—the bigger, scarier one—replies to her in

his native tongue. She shakes her head. "I'm sorry, I don't know what you're saying."

The man frowns, causing his bushy black eyebrows to hood his dark eyes. "The girl. Where is she?" he says in a thick accent.

"I'm the only girl here," Lily smiles, the lie painting her pink-glossed lips. She casually makes her way behind the counter without the slightest inkling of urgency in her step. "But if you'd like to leave a message—"

"Don't play with me, *d'yavol*. Give us the girl, and we might let you live."

Holy. Fuck.

As my eyes quickly scan the small space around me, searching for anything that can be used as a weapon, a set of Italian leather shoes come into view.

"Hello, Eden."

Horror coils my stomach. But before I can run, fight back, respond—something—there are strong hands roughly gripping my arms and pulling me to my feet.

"Here she is."

An iron grip yanks me toward the front of the store despite my violent protests. "Let me go, asshole!" I demand, putting all my strength into fighting his grasp.

"You will come, *сýка*. The master awaits." The Russian thug drags me as if he doesn't even register my one hundred and twenty pounds.

"Let her go," Lily orders, squaring her shoulders. "Or you won't make it home for *borscht*. I can promise you that."

"Too late, *d'yavol*," replies the slick-haired monster on the other side of the counter. "You had your chance to kill her.

Now we've come to collect."

It happens so fast. Too fast for my unreliable, human eyes to fully believe.

Lily flips completely over the enclosed counter, unsheathing razor sharp daggers in each hand. The Russian staggers back, but not before she slices him across the chest. Bright red blood spurts onto the bulletproof glass, but it doesn't slow him down from producing a machine gun from inside his floor length wool coat and spraying bullets in Lily's direction. She rolls and dives with cat-like grace, swiftly taking cover behind a shelf. Her speed, her agility…it's not possible. Not for the girl I thought I knew. Not for anyone.

"Come out, *d'yavol*. I have a big present for you." Blood soaks the man's entire torso, although there are no signs of him slowing down. He nimbly steps around littered potato chips and puddles of soda, the crunch of cellophane and wasted food under his expensive shoes resembling the sound of crushing bones. I don't dare to say a word as he creeps closer to Lily's location, in fear he may turn his attention to me. My captor unsheathes his own gun and jabs it into my side, insuring silence.

"Come on, Vlad. We have the girl. Let's get out of here," says the other goon near the stockroom. He holds his gun with a shaking hand, his nervous eyes darting towards the exit. Out of the three, he looks the youngest, and is clearly rattled.

"No! We will finish the job," the man called Vlad shouts, rounding the corner where Lily escaped. I'm only one aisle over, still being manhandled by the greasy pig bathed in cheap cologne. Lily has nowhere to run. And even if she did, she couldn't possibly dodge their bullets. I should do something.

I should say something. But overwhelming fright has stolen my voice, locking it up tight behind the bars of my chattering teeth.

I catch movement out of the corner of my eye, and divert my terror-stricken gaze to Lily's reflection in the glass doors of the cooler. She's only a dozen feet away, crouched down, those knives still gleaming with blood. Maybe if I struggle, I can cause a diversion, allowing her to escape. Or at least give her a chance to strike and get us the fuck out of this mess.

Do something, Eden. Focus.

You are not a fucking victim.

I open my mouth to scream, but before I can conjure my voice, the sudden ear-splitting sound of breaking glass rattles my skull as the entire storefront window explodes, raining down jagged, crystallized shards. The Russians turn towards the violent blast, training their attention and their guns on the entrance. They only have time to blink once before their vision is painted in blood. It's him. The man with eyes carved of stone. The man I should have known was too alluring not to be deadly.

Without missing a beat, he rushes in, a gun in each hand. My stranger hits the younger thug before he can even get a round off, sending him to the ground before putting a bullet between the eyes of the asshole with the stinky cologne. The corpse slumps on top of me, his dead weight trapping my frame to the dingy floor. Blood gushes over me, staining my clothes and skin, along with chunky bits of brain matter. The smell is overwhelming, and I struggle frantically to turn my head, just in time to vomit.

Oh my God.

Oh my God.

I'm going to die.

I'm going to die tonight.

Death clings to my skin, cradling me in its hot, liquid arms. It's in my eyes…on my tongue. It demands to be felt and revered.

Strong hands yank me from the pool of blood and my own waste, swiftly dragging me deeper into the store, and leaving a smeared trail of red. Between the resounding pops of gunfire, the sight and smell of blood coating me from head to toe, and the violent sickness in my roiling gut, I'm disoriented. Shock and panic rally my rattled senses, and I do the only thing I can. What I should have done the moment the door chimed mere minutes ago, followed by the scent of cheap cologne. I scream at the top of my lungs like a crazed lunatic, shredding my vocal chords like ravaged ribbons. I don't even know what I'm saying or even why I'm screaming. I'm beyond reason—beyond feeling anything but intense dread. Hysteria is all I know.

The blow comes before I can even see it—let alone prevent it. It jolts my skull for only a moment before a dark heaviness cloaks me in oblivion.

Just before it claims me completely, I look up to stare into twin pools of gray moonlight. Then everything shimmers before blurring into black.

TWO

I'VE BEEN BURIED ALIVE.

Deep below the crypt of my darkest nightmares.

My head feels as if it's been split wide open. My eyes are swollen shut. I can't swallow beyond the metallic-tasting sandpaper in my throat, and I hear voices—shouted whispers that I can't comprehend. They're close but my limbs are so heavy that I can't bear to move towards them. Not that I would want to.

I force my brain to retrace my last steps. The icy sidewalk. The corner store. Logan and Lily. Shooting. Screaming. Blood.

Gray.

The breath is sucked from my lungs as I plummet into cold reality. I'm not at the store anymore. I know that for certain. The smells, the sounds, are all unfamiliar. Still, I'm too scared to open my eyes and see what foreign terror lies before me. More scared than I've ever been in my life. More scared than I was as a child when my own mother tried to drown me in the bathtub.

"Why the hell did you bring her here?"

"We couldn't just leave her. They would've killed her."

"And your point exactly? Wasn't that the objective? Fact is, she should be dead. Very, very dead."

"Not if they already know what she is. Death would be a kindness for her. For everyone."

They're talking about me, but I don't understand. *What she is?* I'm a girl. An unimportant, inconsequential, invisible girl. *Forgotten.* What the hell could they want with me? And why…why do they want me dead?

"This wasn't the plan, Lil. Stick to the fucking plan. We can't just make exceptions anytime you feel like taking in a stray."

"No, she's right. They couldn't have left her. Not like this."

Three voices. Two men and…Lily. Lily's here. Shit, they've taken her too. Or…no. Wait. Not taken. She's with them. She's *one* of them.

"It wasn't my call," she says. "L made the choice. If he wants to keep her contained…it's for a good reason."

"Fuck!" It's the first male voice, the one who wanted to leave me. Or kill me. It's gruff, veiled in annoyance. If I could reach out and feel his mind, I'd find hatred and spite festering in his hollow soul. But the blow to my head has left me incapacitated and unable to make a connection. I can't focus through the pain. Good. That type of evil stays with you, echoing in the dark hallways of your subconscious. I don't want that darkness inside of me.

The second man speaks up, his voice much clearer, softer, but a deep, sultry baritone. He has an elegant accent, the type that draws you in and makes you want to listen. "Did he say why?"

"No," Lily replies. "But it must have something to do with the Jumper."

"So L is certain?" the second male asks.

"No, but…can't you *feel* it? Besides, we need to be sure before we dispose of her." *Dispose of her?* What is Lily saying? Why would she…?

"Well, only one way to find out. Let's see what's under those clothes."

Hard, heavy footsteps approach, jumpstarting my better instincts and allowing fear to override the pain in my skull. All at once, I open my eyes and my mouth, and begin to scream at the top of my lungs.

"Get away from me! Get the fuck away from me!"

With fists and feet, I tear at the air in front of me, desperate to keep my captors at bay. Haughty, harsh laughter only pisses me off more. With angry tears burning my eyes, I focus on the sound coming from a tall form a mere three feet away from my place on the cold hardwood.

"This one's a little firecracker. I like it," he sneers. It's the one that wanted to leave me for dead. He's a massive brute with a jagged scar that runs from his right ear to the corner of his mouth, as if someone tried to cut his face into a permanent smirk. His hair is shaved close to his skull, making the grotesque disfigurement even more stark against his fair skin. He's dressed in black leather from head to toe and his arms are exposed, showcasing bulging mounds of muscle. This man is a killer, there's no doubt in my mind. And I don't have to feel the blackness of his thoughts to know that he wouldn't hesitate to snap my neck. And without remorse.

"Leave her alone," Lily says, stepping beside him. She, too, is dressed in all black, so different from her usual wardrobe of floral prints and jeans. I know her—*knew* her—but this woman is not my friend. Her face…her voice…are all the same, but she is a stranger. A wolf in sheep's clothing. I just so desperately wanted to believe there was still goodness and kindness in the world, that I didn't see through the disguise.

I scramble backwards on the floor until my back hits brick, scraping the skin under my blood-crusted sweater. Another man joins Lily at her side. His skin is dark bronze, and his eyes are the shade of spun honey. He doesn't smile at me, but there's something kind about his face. Or maybe that's what I want to see—need to see. He raises a hand to halt the first man from coming towards me and warns him to give me space. He's the second male voice, the one that agreed that they shouldn't have left me. But why take me in the first place?

"Seriously, I'm not sitting around with a thumb up my ass, waiting for her to be *Called*. Lil, you need to check her now, or I will," says the muscle-bound Buzzcut.

Lily looks uncertain, but she takes a step towards me, her palms raised in front of her.

"Don't come near me," I caution with a shaky voice. I try to shuffle back further, but there's nowhere to run. There's a wall to my right and what seems to be an end table to my left. Beyond that, there's a bed. I'm in a bedroom.

Oh no. No.

Not this. Anything but this.

I scream, praying that my pleas for help will penetrate the brick walls. With my eyes still trained on my captors, I search for something—anything—to use against them, but there's virtually nothing lying around. No shoes, no books, no empty water glasses. No signs of life.

I scramble to the nightstand and reach for the lone lamp and launch it with all my might. Without flinching, Scarface plucks it out of the air.

"You'll regret that," he growls, jerking forward and causing me to shrink back.

"L will be pissed if you kill her here," a nameless voice says. Another man steps into view and looks me up and down, his dark, slanted eyes sparkling with amusement. He flashes me a half smile before looking at his accomplices. "You know he hates a mess."

The newcomer, like his criminal friends, is dressed in black, although his unusual garb reminds me of a modern day samurai. He even has twin swords fixed onto his back, forming an X. So is that how I will die? Sliced to ribbons before an audience of sadists?

"Fine. I'll do it," another voice sounds behind him. The samurai is nudged aside by yet another man, a blonde with shoulder-length hair. Is *this* L? Seriously, how many people does it take to kidnap one, defenseless girl?

Surprisingly, he's dressed in jeans and a blue shirt, although his long, muscled frame doesn't lessen the threat. He approaches me, despite my screams, and grips my sweater between long fingers.

"Please. I'll do anything. Just please…please don't do this," I cry, choking on my tears. I try to push him away with violently trembling hands, but I'm still weak from the blow to my head. Either way, I'm no match for him, or the other four psychopaths glaring at me with varying looks of contempt and skepticism.

"Calm down, pet. I'm not here to hurt you," says the blonde man softly. His voice is dipped in sugar, but I can tell it's only to coat the venom on his tongue. I want to believe his words, but something about his ethereal beauty completely alarms me. On the outside, he appears almost angelic—light hair, light eyes, with a tall, languid body. He actually reminds me of Lily. But I was wrong about her. Angels don't abduct innocent women and hold them hostage in a strange bedroom while her friends gang rape her to death.

"What—what do you want with me?" I sputter hoarsely.

"Want with you?" he smiles. *"I* don't want anything with you, pet. Besides, you reek."

"Then…why? Why am I here? I don't have any money. I don't know anything. What…what are you going to do with me?"

The beautiful, blonde man tsks and shakes his head in amusement. "That remains to be seen." Then without warning, he grips my sweater tighter and tugs, attempting to remove it. I thrash and resist his efforts, but his hold is unbreakable. While he may look willowy and elegant, his body is made of stone.

"Please," I beg again, a fresh flood of tears streaming down my face. "You don't want me. You don't have to do this. Just let me go. I swear to God…I won't tell anyone."

The blonde man abruptly takes a step back, freeing my top from his once determined clutches. "Stop."

"I swear to you. I won't say a word. Please don't rape me."

The man looks up at the ceiling, then back to his colleagues, his light blues filled with conflict.

"Oh, for fuck's sake!" a gruff, animalistic roar rumbles the very floor beneath my trembling frame. Then he's here. The man…the gray-eyed stranger from the store appears, pushing through the crowd of captors with an air of annoyance. His beautiful, rugged face is screwed in distaste as he swiftly kneels down and takes my sweater in both his hands, ripping it in two like it's made of paper. I don't even have time to protest. And even if I did, I'm too stunned by his presence…by the menace that seems to encompass his frame…by the feel of his massive hands on my naked skin, to say a single, solitary word.

I scramble to cover myself, but it doesn't dissuade him from twisting my body around so that I'm facing the wall. The blunt of a callused finger runs along the length of my spine, sending dread and unsolicited desire to my quaking core.

"It's true," he spits, as if it disgusts him to touch my body. "She's the one."

Then just as quickly as he entered, stunning the room into silence with his undeniably domineering presence, he exits without another word or glance in my direction.

Satisfied with the his declaration, the others file out one by one until only Lily is left staring at me, her eyes wide with shock…or fear. She opens her mouth to say something, but hesitates, opting to swallow her words and follow her friends out of the room. The door locks behind her, sealing my fate.

I stare at the door until the sun rises into the sky. I don't bother to scream or fight anymore. It wouldn't matter anyway. I won't make it out of here alive.

THREE

It has to be late afternoon by the time I hear the bedroom door unlock. I must've fallen asleep after emptying angry, confused tears into my blood-stained palms. I scramble to sit up from the floor and wrap the ripped sweater around my naked torso.

Lily kicks the door behind her and turns to me with a solemn gaze. There's a tray of what appears to be food in one hand and a duffle bag in the other.

"Hi," she whispers. She doesn't approach me. Maybe in her convoluted mind she's expecting me to invite her in with open arms. And honestly, I'm thankful for the familiar face. I hate it. I hate that I look at her and still see my friend, but I can't help it. I am utterly alone, completely lost. She's the only thing still giving me hope.

"What are you doing here?" I rasp through the extreme

dryness in my throat. I should be begging her to help me, to free me, but I can't. I'm hurt. I let this person—this killer—into my heart and she hurt me.

"I thought you may want to clean up. And eat something."

"You thought wrong," I lie, my stomach growling on cue in an act of betrayal. And the blonde guy was right. After being doused in blood, my own vomit and sweat, I do reek.

Lily looks back towards the door and frowns slightly before fixing her eyes on me. "L will want you to bathe, and he'll want you fed. So…please. It will be easier for you if you just cooperate."

"Why am I here, Lily? Who are these people? Shit…who are *you*?"

"I'm your friend, Eden."

"Bullshit. If you were my friend, you'd tell me where the fuck I am and why the fuck I'm here."

She sighs and rolls her sky blue eyes. "I saved your life."

"Bullshit. You wanted to kill me. You saved me only so you could drag me here and do it yourself."

"Calm down." She approaches with measured steps, sets the tray on the nightstand and the bag on the neatly made bed. "You really shouldn't talk like that."

"Fuck. You."

Lily shakes her head before sitting on the bed. "Look, we can do this two ways. You can go into the bathroom, shower and change on your own, or I can carry you in there, strip you naked and scrub you until you're raw. Your choice."

I open my mouth to retort with something vulgar, or even a threat of violence, but quickly snap my jaw shut. Lily isn't the sweet, dainty princess that I thought she was. This girl is something out of a Marvel movie, complete with blade wielding and acrobatics. I've never seen her move like that. I've never seen *anyone* move like that. I've seen gang bangers and mobsters before. Shit, I've been in a few nightclub brawls myself. But never anything like her.

I try to reach out and touch her mind with mine, hoping to glimpse any signs of menace. If I could do that, maybe I could will her to let me go without harm. But, all I get is static. White noise. I never felt the need to sift through her head, because she never gave me a reason to. Now that I have one, I can't make a connection.

I try again, focusing all my energy on reaching out to where she sits just feet away. Sweat beads on my brow and the bridge of my nose. My breath escapes in short pants and my heartbeat drums in my ears. I'm grasping for her, stretching myself like a worn rubber band until it begins to fray and tear, threatening to shatter my own mind.

Then, just before I give up, I feel it. A crack in her mind. A small fissure that'll give me access to her cerebrum. But the very second I touch the fractured barrier with invisible fingertips, I'm met with excruciating pain. My teeth clench so tight that I'm sure they've been ground to dust in my mouth as I bite through a scream. Tears fill my eyes, spilling down my hot cheeks in salty rivulets. The taste of metal fills my mouth as my nose gushes blood.

I'm dying I'm dying I'm dying.

"Don't," Lily says, flippantly. And with that one word, the pain eases back the way it came as if it was never there, leaving me to cough and sputter. I gulp the precious air that had been strangled from my lungs. Tears and deep red blood drip onto the hardwood. If I didn't see the tiny pools for myself, I'd think my agony had been imagined.

"What did you do to me?" I wheeze, trying to catch my breath.

"Nothing, sweetie. But if you don't cooperate, that'll be the least of your problems."

No. No. No. Not this way. I can't die this way.

Resigned to wallow in my weakness, I lift my heavy head to look across the room to where another door is situated. It must be the en suite bathroom. Honestly, I have to pee so badly it hurts, and even I'm sickened by my stench and the taste of blood staining my teeth, but I won't tell her that. I can't let her know that I'm compliant—that I'm accepting of what's happening to me. Even if she could rip me apart limb from limb. Even if I am virtually defenseless.

"Fine. I'll shower. But only if you tell me what's going on."

She shakes her head. "I can't do that. Not right now."

"Then when?"

She looks towards the closed bedroom door then back at me. "Soon. When L says it's time."

L. There's that name again. Some mob boss? Drug lord? Either way, what would he want with me? I'm nobody.

"Fine. But just answer one question for me—just one. And I'll do what you ask. I won't ask you why I'm here or what you plan to do with me. I just…I need to know."

"One question?" Lily lifts a slender brow.

"Yes. Answer it truthfully, and I'll march into that bathroom without another sound. I'll even eat your food."

She rolls her eyes, and heaves out an exasperated sigh. "Ok. One question. Let's hear it."

I look up from the floor at the girl I had considered one of my only friends. I didn't love easily, and most people found me too cold and guarded to forge a relationship with. But Lily… she never gave up. She never made me feel like an outsider. And she never pitied me. She accepted me—poor, abandoned and forgotten. At least that's what I thought.

"Did you ever truly care for me, or was it all a ploy to capture, and, ultimately, kill me?"

Without blinking, Lily answers with a simple, "Yes."

"Yes, you cared? Or, yes, it was all staged?"

"Yes…to both."

Speechless, I climb to my feet and gingerly pick up the duffel bag. Then I make my way into the bathroom with my trampled heart in my throat.

I hate to admit it, but a shower is exactly what I need. I hadn't realized what a horror show I was until I looked into the vanity mirror. Dried, flaky blood covers my face and chest, along with a good coating of vomit in my hair. What was left of my clothing has been ripped and stained beyond salvage.

The bathroom is immaculate, just as the bedroom, and just as cold. The only toiletries in the shower are a bar of white soap and a bottle of shampoo. I lather, scrub, rinse and repeat, eager to wash the remains of the dead Russian and the night before off of me. Although it's difficult with a golf ball size goose egg on my head, I'm able to restore my hair to its radiant silver tone. I touch my fingertips to the nasty lump and wince. He must've hit me with the blunt of his gun. Or maybe I was mistaking his fist for hardened steel. Either way, the fucker knocked me out cold like I was no more than a mangy, rabid animal. And without a single tinge of remorse. My eyes water at the remembrance, and I quickly dash away spiteful tears.

After drying off with an oversized towel that's surprisingly fluffy, I unzip the duffel bag. I expect to find the basics: nondescript pants, t-shirt, hopefully some undergarments. But what I don't expect to see are my clothes. Clothes from *my* room. In *my* apartment. *Oh shit.* They've been to my home. To *our* home.

I leave the water running in the shower, creating a veil of steam within the confined space, as I rummage through the drawers and cabinets. There's nothing—nothing that I could use as a weapon. Nothing that would allude to my captor. Not even a razor or a safety pin. Everything is bare and cold and harsh. Stainless steel against brick.

I give up my search, and reluctantly turn off the water, then leave the temporary haven of the bathroom. Lily is gone, and something within my chest stirs. I hate her. I hate her for deceiving me. But I also know that I need her. She's my best bet at getting out of here. She admitted it—she cared for me. And if any of that affection still exists in her heart, maybe I can manipulate her into letting me go. It'll take time, and every ounce of my will, but if I can just tap into that little crack in her conscience, then maybe I can make it out of here alive.

As quietly as I can, I search the room from top to bottom, taking inventory of anything out of place. The door is locked—no surprise there. The drawers are filled with nothing but plain men's clothing and there doesn't seem to be any grooming products or jewelry lying about. There's a closet, but it's locked behind what appears to be a steel door. There. That's where I need to be. That's the ticket to my freedom. Or maybe just the opposite. The samurai said that *L* didn't like a mess. Maybe that's where they plan to kill me.

There's a single window in the bedroom, painted shut and locked behind metal bars. I touch my fingertips to the freezing cold, frosted glass and peer down onto the street, watching the world zip by me like a faded silent film. I'm still in Chicago. I should be relieved by that fact. Instead, realization chokes me, and I push away, refusing to see any more.

It's quiet. In the twenty-two years I've lived in this city, it's never been quiet. Ever. The window is soundproof. Screaming for help would be futile.

Defeated, exhausted, and utterly drained, I plop onto the bed. It's massive, bigger than any bed I've ever seen. The steel-colored comforter is surprisingly soft under my palms, and the pillows are full and fluffy. It's odd and out of place against the stark harshness of the rest of the room.

The tray of food still sits on the nightstand, so I give into the near-debilitating hunger pangs and lift the metal-hooded plate. A burger and fries. Food that doesn't require a knife and fork. Smart. With a ravenous bite, I devour half of the burger and wash it down with the entire bottle of water. The food has turned cold, but it's delicious. Probably the best thing I've ever tasted, considering I haven't eaten in almost twenty-four hours. Maybe even longer. I can't be sure how much time has passed.

The numbness starts at my tongue, slowly slithering its

way down my throat like a toxic slug. I drop the French fry at my lips and clutch my neck in a hopeless attempt to rip the venom from my deadening esophagus. I gulp air, drinking in life to wash away the death strangling my soundless screams. Choking on tears, I cry out for help, but the voice has been wretched from my throat. I'm drowning in my own saliva, thrashing in a sea of sheets the color of clouds fat with rain. I fight for the surface, but I've fallen too deep...too deep...too deep within my own demise.

With eyes so wide I can see each frame of my life flash by in brilliant color, I see a familiar face come into view. Smirking. Waiting. Watching me die.

FOUR

I'M NOT ALONE. I CAN SENSE IT. I CAN FEEL THEIR CRUEL eyes on me, waiting for me to entertain them with my stubborn mortality.

"You're awake," an accented voice says. It's French, I think. French…and something else. "Good. We've been waiting."

My heartbeat stutters as I leap out of my skin. With uncoordinated limbs, I struggle to sit up and drag my body to the other side of the bed. The dark-skinned man with honeyed eyes sits mere feet away, his expression curious—maybe even a little amused by my floundering. I look up to find that another man the color of sunbaked desert sand stands at the foot of the bed, silently watching me with irises the shade of soot.

"What do you want?" I rasp, my throat tight. The man the color of night hands me a bottle of water. I go to grab it then stop, remembering myself. "You drugged me."

"I did not personally, but yes, you have been drugged. I apologize for the inconvenience." He sets the water on the nightstand, which has since been cleared of the remnants of my poisoned meal. "We didn't want to risk you getting hurt during the medical exam. But I assure you, you were safe. It was not invasive. And the water is clean."

His words pierce through the smog in my brain, and I frantically assess my body. To my relief, I'm fully dressed. But the thought of this stranger…this monster…touching my naked skin…

"You *examined* me?"

"Briefly, yes. I'm a medical physician, among other things. I wanted to treat your contusion and make notes of any distinguishing marks."

"You *touched* me?" I mean to shout, but it comes out in a strangled wheeze.

"Please, Eden. Calm down. I do not wish to harm you."

"You drugged and kidnapped and touched me without a word of why I'm here. And I'm supposed to believe you? Some freak I don't even know!"

The man nods once. "That would be ideal. I am Phenex. My companion is Jinn. I was hoping to speak with you."

I look from Phenex to Jinn, whose expression is stony. "I told you—I don't have anything. I don't know anything. You must have the wrong person."

Phenex shakes his head, causing the long, coiled dreadlocks tied at his nape to brush against his dark tunic. "I don't believe we do. You're the one we've been seeking for some time now. However, there has been a…discrepancy. My hope is that you'll speak with me so we can figure this out as amicably as possible. You'll find that my methods are a bit more… *desirable*…than those of my counterparts."

I struggle against the toxins clouding my mind, trying to find reason in his words. "Desirable?" I recoil as far as my sluggish body will go. Leaving the bed would prove pointless; my legs feel like they've been asleep for a year.

"My friends persuade with brute force," he answers, regarding me from his side of the bed. "I choose to use intellect."

"And him?" I ask, jutting my chin toward Jinn. He's as still as a statue, only his dark eyes moving beneath the wrap of fabric atop his head. I don't even think he's breathing.

Phenex looks back at his friend before answering. "Jinn lives by a stringent code of ethics much different from all of ours. I assure you, he is not a threat."

"Yet, I'm here against my will. He's an accomplice to my kidnapping." I shoot Jinn an accusing look, just in time to see the faintest twitch of the corner of his mouth. His fists ball at his sides. I'm definitely poking the beast here, but that's good. That miniscule reaction tells me what I need to know. It gives me hope.

Remorse. He feels remorse for what's been done to me. Maybe he even disagrees.

"Not everything is what it seems," Phenex responds, drawing my attention back to him. "You will see that soon. Or maybe you won't." He picks up a notepad and a pen that I hadn't noticed on the bed. "It's imperative that we get started. L won't want to wait much longer."

L. There's that name again. The keeper of my fate.

In an act of good faith, I scoot a fraction towards the middle of the bed. I won't persuade him with vulgarity. Maybe I can charm him into getting some answers. "Who's L?" I ask, using my softest, sweetest voice.

Phenex smiles, his full lips curling over perfect, gleaming white teeth. He's a beautiful man. It's hard not to admit it. But there's something about his beauty that just doesn't seem... real? He's a criminal. He shouldn't be extraordinarily handsome. I shouldn't notice the way his dark lashes flawlessly frame almond-shaped, deep-set eyes. I shouldn't wonder if his skin over the apples of his cheeks is as smooth as marble. This is a trick. A side effect from the drugs still in my system.

I take a deep breath and push myself outside my body like an outstretched hand, seeking the feel of his mind pressed against mine. I want to trust him. I want to believe that I haven't been brought here to be executed. But I can't trust the guise of a smile anymore. His words are worthless. But the soul never lies.

Pain. Debilitating pain slices through my scalp, retching a harrowing scream from my hoarse throat. I grip the sides of my head, begging through sobs for it to ease. I can feel my brain throbbing as it swells against the cage of my skull. I imagine it seeping from my ears, a pulpy mess of twisted pink flesh turned to blood soup.

And then it stops.

"I wouldn't do that again if I were you," Phenex remarks, his eyes roaming my sweat-slickened face. "You'll hurt yourself."

"Huh?" I pant, blinking through tears. The pain is gone, save for the dull headache I've had since I woke up from my drug-induced slumber. A second ago, I could have sworn my brain had been pulverized, but now...nothing.

"You're trying to read my soul. It won't work. Just like it didn't work with Lil."

"Wha…?" How? How did he know? No one knows about me. Not since I made the mistake of telling my mother what I could do. She was certain I was possessed, and tried to *beat* the devil out of me. After that, I never spoke another word about it.

Phenex smiles, and it looks like pity. "Your tricks won't work on me, or anyone else here. You cannot bend our wills. But you will give yourself an aneurism if one of us decides to let you in."

"But…how?" I stammer, pressing a trembling hand to my dry, cracked lips. "How did you know? Are you like *me?*"

He shakes his head, before turning his gaze to the notepad as he scribbles something down in characters I can't read. "Not exactly."

"Then how did you know?" Hell, *I* don't even know what I am.

A slow, sinuous smile spreads against his lips. "We know everything about you, Eden Faith Harris. I told you…we've been looking for you for a long time."

Phenex asks me simple questions at first. Weight. Height. Age. Things he would already know. He's testing me, trying to see if I'd lie, even about something inconsequential. Then he moves on to the heavier shit. The shit I'd buried a long time ago.

"Tell me about your parents."

I shrug, feigning nonchalance. "My father was a no-show. My mom was a nutcase."

"Is that all?"

"What else is there to tell?"

Phenex sets the notebook down and trains his amber eyes on me. There's empathy in his gaze. "What was your father like?"

I shrug again. "How should I know? He left when I was a baby. My mom said he was a minister. I guess he felt his God needed him more than his family did. Not that I blame him."

"And why's that?"

I look down where my hands are clasped tightly in my lap. I don't want to think about this, let alone talk about it. I haven't talked about this shit in years, not even to Mary, the foster sister I've affectionately called Sister since we were placed together. I was just a snot-nosed kid, and we were forever bonded by pain and loss and loneliness.

"My mother was sick. Drugs, alcohol, you name it…she was a junkie. But more than that, she was literally out of her fucking mind."

Phenex winces at my words before frowning. "Why do you say that?"

"Because she was. She was psycho. She was the reason why my father left us, thinking I wasn't his child. She was convinced that she had been seduced by the devil while pregnant with me. She told anyone who would listen. She even tried to get the doctors to abort me, claiming I was tainted. When they turned her away, she tried to cut me out herself with a kitchen knife."

Phenex blanches then swallows thickly. Something like sorrow clouds his chiseled features. That was something he didn't know.

"What happened?"

I shake my head and try to smile through the ache in my chest. "She went into premature labor and hemorrhaged. And I have a nice little scar from my shoulder to my elbow as a reminder." I lift the sleeve of my shirt to show him the raised sliver of skin which has since been covered in a colorful inked mural of lace, skulls and roses.

A strange silence stretches between us. Even his quiet companion shifts uncomfortably on his feet.

"It's ok," I remark, pulling my sleeve down. "It couldn't have been all that bad. After we were both healthy enough, they sent me home…with her."

Rage flickers in Phenex's golden irises, and for a moment, I swear black eclipses the whites of his eyes. "How could that be? Why didn't anyone intervene?" He shakes his head, as if trying to rid himself of the image. "I'm sorry," he whispers, the sound just a rumble of his deep voice.

I lift my marred shoulder. "That's what happens when you're poor. Keeping us any longer would rack up a bill that my mother couldn't pay. We were a problem, but just not *their* problem."

I don't know why I'm telling him all this. I don't know why I'm divulging my scars to not only a complete stranger, but to someone who had a hand in my abduction. But there's something about Phenex—something warm and comforting—that makes him familiar. Like maybe we were friends in a past life.

He closes his eyes and takes a deep, cleansing breath, as if he's trying to exorcise his own demons. With lips slightly parted, he looks at me with the face of a man that has dreamt my nightmares, and has felt my agony.

"When did the graying begin?"

I gasp. How did…how did he know?

"It's one of the first signs," he continues, as if hearing my thoughts. "Your hair turns gray around the age of eighteen. It's almost instantaneous."

"How did you know about my hair?" I ask in disbelief.

He smiles that smile that makes me scoot a little closer and lets my gaze settle on him just a little longer. "I told you—I know everything about you. Almost, at least. And the signs are quite predictable. The hair, the cluster of freckles on your spine, the nightmares, the aversion to silver." He nods toward the hoop threaded through my nose. "Maybe we still have time."

"It's titanium," I blurt out before I can stop myself. "I'm allergic to silver. How did you…how did you know all this? What does it all even mean?" I hadn't told anyone—not a single, living, breathing soul—about what had been going on with me. Not even Sister, although she knew about the hair and the nightmares. Considering our entire apartment was about as big as this bedroom, it was hard for her not to know about the terrors sleep would bring. That's why I chose the nightshift. She'd be left to sleep in peace every night. And I'd be left to thrash and scream and cry in the daytime…alone.

Phenex looks back at Jinn as if asking for permission. Of course, he receives no response.

"There are seven signs. Seven physical symptoms that will lead up to your *Calling*. Some are as simple as your hair losing its pigment. Others can be more…alarming."

I shake my head, unable to absorb his words. "Wait. Back up. I don't understand a word you just said. My *Calling*? Calling for what? That makes zero sense."

Abruptly, as if some internal switch has been triggered, Phenex jumps to his feet, clutching the pen and pad in his large hand. "L will tell you. When it's time." He and Jinn both turn on cue and begin to make their way to the door. No explanation. No goodbye. No promise of rescue or release.

"Wait! Who is L? And why can't you tell me why I'm here? What the hell is going on?"

Phenex pauses mid-step and turns his head to one side, giving me a view of his sculpted profile. "Your mother was telling the truth."

Before I can even grasp what he's said, he's gone, leaving me to dangle somewhere between confusion and disbelief.

FIVE

It's hours before I hear the door unlock again.

Darkness has fallen. The kind of darkness that only breeds violence and crime. The kind of darkness that shrouds our deepest depravities.

I rub my tired eyes and try to focus on the shadowy figure entering the room. He locks himself inside with me before taking the armchair at the opposite wall. The sight of him turns the blood in my veins into molten lava. My breath catches reflexively, as if breathing in his presence is forbidden. The sound of my heartbeat serves as a sort of hedonistic soundtrack—a carnal, infectious beat that preludes the promise of corruption.

He looks at me with a gaze filled with ire. Even in the dark, it seems as if those silver eyes glow. Nervously, I grab a pillow and squeeze it to my chest.

"What do you want with me?" I whisper.

Dead. Silence.

"Why am I here? Who are you?"

He doesn't reply. He just watches me…unnerving me like he did the first time he set foot in the store. He wants me to fear him, and I can't help but give him what he desires.

"Are you…are you going to kill me?" My voice cracks on the last two words, barely audible to even my own ears.

I think I hear him snicker in response, but I can't be sure. Night shrouds his face, making the moment all the more menacing. He could attack, and I wouldn't even see it coming.

"Dammit, answer me!" Red-hot anger simmers beneath icy trepidation. "Why am I here? What do you want from me?"

"I've been waiting for you for a long time, Eden."

The sound of his voice is the bass line of a sensual song—deep, penetrating and melodic—vibrating my insides into liquid. I squeeze the pillow tighter to my chest, holding myself together and praying his words won't find me in the dark.

"Why?"

Minutes pass. I don't even think he hears me until he responds.

"You're the next one. But you cheated your death."

"What? I don't even know what you're talking about. I'm not—"

"You are. You were bred for destruction. I was sent to stop you."

I swallow against the desert dryness in my throat and force myself into a sitting position. My head still throbs from the blow to my head. The blow *he* inflicted.

"Who are you?" I ask again.

Before my befuddled mind can register his advance, he's on the bed, crouched over me. He stabs a fist in the headboard above my head, pinning me in with his body. Heat rolls off his panting frame in feverish waves of fury.

If we were lovers, he'd be sliding inside of me, fucking me while gripping the heavy oak wood against the wall. I'd be clawing at his back, chanting his name, begging for him not to stop…

The forged image flashes in my mind for merely a heartbeat then fractures into a million broken pieces. I blink once, trying to remember where I am…who I am. But it felt so real. So vivid that I twitch between my thighs. I reach out to reality, struggling to come back to the here and now.

This man—this monster—is not my lover. He's not here for pleasure. He only revels in pain.

"You know exactly who the fuck I am," he sneers, the venom of violence dripping from his tongue.

"What? Get off me!"

"How long have you had her?" he shouts, his nose just a mere inch from mine. "Show yourself, you coward! You have no idea what you've just done!"

"I don't know what the hell you're talking about!" I scream, pushing against his chest. He's made of cut steel and smooth marble. I doubt he even feels my hands pressed against him.

He grabs my face with the other hand, roughly gripping my chin. His fingers are ice picks digging into my skin. "Come out now! You can't hide in there," he fumes, bringing his face as close to mine as humanly possible. So close that I can feel the heat of his breath and the brush of scruff along his jaw.

"I don't understand what you want! Get off me!"

Anger chokes my voice, and frustrated tears sting my eyes. I lift my fists to strike him but he easily defers them by knocking them out of the way. I try to buck and kick myself free, but he locks my thighs between his knees. I'm caged in by his massive body like a broken-winged bird, utterly helpless and defeated. His eyes bore into mine, emitting a thousand shades of contempt and disgust. He hates me. It's evident in those striking eyes made of frosted moonlight.

I'm ready to give up, to let the fear and anger swallow me whole. And then I feel the brush of his dark hair against my brow. I yelp in surprise when he dips his head and presses his forehead against mine, our noses, our chins, our lips, just a breath away. I feel his entire frame shudder above mine, and he gasps aloud.

"What are you *doing?*" I shout, pushing him away with all my might. I somehow muster enough strength to heave his body off me. He remains on the bed, yet looks at me with a mix of alarm and awe.

"*Adriel*," he breathes.

"What? What the hell is wrong with you?" I scurry from the bed and press my back against the wall, trying to put as much space between us as possible. My skin still burns from his phantom touch.

I watch in disbelief as he struggles to compose himself. His breathing labored, he fists the sheets at his sides. Ripped mounds of cut muscle flex from wrist to shoulder, making the dark ink embedded in his skin dance in the shadows. When he turns his head towards me, his eyes are closed, his mouth screwed in a grimace carved out of pain.

"Adriel." His voice is strained, as if a foreign feeling is stuck in his throat.

"Eden. You know my name is Eden. I'm not Adriel. I don't even know who Adriel is."

"Adriel, you can't do this. You know what he'll do to you." The words crack under the weight of his obvious torment. He opens his eyes and reveals full moons of desperation. I don't understand, and I don't want to.

"Are you deaf? I just told you, my name is not Adriel!"

"Don't do this," he continues without hearing me. "You won't survive. He'll use you. You'll never find your way back."

"Stop it! You're insane!" I scream. Fueled by frustration, I launch myself from the wall until the tops of my thighs hit the bed. "Just please, let me go. You have the wrong girl."

He shakes his head. "I can't. I can't."

"You can't?" Maybe I'm still delirious from the drugs or woozy from the bump on my head. Or maybe seeing him so dejected makes him appear like less of a threat. But, stupidly, I press into the mattress, getting so close that I make out the inscription etched on his forearm in the dim moonlight. It's… Bible scripture? Ironic, considering everything about him is sin incarnate. "Listen here, asshole. Obviously you're off your meds and grabbed the wrong person, thinking I'm this *Adriel*. Just let me go now before shit gets worse. I won't go to the police. I won't tell anyone. I just want to go home."

"No."

"No? Why not? I'm not who you want!"

"No."

"What the fuck is wrong with you?" I scream, heat snaking up my arms from tightly clenched fists. "Are you deaf? I said I'm not Adriel!"

Emboldened and stupid, I grab the pillow closest to me and fling it at his head. It hits him with a soft thud and tumbles off the bed. It's a whisper of an assault, and probably felt like nothing more than fluttering butterfly wings against his tense, squared jaw, but something in him…snaps. Like whatever spell he was just under two seconds ago that left him raw and open has been broken. That wasn't weakness I saw before. That was mercy.

In a blur of movement, he snatches me by my hair and hurls me onto the bed. My scalp stings from the sudden force, yet I don't even have time to cradle my aching head before his hand grips my throat, impeding precious oxygen from my shrieking lungs.

"Don't *ever*. Do. That. Again," he sneers, fixing that cold, stormy gaze on me. "Listen very closely. Your existence is dangling from a very thin thread. Try me again, and I'll snap *it*, by way of your neck. An eternity of damnation has not made me a patient man."

I open my mouth, but no sound escapes. Hardly a whistle of air. I'm held hostage by his stare, brewing with centuries of destruction and rage. They swirl with delicate tendrils of chaos, coaxing me, pulling me into hopeless depths of despair. *Don't look. Don't look.* But his glower is magnetic, holding me in place. And I feel it.

Agony.

Horror.

Evil.

Wickedness so black and so bleak that it brings tears to my wide, unblinking eyes. My soul cries, thrashing against the hold of his malevolent gaze. Physical pain racks through my body, a million shades of torture painting my nerve endings. I want to scream—need to scream. But I can't. Just as my body is bound and gagged, a prisoner beneath powerful muscle, my senses have been taken captive. I can't blink, can't speak, can't move. I am nothing but a sack of burning flesh, writhing within from the terror reflected in those gray eyes.

From far away, I hear a voice, calling not to me, but to him. Through my own inner anguish, I can't make out the words, but it's enough for him to slowly pull away, taking that sin-speckled stare with him. I cough and sputter as oxygen floods my lungs and force myself up on trembling elbows, gulping air. Lily stands at the doorway, her face a mask of alarm. Not for me, but for the cell phone outstretched in her palm.

"I'm sorry to interrupt but..." She looks to me as I clutch my neck, tears streaming down my hot cheeks, then looks to the animal leaning back on his knees, still snarling with disdain. "L, we have a problem."

SIX

I SHOULD HAVE KNOWN. I THINK I ALREADY DID.

Lily steps into the room, her eyes darting between me and…L. He was the man who took me. The man who makes the decision whether I live or die. The man who pulled me out from under a bloody corpse and knocked me out cold with a blow to the head. My skull continues to throb with the remembrance.

"What's wrong?" His voice is flat, unfeeling. As if he hadn't just been choking me a second ago, while hypnotizing me with his vicious stare. I still can't be sure of what I saw, what I felt.

"Her sister…she's calling."

Sister.

"So?"

"So…she's left at least a dozen messages, and has resorted

to calling everyone Eden knows. Left me a voice mail, threatening to file a missing persons report. It's more trouble than it's worth." Her keen, blue eyes slide to me, as if to say, *"It's more trouble than* she's *worth."*

L rakes a hand through his midnight black hair, a heavy, irritated breath flaring his nostrils. "Fine. Take care of it."

"No!" I cry out, despite the hoarseness in my voice. "Please, I'll do anything. Whatever you want. I'll cooperate. Just please don't hurt her."

They both look at me, perplexity resting on furrowed brows. I've just handed over my ultimate weakness.

L bounds off the bed with a seamless swoop of his legs and takes the cell phone from Lily. *My* cell phone. "Is Toyol on patrol?"

Lily nods. "Already on it. And Andras is monitoring the CPD mainframe."

"Good. Have him listen in."

Lily swiftly leaves, shutting the door behind her. L turns to me then, eyes wary, calculating. "Call her."

Without a second thought, I lunge to grab my phone from his grasp. He pulls away, causing me to nearly collide with his rock hard chest. "Tell her you're fine; you're with Lily. Tell her you decided to move in with her to give her space with her boyfriend. Tell her you'll be back to get your things and that you love her. Make her believe it all. But if you allude to anything about us, this place, why you're here…she'll be dead before she can even press the End button. Understand?"

Why I'm here…? How could I tell her something that I don't have the slightest clue about?

My voice quivers. "Yes. And when should I tell her I'll be

back?"

He tosses the phone on the bed, and strides to the armchair across the room, folding his muscled frame in with complete control and grace. "You won't be back."

I tear my eyes from him, afraid to let him see the tears welling in my eyes. I've cried so much in the past days. More than I've ever cried before. More than I cried when the state locked my mother away and placed me into foster care. More than I cried when the nightmares began when I was twelve. More than I cried when they tried to separate me and Sister, the only person that ever showed me a shred of kindness and love.

I have to protect her. I have to do everything in my power to keep her safe from these monsters. I don't doubt that he'll kill her if she goes to the police. Hell, I'm pretty convinced that I'll meet the same fate sooner or later.

But I'm expendable. No one would miss me. No one's life would be irrevocably rocked by my passing. And honestly, no one would be surprised that I had fallen into the wrong crowd. So it's fitting that I was taken, not Sister. Not an innocent equally as good and kind. I'd been forgotten a long time ago.

I pick up my cell phone, still warm from his palm. It brings me back…back to having that same hand around my neck just minutes ago. Back to him ripping my sweater to shreds and touching my naked skin.

The image hits me so hard that I gasp aloud. His hands on my bare thighs, creeping higher, higher until they are beneath my white slip. Those long, thick, commanding fingers finding the wetness at my apex. Teasing, stroking, punishing…

I suck in a harsh breath as the vision dissipates as quickly as it flooded my mind. I saw it. *Felt it.* My panties grow damp at the haunted memory as if it's a part of me. As if he was inside me. I shift uncomfortably on my knees.

"Something wrong?" The asshole has the nerve to look smug—amused, even—as if he dug into my mind and planted the forged remembrance himself.

"No," I lie, refusing to give him the satisfaction of knowing that he's rattled me.

"Well…" He waves a hand in my direction, bored and ready to get back to whatever dungeon he crawled out of. "Get on with it."

I look down at the phone in my sweaty palms. It would be so easy…a two word text to tell her to call the police. Or I could simply press 911 and pretend to be talking to Sister. He'd never know. He'd never even suspect I'd be so bold to defy him. But then I remember his words to Lily, instructing someone—Andras—to listen in. I don't doubt that they've tapped my phone, and probably Sister's phone as well. But maybe it'll be enough…enough to warn her. Maybe he'll be too distracted with slaughtering me that Sister will get to safety.

"Don't try to be a hero," L says from his spot across the room, the shadows casting a mask of midnight across his face. Yet somehow, it just makes those moonlight eyes seem brighter. As if they actually glowed—thrived—in the darkness. As if they were carved of darkness itself.

He knows. He knows everything. This is no ordinary man. He's a killer, trained to destroy anything that stands in his path. Trained to destroy *me.*

Heeding his warning, I press a button. Then another and

another. I won't let him win. He wants me to defy him, if only to have an excuse to kill me. I won't give him what he wants. Not yet.

"Sister?"

"Oh my God…Eden?" Her voice is heavy with sleep, but she quickly perks up. "Where the hell have you been? I've been calling you for days. It's all over the news—the fire at the store. I was scared out of my mind! I thought…I thought… It's been 72 hours since anyone has seen or heard from you."

72 hours. It's been three days since I was taken. I hadn't realized it had been that long.

A knife twists in my gut. I hate lying to her. Out of everyone—out of all the people I've pushed away, all the relationships I've tarnished, all the suffering I've caused—she was the one person that tethered me to the last shred of my humanity. If saving her life means losing her—losing *me*—then I have to do it. I have to make her believe what I've always known: I'm not worth it.

"Yeah, I know," I say into the receiver, swallowing the lump in my throat. "Listen…it's not going to work out anymore…me living there. I decided to move in with Lily."

"What?"

"Yeah. It's better that way. For both of us. She'll work days, I'll work nights. We'll hardly see each other. I just…I need to get away for a little while. I need space."

"Eden." Her voice breaks in two, a sound that I'd always hated hearing. She's cried for me too many times. Tears I didn't deserve. "Eden, I know things have been hard. I know you've been low lately, and I haven't been a great big sister. I promise…I promise I'll do better. I'll work less. I'll spend less time with Ben. Just please…don't shut yourself off from the world. Don't pretend like it doesn't bother you—like it doesn't hurt you—because you think being alone is easier than being forgotten."

Forgotten.

That was the word CPS used when they found me. When they finally followed up on our case. They knew I was at risk. They knew my mother was sick, but they had forgotten. By the time they got around to us, I was no more than skin and bones, bruised and scarred from countless instances of my mother trying to "beat the devil out of me." They knew she'd kill me; she had already tried years before. She said she was trying to baptize me in the bathtub. Trying to cleanse my soul of the evil festering inside. She held me down long enough that my fragile five-year-old body had given up. Had stopped kicking and thrashing and clawing for help. I should have died that day, but I didn't. I wish I had, if only to spare Sister this pain.

I look over at L, whose silver eyes watch me like a lethal viper. I wonder if he can see the fractured pieces of me falling to the floor, scattering like ash in the wind. The tattoos, the piercings, the hair…they served as my armor. But something about his penetrating stare told me that he could see right through it all. Right through to my cold, hollow chest.

"It's not you, Sister. I just need…" Time. Space. Quiet from the whispers in my head.

"You don't have to do this," she whispers. "You don't have to be alone."

I know that I'm supposed to lie, but my tongue is coated in truth. Every word I speak is excruciatingly sincere. "Yes.

Yes, I do."

She's sobbing, so I pull the phone away from my ear, refusing to hear it. *Don't cry for me, Sister. It'll be ok. Just let me go.*

Let me go.

"This isn't like last time, is it?" I hear her say when I finally find the strength to place the phone to my ear.

"No, it's not." Or the time before that. Or the time before that.

"Just…just take care of yourself. And remember…remember that I love you. Someone loves you, Eden. And I won't give up on you. I won't forget you."

I hang up before she can say any more and toss the phone across the bed. I don't say goodbye. I don't tell her that I love her too. It doesn't matter anymore.

You won't be back.

I believe him.

L stands and makes his way over to the bed to retrieve the cell phone. I'm either too numb or too stupid to recoil.

"Lily will be back in with food and water," he says flatly. I don't know why they bother. Why keep me alive only to kill me? Maybe the next time they drug my food, it'll be my last meal.

I remain still, frozen in my own selfish pain. But I don't crack. I won't let him see what he's done to me.

"Why do you call her that?"

I think I hear him but I can't be sure. I look up with glazed eyes.

"Why do you call her Sister?" he asks, his expression blank, save for the slight furrow of his brow. I can't tell if he's being condescending or sincere. I don't even care.

"When I was placed in foster care, she was there. Since she was older, she looked out for me. Taught me how to tie my shoes. Braided my hair. I had always wanted a sister, so she said she would be mine. She raised me. She…loved me… when no one else did. I thought she was my guardian angel."

L looks down at me, a deep frown dented between those starlit eyes, before turning to stalk out of the room. He pauses at the doorframe just before exiting.

"Maybe she was."

SEVEN

I try to feign disinterest when Lily enters with a fresh tray of food, the billowing tendrils of steam emitting mouthwatering aromas of spices and melted butter.

"You expect me to eat that? After you poisoned me?" I eye the food suspiciously, hating the hunger pangs stabbing me from within my belly.

"Drugged, not poisoned. Although Cain wouldn't object to the latter." She heaves out a breath and rolls her eyes. "It's safe. See?"

I watch with envious eyes as Lily picks up a crisp, buttery green bean and takes a bite.

"And how am I supposed to eat this?" Roasted chicken, creamy mashed potatoes, steamed veggies and a dinner roll. It looks delicious as if someone took great care in preparing it. However, they've only provided me with a fork, no knife to cut the quarter piece of chicken.

Lily unsheathes a blade from behind her back, one of the very same daggers she used on the Russian back at the store... three days ago. With a swift maneuver, she sinks it into the flesh of the chicken. It cuts right through to the plate without hardly any effort, sawing through meat and bone as if they were cotton candy. I gulp loudly.

"There," she smiles smugly. She grabs my linen napkin to clean the four and a half inch blade and swiftly secures it behind her back. As if I'd ever be so bold as to try to swipe it. "Eat."

I look down at the food, imagining phantom splotches of blood tainting the meat. I pick up the bread in a compromise, forcing it down my sore, bruised throat.

"So...is it true?" she asks, watching me intently as I pick up my fork to stab a butter-glazed green bean.

"Is what true?"

"About...Adriel?"

I shake my head. "I don't even know who Adriel is. Your friend, L, is a raging lunatic. I told him a million times that I have no idea who or what he's talking about." I let my fork clang to the plate and turn to look at her, not even bothering to hide my rage. "Seriously, you guys are all fucking nuts. You're holding the wrong person hostage yet you won't let me go. What the hell do you want? Money? I told you, I don't have any. *No one* has any. You're wasting your fucking time."

"We're not holding you hostage," Lily replies stonily. "We're trying to protect you."

"Protect me?" I bark out a sardonic laugh. "By drugging me? Assaulting me? My life was fine before you and your merry band of ingrates showed up and locked me in here."

Lily raises a haughty brow. "Was it?"

No. It wasn't.

I shake my head, refusing to give her the satisfaction of my unease. "This is only going to get worse. The longer you hold me, the harder it will be for you. You know that. So if you want to spare your friends from getting butt raped in prison, you should just let me go."

Lily smiles emphatically. "You know that won't happen. And I wouldn't let L hear you say that if I were you."

I push the tray of food away from my lap, too incensed by the sound of his name to take another bite. "L? Why do I give a shit about what he thinks? I'm not afraid of him. I'm not afraid of any of you."

"You should be," she snorts.

I cross my arms in front of my chest like a petulant child. "Who is he anyway? Why do you let him make the rules around here?"

Lily sighs and gingerly leans back on the bed, as if she doesn't have a care in the world. As if a blade the size of my arm isn't jammed in her back.

"L is…he is our leader of sorts. He started all this. He brought us together. He made us believe that there was something greater…much bigger than what we were told. He gave us hope."

I blanch, the foul taste of disgust invading my mouth. "And killing innocent people is *hope?*"

"When it serves the greater good—yes. We don't kill because we want to, Eden. We kill because we have to. We we're *called* to."

"And somehow, you were called to kill me." It's not a question.

"Initially, yes."

I can feel the blood leach from my cheeks. "But now?"

"Now..." Eyes trained on the ceiling, she nonchalantly drums her pink painted fingers on top of her flat belly. "Now, we're called for something else. Something that we weren't prepared for."

I lean forward just a fraction. She's talking, telling me things that may aid in my escape. "And what exactly *are* you all?"

Fast—too fast—she turns her head to me, those blue eyes growing brighter than I've ever seen. A smile etched in malice spreads across her lips. "We're called the Se7en. We sin so that your kind may find salvation."

"*My* kind?" A dozen different images flash through my head. The horrified confusion on my face only seems to spur her on.

"The world is a wicked, wicked place, Eden. Full of evils that cannot be seen. But you already know that."

I struggle to swallow my trepidation. "What are you?" I ask again.

"Something..." she redirects her gaze to the ceiling as I hang on to every rasp of her breath, every blink of her haunting eyes.

Say decent. *Say kind.*

Say human.

"Something different."

"Different as in...?" Part of me doesn't want to know. Part of me *needs* to know.

Without warning, Lily sits up in one swift, lithe movement. She's not even trying to pretend anymore. She grins at the obvious shock written on my face.

"I'll let L tell you. You're his now."

"What… His?" I stammer. But before I can get an answer, she takes the tray at my crossed knees and turns to leave. When she opens the door, I nearly leap out of my skin.

He stands as if he is made of stone—unbreakable, impenetrable. Forged of the earth and elements, yet he moves in shadow. Darkness molds to his daunting frame, sweeping over broad shoulders, chiseled arms, a taut chest. Silver eyes take me in, studying the rise and fall of every one of my breaths. Contemplating my fragile mortality. I wrap my arms around my knees, hoping it will block him from seeing my heart beating out of my chest.

"Goodnight," Lily coos amusingly, brushing past him. I had forgotten she was there.

He enters the room and closes the door behind him, commanding the enclosed space with his massive presence. Every step towards me is a breath stolen. I don't know what to do. What to say. This man…this monster…brutalized me. Cursed me. Threatened to kill me. He's an animal waiting to strike, and considering the wicked gleam in his gaze, I am his favorite type of prey.

He walks over to the dresser and retrieves a bundle of clothing, and without a word, enters the en suite bathroom. As soon as I hear the water running, I bound from the bed, my limbs trembling uncontrollably.

What is he doing here? What does he want from me? The thought of him naked and wet just feet away disgusts me. So arrogant, certain that he has me under his hold. I try the door. Of course, it's locked. With trembling fingers, I pat the front of my pants, feeling the metal tines of the fork under my waistband. Lily was too busy being smug that she didn't even notice when she retrieved the tray. Since I can't penetrate his mind and make him let me go, I'll have to fight my way out of here. I need to be smart. Gain his trust. Make him think I'll cooperate. He has to have a weakness. Maybe this *Adriel* is it. Now to find out who and what Adriel is and use it against him.

I suck in a breath when I hear the water shut off. I have to keep my wits about me. If I'm going to live long enough to get the hell out of here, I can't risk stupid mistakes.

The door opens, sending billowing clouds of steam into the bedroom. L walks out in nothing more than black sweatpants, his golden, ink-adorned skin slick with rogue droplets of water. A small, white towel straddles his neck, grazing the dark, wet hair curling at his nape. Bare feet pad across the room to the bed.

"What are you doing?" I ask, clamping down on the quiver in my voice.

"Going to bed."

"Here?" I screech.

"Yes. And you should too. Tomorrow, we begin."

"Begin what?"

He doesn't answer. He simply lifts the comforter and slides his muscled, half naked frame inside the sheets. Sheets that I've slept on, cried on. Sheets that smell of clean cotton, winter rain and fragrant smoke.

"And where exactly do you expect me to sleep?"

He heaves out a heavy sigh of annoyance. "Where ever

you want to, Eden."

My heart tumbles at the sound of my name brushing his lips, slipping across his tongue. There's no way I can sleep with him in this room, let alone in this bed.

With more force than necessary, I snatch a pillow and toss it into the corner farthest away from him. He wants to be an asshole and make me even more uncomfortable, fine. I won't beg him for any favors.

"You don't have to do that," he grits, his jaw tight.

"I'd rather sleep on the hard floor than be anywhere near you," I spit back.

"Fine. Suit yourself."

He reaches across the bed, across the space he had left for me, and turns out the light. I hear him sigh, releasing his tension into the charged air. Begrudgingly, I lay back onto the pillow, the cold ground biting into my back through the knit fabric of my sweater.

Minutes tick by, but my eyes stay wide, alert. I listen to his breathing, waiting for it to grow heavy with exhaustion. Maybe I should have taken him up on his offer. It would have been easier to jab the fork into his jugular as soon as he drifted off to sleep.

"I'm sorry," he says softly, the words echoing in the enveloping darkness.

"What?"

"I'm sorry. For hurting you. At the store and…here." I don't miss the sharp edge on the word "sorry" as if he's not used to saying it. Or hearing it.

"It's fine," I lie.

"No, it's not. I shouldn't have…" I can't see him from my

spot on the floor, but I imagine his brows pulling together in frustration. "I shouldn't have done that. It's easy to forget myself. The draw is…overwhelming at times."

I roll my eyes. The guy is off his fucking rocker. He's a killer. Why does a morally corrupt monster like him even care?

"I just wanted you to know," he says, answering my silent question. "That…I'm sorry."

I don't dignify his bullshit apology with a response. He doesn't deserve my forgiveness.

I clutch the cold serrated steel in my palms, feeling the bite of the tines against my sensitive skin. It's delightfully sharp. Sharp enough to turn flesh and bone into melted butter. Wetness pools between my thighs at the thought of the impending violence. The sound of stubborn tendon being ripped to shreds. The warmth of fresh blood gurgling over my hands. The sight of the light fading out of their eyes, their faces left frozen and pale.

He'll be so pleased. So happy at what I've done for him.

In reward, he'll fuck me amidst the corpses as they watch with dead, horrified gazes. I'll worship at the altar of his thick length, singing his praises as he pounds me into submission. He'll paint runes of blood across my naked belly, my nipples, my ass, between my thighs.

But first, I'll make them scream so loudly that their lips split at the seams. I'll make them choke on spit and bile as I slice them open and spill their insides. I'll do it slow, so slow that they'll beg for death. So slow that they'll witness it up until the very last second.

He'll be so proud of me.

My Lord.

My Master.

I thrash to consciousness surrounded by heat. An ear-splitting, animal-like screech pierces the night, ripping it wide open into a black expanse full of silver stars. No, not stars. Eyes. And there is no animal being slaughtered. The screaming is coming from me.

"Shhhhh," L whispers, holding me tight to his bare chest. "It's ok. You're ok. It was just a dream."

He's cradling me, blocking me from the terrors manifested in my mind. Whispering gentle words of comfort into hair matted with tears.

His scent of scorched earth and midnight jasmine envelop me, smothering the horror behind my eyelids, extinguishing my fear. It seemed so real, so vivid. I could smell the blood pooling at my feet. I could hear their desperate pleas for mercy. And I could feel him inside me, punishing me, fucking me into blissful oblivion.

"It was just a dream. It's over. I've got you now."

Lily's words echo in my head, charging L's proclamation with a different meaning.

You're his now.

I don't know what it all means. All I can comprehend in

this moment is his sweltering heat. His soothing voice. His smooth, marble skin against my cheek.

Somewhere in a distant corner of my mind, I remember that I should hate him. Should fear him. But now I fear something else entirely.

I fear myself.

EIGHT

WARM SUNLIGHT STREAMS THROUGH THE BARRED window, painting golden stripes across my face. I press the heels of my palms into gritty eyes and yawn, stretching my stiff, sore joints. L is nowhere to be found, and I'm glad for it. I can't breathe when he's around. My thoughts become disjointed words and mumbled sounds whenever he's near. How I survived last night, I'll never know. But I know I'm grateful. Having him here, holding me, comforting me—I never knew what that felt like. For someone to tell me it was just a bad dream and that it wasn't real. I'd learned to swallow my bouts of hysteria a long time ago for fear that someone would think I'm crazy.

Like her. Like my mother.

A fresh bundle of clothes, a toothbrush, toothpaste and a hairbrush sit in the place where his naked skin had kissed the sheets. Unconsciously, I slide my hand over the soft, crisp cotton, wondering if I could still feel his stifling heat. Being in his arms, my cheek pressed to his firm chest—it had been almost too much. But not just his body temperature. *He's* too much. Too intense. Too gruff. Too frightening. Too much of everything all at one time.

I retreat to the bathroom to shower and change, thankful for hot water and clean clothes. The thought that L had been here—naked…wet—just hours before is not lost on me. I shake the image from my head, frustrated at my own weakness. He showed me a bit of kindness, a smidgen of compassion.

Big fuckin' deal. That shouldn't make him any less of a murderous creep. That doesn't excuse him for nearly choking me to death and kidnapping me. If anything, it just makes him an even bigger piece of shit, because he actually is capable of knowing right from wrong. He knows what he's doing. If he was insane, I'd be able to understand it more.

I bypass the opportunity to look at myself in the mirror. It wouldn't matter anyway. I've always been somewhat proud of my edgy, eccentric look, but I don't want to see the wild terror swirling in my eyes. I hate that I don't have control—something I had fought long and hard to grasp most of my life.

Someone has brought my favorite, faded black denim jeans and my most comfortable sweater. I wonder just how much of my clothing they've stolen from my apartment. Maybe my little shoebox of a room has already been packed up and relocated, considering I told Sister that I'm moving. I don't doubt that they've covered all their bases.

When I exit the bathroom, my blood runs cold, the

warmth of the water quickly forgotten. L sits on the bed, on the side I'd slept on. He's wearing a long sleeved black thermal top cut close to his body, tight enough for me to glimpse shadows of cut muscle. His jeans are also black, as well as his boots. Hands clasped in his lap, making him look somewhat contemplative, he lifts his head to look at me, those silver eyes studying every inch of my frame.

"Don't you knock?" I blurt out.

He lifts a dark, sinister brow. "Knock? To enter my own bedroom?"

His bedroom. I've been sleeping—with him—in his bedroom. This isn't just a holding room for his captives. It's his personal living space. I feel the blood drain from my face.

L scrubs a hand on the back of his neck and frowns. "You look…rested."

A compliment? But why does he look like he's in pain? Whatever. I don't respond.

He stands and strides towards the bedroom door. "Come," he commands, without looking at me.

He's letting me out of this room. After almost four days—half of them spent unconscious and drugged—he's letting me out. Maybe for good? This could be it. My freedom could be waiting on the other side of that door.

Or maybe something worse. Maybe he's not leading me to my freedom. Maybe he's leading me to my death.

Stealthily, I pat the fork secured on the inside of my jeans. It may not do much, but if it's my time to go, I'm taking someone with me.

On shaky legs, I follow him out of the room, which leads to a long hallway. Five doors, all closed, give me no indication of where I'm being held. Are there other girls in those rooms? Has his quest to find Adriel led him to kidnap random women on the street? I'd never heard any screaming, but if the windows were soundproof, I'd imagine the door is too. However, as we get further from the bedroom, I do hear something. Something familiar.

Music.

L leads me to a wide, open room that resembles a living room. No, not resembles. It *is* a living room. And there's a large kitchen off to the right. I'm in an apartment. And it's full of killers.

Lily. Phenex. Jinn.

The tall blonde man. The samurai. Scarface.

They're all walking around, doing regular, normal people things as if they don't have a care in the world. I don't know if I should be pissed off or relieved.

Jinn and Phenex are in the kitchen, and they appear to be cooking a feast. Lily carries platters of scrumptious-smelling food to a long, marble-top table while the blonde man organizes place settings. The scarred guy and the samurai are sprawled out on the floor of the living room. They're playing video games. Fucking video games! I blink once…twice. Surely I'm seeing things. Murderers don't play X-Box One. They should be skinning cats or designing necklaces made of ears.

Without a word, L goes to the living room and flops into the oversized, plush sectional, leaving me to stand in disbelief. I'm in quicksand, being sucked in by the illusion playing out before me. They have the nerve to act normal. Like they're friends or…family. It has to be a trick—a ploy to get me to trust them. Shit, maybe *I'm* part of the meal.

"Hey, Eden!" Lily trills, noticing me at the threshold. She sets a bowl of yogurt dressed with fresh berries on the ornate table and damn near skips over to me, a wide grin on her face.

Everyone turns to look at me, not one of them wearing a mask of surprise. Like this was all premeditated. The Asian guy even flashes me a wide grin.

"Hey, Eden. Pretty dope playlists. You've got good taste." He tips his head towards my phone sitting beside a wireless speaker.

"You went through my phone?" I blurt out, my voice full of annoyance. He has the gall to smile sheepishly and shrug his shoulders before turning back to his video game. The scarred guy takes advantage of the distraction and sends a barrage of bullets to his camo-clad man.

"Aw shit! You dirty motherfucker!" the Asian guy laughs, his thumbs furiously trying to save what little life he has left. Bizarre.

"Welcome, Eden," Phenex says, approaching me. He wipes his hands with a kitchen towel before extending a palm. I simply glance at it before looking up at his seemingly kind face, my own etched in a frown.

"What is this place?" I ask, my tone demanding.

Phenex pulls back his hand and waves it around the room. "This is our home. You're just in time for brunch."

"Brunch?"

"Yes. Since we take shifts, it's rare that we're all together. But Tuesdays are our slow days, so we have a mandatory meal."

"Jinn is a fabulous cook," Lily chimes in. "He's actually a trained chef, which is ridiculous, because he hardly eats anything."

Phenex gives her a pointed look but quickly recovers. "Yes. I'm so glad you'll be joining us. And FYI…I made the mac and cheese. That's your favorite, right?"

"Um…yeah?" I fail to keep the wariness from my face, but it doesn't seem to offend him.

"Good! I hope you like it. I didn't want to insult you with the blue box kind. Besides, L has outlawed most processed foods from the apartment." Before I can yelp and jump back, he dips his head closer and winks conspiratorially. "But if you have any other favorites, don't hesitate to make a request, and I'll do my best."

"Ok, everyone! Time to eat!" the blonde guy announces from the table. A beautiful centerpiece sits in the middle, vibrant with rich golds, reds and ochres. Thanksgiving colors. Expensive looking plates and flatware are expertly placed in front of each of the eight seats. They were expecting me. As if I'm a part of this twisted little game.

"About damn time," Scarface bellows, tossing his controller on a nearby chaise. "I'm fucking starving."

"Well, we had to wait for Eden," Lily retorts, grasping my hand and pulling me towards the open dining area. I'd pull away from her hold, but I'm too disturbed when that disfigured thug looks me up and down, and sneers.

Lily leads me to a seat, the space right beside L, who takes one of the end chairs. Phenex takes the seat across from me, and Lily sits on my other side. I'm grateful. The leering asshole takes the other end chair, flanked by Jinn and the Asian guy. The gorgeous blonde man sits beside Phenex.

I look around the table, amazed by the amount of food

prepared for this one meal. Pancakes, waffles, three different types of eggs, cereals, sliced fruit, freshly baked pastries, every type of breakfast meat imaginable, and of course, macaroni and cheese. It's more food than I could eat in a month, and more food than I could afford in that time, as well.

Without warning, Lily slides her palm into mine. Startled, I find that everyone is grasping hands. My focus shifts to L.

"Please," he bites out, as if the word pains him. He slides a callused hand towards me, palm side up. An offering. A choice.

I swallow and divert my gaze to the faces around the table, all staring at me. Last night was a fluke. I don't need to be touching him. I don't need to be touching any of them. But there's something in their earnest gazes—something pleading…encouraging—that has me inching my hand closer to L's. Even the scary one looks on with anticipation.

I let my fingers rest atop his, the farthest that I'm willing to go in this ridiculous charade. The heat of his touch sears my skin in a way that sends warmth to the pit of my traitorous belly. I tell myself I'm imagining it. It doesn't matter. None of it does in the end.

If they want to pretend all is well—fine. I'll play along. I'll act as if everything about this scene isn't royally fucked up. And once they turn their backs, thinking I'm docile, I'll act.

In unison, every head bows and every eye closes—all except mine. They're…praying. These criminals, these heathens. All silently praying with joined hands. At precisely the same moment, they lift their heads and end with *Amen*, before filling their plates. I snatch my hands away and shove them in my lap.

"What's wrong, Eden?" Lily asks, stacking at least eight waffles onto her plate before drowning them with butter, homemade syrup, fresh whipped cream and plump blueberries. "Not hungry?"

I gawk at her overflowing plate and look around me. All of them—save for Jinn, who settles for yogurt and plain hot cereal—have more food on their plates than they could possibly eat. More food than *anyone* could eat.

"Here," Lily says around a mouthful of bacon. She takes it upon herself to dish out a heaping portion of mac and cheese onto my plate.

I open my mouth to thank her but something else entirely comes out. "What the hell is going on?"

Forks clang onto plates. Mouths stop chewing.

"You didn't tell her?" Phenex questions, frowning at L, who couldn't be bothered to look up from his plate to respond.

"I thought we could eat first."

"Tell me what?" Fuck eating. Even though the piping hot pasta and gooey cheese on my plate smells delicious, I want answers. I'll eat later.

"Eden…" Phenex tips his head to one side, as if he's trying to find the right words. "My brothers and sister and I…we're not what you think."

Killers. Liars. Freaks.

"Oh? So what in God's name are you?"

His brows raise at my brash turn of phrase. "We may have brought you here under false pretenses. I apologize for that." He shoots a scowl at L who seems oddly engrossed in his mountain of pancakes and sausage. When he looks back at me, his amber eyes are full of warmth and remorse. "Eden… what do you know about the Bible?"

"What?"

"The Bible. Specifically, angels and demons."

A snicker sounds from the other side of the table. "Not much. My mom was a bit of a fanatic, and we know how well that went. So when I was old enough, I rebelled against it all. It's bullshit, if you ask me."

"Is it?" Phenex lifts a dark brow.

"I suppose you'll tell me I'm wrong." I roll my eyes, and pick up my fork, daring a bite of the mac and cheese. It's Heaven in my mouth, and it's a great effort to keep my eyes from rolling into the back of my head.

"I won't say *wrong*. Misled. I believe your life's circumstances have guided you to believe otherwise."

"And why's that?" I shovel another forkful into my mouth, and even reach for a strip of bacon from a nearby platter.

"Because how could angels exist and not help you? Not save you? How could such evil exist in the world without the reprieve of goodness?"

I try to focus every ounce of my attention on the food in front of me, although my stomach has turned to lead. "I stopped believing in that a long time ago."

"That's sad. So utterly sad."

I shrug and force a strained smile on my face. "But it's true."

"I can see why you'd believe that. But you were never alone. I think you knew that too."

I look up from my food that has lost its flavor. My mouth fills with ash.

"What do you mean?"

The beautiful, ebony man smiles, the movement causing his hazel eyes to spark with radiant gold. "Eden, we are not from this earth. Our origins date back to the beginning of time, long before your world was a sparkle in the Creator's eye. By origin, we are passengers of the dark—ambassadors of evil. We were forged in fire and filth and the blood of the damned. Eden, we are demons."

Flames snake up my neck, scorching my cheeks. My tongue feels heavy. Blood rushes my head, roaring in my ears.

"What?" I didn't hear him right. I must've misunderstood what he was saying. Demons, as in *bad people*. Criminals. Not in the literal sense.

"Demons," someone says from the other end of the table. I don't even look to see who it is.

"But that's…that's…" Impossible. Ridiculous. Insane. Terrifying.

"I know it's hard for you to digest—

"Hard?" I swallow thickly, and shake my head. "You think it's hard for me to believe that I've been abducted by….by…" I can't say it. I won't say it. Saying it would make it real.

"Not abducted. Rescued," Lily chimes in, turning to me. "We rescued you, Eden. Those men at the store weren't just common thugs. They were *Called*. Exactly what we were trying to stop from happening to you."

Called? Called to what? Or by who?

Reading the questions splayed across my pale face, she continues her horrifying…*lies*. "There are those who will be Called. Before they are born, they are chosen to become weapons of evil—serial killers, terrorists, mass shooters. They don't know it, and once they are activated, they have no control. They're sole purpose is pain and destruction."

I muster my courage, but it's deflated in my gut. I force the words from my dry throat. "And you're saying that I am one of these…weapons. Or bred to be."

"Yes," Phenex answers, his gaze full of empathy. I don't want it. I don't want any of it.

"And you…you want to stop it."

"Yes," he nods.

"But you're…" Say it. Just say it. Spit it out and be done with it. *"Demons?"*

"We have spent over a century battling our true nature, in hopes of restoring mercy and peace amongst your kind. There's been too much…too much pain and turmoil. This is not how it was supposed to be. There has to be a balance. The balance has been skewed."

"But we've tried to fix it," Lily adds. "We've been hunting those that are chosen, ending them before they are Called. Hoping that by ending one, we will save thousands…millions. Hoping we can save your world."

The room spins, blurring light and color into a prismatic smear of painted chaos. It dips and rolls, taking my equilibrium with it. I risk a hazy glance at L, who appears still, even in my vision's roller coaster.

"It's true," he says, the two words bearing down on me like two-ton boulders.

"You want to kill me," I gasp, realization creeping in.

"Not anymore. We want to save you. We *have* to save you."

Not anymore.

Not anymore.

I hear the words but they don't make sense. They still don't bring me comfort. I was born to be a weapon. A murderer. And I'm sitting at a table, dining with demons that have made it their mission to kill people like me. People that are otherwise good, innocent humans with no control over what they'll become.

With legs too rubbery to be tangible, I struggle to scoot away from the table. I can't breathe through the tightness in my chest, causing my lungs to scream with effort. I can't think through the fog of panic in my head, shouting for me to flee. I have to go. I don't know where, or how, but I have to get out of here.

"I have to…" I begin, my slurred words foreign to my ears. I heave my leaden body up with numb, sweaty hands. "I have to get some air."

I hear a chair screech against the hardwood before I plunge into speckled blackness.

NINE

I wake up in the familiar bed—L's bed—with the blanket pulled up to my chin. My limbs still heavy with sleep, I do a quick assessment of my frame. I'm fully clothed, and even the fork under my waistband is still intact. There's a glass of orange juice on the nightstand that I gratefully gulp down. I'm alone, but the bedroom door is open. An invitation.

I've already spent too much time cowering between these four walls. If what they claim is true—if I'm not a prisoner—then I shouldn't hide any longer. Even if I can't shake the dread that creeps up my spine every time I think of what they are.

Demons.

Creatures of myth. Pure fantasy. Still, the feeling in my gut—a strange, twisting notion that make my insides turn liquid—tells me what they're saying is true. I can't deny that I've felt it. I've seen what unexplainable power can do. And if I am able to walk this earth—an inconsequential girl with the ability to bend the wills of others with just a whisper—then I have to believe that there is more out there. Something greater… bigger than all of us.

I have to decide to trust their words. I have to have faith that they won't hurt me. Realistically, they could have snapped me like a twig a long time ago. Lily could have plunged one of her knives right through my heart before I even knew what was happening.

I shiver.

A haunted memory of a blade in my hands flashes in hues of red before I banish it back to the dark recesses of my mind.

I hear chatter as I slowly make my way down the dimly lit hallway. Now that I have time and the stomach to take this place in, I realize that it's enormous and incredibly stylish with its exposed brick walls and steel accents. We have to be in some expensive high rise in Near North Side or the Loop. Either way, it's a far cry from the ramshackle two-bedroom I shared with Sister on the Southside.

Sister.

I pause and close my eyes for just a moment. Another memory for my dark place. I can't go back there. If I do, it'll break me.

I enter the open living area and allow myself to see it for the first time. To the left is the living room, complete with panoramic views of the harbor. To the right is a kitchen fit for a gourmet chef, with every high-end appliance imaginable, all in gleaming stainless steel, of course. Beyond that is a wide, heavy door, armed with locks and alarms, and across from where I stand at the mouth of the hallway is the dining area.

The space is filled with light and opulence, the complete opposite of what I'd expect. It's somewhat cold, yet comfortable. Sleek and elegant in a rugged type of way. This isn't a dark, decrepit dungeon scattered with the skeletons of innocents. This is a *home*. And it's exactly what I would have dreamt for myself—for Sister—if my dreams didn't horrify me.

"Good! You're awake!" Lily trills when she sees me stalking in the shadows. She sets her book down on the glass top coffee table and jumps from the plush sectional, waving me over. "Come. Sit with us."

My eyes dart to the others, who seem completely oblivious to my presence. Yet, I know they're aware of each one of my movements. Every heartbeat, every intake of breath. I'm almost positive that Lily just made a big show of my arrival for my sake.

The samurai looks up from the laptop balancing on his lap and gives me a smile. He's beautiful—all of them are. But there's a cunning to him that screams of trouble. "Hey Eden. Want me to throw on some music?"

I shake my head as I make my way over on wobbly legs. "No, thanks."

"I added some of my favorite playlists to your library. Hope you don't mind."

I merely blink in response. *Do* I mind? Shit, considering my predicament, should I?

"That's Toyol," Lily chimes in, waving towards the exotic assassin. He's stowed the swords for today—thank God. But I highly doubt he's any less lethal without them.

He dips his head towards me, causing a lock of jet-black

hair to fall into his almond-shaped eyes. "Demon of mischief and thievery. The legends depict me as some half-dead baby creature, but I assure you, I'm all male." He winks, and I hate to say, I almost want to chuckle.

"And this is Andras," Lily states, tipping her head to the beautiful blonde man with Nordic features. They could be twins.

Andras lifts his regal head from a magazine and gives me a grin. "Nice to formally meet you, Eden."

"He's the demon of instigation and conflict. Don't let the pretty face fool you. He loves to start shit."

Andras brushes a golden lock from his shoulder before admiring his nail beds. "Oh, please, Lilith. You're just mad because you're old and ornery. You'll never keep a man like that."

My eyes widen. "Lilith?"

She curtsies gracefully and smiles that smile that I had grown to know and adore. Before I learned of the treachery behind it, that is. "That I am."

"The original scorned ex-wife," Andras jibes. "The demoness of disease and death. Such a killjoy at parties."

I look to Andras, then back to Lilith, waiting for clarification. "Ex-wife?"

She rolls her eyes and flops back onto the couch. "I was Adam's first wife. The one everyone seems to forget."

"You were a barren old hag. No one wants to remember all the foul shit you did."

Toyol. Andras. Lilith.

Holy shit.

I'd heard of them—read about them. Daily bible study was mandatory while living with my mother. Forfeiting that meant a beating with the good book. I was too young to understand, but as I got older, I sought out to debunk my mother's teachings and researched on my own. Heaven, Hell, the Creation. All different religions in all countries around the world. I *remember* them.

"Where…where are the others?" I stammer, resigning to a seat on the huge sofa. It's as soft and plush as it looks.

"Out on patrol. Jinn is in his room meditating," Toyol answers. "He's got a pretty intriguing story. Ever hear of the Jinn in Islam?"

I shrug. "Vaguely."

"Well, they're actually like the urban legends of your world. People like to romanticize what they find too dark and disturbing to understand. Your books state that there are several, all serving different purposes, all depicted as different beings. Genies, vampires, shifters, zombies. But really, they're all just him. So naturally, he's a master of disguise, able to appear as one desires. Pretty creepy, right?"

Creepy? I may not sleep for a week.

"So is he a demon? Or something else?"

Toyol nods. "Anything that is not of the Creator, is evil. Your people can glamorize it all you want with movies and cheesy romance novels, but he is demon."

"And Phenex?"

"The conjurer," Andras answers without looking up. "Master of all sciences, literature, and song. But that's how he gets you. He lures you in with the kind words and gentle voice. But truly, he is demon. A very old demon, at that."

"He's fallen," Lily—Lilith adds. "He fell from Heaven, and a former angel. He's been searching for a way to get back ever since."

"Is he the oldest of all of you?"

The three shake their head. "No," Lilith answers. "L is older. And stronger."

"Don't let Cain hear you say that," Toyol smirks. "His blemished ego would level Chicago."

The scarred beast. Cain.

"I thought he was mortal—the son of Adam and Eve?"

I hear Lilith snort from her spot on the couch.

"He made a deal that landed him in Hell. Stupid fool." Toyol shakes his head. "Plus he has a thing for murder, so there's that. Probably wouldn't pan out upstairs."

It doesn't go without notice that I haven't asked about L. L, the leader, the elder. L, the demon that held me while I cried into his chest.

You're his now.

I know I shouldn't press for more; they've already told me so much. Much more than I can digest over a casual conversation. But if there is something I should know about him—something that would explain his obsession with this Adriel—I need to know.

"And, L. Who is he?"

Lilith perks up like she can't wait to divulge a piece of juicy gossip. "Oh, L is—"

"Just L."

The four of us whirl around to find L standing behind us, his expression etched in stone. Those haunted eyes bore through me, searing me with molten silver. His mere presence radiates strength and unrelenting power.

"You're here." The sound of my voice… Surprise? Fear?

Eagerness? Even I can't decipher it.

Without so much as a blink, he tears his gaze from mine and looks at Toyol. "Pull up surveillance for Lincoln Park. Cain detected some activity in that area."

With just a press of a button on a small remote, a large, flat screen descends from the ceiling, completely eclipsing the 85 inch television. Toyol hits another button, splitting the screen into eight different picture angles. Holy shit. It's feed from live cameras.

"How many cameras do you have around the city?" I dare to ask.

Toyol shrugs. "Two hundred or so, most of them centrally located around the downtown and lower income areas."

Lower income. Like where they found me.

"A human that is Called tends to lead an unsuspecting, inconsequential life," he continues. "They go unnoticed, fly under the radar. That's when you hear about school shootings or church massacres, their friends and family are caught off guard. They can't believe that the quiet, reserved person they thought they knew is actually murderous scum."

Hmph. Inconsequential life…

It stings, but it's true. I fit the profile.

"And after it's done…after they've been activated…or Called…or whatever. Do they remember what they've done?" I can't stomach the thought of walking into an elementary school and spraying the cafeteria with bullets while innocent, little kids wolf down PBJ and milk. I can't imagine strolling into Sunday Mass and detonating a bomb during communion. What type of animal would do such a thing? How could they not fight against the impulse to kill? And how…how do you possibly live with yourself after the fact?

"No. Because 9 times out of 10, they kill themselves, if they're not killed first. He doesn't give them an opportunity to repent or feel remorse. Their lives are not his concern; just wants them to do his bidding."

"Who does?"

Toyol turns his attention from the black and white boxes on the screen, an edge of malice rimming his black eyes. "Lucifer."

Lucifer.

As in…

"Satan?" I whisper so quietly that no human ears could hear. As if saying his name would make him appear.

"Satan. Beezlebub. The devil. Abaddon. Apollyon," Andras answers. "Many names for a very large ego. But yes. He is responsible. He infects them before birth, while still in their mother's womb. They are born sinner, and will die sinner."

"But that won't be you," L suddenly declares, his deep voice heavy with conviction. "I won't let anyone, or anything, hurt you."

I turn to face him, my gaze sweeping over his taut frame. His large hands gripping the back of the sofa, the tension in those powerful shoulders flexing through his form fitting shirt…he always looks like a rubber band on the verge of snapping. If intimidation had a face—a body—it'd be him. Yet, there's something about him…something familiar and comforting. Maybe it's the way he held me, or the calm words he whispered over and over while I sobbed myself to sleep. Maybe it's the images that randomly flash before my eyes that I can't explain. I've felt his hands on my body—those thick, callused fingers much gentler than they appear as they roamed my sensitive flesh. I've tasted every inch of his skin, just as he has feasted on every inch of mine. I've heard his laughter and basked in his smile.

I know this man, yet I don't. Not at all.

"Eden? Eden?"

I blink furiously, breaking the spell at the sound of my name. "Um, huh?"

Lilith giggles. "I said, are you hungry? You didn't eat much before you passed out, and I'm hoping that doesn't happen again. There's a lot you need to learn."

"Learn?" I frown. Lucifer infected me with evil while I was still a growing fetus. My mother was right—I have the devil inside me. How much more do I need to know?

"What you are," L interjects. "You need to know what you are so we can stop the Calling. So *I'm* not forced to kill you."

"But you told me already. I already know that I'm one of these *Called* freaks, and I need to be locked away before I do something terrible. What else is there to know?"

A slow, sinuous smirk curls itself on the edge of his full lips. Lips I've kissed, yet haven't. "Food first. You'll need it."

TEN

Phenex arrives with Cain while Jinn makes me a bowl of homemade soup. I insist that I can just heat up some leftovers or make a sandwich, but he simply ignores me, his focus on the vegetables on his chopping board.

"He doesn't like me, does he?" I whisper to Lily—*dammit*—Lilith. It's easy to fall back into friendship with her. She just seems…normal to me.

"Who Jinn? Why do you say that?"

"Well…" I look over at the bronze, bearded man, praying furiously that he can't hear me from the dining room table. If what Toyol said was true, I do *not* want to get on his bad side. "He won't talk to me."

Lilith laughs gleefully, causing me to look around to see if I've missed something. "He won't talk to you, because he can't, silly! His tongue is cut out."

"Oh my God. I'm so sorry." I cover my mouth with trembling fingers. I'm not sure why I'm apologizing to her, but it seems like the right thing to say. And then there's the G-word. I'm locked in a high-rise apartment with a posse of demons. Isn't that kinda like playing Biggie at a Death Row party?

She shrugs. "Happened a long time ago. Cooking helps him relax."

"So…did L-Lucifer do it? For killing his pawns?"

"Nope. He did it himself." She says it so casually, as if she was telling me what she had for breakfast. He cut out his own tongue. What drives a person to mutilate himself?

"But…why?" I know they have cat-like reflexes—I've seen them. And superhuman strength as well. But I really, *really* hope Jinn can't hear me prying into his past.

"The Jinn uses his influence to inflict harm on his victims. He whispers in their ear, glamours them with their own desires. He doesn't infringe on their free will, yet makes them believe that they want to do vicious, lustful acts. You sleep with your best friend's husband because you're so owned by your basal desires. You steal money from your neighbor because you trust you need it more than they do. You slit someone's throat because the thought of their blood spilling over your hands arouses you. He takes your weakness—your faults—and gives it that little nudge over the edge." She takes a beat to look at the strong, silent man gently plucking fresh herbs for the soup, and sighs. "It can take a toll on you… the constant treachery and deceit. Constantly evoking pain and anger and misery. It can suck you dry until there's nothing left. Until you begin to feel just like your victims."

I blink at her humble testimony. "But isn't that what you

want? For us all to hurt? For the world to bow to evil?"

She turns back to me, the remnants of a wince still resting on her brow. "We're demons, Eden. That doesn't mean we don't have a conscience."

"Speak for yourself," a gruff voice says from across the table. Cain. Son of Adam and Eve, Killer of Abel. Demon of Murder. There's a slight squint in his jet black eyes as he glares at me, picking me apart like a vulture. Trying to unhinge me with his venomous leer. I feel spiders crawl all over my body, scraping and scratching my skin with their spiny, little legs. But still, I hold his stare.

I won't let him see how much he terrifies me, and how just by looking at that grotesque scar makes my stomach roil. I won't give him the satisfaction that he so craves.

I believe he may have been beautiful once. And he still could be now, even with the disfigurement. But he doesn't want to be. He relishes the fear, the disgust. He wants people to grimace and avoid eye contact. He delights in making women clutch their purses to scurry to the opposite side of the street when he approaches. He takes joy in intimidating lesser men, reducing them to cowering little boys.

I know him, because I *am* him.

Isolation is a much better option than rejection.

Showing fear at this point would only prove how truly helpless I am. I've fainted over brunch, cried until snot bubbled from my nose, vomited in my hair. I seem like all the rest to him—pathetic, weak. He hates that I'm here; that much is evident. Yet he's one of them. So maybe he doesn't despise me as much as he appears to. Maybe he has no choice in the matter.

"I despise you," he sneers, showing his teeth. So much for that theory.

"Huh?" His words coupled with the harshness of his tone catch me off guard.

"I said, I despise you. What you are…what you're capable of. Yet you're cheating your fate. Coward."

"Give it a rest, Cain," Lilith retorts, waving him off. "He's just mad because he hasn't had a kill in the last six weeks."

"I should have been there the other night! I was en route!" he shouts, flailing his arms. No one even gives him a second glance.

"L and I handled it just fine."

"Huh," he snorts. "You mean, *L* handled it. You were about to be rat food. You know…I'm disappointed in you, Lil. You're usually much more focused. Maybe three decades without dick is making you lose your edge. And we all know your roomie, Andras, isn't giving it to you. Tell me, do you two share dildos?"

It happens so fast that I don't even have a chance to scream or take cover, yet the sheer velocity itself knocks me backwards in my chair. I scramble from the ground just in time to see Lilith lift Cain a foot off the ground with one hand grasping his collar. Then she slams him back onto the marble tabletop with a resounding crack, hard enough to shatter his skull into dust.

"Watch your tongue, Cain. Or I'll carve you up and give you a full smile," she hisses, crawling up his body like a creature devoid of bones and joints. Her arms and legs bend at opposite angles. Her neck stretches impossibly long and serpent-like, and I could have sworn actual fangs descended from her mouth.

She lifts a clawed hand, aiming to strike, just as L decides to enter the common area from his bedroom. He stops several feet from the scene and shakes his head.

"Knock it off, you two. I'm not buying another table."

With a sinister smile that definitely showcases razor sharp canines, Lilith slowly climbs down Cain's hulking frame. The mountain-sized man jumps up without any signs of injury, and smoothes his clothing.

"Dammit, Lil, this is a new shirt! I was just fucking around. Stop being so sensitive."

Lilith gingerly picks up the scattered chairs and sits down with all the grace of a ballerina. "Apologize," she demands flippantly, fluffing her blonde hair to its original perfection.

"Sorry. Shit." Cain flops back into his own seat, his face red with anger…or embarrassment.

"Not to me." She waves a manicured hand to where I still stand, eyes wide. "Her."

"What? I'm not apologizing to some filthy human—"

"Apologize or I'll cut your nuts off with a butter knife."

Begrudgingly, Cain turns to me, his mouth fixed in a severe line. He heaves out an aggravated breath and crosses his arms, his bulging biceps lined with veins. "I apologize."

"For what?" Lilith asks sweetly.

He releases a resigning breath and flares his nostrils like a bull. "For being a dick to you."

"Good! That's much better!"

L coughs loudly, a hand cupped over his mouth to stifle his laughter. A low growl from Cain's side of the table rumbles the floor.

The ruckus seemingly over, Jinn brings over a piping hot bowl of soup and sets it in front of my seat, along with a basket of fresh baked breads. I timidly slink back to my chair, my belly leading the way. The first spoonful nearly scorches my tongue, but it's worth it. Oh so worth it. Juicy morsels of chicken, tender vegetables, al dente pasta and fresh herbs and spices. I could eat this soup every day for the rest of my life and never tire of it. I pick up a slice of warm bread and dip it into the broth, letting the flavor seep into each nook and cranny. It's Heaven—actual Heaven—in my mouth.

"I still despise you," Cain grumbles, watching me like a malnourished hawk.

I finish chewing before gently dabbing my mouth with a cloth napkin. "That's ok. I don't particularly like you either. You should really get some help for those anger issues. Roid rage is a serious thing, ya know." Then I take another bite, my eyes never leaving his.

The redness in Cain's face seeps into his ears, and his arms flex so tight that his new shirt begins to tear at the biceps. L *coughs* a little harder.

Jinn returns to the table with another bowl, setting it in front of Cain. A small Band-Aid for his fractured ego. When he turns back towards the kitchen, I swear I see a smile tugging on his lips.

"I know you have questions about why you're here…and what we plan to do with you," L says from the head of the table.

Again, I sit to his right, wedged between him and Lilith. Phenex sits across from me, those russet eyes emitting calm and serenity.

"I do." That's an understatement. I don't understand any of this. I don't get why I was chosen to be Called. And furthermore, I don't get why a band of demon assassins have vowed to protect me.

"Eden, what happened when you were five?"

Warmth leeches from my face despite the warm temperature in the apartment. I look down at my hands knotted in my lap. "I don't know what you mean."

"It's ok, Eden," Lilith whispers soothingly. She reaches over and unknots my fingers, taking my hand in hers. She's hot—burning up—just like L. I hadn't noticed before, but then again, I can't remember touching her. We only really saw each other at the store where it was always freezing. I'm starting to guess why, and it has nothing to do with Eduardo's frugalness.

I look up and glance around the table. Seven sets of eager eyes stare back, waiting for me to confirm my fate.

"My mother…she said the only way she could cleanse my soul was to baptize me. One morning, she made me pancakes. I had never had them before. Then she lit candles all around the bathroom. She recited scripture and sang hymns." I swallow through the tightness in my throat. "She put me in the tub filled with water and held me down. I fought and clawed to get to the surface, but she wouldn't let go. She wouldn't let me up. Eventually, I stopped fighting."

Phenex nods, his mouth in a tight, grim line. "You drowned."

"Yes."

"And after?"

"After…" I close my eyes, conjuring the memory that I'd vowed to never unearth. It had been locked up tight, behind chained doors and brick walls. Far beyond forgotten birthdays, freezing nights on a hard cot and empty, roach-infested cabinets. Only two memories sat covered in blankets of dust in that small, dark space. This was one of them. "After I woke up under water, I was cold, pale. But I was alive. And it was nighttime."

It's completely silent, save for the beating of one heart. My heart.

"Was there anyone else in the house?" L asks, his voice devoid of its usual timbre.

I shake my head. "No one ever came to visit. The entire neighborhood knew my mother was crazy."

"Any animals…pets?"

"A dog," I nod. "A stray. I don't know why it kept coming around. We didn't have any food save for the scraps I'd feed it whenever I could spare a little extra. It was my only friend. My mom hated that dog. She must've chased it away for good once she thought…once she…" I swallow the bile in my throat, determined to get through it without cracking. Without showing them how irrevocably weak and broken I am. "…thought I was dead."

L looks to Phenex who nods once in response. They don't seem surprised at all by my account.

"Eden, you survived because you were inhabited by what we call a Jumper," the mahogany angel-demon explains. "Your canine companion wasn't just there for table scraps. She was there to save you."

"She?" This doesn't make sense. None of it does. I had just chalked that incident up as one of the many bizarrely tragic occurrences of my life.

"Adriel," L answers.

I frown and shake my head. Not this shit again. "Look, I told you I don't know—"

"Adriel is an angel. She had to have fallen in order to find you…in order to save you. She used the dog as a vessel. That's why it came into your life. She knew…she knew it was only a matter of time. She jumped into your body before it was too late."

I blink once…twice. Panic fills my lungs, causing each breath to escape in short pants. *Angel. Adriel is an angel. Inside* me.

"But that…that can't *be*."

"You have abilities you can't explain. You're able to bend the wills of humans with just a single word. Why do you think that's so?"

I shake my head furiously. Lilith gives my hand a comforting squeeze, but I snatch it out of her grasp. "No. No, that's not possible. *None* of this is possible." Angels, demons…it's ludicrous.

"Eden, we can help you," Phenex assures. "That's what we've been trying to get you to understand. If you're Called—if Lucifer activates you while Adriel still inhabits your soul…"

"You'll have the ability to wipe out mankind," L concludes, his silver eyes glowing like orbs of moonstone.

"No!" Sweat slickens my palms as I push away from the table and jump to my feet. "You're wrong!" I scream, desperately trying to believe my own claims.

Accepting their outlandish theory would be accepting that there truly is no good left in the world. Because how could an angel stand by and watch a child suffer? How could an angel endure beating after beating? How could an angel command me to hurt people, deceive people…murder people?

I believed them when they told me I was born with a touch of evil running through my veins. *That* I could imagine. *That* I could grasp as an explanation for all the wrong I've done. But this? I'm no angel. An angel wouldn't revel in the suffering of others.

"You don't know what you're talking about," I say, my voice as hollow as my soul. "You don't know *anything* about me and the things I've done."

L climbs to his feet in one swift movement, his fists balled at his sides. He pins me with that starlit stare, swimming with his own ancient pains. "Yes. I do," he grits, his jaw quivering under the weight of his earnest declaration.

"How? You weren't there. You don't know…" *What I did. What I caused.* "You can't know for sure."

He steps around the table and comes to stand before me, close enough that I can feel his fire. "Yes. I do."

"How?" I whisper, daring to look at him. Daring to gaze at that devastatingly handsome faced carved of stone and bone.

"Because I once was seraphim," he pronounces, his all-commanding tone rumbling the floor beneath my socked feet. A blast of sweltering heat radiates around his entire frame, forcing me back. "But now… I… Am… Legion."

ELEVEN

We sit around the table, cloaked in the silent aftermath of truth. No one has spoken in several minutes, yet I can hear their questions. I can feel their probing gazes fixed on me, wondering if I'll run, scream, cry.

I'm too numb to do any of that.

I open my mouth, but quickly close it, words escaping me. What do you say to one of the most powerful and feared demons in history? To the beast that terrorized innocents and destroyed whole villages? I don't even know how I can ever look at him again. That wasn't understanding or hurt swirling in his eyes. It was the ashen faces of many…many…demons that amount to the monster sitting beside me.

"That's enough for today," he announces, jumping to his feet as if his chair were on fire. Without a word, he strides to the front door and yanks it open, disappearing into the darkened hall.

"I'll go," Cain says, heaving out a sigh. He makes his way towards the exit as the other males quickly scatter, retreating to different areas of the apartment.

I look to Lilith, my brow furrowed in question.

"He feels more than anyone. Hurts more than anyone. When your very being is comprised of dozens of lost souls, your misery becomes interminable. You can't determine what's truly you, and what's them. He's been fighting for millennia, seeking penance for each one of them. He won't give up. He thinks...he thinks one day, he'll somehow make his way back into Heaven. And by saving you, he believes it will help him earn God's favor and mercy."

I look towards the closed front door. Not even Legion's ghost remains.

Lilith, Andras and Toyol head out for the next patrol shift, leaving me with Jinn and Phenex. While the pair doesn't invoke any more fear than the others do, I turn down Phenex's offer of a game of chess and resign myself to the confines of Legion's bedroom. Luckily, Lilith lent me a few books to pass the time.

"This one, you have to read," she'd beamed, holding up a red hardback book with bold lettering. I touched my fingers to the artwork on the cover—a girl with a swirling tattoo spanning the length of her forearm. It doesn't look like the tales I usually choose for myself, as I'd always opted for more contemporary reads.

"What's it about?" I had inquired.

She shook her head. "If I tell you, you won't read it. Just trust me on this one, ok? Have a little faith."

She was right. I wouldn't have read it.

But as I flip through the pages, my eyes eager to absorb every word as my heart flutters in my chest, I'm so glad I took her advice. I lose myself in the fantastical journey, feeling the heroine's anger, desperation…terror. I even feel a little kernel of something else. Hope. Maybe even love.

"Knock, knock," Phenex says at the doorway, his face shrouded in shadows. Night has already fallen. I didn't even realize so much time had passed.

"Hey," I say with a tight smile.

"I thought I could give you a tour while Jinn prepares dinner. I have to say—I think he likes having you here. It's not often that he gets to cook three meals a day."

I save my place with a bookmark and reluctantly slide off the bed. "He doesn't usually do that?"

Phenex shakes his head. "When we're not patrolling, we rest or train. Besides, we don't require sustenance as regularly as humans."

"Oh. Well, please don't trouble yourselves on my account. I just had soup not long ago, and I usually don't eat much." Or usually have such good food at my disposable.

"No trouble at all. The others will appreciate something warm in their bellies when they get home later tonight. Come. I'll show you where everything is so you can make yourself at home."

Home.

This isn't my home. It will *never* be my home.

I can't be certain that I even know what home is.

Phenex leads me down the hallway, stopping at the door closest to Legion's room. "Here is Lilith and Andras's quarters," he explains, waving his hand around the vast space. It's huge. One side is clearly Lilith's, decked out in soft pinks and purples and teals. Her section is partitioned by a divider bedecked with twinkle lights, while Andras's living quarters is separated by an Asian-style screen. Between their respective sections is a grouping of plush, funky-colored chairs, a 65 inch television, bookcases and a desk. A door leading to an en suite bathroom is situated to the left. The setup reminds me of dorm room, if dorms were three times their size and furnished with the finest accoutrements money could buy.

"This building was once a warehouse," Phenex explains, noting my amazement. "We completely refurbished it and now live on the entire top floor. Below us, in this building, there's a bar, a restaurant and a couple boutiques."

No wonder this place is so big. They have an entire block to live on.

Across from Lilith and Andras's room is Phenex and Jinn's living area. The set-up is pretty much the same, although the décor is starkly different. While the blonde demons adorned their space with colors and textures and finery, Jinn and Phenex had kept theirs fairly simple, opting for muted earth tones and rich woods. There is no television, I note, however, the common area is filled with wall-to-wall books. Every language, ranging from ancient tomes to more recent works. A heavy, dark mahogany desk is centrally located against the wall.

"If you all have so much space here, why not just make individual bedrooms?" I ask, not meaning to offend. I offer a small smile to show my intent.

"It's better for us to be close to our own kind. The temptation to revert to our old nature can be hard to ignore in isolation. Being together keeps us accountable. It keeps us connected to each other."

I nod, understanding. "But…L…" I still can't say his name out loud.

"Legion has enough souls of his own to keep him company." One side of his mouth curls up and he shrugs sheepishly.

The door beside their room contains an infirmary stocked with a variety of bandages, high tech machines that I've only seen on *House* and even a hospital bed. Phenex said he was a medical doctor. I vaguely wonder how many times he's had to patch up a nasty cut or reset a bone. Demons were said to be immortal. Wouldn't they just regenerate or heal themselves?

"Our bodies on Earth are somewhat susceptible to harm, much like humans," Phenex says, answering my unspoken musings. "We can heal from most superficial wounds on our own within minutes, but more serious injuries can render us debilitated, and unable to recover. That's where modern medicine comes in."

I run my fingers over a machine consisting of about a dozen different buttons and a screened monitor. "Is it more difficult to treat your kind? Or is it much like treating a human?"

"It's essentially the same. We aren't able to use anesthesia so—"

"Wait. You don't use any painkillers?"

Phenex smiles in that easy way that makes his eyes sparkle with golden sunlight. "It's unnecessary. Since our bodies run at about 103 degrees, we'd burn it off before it could even take effect."

"So they're wide awake, feeling *everything*? Even for surgical procedures?"

He nods. "If they don't pass out from the pain first."

A cold shiver snakes its way up my spine. How…awful.

We step into the hall and I point to a door across from the infirmary. "Hey, what's in there?"

"Storage," he answers coolly, before ushering me to Cain and Toyol's quarters.

It is exactly as I'd expected. Dark in color, and jam-packed with endless entertainment and gadgets. Other than the king-sized beds and clothing strewn about, you'd think you just walked into Best Buy. It's also littered with random weapons—guns, hunting knives, and swords, as well as some other things I'm not familiar with. We don't stay in there more than a couple minutes.

"Can I ask you something?" I say as we make our way to the living room.

"Of course." Phenex settles onto the couch, prompting me to take the seat across from him.

"Why can't I leave? Why can't I see my sister?"

He takes a deep breath, steepling his fingers in front of his chin. "You're still a risk to the general population. If you're Called while out there, you would be a danger to everyone around you, especially your sister. We're keeping you here for your safety, and theirs. Not because we want to be cruel. Just the opposite, actually."

"But what if I'm Called here? What could you do to stop it?"

"Well, you can't bend our wills, so your only method of attack would be physical. And we could…deal with it."

Translation: *We would kill you.*

He doesn't have to say the words. I can read it clearly on his beautiful face.

"But…for how long? I can't stay here forever. I can't be locked away from the outside world for the rest of my life." The thought of never interacting with another human being, never feeling the sunlight on my face, never dipping my toes in the freezing waters of Lake Michigan…honestly, it's no better than being dead.

"We've been searching for a way to intercept the Calling. Maybe with training and careful guidance, we can detect the signs in time to avoid tragedy." He opens and closes his hands as if trying to capture my anxiety in his palms.

"And if I don't fulfill what I was Called for? If you somehow avoid an attack? What then?"

His eyes fall to the floor for just a moment, as if the sheer weight of his remorse is too much to bear all at once. When he looks back up at me, his expression is grim…hopeless. "We keep you from committing suicide."

I'm trapped by my own destiny, caged in by the hand this life—my *insignificant, inconsequential* human life—has dealt me. If I stay, I remain isolated from everything I know. No more than a prisoner in a cushy jail cell. If I go, I risk hurting people—killing people. There's no way to stop what's coming. No way to fight against it. Andras was right. I was born sinner, and I will die sinner. Even if it's at my own hands.

"There may be a way..." Phenex offers. He twists his full lips, as if struggling with the decision to tell me. "We may be able to find out what you were bred for, and help you—teach you—to battle against the urge. Especially with Adriel..."

"Adriel? Why would she help me? She's done nothing but prolong the inevitable anyway."

Phenex frowns. "She saved your life, Eden."

"I would have been better off dead!" The words tumble out of me before I can slow their momentum. I don't mean to yell, especially at one who's shown me nothing but kindness and caring since I was taken. I'm not used to that. I'm not used to *any* of this.

"I don't believe that," he says, shaking his head. "And neither do you. You have a purpose, Eden. A purpose bigger than you, bigger than me, bigger than all of us. Adriel must have seen that. We don't know why she fell, but she did so for a reason. Maybe she..." He shakes his head. "Never mind."

"What?"

"I don't believe she would have risked the fall if she knew all hope was lost. If she knew there was no way to get back."

I want to tell him that he's wrong. Adriel is not what he thinks she is. Whispering in my head, telling me to hurt people to satisfy my own irrational anger, does not earn you a ticket back into Heaven. Adriel didn't fall to bring me to salvation. She fell to bring us to our knees.

Legion and Cain don't make it back in time for dinner. I don't miss the forced chatter around the table as we dine on venison stew and sweet corn bread. It's divine, of course, but all I can taste is the bitter flavor of my fate.

I'm going to die here.

I jerk awake at the deafening sound of a metal against metal. My first instinct is to scream, run, but my voice is merely a choked whisper when I see two dark, daunting figures stagger inside the bedroom, lit only by shimmering moonlight streaming from the window.

"Shit, L, you weigh a fucking ton!" Cain barks, leading the taller man to the bed. I sit up and pull the sheets up to my chin. Lilith gave me a nightgown to wear, and while beautiful, it's more than a bit thin. Thick flannel pajamas just wouldn't work for her and her elevated body temp.

My first thought is that he's hurt, and I bite down on the foolish panic rising in my gut. But then I hear something that completely confounds me.

Legion…laughs.

Cain has him hoisted up with one of Legion's tattooed arms around his shoulders. As soon as he sets him on the edge of the bed, he tumbles back, his blissed-out face landing just inches from my leg.

"What happened to him?" I whisper to the scarred demon.

Cain looks at me, and oddly enough, his gaze is devoid of its usual spite. Instead, he looks…amused. "Your boy here is a lightweight."

"He's drunk?"

"No, I'm not!" Legion slurs before breaking into a fit of

chuckles. "I'll take any of you…any of you on right this second. Help me up. I'll show you. Ain't shit light about me!"

I had been worried, as much as I hate to admit it. Worried that something was happening. And all this time, he had been out *drinking*.

"Easy, big man," Cain bristles, pulling off his friend's boots. "Maybe some other time. I wouldn't want to blemish that pretty face of yours."

"Bull. Shit." Legion looks up, turning those silver eyes on my stunned expression, before letting them move over my bare shoulders and exposed arms. His mouth parts slightly, and something else entirely fills his gaze.

Hunger.

I can't look away.

"Ok, pretty boy," Cain says, straightening his back. "Time to get some sleep. You're on your own with undressing. Fuck that."

I want to tell him to stay, to save me from the raging beast hidden in Legion's stare.

Save me from the turmoil I feel for this monster of a man. Save me from myself.

But Cain swaggers out of the room, a devious smirk on his marred face. He's playing a dangerous game. Maybe we both are.

I can't stand the quiet. Can't stand the way he just…stares. I swallow, washing away my trepidation.

"Come on. You should get into bed."

"Yeah." He finally blinks, remembering who he is. Remembering who I am. With some effort, he flips over and places his knees on the bed, moving as if the weight of his massive frame is leaden with exhaustion. He's on all fours like the animal he is, that ghostly gaze whispering over my chill-bumped skin. I can feel his heat wafting over me, caressing my neck, kissing my lips, sliding over my satin-covered nipples.

He slowly crawls towards the top of the bed, his movements lithe and deadly like a panther. I hold my breath for what seems like eternity, counting each of my frantic heartbeats as he gets closer…closer…closer…until he's right in front of me. I once thought the size of this bed was ridiculous. Now I'm not so sure if I'm grateful or frustrated for it.

When he hovers over my bent knees, those muscled forearms on either side of my thighs, I gasp. He moves in just a fraction closer, aligning his face with mine. *Seeing me.* He sees me to my soul. He sees all the ugly, all the pain. All the desire kindling within my trembling flesh.

I don't expel a breath until he suddenly rolls his body over, settling onto his back. He grips his pillow behind his head, his knuckles so taut that I fear he may rip it in two. Impossibly long, dark lashes fan over proud cheekbones as he closes his eyes. Within seconds, his breathing becomes heavy and deep.

I don't think I'll be able to sleep a wink.

TWELVE

IT BEGINS LIKE THEY ALWAYS DO.

Cold concrete bites the bottom of my bare feet. The blade in my hand feels weightless, and I stroke it over my naked bosom like a silken feather. I gasp at the sensation of tiny thorns pricking my nipples and let it drift down to my belly, carving phantom symbols along my ribs. I sway my hips from side to side, dipping and rolling so he can see every inch of my body in all its glory. So he can see what pleasure I can bring him.

I hear their cries, a sweet, erotic symphony to my slow, sinuous dance. They beg me to let them go. Beg me to spare their pathetic little lives. I dip my head back and laugh, allowing them to take in the view of my heavy breasts quaking with my amusement. I part my thighs and tease my slick lips with the very tip of the blade. I moan at the sensation of sharp steel against wet warmth. With eyes pinned on my captives, I bring the knife to my waiting tongue and lick it clean.

They want it too. They just don't know it yet. But I plan to make them want it.

I know the faster I slaughter them, the faster I can take him inside me. I burn for him, but this game is too fun. The anticipation, the longing, it's just as sweet as the kill. And when I get my reward—when he bends me over in a pool of fresh, warm blood and buries himself inside me to the hilt—it will be even sweeter.

A blinding flash of light envelops the room, swallowing it whole like a supernova. When my eyes adjust to the strange, bright blaze, I find that I'm in a bed draped in silk and satin the color of morning mist. There's no more cold at my feet, no blade in my hands. My body is warm and soft and eager. I stretch my limbs and smile, a soft sigh escaping my upturned lips.

He crawls over my body, wearing that devilish smirk that makes me weak in the knees. I feign fright and try to escape his approach, but he swiftly catches my thigh and pulls me to him.

"You can't run away from me," he smiles lazily.

I look up into those eyes the shade of summer rain and lift a hand to play in his midnight hair. He shivers under my touch. "Why would I want to?"

"Never," he breathes, dipping his head so that lips brush against mine. I shiver at the feeling of his short scuff tickling my face. "Never be afraid of me. Never run from me."

"Never," I promise, meaning the word more than the promise of my next heartbeat.

He parts my thighs gently with a push of his knee and settles between my legs. I feel him against me, throbbing, growing harder and longer still. It pushes at my entrance without him even flexing his hips.

"Never," I repeat, on a breathless moan. The tip of him eases into my body, the burning, aching sensation a balm to my trembling flesh. "Never," I moan into his mouth as his tongue tastes mine.

He sits upright, taking me with him so I slowly slide onto his length, fitting around him like a glove. I want to move—want to feel him as deep as my body will take him…as deep as he can go—but he cradles me, gripping my back, my hips, while I clutch his chiseled shoulders. *Hold on to him*, a voice whispers. *Hold on and never let go…*

I gasp awake in the earliest moments of dawn, my limbs tangled with Legion's under the sheets. He sleeps soundly on his back, my cheek pressed to his chest, his arm wrapped around my body protectively. We're both on his side of the bed. Either he pulled me to him or I must've rolled towards him in the night, seeking his heat against the frigid air. He holds me so tight, as if he's afraid I'll slip away. As if some unspeakable evil will rip me from his clutches in the midnight hours.

I dare a glance at his face, wondering if he can feel my eyes on him. Wondering if he's aware of the way my bare leg is hitched up onto his thigh. I should pull myself away from him and go back to my side of this stupidly large bed, but I fear it will wake him. And he's so warm. So warm when my heart is so cold.

I'm not ready to wake up. I'm not ready to leave the safety

and serenity of this cocoon and face another day of learning my fate.

I close my eyes against the rising sun, and long for night for just a little longer. Just a few more minutes of his darkness to make me feel fragile and human again. The day brings questions that dissolve in morbid answers. Truths that leave me even more confused and angry. I don't want to leave this bed, or his arms, or this charade. Not yet.

I hear a voice beckoning, but the blanket of sleep has already covered me. I let it sing me a lullaby, soft and melodic, until all I feel is heat and smooth stone and satin the color of rain clouds. Until obscurity eclipses the sun through my closed eyelids.

Hold on to him. Hold on and never let go.

"Never," I whisper into Legion's chest before drifting back to sleep.

Legion isn't in bed when I wake up for the second time around mid-morning, and I'm grateful. I can't imagine what had to have been going through his mind when he awoke to me nestled in his arms. Honestly, I don't even know what was going through *my* mind. He's a demon. A creature of filth and destruction. A monster that brutalized me when I was scared and confused. Yet his touch brought me safety. His words brought me comfort. His very presence chased away the terrors in my dreams and replaced them with something else. Something sweet and tender. He replaced that wickedness with…himself.

I'd been having the nightmares for years now, each one leaving me shaken to my core. It was always the same: cold, cement room without doors and windows, me naked and writhing…and their cries. Their blood. And eventually, me and someone or something I can't see—can't quite touch—fucking me senseless among the gore of slaughtered corpses.

I always scream for him. I always beg for more and more. He pummels my insides until my flesh is inflamed and sore, yet I don't want him to stop. It's as if I yearn for the cruelty. I know it's wrong, but some part of me—something sick and twisted and depraved—feels like it's right. Like his brand of wicked calls to me.

I fist my tousled hair in frustration, as if to pull the sadistic thoughts from my head. I'm in desperate need of a good, cleansing shower to wash away the lingering terror. There isn't a stack of clean clothes on the bed, but there is a large cardboard box by the dresser. Apparently someone got tired of smuggling my things from my old apartment and decided to pack up my stuff. Clothes, shoes, toiletries, books, my phone charger. No photos or any other reminders of the life I've been forced to leave behind. I'm glad for it. I've already boxed up those memories and stored them away for good.

I shower and dress in black yoga pants and a sweatshirt, opting for comfort over fashion, before padding out to the living room. To my surprise, everyone is gone, save for Andras and…Legion.

He sits at the dining room table, staring into a cup of coffee. His forehead is in his hand, his elbow pressed to the marble as if it's a great effort to keep from falling face first into the hot brew.

I make my way to the couch where Andras is watching television. He seems like the lesser of two evils.

"Morning, sleepyhead," he says in greeting. "Jinn left you breakfast on the stove."

I nod and give him a tight smile. "Where is everyone?"

"Patrol mostly. Lilith wanted to go shopping. Such a vain little creature." He flips the channel to something on HBO, an older movie starring Al Pacino. He snorts a laugh. "I swear, they always depict him as some dark haired, old guy. Humans."

"Who?"

"Lucifer," he answers flippantly. "Doesn't anyone crack a book these days? He was God's favorite, the most talented and beautiful of all the angels. Why the hell would he look like an over-the-hill, saggy-balled, short dude?"

Lucifer.

Just imagining him as anything other than a red, horned beast unnerves me.

"So…what does he look like?"

Andras shrugs. "Gorgeous. Tall. Sensual. Just as the Creator made his people in his image, Lucifer made us in his. Well, most of us anyway."

My curious eyes unabashedly roam the beautiful blonde man from head to toe. Deep-set crystal blue eyes, a straight perfect nose, full, pouty lips. His shoulder-length blonde hair is tied back into a man-bun, which normally would make me cringe. However, it's stylish and sleek on him. I have no doubt in my mind that he could wear a bag over his head and somehow pull it off as alluring and mysterious.

If this is the work of Satan, I can't fathom what *he* looks like.

"I thought there were only male angels and demons," I say, switching gears. "There's Lilith and…Adriel."

"The Bible was written by misogynists who thought it was God's Will to beat women and sacrifice virgins. And some of the *holiest* men had several wives and concubines, viewing women as merely incubators for their righteous seed. Don't believe the hype."

I nod in agreement. Unfortunately, too many micro-dicked egomaniacs have adopted the same thinking in the modern world.

I allow myself just the tiniest glance over at Legion, who still sits with his head in his palm, his coffee untouched. Andras follows my line of vision and flashes a cunning half smile.

"He's been there all morning," he almost whispers.

"Huh?"

"I think last night really did him in. He's not much of a drinker. To imbibe to excess is…sinful."

That's an odd thing to say. I frown, confused. "Why would he care about what's sinful. I mean, considering what you are, and what he is…" Just the word feels wrong on my tongue.

Andras shrugs. "Legion isn't like other demons. What he believes…what he's been searching for…it's not just for show. He wants to live the life of the righteous. Shit, after roughing you up, he put himself through the ringer. He fasted, he begged for repentance. He wants this more than any of us."

"And what do you want?" I ask, my voice shaky.

"Salvation." The earnest in his eyes is so clear that I can see my reflection in those pools of blue. "It's more attainable for some of us more than others. I'm a card-carrying member of the All Boys Club. According to the good book, I'm damned no matter what."

"You're *gay?*" I don't mean for it to come out so brash, but…he's gay? I guess even demons can't deny who they are. I'm not surprised though. Andras is just too damn pretty. Any woman would be jealous.

"Last I checked," he chuckles. "I was birthed to be angelic and alluring. I was known for…tempting the flesh of men."

Interesting. I've heard of straight men being turned out, but I always just thought they were truly homosexual deep down inside and too scared or stubborn to admit it. Maybe Andras was responsible for more than a few sexual awakenings.

Andras looks over at his leader, his friend…his brother. When his eyes find mine again, he dips his head in Legion's direction. "Go talk to him. I bet he'd appreciate the distraction."

I can't be sure he's right, but something in me stirs. Something sad, lonely and confused. Something I think Legion knows all too well.

Disguising my intrusion with the need for sustenance, I pad into the kitchen for the breakfast Jinn has so graciously left for me: eggs, bacon and homemade biscuits. There's even fresh coffee in the French press. I help myself and take a seat at the dining room table, choosing my usual spot…beside Legion. He doesn't even look up.

"Are you ok?" I finally muster up the courage to ask. He grunts out something resembling *Yeah*.

I silently eat my food, resigned to let him wallow in his guilt and misery. We aren't friends. We aren't anything. He doesn't owe me an explanation or even small talk. I can't expect someone to offer a shred of kindness just because I slept in his arms for the past two nights. Hell, that could very well be the reason he's ignoring me now.

Suddenly feeling insecure and a little bit—no a lot—embarrassed, I decide to cut my meal short and escape to the bedroom. But before I can stand to take my plate to the kitchen, he lifts his face from his hand.

"You were crying."

The napkin falls from my fingertips and lands in my half-eaten eggs. "What?"

"Last night. You were crying in your sleep. I didn't want to wake you so I…" He swallows and looks back down at his coffee. So he did pull me to him. "You were reaching out… searching for someone." *Searching for me.*

I don't know what to say or do. Do I thank him? Do I pretend like nothing happened? No words seem like the right ones so I go with, "Did I…say anything?"

Thankfully, he shakes his head, wincing as if the movement has rattled his aching brains. I'd offer him some Advil but it wouldn't make a difference.

"Oh. I guess that's good."

I look down at my plate. Now I'm wishing I would have continued eating just to have something to do with my mouth.

"I'm sorry."

I lift my head, wondering if I heard him right. "Why?"

"I shouldn't have gotten drunk. It was stupid of me, especially with you in my bed."

"It was fine."

"No, it wasn't," he says with more force than I expect. It's enough to make me shrink back a fraction. "I could have done something you wouldn't have liked. Something unforgiveable."

"I was fine, L," That's the closest to his name I can get. "You didn't hurt me. We just went to sleep."

"Yeah, but I could've. I would've. Don't misunderstand, Eden. I'm a demon. My nature is evil. Just because I've chosen a different path, doesn't mean I'm not prone to lust."

Lust.

Legion...lusts for me?

I take a long sip of strong coffee.

"Eden, there's something you need to know about me."

"Yes?" The word nearly gets caught in my throat.

"When I was—"

Before he can finish his thought, the front door bursts open, spilling darkness into the otherwise brightly lit room. Legion is on his feet within a fraction of a second, fists balled at his sides, and wedged between me and the table. I'd appreciate the fact that I have a full, up-close-and-personal view of his backside if it weren't for the frantic shouts reverberating around the room. I move around Legion's rock-solid frame and see...

Blood.

So much blood everywhere.

On their skin. Soaking their clothes. Splattered on their heavy boots.

That much blood means something is seriously wrong.

That much blood means someone is dead.

THIRTEEN

"**What the fuck happened?**" Legion shouts, his deep roar rattling the windows.

"We were ambushed," Toyol answers, hoisting up Phenex with an arm under his shoulders. Jinn is on his other side. "A dozen of them. It's as if they knew our patrol routes."

Oh no, Phenex. His head lobs back as if he's holding on to consciousness. I look on in horror as I take in the large tear in his pants, exposing a ravaged thigh. It looks as if he had been mauled by a bear. Or worse.

"These fuckers are getting bold. Attacking during daylight? He's getting desperate, L. They want her and they know she's under our protection."

Legion's jaw ticks as he digests his brothers' words. "Get him in the infirmary. We need to get that wound treated before he loses too much blood. Cain, how many are still out there?"

"We killed all but two. They got away when Phenex was hit. *Shit!*" I can read the rage mixed with guilt on his face. His friend was injured and two of whatever they were fighting escaped. He feels responsible.

"Lilith," Andras gasps, his face pale and eyes wide. Legion nods, understanding his anxiety.

"Get her and bring her back. Cain, go with him."

Andras escapes for just a moment, returning to the front of the apartment armed to the teeth and dressed for battle. So different from the blonde angelic man who was just lounging on the couch, flipping through the channels and pretending not to eavesdrop.

Legion turns towards the infirmary once the two demon warriors are out the door.

"I can help," I find myself saying to his back. He doesn't turn around, but he pauses, so I continue. We don't have time for niceties. "Sister…she's an ER nurse. She taught me things. There looks to be arterial damage. I might be able to help."

He's deathly silent for a half a heartbeat before nodding. "Come on."

Ignoring the deep red blood trailing from the door to the hallway, I quickly race to the infirmary, trying to keep up with Legion's strides. Phenex is in bad shape, and barely alert, so I can't ask for guidance. His brothers are not much help either, too stunned and angry to do more than stand there and watch him bleed, their own blood drained from their faces. There's no way I can count on any of them, so I rack my brain, trying to remember everything Sister taught me, everything I picked up while helping her study through nursing school.

Toyol looks up at me, his slanted eyes much wider than I've ever seen them. "Poison."

I inspect his leg. I was right. Blood spurts like a fountain, coating the white tiled floor. Whatever attacked him hit an artery.

"Ok, we need a tourniquet and lots of gauze. L, can you adjust this table and elevate that leg? Jinn, here take this gauze and apply direct pressure. Toyol, help me tie the tourniquet," I instruct, tossing them all latex gloves. The action seems to snap them back to reality, and we quickly spring into action. "Ok, good, above the wound, so it's closer to the heart. Don't make it too tight."

Once the leg is elevated and the blood loss has slowed from a vicious spurt to a steady trickle, I rummage through the large white cabinet containing about a thousand different vials.

"What are you looking for?" Legion asks.

"Adrenaline. I don't know what type of poison is in his system but if you have some secret miracle cure lying around, I suggest you give it to me now. He's losing too much blood. And with his elevated temp, he has minutes. Maybe seconds."

Legion disappears from the room, racing to some undisclosed location and leaving me to read the foreign scrawl on the tiny glass jars. Sweat covers my brow as I squint at the nonsensical characters. It all looks the same to me. I'm in way over my head, but I have to do something other than stand around with my thumb up my ass while someone bleeds out in front of me.

"Here. The antidote," Legion pants, suddenly beside me.

I don't have time to be stunned before he shoves a small, red container in my palm and plucks up a vial containing a clear liquid. "And adrenaline. What do you need that for?"

"You're about to see. Pass me the rubbing alcohol, and hold his shoulders. Jinn, you take his legs. This is going to hurt."

I remove the blood-soaked gauze over the nasty gash and take a deep breath before pouring it directly onto the leg. He screams out in excruciating pain, but I just try to stay focused, swallowing down the lump in my throat. I know I'm doing this all wrong, but I don't know what else to do. All I can think about is saving Phenex's leg…and his life.

"Toyol, I need fresh gauze," I say, clawing at the top of the adrenaline vial. He hands me the fresh, white cloth just as I get it open. I completely soak it before holding it directly onto the wound.

"What are you doing?" Legion questions. He still hasn't let go of his friend's shoulders.

"Boxing trick. It helps clot the wound and speed healing."

"Does it actually work?"

I say a silent prayer. "I guess we'll see."

The mix of the adrenaline and Phenex's accelerated healing allow the cut to clot within minutes, and the blood slows to just a dribble. The tourniquet is no longer necessary and Phenex has stopped screaming in pain. However, he's too still. Too pale. Too cold.

"It's the poison," Toyol explains. "Their blades were coated in it. It's deadly for our kind."

With great effort, I fill a large, sterile syringe with as much antivenom as it will take. It's an odd smoky pearlescent color, nothing like I'd expect for a medical serum. But I don't have time for second guesses. We're losing him fast. If I don't get this right, the Se7en will become six.

Deep breaths, Eden.

I place my ear to his chest, hoping—praying—for a heartbeat to guide my next move. Nothing but a low hum vibrates the space where a human heart would be. I don't have any other alternatives. I look to Legion, searching for any indication that I'm on the right path. Thankfully, he gives me a stiff nod.

Stepping out on faith, I plunge the needle straight into his chest, piercing through flesh and bone. The sickening sounds of metal slicing through thick tissue makes my stomach roil, but I shake it off, pushing down on the plunger. I don't think any of us breathe until Phenex gasps for air, taking in as much oxygen as his lungs can contain. His skin begins to morph from ashen to its normal smooth mahogany. And right before my astonished eyes, tendon and muscle begin to sew themselves back together. It's *working*.

I step back to give them space, knowing that I'm no longer required. Various shades of relief paint all their faces. I smile to myself. I did something…something I never thought I could. Something *good* for a change.

"Hey," Legion says, sidling up next to me, as I scrub the blood off my hands, arms and face. Luckily there's a large basin sink and plenty of soap in the infirmary. Unluckily, there's a deep red trail from the door, filling the enclosed space with a distinct metallic odor tinged with an odd sweetness. Like honeysuckle and sunshine.

"Hey," I reply, casting my gaze down to the whirls of rust trickling down the drain.

"You...were incredible. You saved my brother's life, and for that, I owe you a great debt."

I look up to find him staring at me, his piercing gaze so intense that it steals my breath. Words abandon me, leaving my lips suspended in a soundless gasp. My mind is a scattered jigsaw puzzle, the pieces not quite fitting together to form coherent thoughts. I'm searching...searching for a way to convey what I feel. But even I don't know what it is. This man—this monster—is my would-be killer. Yet every time I touch his skin, his arms wrapped tight around my body, I never feel more alive.

I shake my head, dispelling the insane notion. It's adrenaline, or shock, or a mixture of both. I feel for him what he obviously feels for me. Not a damn thing.

"It's...nothing," I finally reply, mimicking the revelation ringing in my mind. "You don't owe me anything. I don't even know what I did. We just got lucky, honestly."

"No. You helped him, Eden, and as a result, you helped us. You didn't have to. You could have stood by and watched him die, and no one would have faulted you." A frown dimples his brow as if suddenly remembering who I am and what I represent. "Why?"

"I don't know," I shrug, meaning it. "I guess...I guess I couldn't allow someone to die, even a...demon...because of me. Because of trying to protect me." I laugh sardonically, the sound wrong and sad to my own ears. "It wouldn't be worth it."

The frown deepens, seeping into his eyes until they flash with a raging, ancient storm. He steps forward, the movements of his body so fluid...so predatory. Like the panther in my dream. Like the prowling beast from last night.

He opens his mouth, ire on the tip of his tongue. But before he can unleash it on me, Toyol claps him on his shoulder, stealing his attention. I release a breath.

"Hey, man. The others are on their way." Those slanted eyes fall on me, so full of gratitude and relief. He smiles genuinely, easily, like it's second nature. Like he's…happy. "Thank you, Eden. You don't know…thank you." He bows at the waist.

"Um, it was nothing, really. I'm glad he'll be ok."

"He will be," he says, standing upright. "Thanks to you. We're fortunate you were here."

I dry my hands quickly, eager to escape the smell of honeyed blood and their overwhelming appreciation. I'm not used to it…people being pleased by my presence. From the day I was born, I was told I was a burden—a stain on what should have been a happy life. My mother never let me forget what I had ruined. It didn't get better after she was free of me either. Not until I met Sister, did I ever feel a modicum of normalcy. And love.

I make my way to the infirmary exit, smiling stiffly at Jinn when he nods in my direction, his eyes shining with—holy shit—tears. Phenex seems to be resting as his body heals. The wound is completely sealed, although a bit inflamed. It's a miracle. An injury like that would have killed a mortal within minutes, even without the poison.

I nearly burst into a sprint when I hit the hallway, and I don't slow until I get to the bathroom in Legion's bedroom. I need to get these blood-stained clothes off me. I need to scrub the smell of death and ruin from my skin. I can't get the water hot enough. I can't make the shower's jets strong enough. I can't escape what's been done, and who I am, and what will happen as long as I'm alive.

I step out of the shower, not even bothering with a towel, and swipe a hand over the steam-clouded mirror. A girl stares back me, her pain so deep that it pales her complexion.

I don't see an angel. I don't even see the devil.

I see a stranger wearing my silver hair, looking through my brown eyes, breathing my breaths as if each lungful of life belongs to her.

She is not insignificant. Her life is not inconsequential. She is brave, strong, innovative. She saved someone's life today. Someone who would have taken part in her own murder before last week.

She was needed today. She was not a burden. She was not a mistake.

This girl had chosen to be an asset rather than a victim. She would not be a martyr in the face of adversity. She would stand and fight, despite her mortal weakness. Despite her destiny. She would fight…and win.

I take one last look at her before turning away and grabbing a towel. In my haste to get clean, I had forgotten to grab fresh clothes, so I wrap the fluffy terrycloth around my body and open the door, surrendering the solitude of steam and quiet.

Legion sits on the bed, his stoic gaze trained on the bathroom. I yelp in surprise and clutch my chest, careful to keep the towel intact.

"Sorry, I…" His usual scowl adorns his face, his jaw ticking with rage. Or is that frustration? Eyes of quicksilver roam my still-wet body as if he's disgusted by the sight of my exposed flesh. I grip the towel tighter.

Without a word, he stands in a huff, tossing a small bundle on the bed. He stalks from the room without so much as a glance over his shoulder and slams the bedroom door.

There, sitting amongst a sea of storm clouds and satin, are my ear buds, my cell phone and the stolen fork.

A smart person would have called 911. Maybe even called Sister and explained what had happened to me. But a realistic person knew that she'd be signing her death wish.

I had no doubt that my phone was bugged and my activity would be closely monitored. Besides, I couldn't drag anyone else into this. Even a trained human couldn't stand against whatever supernatural forces were out there. And if the Se7en had tapped my phone, who's to say an even greater evil hadn't done the same? I could be leading their enemies—our enemies—right to their front door.

I accept the peace offering for what it is—a small act of faith. He wants to see if he can trust me. He's trying to prove that I'm not a prisoner. I would be a fool to screw that up by testing the limits of kindness.

I lodge the small buds into my ears, scroll to my favorite playlist and pick up the book Lilith had lent me. I lose myself in smooth bass lines and hard-driven lyrics while delving into a fictional world full of fantastical fantasy. I don't even blink until a creeping sensation crawls its way from the top of my shoulders to the base of my spine. I'm not alone. A mountain of unyielding muscle and a hard face carved in a permanent snarl stands less than a yard away at the foot of the bed.

FOURTEEN

"I KNOCKED," CAIN SAYS BEFORE I CAN SCREAM. HIS flat, black eyes go to the headphones dangling from my white knuckled fist, still blasting the sounds of A$AP Rocky. "Your music is too loud."

I swallow down my fear. "What do you want?"

"Family meeting in 5."

Brows raised, I look from side to side, as if to say, *Aaaaaaaand?*

"You need to be there," he responds, reading my expression.

"Why?"

Cain's lips flatten into a thin slash across his marred face before replying, "You saved my brother's life. You're one of us now." He turns and stalks out of the room before I have a chance to object.

BORN SINNER

One of them? I don't know if I should be flattered or insulted. Still, I can't deny the warm feeling in my chest that wraps itself around my cold heart, smothering the dead remains of abandonment and loneliness. I'm ridiculous, I know, but...it feels good to belong. Even if it means I belong to inherent evil.

You're his now.

I shake the foolish notion and climb to my feet. I'm not his. I'm not anybody's.

On timid feet, I enter the dining room area, finding them seated around the marble-top table. Even Phenex sits beside Legion, his reverent, golden eyes gleaming with emotion. He smiles and dips his head as I take the space across from him and beside Legion.

I should have said no...I should have stayed hidden in the room for this reason alone. I don't know what to say, or how to act. Graciously accepting gratitude is completely foreign to me.

Legion pins me with his icy glare, and I can't be sure if he's surprised or upset that I've intruded on their family meeting. I wring my hands in my lap, refusing to acknowledge him. Maybe if I don't speak, or even breathe, I'll be invisible.

"Before we begin," his deep voice echoes in the otherwise silent space, "we need to address something."

Oh, no. No, no, no, no.

I can feel their eyes crawling all over me, picking me apart. Silent questions of how and why ghost across my hot ears. I pull my shoulders inward, hoping they will keep the anxiety from bubbling up from my chest.

"I fucked up," Legion announces, drawing my eyes up to his face. He stares straight ahead, chin held high in defiance.

"I should have been out there with you all this morning. It was my shift, and Phenex stepped in because I was too hungover to get my shit together. Today is on me. And I apologize."

I frown, but say a silent prayer of thanks. I don't know what he's doing, but…

Why?

"Now that that's out of the way… Cain, tell us what you know."

The scarred man nods. "There's been more demon activity than normal in the past 72 hours, centralizing around the southern neighborhoods…"

He recites his detailed report, informing his fellow comrades of the unexplainable increase of demon attacks around the city. Strangers slain on the streets. Entire families slaughtered in their homes. It's Chicago, so the media is chalking it up as inflamed turf wars between rival gangs, but they know differently. They're provoking them. Forcing the Se7en to make a choice: give me up or innocents will die. My mouth dries.

"And do we have a lead on the poison?" Legion asks.

"No," Toyol answers, shaking his head. "It doesn't make sense. Why would the angels give up their only weapon of offense to their enemy? Why surrender the one thing that could lose them the war?"

"What?" I interject before I can stop myself. "What did you say?"

"The angels," Phenex replies, his voice hoarse from screaming. "Their venom is poison to us. The demons earlier today had coated their weapons in it. Someone is supplying them, and only the Seraph, the most exalted, have the resources to do so."

But that…that doesn't make sense. Why would angels work with demons to kill defenseless humans that have absolutely nothing to do with me? And why would something that's supposed to be good and just allow for such death and destruction to sweep through the mortal world? I shake my head, refusing to believe it.

"Why? How?" But even as I ask the questions, I already know the answers. They rest in the corners of his tight lips, the whites of his knuckles, the tightness of his pulsing jaw.

"We don't know," Legion responds, without looking at me.

"You know who may though," Lilith says beside me. I turn to her to find a small smirk on her pink lips. Blonde hair unruffled, clothing without a wrinkle. No signs of brutality. I don't fight the warmth that floods my chest.

"No," is all Legion says, the word sharp and final. He turns away from the mischief in her gaze.

"Come on, L. You know it's our best bet. We can't go out defenseless and expect to protect her when we can't protect ourselves. Whoever is behind these attacks needs to be stopped, or next time it could be worse. Any one of us could have been Phenex. Even *you*."

"No," he repeats. The thunderous timbre of his voice vibrates the heavy marble under his elbows.

"She's right," Andras chimes in. "She's right and you know it. We're practically sitting ducks out there. And that was the final drop of antidote we had left. I highly doubt Lucifer would like to supply us with more of his blood."

"And we could get answers," Lilith adds. "Answers about

why Eden was chosen and what she'll be Called for. If we could pinpoint the nature of her Calling, maybe we could intercept it. Or teach her to fight it. We have to do something other than sitting around with a ticking time bomb waiting to detonate."

I sit up straighter, my face a mask of foolish relief. There's a way…a way to stop the Calling. A way to stop *me*.

"Who?" I ask, my voice tinged with hope.

"The Watcher," Lilith answers, her earnest expression still trained on Legion. "You know I'm right, L. This is the only way."

He doesn't say a word, his tongue seized with selfish pride. How could he just sit there when people are dying? When his own family is at risk? When there's a chance—even a slim one—of stopping me from becoming a killer?

"Please," I whisper, that one word weighted with every ounce of my anxiety. "Please."

His eyes snap to mine, and just for a moment, almost too fast for me to see, he lets his mask slip a fraction, revealing warmth and tenderness. Revealing the Legion from my visions.

He sucks in a deep breath, and closes his eyes on exhale. "Fine. But we stick together and do things my way. Toyol, locate The Watcher's whereabouts. Phenex, how are you healing?"

"About 80%. I'll be fine by morning."

"Good. The Watcher will require an audience, and you have a rapport." Phenex lifts his brows but Legion ignores the silent question. "Lil, make sure Eden is properly prepped and attired. I want a tracker on her."

"Wait…I'm going?" I sputter. I had prepared for them to

go seek out this Watcher, but me… I could be walking into something far more deadly than the Se7en's lair.

"We won't get answers unless you're there," Lilith answers. "Don't worry. You'll be safe."

"Party tomorrow night," Toyol interjects from two seats down, scrolling through his cell phone. "And you'll love the theme."

Legion rolls his eyes and leans back in his seat, crossing the chiseled forearms in front of his chest. "What now?"

"Saints and Sinners," Toyols grins sheepishly.

Legion snorts sardonically. "The Watcher is a twisted motherfucker."

When Toyol said there was a theme, I thought it just pertained to the décor, maybe some festive punch and snacks. No. That would be much too normal. It's a damn costume party.

"Do I *have* to wear this?" I whine, tugging down my skin-tight skirt. We're in Lilith and Andras's room and they've been having a little too much fun at my expense.

"Yes. You'll need to look the part. If you don't, you'll stand out for the wrong reasons. The Watcher loves all things kitschy and extravagant."

I release a huff of air and dare a look into the floor length mirror. My skin has been exfoliated into silk and brushed with oil mixed with gold flecks. The only parts of me that are covered are draped in stark white lace and satin, covering little more than my bikini area and breasts. Gold bangles adorn my wrists along with a cuff around both arms. My heels are strappy and obscenely tall, adding an extra four inches to my average frame. Silver, thick curls cascade down my back and frame a face completely painted with more makeup than they sell at Sephora.

I look like a model for a lingerie brand, or the star in a sacrilegious porno. I am pure sin wrapped in the shade of innocence.

"You look…" Andras muses, looking me up and down. He did my hair while Lilith did my makeup. I swear, those two could make Cain look like Henry Cavill.

"Ridiculous?" I answer. "Slutty? Whorish?"

"Sexy as hell!" he exclaims. "I swear, Eden, if I wasn't into cock, I'd definitely give you the ride of your life. I may make an exception after tonight. You are…more tempting than usual."

"Huh?" I try and fail at hiding the blush from my already bronzed cheeks.

"That Jumper in you?" He explains, grazing a long finger down the thin bodice that stops just under my breasts. "We can feel it…seducing us. Taunting us. Our baser senses have been on overdrive since you got here. That's why it was Lil that was sent to befriend you. Any one of us would have fucked you a long time ago, making it really awkward when we had to kill you."

"Don't count me out just yet," Lilith chimes, coming to stand beside him. "It's been a long, *long* time, and it's not like I haven't dipped a toe or two in the lady pond."

I swallow. Hard.

"So I make you all…" My face flames hot, challenging the staying power of the makeup.

"Horny?" Andras answers. "Incredibly. I don't know how L is resisting you every night. Unless there's something you're not telling us…"

Lilith smacks him playfully on the arm, slicing through the tense intimacy of the moment. "You know that wouldn't happen. Legion would *never*."

I have the nerve to feel affronted, maybe even a little hurt. My pride wounded, I turn back to the strange, sultry girl in the mirror.

"It's not you, love," Lilith quickly says, reading my solemn expression. I feel even dumber. "But Legion doesn't…"

"He's celibate," Andras says, finishing her thought.

"Celibate?" My eyes grow twice in size.

He nods. "Remember how I told you that he doesn't drink to excess? It's like that with all sins. Well, mostly. But sex? Nope. Never. Not for almost a century."

"He hasn't had sex in a hundred years?" I shriek, much louder than I should. I clamp my lips closed. Holy shit. Holy *shit!* How? His balls must be elephantine. And shit, why am I thinking about his balls? I swear, my eyes are so wide that my false lashes are melting onto my perfectly shaped brows.

"Could be longer. Legion was…very much sought after in the underworld. He was strong, powerful, enigmatic and extremely beautiful," Lilith sighs, as if remembering him from his glory years. "He's still handsome, and strong, but that's only a fraction of what he was."

Legion was even *more* gorgeous? I don't know how that's possible. His is the type of body that is built for only two things: bringing men to death and women to orgasm. Eyes plucked from the stars, proud cheekbones, a straight nose and full lips framed by neat facial hair make up his face. He isn't as pretty as Andras, or as exotic as Toyol, or even as regal as Phenex. But he's flawless. Well over six feet of pure male perfection.

And that makes me even more appalled with myself.

How can I be thinking of him like that? How can I feel anything but apathy about his celibacy? It has nothing to do with me. *He* has nothing to do with me. What he does and doesn't do with his dick is none of my business.

"Ok, I think you're ready!" Lilith exclaims. I take in her shiny, vinyl one-piece jumper that dips down to her navel, showing off full breasts and a toned stomach. How she plans to walk in her six-inch platform heels, I'll never know. Her smoky eyes and blood red lips really bring the look together. She looks more dominatrix than demon, not that she looked like one before.

Andras is dressed in a tailored, black-on-black three-piece suit cut close to his body. His blonde locks are swept into a bun and, if I'm not mistaken, he's wearing guy-liner. It actually doesn't look bad on him. Honestly, it looks pretty fuckin' hot. His words replay in my head. I tempt him. I make him burn for me. Not me, though. They're all drawn to Adriel.

Of course they are.

I take one last look in the mirror and steel my nerves before exiting the room. Legion still needs to hook up my tracking device, so I take a deep breath and open the door to his bedroom.

He's sitting on the bed we share, slouched over with his elbows to his knees, hands clasped together. He lifts his head slowly, his silver eyes taking the agonizing journey from my high heels to my long, gold-specked legs to my tiny scrap of skirt to my naked belly. His molten stare grazes my breasts for just a heartbeat before flicking up to my face. I know he's celibate. I know he has no interest in me. But the look in his gaze is pure, unadulterated sin and sex.

He closes his eyes for a moment too long to be considered a blink, clearing the lust from his vision. He's back. Just like that, the spell is broken, and he's back to regarding me with cold indifference. I step into the room, my cheeks hot. He doesn't want me. And even if he did, it wouldn't be me he was attracted to.

"Come here," he commands, his voice gruff, thick with some unnamed emotion. I obey. No thoughts, no hesitations. I slowly slink to where he sits, the clack of my heels mimicking my heartbeats.

When I'm standing nearly between his legs, he climbs to his feet, looming over me with his daunting frame. Even with the heels, I only come up to his chin. High enough to kiss his neck, or lick the patch of exposed tanned skin peeking through the top unclasped button of his black shirt.

He reaches into the pocket of his matching slacks, and pulls out a small button no bigger than my thumb. "This is a tracking device. It'll tell me where you're located as well as read your pulse and heart rate, alerting me of any distress."

"Is that really necessary?"

"Yes," he replies holding it between his fingertips. "The Watcher's property is sacred ground, meaning no weapons or violence allowed. Breaking those laws results in sudden, absolute death. I won't be able to protect you. So I need to…feel you."

I suck in a breath. "What?"

"I'll be wearing the receiver so I can physically feel if anything is wrong. If I need to find you, it emits a signal to my nervous system and actually leads me to you without causing a scene."

"Wow. That's pretty neat." It is. I'm genuinely impressed that they've thought of everything. A device like that should be in the hands of every parent of small children.

"Yeah, Toyol designed it."

"Toyol? He designed it?" Holy crap. I knew the guy was a tech geek, but damn… "Then why isn't he installing it?"

He looks down into my eyes, steel gray plunging into chocolate brown. "Because I didn't think you wanted his hands on your body."

Breathless, I hold his stare. His overwhelming warmth surrounds me, wrapping me in a cocoon of fire. I should tell him that I don't want *anyone's* hands on my body, especially his. I should refuse whatever treachery his touch will bring.

But I don't. Because I can't.

"I apologize, I…" His mouth works from side to side, as if he's searching for the words. "Please…"

I don't tell him to do it, but I don't object when he slowly slides a fingertip along the low neckline of my top. He gently inches the fabric down, revealing the milky white tops of my breasts. I hold my breath, but I don't register the burn of my lungs. All I can feel is his skin on mine, brushing against the sensitive place where his scruff had tickled me in my visions. All I can imagine is his large, callused hands kneading, exploring, grasping as he dips his head down to take a pebbled nipple into his mouth.

"This won't hurt," he says, slipping the lace-trimmed satin down just a bit further. "I just have to place it right over your heart."

I don't dare respond. I doubt I even can.

With an agonizingly soft brush of his fingers down the middle of my chest, he finds the spot where my heart races wildly. A loud, erratic rhythm that plays just for him. He pauses for just a second, taking that hypnotic beat into his body then he swiftly attaches the sensor to my skin.

All while watching me through orbs of swirling silver.

"There," he says, gingerly placing my bodice back over the tops of my breasts. "The receiver is behind my ear. It'll transmit a signal straight to my brain."

"Do you plan to leave me alone there?" I hate the panic in my voice.

"No. But it will be crowded. The Watcher's parties are… lively…to say the least. You'll be expected to enjoy yourself."

I raise a brow. "And what if I escape?"

"You're not a prisoner, Eden," Legion deadpans, stepping around me, taking his warmth with him. "You're here because you need to be protected. You're free to leave whenever you wish."

"It hasn't felt like that," I challenge.

"Because I knew if we didn't have time to make you understand—to explain everything—you'd leave without a second thought. And you'd be taken the moment you set foot out of this building."

He's right. And I hate it. I would've left without hearing them out. I wouldn't have believed any of it if they tried to explain in haste. I would have run home to Sister and led whoever and whatever right to our doorstep. Or worse. I would've been activated and may have killed Sister myself.

I shudder at the thought.

"I can't cook."

He frowns. "What?"

"I can't cook, and neither can Sister. We ate instant mac and cheese and frozen food every single day. Our idea of a gourmet meal was Stouffer's lasagna. The food here is much better."

He nods once, the slightest curve of a smile tugging on one corner of his lips, before turning towards the bedroom door. I stop him just as he hits the threshold.

"How did you know it was ok for *you* to put your hands on me?" I ask, a fist resting against a curvy, exposed hip. "How did you know I wouldn't push you away?"

Legion looks over his shoulder, a sinister smirk playing on his face.

"I didn't."

FIFTEEN

My stomach is twisted in knots as we step into the elevator outside the front door. There's nothing else in the hallway. No other units or décor. Just the elevator.

If feels like forever since I've been outside, and while I'm excited, part of me is riddled with anxiety. Who or what could be waiting for us when we step onto the street? What if I see someone from before and have to explain?

Luckily, all those worries are dispelled when the elevator car opens, leading out to an underground parking garage. There are cars. And more cars. And more cars after that. SUVs, convertibles, sedans. Even something that resembles a tank. All black, all heavily tinted. I don't have to ask why. I've been around enough drug dealers to know that flashy colors, bells and whistles attract attention. And while each vehicle appears new and luxurious, they're not decked out with chrome rims or ostentatious racing stripes.

We decide to take two cars: a GMC Yukon Denali XL, the proverbial beast of SUVs, and a Jaguar XJ, a much sleeker, sexier ride. The majority of us pile into the Denali, leaving Legion, Cain and Phenex in the Jaguar to discuss strategy. I work to conceal my disappointment.

"Don't you all worry about someone sneaking in through the garage?" I ask, staring out the window from my seat behind the passenger side. Jinn is driving, and Toyol took the other front seat, leaving Lilith, Andras and me in the back.

"The building is heavily armed with alarms," Toyol replies. "The system that secures our garage and apartment is very complex, to say the least."

"How so?"

"It's controlled by blood. Our blood, to be exact. It's a series of very detailed mechanics along with a touch of blood magic. Wards, actually. They keep enemies from finding the place—but even if they could—they'd be killed the moment they set foot on the property."

Blood magic? "But what about me?"

"The blood magic wards against the supernatural. Whoever else slips by without our consent won't make it five feet before they're blown back to their maker. You're good." He looks back at us, his eyes dancing with sinister delight in the dark. "Hey, Lil. Think The Watcher will have some live entertainment this time?"

"Oh hell, I hope not. Last time, I had to throw out a brand new dress because I couldn't get the damn paint out of it."

"Paint?" Blood I could understand. Even more…intimate…bodily fluids. But paint?

"Body painting party. The Watcher's concubines were completely naked, save for intricately designed murals on their bodies. Even many of the guests abandoned their clothing for the feel of a new second skin. It was a very messy night, to say the least."

Wow. I can imagine. Naked people coupled with alcohol just asks for trouble.

"So…what is The Watcher exactly?" I had meant to ask Legion, but I'd been much too distracted.

"Neither demon nor angel, but immortal. Very old and very bored. Imagine a bookkeeper for the human realm, someone who sees all and knows all. They hold no allegiance to either side, and will snitch if you break the rules. That's The Watcher."

"So like an angel-demon babysitter?"

"Exactly. But with questionable morals and an affinity for pretty, shiny things."

I look down at my skimpy outfit and wince. Other than a silk shawl on my shoulders, I'm more exposed than I've ever been. Lilith insisted that I go sans jacket, afraid that I would smudge the gold flecks on my skin. She said I needed to look perfect, like I belonged there. Thank God the combined body heat in the car is enough to warm me. I guess that's the plus side of rolling with demons—I get my own personal furnace.

The Watcher's home, which I learn is one of many, is located outside of the city in Winnetka aka "where the rich folks live." The enormous mansion is situated on acres upon acres of land right on the water. It's dark, so I can't really take in the view. However, the house is illuminated by red and white tinted floodlights, signaling that the party is underway. Luxury vehicles neatly line the circular drive, while valets works to keep the receiving line moving. It's packed. More so than any club I've ever been to. I've never seen such opulence, such wealth. And we haven't even left the car yet.

"I guess it's going to be one of those nights," Andras groans from the seat behind me.

"Why do you say that?"

"The Watcher is known for lavish parties teeming with debauchery. It's all in good fun though. No violence, no maliciousness. Just the type of sin that straddles the line. You know it's wrong, but it feels so good. And since this is sacred ground, and all creatures of the night and day are welcome, temptation will be at its peak." He looks me up and down, mischief gleaming behind blue irises. "Even moreso with you here."

"Ok, people, look sharp," Toyol commands from the front. He presses a finger to his ear, and mumbles something too low for me to hear. "Eden, it's in your best interest that you stay close. Always be with one of us. No one can hurt you while on these grounds, but that doesn't necessarily mean you're safe."

"What does that mean?" A chill scrapes dagger-sharp shards of ice up my spine.

"It means that you may see things…feel things…that you normally wouldn't," Lilith explains. "There will be beasts from all walks of life within those doors. Many of them have a sense of humor."

"And stay away from the punch," Andras warns. "It'll knock you on your ass. Trust me."

I roll my eyes. What was the point of bringing me if I'm just a party favor? To stand there and look pretty while the *grown-ups* plot and scheme? I could have stayed at the apartment with my book and my music. "Anything else?"

"Yeah," Lilith replies, just as parking attendants approach the blacked-out vehicle. "Try not to let your hormones get the best of you. You're ovulating. Nephilim and Cambion are highly coveted."

On that note, she exits the car, leaving me with my mouth hanging down to my overexposed cleavage.

With measured steps, conjuring all the confidence I can in my scantily clad body, I walk into the mansion flanked by Jinn and Toyol, with Lilith and Andras taking the lead. Legion, Phenex and Cain have gone ahead to sweep the scene, and are somehow communicating with the rest of their team through invisible earpieces. The hypnotic sounds of *Panic! At The Disco* vibrate the vast space, setting the hedonistic scene before me. I stifle a gasp. Beautiful beings of all walks of life dance and mingle and flirt, dressed in faux angel wings and red pointed tails, each outfit more daring than the next. I thought *I* was naked. Some of these people actually are. One gorgeous woman, who has to be a model by day, strolls past us wearing little more than strategically placed ivory feathers over her nipples and a diamond-crusted thong. She licks her cherry lips and winks at Toyol before disappearing into a crowd of partygoers, swaying seductively to the beat under a sky of twinkling chandeliers.

"Are all these people angels or demons?" I whisper to him.

"Some. Some are humans. Some are…other."

"And how do you know we can trust them?" *How do you know they aren't trying to kill me?*

"You'd be surprised how many of us just want to fit in. Just want to lead normal lives. Mortals are fascinating to us. Your lifespans are so short, so fragile, yet you feel so much. Love, hatred, pain, joy, lust, rage. You are ruled entirely by your emotions without the burden of *why* and the consequences of *how*. You'll never know who was slain so that you may feel that joy, or the souls destroyed to ease your pain. You just take them inside of you, ruthlessly, arrogantly, never knowing of the wars that rage in the name of your all-consuming love. We rather envy that ignorance."

I'm stunned speechless. To think that an immortal—an ancient being as old as time and as powerful as a god—envies a puny, insignificant human like *me*?

Luckily, I don't have to think about my wasted mortality for much longer. Lilith leads us to an open ballroom where the music seems to be centralized. *Panic!* still plays from the surrounding speakers, spinning tales of salacious affairs, fitting for the electric vibe of the party. But it's not just their music I'm seduced by. It's *them*. Playing on a stage not twenty yards from where I stand. Frontman Brendon Urie is in his usual attire of black leather pants sans shirt, whipping his signature hair while serenading fans.

I freeze on my stilettos. Holy shit. Where the hell am I? And who the hell is The Watcher to have this kind of pull?

"Come on," Andras coaxes, pulling me by the elbow. We sidle up to bar that has to be close to 50 feet long, decked out in gold painted leaves, black and white feathers, and blood red roses.

"She'll have a glass of champagne," he says to a bartender. Punch for him and Lilith.

"I thought that stuff was dangerous?" I ask, when he distributes the glasses, my brow raised in suspicion.

"For you. Not for us."

Toyol and Jinn have disappeared into the crowd, and I haven't spotted Legion since we arrived. I'm not surprised; this place is a museum, and positively alive with activity. Red-tinted strobe lights cast enticing shadows over writhing bodies. Drinks overflow from every glass—champagne, shots and a pink-tinged, sparkling punch. Complete strangers dressed in blasphemous lingerie kiss and fondle each other with abandon. It's hard to not feel swallowed up by it all.

"Where is everyone?" I ask, suddenly feeling very small and very insecure. I follow Andras's line of vision as he stares at two men just yards away wearing nothing more than tight boxer briefs. They're pressed chest-to-chest as their tongues tangle in a slow, sinuous dance of eager, explorative limbs.

"Waiting to see The Watcher," he responds without looking at me. He licks his lips as the men rub their obvious erections against one another.

"Shouldn't we go with them?"

"They'll call when we're required." Then without word, he downs the last remains of his drink and swaggers over to the two lip-locked men. I watch them flutter with anticipation on his approach. When he stops in front of them, hands tucked in the pockets of his black slacks, they turn to him coyly, their bronze-dusted cheeks flamed with passion and excitement. He doesn't even seem to say anything to them. He just stands there, watching them squirm in his overwhelming presence. Their breathing is choked into short, labored pants. Their skin slickens with a glittering sheen of sweat. Eyes glaze in unadulterated arousal. And while I hate myself for looking, I can see the hardness in their shorts grow thicker, longer.

Wordlessly, Andras turns to make his away across the ballroom. The two men follow, allowing him to lead them to an undisclosed area outfitted with a canopy bed. There are dozens of them—small coves adorned with large loungers built for two, suspended beds and giant throw pillows draped in jewel-tone silks. A place for every pleasure. Almost all of them are occupied with people talking, eating fresh, exotic fruit, kissing, and even more than that. I turn away from a scene that causes my mouth to dry and my belly to warm with a distant remembrance. A man and a woman kiss intimately on a low bed covered with stark white rose petals. He lavishes her with teeth and tongue while his hand hikes up her bare thigh, giving another male companion access to her naked sex. The men lick and suck both sets of her quivering lips, worshipping her body like a virgin goddess on a bed the color of her creamy skin.

My breath catches. To be loved like that, pleasured like that for all to see…it must be the ultimate rush. She doesn't seem meek or submissive under their touch. She looks liberated—free to explore her body's desires with a beautiful boldness that has me imaging myself in her shoes. To be that woman…to feel what she feels…just the thought makes dampness collect on the scrap of lace between my legs.

"Showtime," Lilith announces, pulling me from my dark, sensual thoughts. She takes the empty flute from my fingertips. I don't even remember finishing the champagne.

Lilith slides her palm against mine and gently tugs, coaxing me to follow her to another part of the house. We bypass the beds and extra-large chaises, to enter a long hallway, lined with several doors. I can't imagine what's happening in there, but I can hear it. Raucous laughing, the sounds of wet slapping, and undeniable panting breaths. I force my chin up and keep my eyes forward.

We stop at a set of carved double doors fit for a palace, bejeweled with gold grommets and rubies that glitter under the dim lighting. In the middle of each door is an ornate eye made of a thousand sparkling black diamonds. The Watcher's quarters.

"Answer every question honestly. Lying is pointless and offensive, so be direct and firm. Do not cower. The Watcher will eat you alive if you act like a scared little mouse. And don't, under any circumstances, try to infiltrate anyone's mind. You can and will be killed before any of us can intervene. Ready?"

I nod before I lose my nerve. "Ready."

She lifts her fist to knock, but before her knuckles connect with the polished wood, it opens, revealing red jacquard walls trimmed in ornate gold. I hear them before I can see them, yet their raucous laughter doesn't do much to alleviate my anxiety. After all I've seen—all I've felt—since entering this mansion, I can only imagine what waits for me beyond the door's prying eyes.

"Come, come," an unfamiliar voice beckons.

My hand still in Lilith's grasp, and my heart in my throat, I command my shaky knees to take a step. Then another. And another. Until we've cleared the hallway swathed in cherry blood.

We turn a corner, and enter what looks to be a lounge or day room, and I nearly gasp in surprise at the languid figure lounging on a canopied dais of roses and cut marble.

The Watcher…is a woman?

"Hello, Eden. It's so nice to finally meet you."

She rises from her cushioned throne with the grace of an empress, and slinks over to me, her curvaceous body adorned in nothing more than a sheer sarong and a jeweled bra. Legion, Phenex and Cain watch her with close, careful eyes as she stops right in front of me, leaving just inches between us.

"You're prettier than I expected," she smiles, spreading her candy-coated lips over bright white teeth.

"So are you," I reply.

Her laugh is deep and animated as she tips her head back, causing her black severe bob to brush against her bare shoulders. "Am I now? You expected a horned creature with fangs?"

I dare a glance over her shoulder at Legion, whose full lips are pressed into a grim line. "No. I expected a man."

"Oh? It seems as if your friends did not properly inform you." She flicks her gaze to Lilith, giving her the same sinuous smile. "Lil, darling. Why are we keeping secrets from our young Eden?"

"Apologies, Irin. She didn't ask."

"Ah," she tsks. "Always ask the right questions, Eden. They will provide the right answers. Come! Sit!" she commands, waving us over to the dais. She strolls over to her designated seat, which resembles an oversized, lush cabana with large throw pillows, and folds her petite frame onto a spot in the middle, tucking her bare feet into the cushions.

I take a spot to her far left, prompting her to say, "Don't be silly, Eden. Come closer. I won't bite." Another predatory smile.

I do as she demands, and scoot closer. "Thank you for

having me."

"Of course! I invite the Se7en to all my parties. However, they often refuse. Do you want to know why?" I look over at Legion who stands several feet away, his arms crossed over his broad chest. Luckily, Lilith has chosen to join us on the dais.

"Sure," I answer plainly.

"I take great pleasure in Earth's indulgences, as you can see. Sexuality is powerful. And power is coveted by all. Don't you agree?"

I nod just as a beautiful bronze man wearing nothing more than tight black briefs offers me a glass of champagne. I accept with a tight smile. "I do."

"And do you believe that *you* are powerful?" she questions, watching me as I take in a mouthful of the fizzy, slightly sweet liquid.

"Not exactly. No."

"Ah, but you are. Extremely powerful. You have knowledge of the Jumper inside you, correct? The angel Adriel?"

Another long sip. "Yes, I've been told."

"So you know that you have certain abilities, giving you access to the minds of humans. Making it possible for you to glimpse the intent of their souls."

Holy shit. She's reading me like a book.

I finish the last of my champagne and am met with another not even seconds later. I happily accept, despite a gruff sound of objection feet away.

"I can. Yes."

"Adriel," she grins. "Angels and demons do not have the ability to bend the wills of humans. But you are neither, which gives you usage of her powers without any of the red tape. Isn't it wonderful?"

I shrug. "I guess."

"Don't you see, Eden? She chose you specifically because there is a plan for you. A plan to be someone great in this world. A plan to touch the lives of many." She speaks the words with so much fervor, as if she actually believes it. As if she wants me to believe it too. I simply shake my head and drink my champagne.

"You don't agree." She lifts a slender black brow.

"I don't. I think she chose me because I'm weak. I don't touch people's lives. I don't do anything that surmounts to greatness. I..."

I can't say it. I can't be the one to tell them that their precious Adriel is no more than a sycophant with a dark agenda. One that makes me do and say things that unleash pain and suffering.

She sighs and leans back onto a pillow. Another beautiful man—this one the color of fresh cream—brings her a short tumbler of punch. "I see it now. You believe Adriel influences you to do things out of rage and hurt. You think she makes you a monster."

Stunned, I open my mouth to disagree, but then I remember Lilith's warning. The Watcher sees all, hears all. She knows what I've done.

"I do."

"Would that make it easier? To believe it is Adriel's doing?"

"I don't understand," I frown.

The impish woman looks up to the ceiling, gazing at a mural of intricately painted cherubs with rosy cheeks and curly blonde hair. "Gaudy, isn't it? I told the artist I wanted angels, not children. I swear, good help is so hard to find."

"Huh?"

"Ask the right questions, Eden," she gently scolds.

I take another sip for courage. "Why does Adriel make me think things—say things—that will hurt people?" *Or worse. I don't have to say it. She's already seen it.*

"She doesn't," she simply answers, still gazing at the ceiling.

"So the Calling? Am I influenced by whatever evil was implanted in me?"

She yawns, bored with the conversation. "No."

"Then who? Who is telling me to do these things?"

Slowly, The Watcher tears her gaze away from the mural of cherubs. "You."

"What?" I couldn't have possibly heard her correctly. "But that doesn't make sense."

"Of course it does. The pain you've inflicted, the wrong you've done—all derived from your own inner turmoil. Adriel gave you the gun, but you loaded the ammunition and fired."

"But…" It's not rational. The voices whispering to me, telling me to make people trip over their own feet or drop their cash on the ground or spill their drink on their shirts.

Or walk in front of a bus.

I'm not capable of that type of evil.

Right?

"It doesn't make you a bad person," she says, a flare of empathy in her dark eyes. "It makes you human."

Blood rushes my ears, carrying with it my rapid beating heart. The taste of champagne becomes stale on my tongue.

My brown eyes grow wide with confusion.

I'm evil.

I'm evil.

I'm evil.

Me. Not Adriel. Not Lucifer. *Me.*

Unable to face the truth in The Watcher's gaze, I look down at my lap. I'm dressed in white, yet stained with my own wickedness. *I* have been the wolf in sheep's clothing all along.

"Irin," I hear Legion say. "There are more important matters to discuss other than Eden's petty, mortal defects." His words sting, but there's no bite in his words. He's trying to spare me, just like he did yesterday. I lift my head to watch him come sit beside her.

"Oh, Legion," she trills, gripping his knee with red, pointed fingernails. "I'm just having a little fun! But you're right. Business first. Then pleasure."

"The Calling, Irin. When will it happen? And where?"

"Ah, ah, ah," she admonishes, waving a finger from side-to-side. "First, we must discuss the terms. You know that." She gazes up into his face with black stars glittering in her eyes. She bites her sensuous bottom lip seductively.

Legion replies, boredom in his tone. "Name your price."

"You know what I want. You always know what I want." Then The Watcher's—*Irin's*—low-lidded stare slides to me. "Does she?"

"Irrelevant." Legion's nostril's flare.

"Are you sure about that?" she teases, the hand on his thigh crawling up higher with lazy strokes. I feel fire in my cheeks.

"Get on with it, Irin."

"Fine," she says with a huff, flinging her hair behind her ear with more effort than necessary. "As you know, I am not a soothsayer, so I can't see into the future. I have no idea when or where she'll be Called."

"Then we're done here," Legion says, brushing her hand from his lap. Something inside me secretly rejoices.

"But…there is a way," Irin quickly adds before Legion can recoil completely.

Legion's jaw works in annoyance before demanding, "Talk."

"You'll need to seek an outside source. Someone that can glimpse into her past in order to unearth her future."

My past.

I shake my head reflexively.

"Something to hide, dear?" Irin drawls. She replaces her hand on Legion's leg, grazing it with her pointed fingernails while turning her venomous leer on me. She's provoking me… toying with me. Why? What the hell do I care?

"No," I deadpan.

"Lies." She says it like my dishonesty amuses her.

Legion clears his throat, drawing her attention back to him. "You have minutes, Irin. Seconds."

"Certainly, sweetie," she grins at him. "But first, I require payment."

He shakes his head. "That's not how this works."

"Ah, but it is. If you want this piece of information, you'll play by my rules. If not, you can go enjoy the party. Maybe our little Eden will be Called tonight? Pity. I have so many human souls in attendance—many that Lucifer would love to claim for himself. Such a shame that my guards will have to put her down immediately for breaking the rules." She sighs as if the thought of killing me bores her. As if the sight of my blood sprayed on the jacquard walls would be no more than a nuisance.

"Fine. What do you want from me?"

Irin shifts her body to face Legion, pressing her pert breasts against his bicep. A sick feeling enters my gut, and I feel the champagne churn its way up my throat.

"A kiss. Kiss me, Legion. Make me feel that fire that burns so bright and hot within you. Make it kindle down in my toes and lick up my thighs. Brand my lips with your wickedness, and the knowledge you seek is yours."

I swallow down the rising bile and roll my eyes. Is this woman for real?

Who makes a deal like that? Who the hell does she think she is to request something so paltry and immature and intimate from another individual? She's the ultimate narcissist. And I know Legion will see right through her bullshit.

"Deal."

My head whips so fast that my vision blurs. No. He can't. He won't.

Lilith stiffens beside me, but doesn't say a word. I look to Phenex, to Cain, but both of their expressions are impassive. Why are they letting her manipulate them? And why is Legion—the scariest, strongest person I've ever met—being reduced to no more than a prostitute?

I want to force myself to look away when Irin sits up on her knees, aligning her face with his, but I can't. She strokes the apple of his cheek before raking her fingers through his hair. She's trying to make this romantic, tender. She's trying to seduce him.

    Legion stays perfectly still as Irin caresses him as a lover would. He's not even fighting this farce. It's like he wants this. He wants *her*.

    She moves in closer, licking her lips in preparation. His own lips part, ready to accept. Red painted claws grip his nape as his hands press against her lower back. Oh God, he *does* want this. He's into this. It doesn't matter that Irin is a snake. All he sees is tits and ass, and he's reduced to a typical male. Why did I believe he would react any differently? Why did I expect him to show just a modicum of self-respect?

    My blood runs ice cold in my veins as I watch their lips collide with so much passion that Irin moans into his mouth, giving Legion entrance. Tongues slide against each other in an erotic dance, teeth gnash against each other in fervor. He palms her ass through the sheer fabric, kneading and pulling her closer into his body. Irin grasps his hair, eager to take more of him inside her.

    I can't see this. I can't pretend that this is ok. That this doesn't disgust me. That this doesn't…

    The glass flute in my hand shatters against the pearl and marble floor as I all but run for the double doors, desperate to escape the sounds of their frantic kissing.

    They don't even flinch.

SIXTEEN

In my haste to flee the soft-core porn behind the doors adorned with black diamond eyes, I find myself back in the ballroom. It's even more crowded. Even the music seems louder. I scan the mass of partygoers for any signs of familiarity, but I don't see any of them. Andras must be busy with his boys, and I have no clue where Jinn and Toyol could be.

I'm lost in a sea of writhing, wicked bodies, slickened in sweat and sin. They're all just a blur…just a blur of lust and greed and poison desire. I stagger through the haze of sex and smoke on shaky legs until I reach the bar. The polished wood is cold under my fingers as I grip the edge of the bar top. I slide onto a stool, grateful to rest my feet and my weary mind.

"Can I get you something? Champagne?" a bartender asks, holding a bottle of effervescent pink liquid. He's oddly attractive, his features too soft, too pretty for his hard, muscular body draped in nothing but tight, black shorts.

I fix my lips to decline, but stop myself. I've been snatched from my home, ridiculed and beaten and humiliated. Dressed up like a doll only so I could be taunted by a five-foot-tall temptress. Then I was forced to watch her make out with my captor, the very same man that took me to keep me as his pet. I'm done being told what to say, what to wear, what to drink. No more. They want me to be docile and meek. They want me to be the weak little human that I'm supposed to be.

I can't.

I can't pretend anymore.

I can't ignore the fire coiling in my gut and slithering in my veins.

I can't ignore what I am.

"No. I'll have the punch."

The pretty bartender looks at me and squints, as if he can see right through to my mortal soul. I lift my chin a fraction, steeling my nerves.

"You got it," is all he says before grabbing a glass and sliding it across the bar top. I down it in three giant gulps.

"Another."

"Careful, sweetie, this stuff'll—"

"I'm a big girl. Another."

He lifts his perfectly arched brows in speculation, but refills my glass. I down it just as quickly as the first.

"Thanks," I slur before he can saunter away to serve another patron.

Then I feel it.

Liquid fireworks burst in my bloodstream, carrying

the toxic ecstasy to the tips of my toes. My fingers tingle as if they're being brushed with feathers, and the surface of my skin burns with golden heat. I'm on fire. My vision turns a glittering blue, then red, then green. Everything around me sparkles like morning dew on blades of grass, a million tiny teardrop prisms bursting with light and color. I gasp at the way rainbows dance on bare shoulders and slither down legs. Music not only caresses my ears, but glides across my lips. I can taste the notes, salty and sweet on my tongue. I swallow it down and let the melody move through me, leading me to the dance floor.

I glide across galaxies on heels made of papier-mâché clouds. The crowd swallows me up, fondling me with eager fingers and thrusting hips. I move with them, become one with them. There's no judgment here. No shame or fear of persecution. Just movement and sound and sensation. I'm as light as a bird on wings borne of stardust—a tiny speck of blinding light in a vast universe.

I dance through song after song, eyes closed and hands high. My body tells me I need to relieve myself, but I can't stop. I can't stop the feeling of brilliant bliss tethered to my veins, controlling me like a marionette on spider web strings.

Minutes, or maybe hours, later, the needs of my bladder become too intense to ignore. The crowd purges me as if it knows that I must go, pushing me on a gold-dusted tidal wave. I stagger to a hallway I've never seen before, wriggle the knob of the first door. Locked. I try another. And another. Until I find one that twists easily.

The good news: it's a bathroom.

The bad news: it's occupied.

Very, very occupied.

"Oh my God, I'm so sorry," I shriek, shielding my eyes. But not before I get an eyeful of the orgy going down on the toilet seat.

"No need to apologize, sweetheart. Come in."

No. No, I don't want to come in. But I do. Shit, I have to.

I take a step inside the bathroom cast in gold and red and black. Much like the rest of the house. My feet tremble on my strappy heels.

"Now close the door."

My hand reaches back for the knob until my quaking fingertips meet the lock. Mindlessly, I click it.

"Now…lift your head. Lift your head and look at me."

A voice in my head screams no, begging me to keep my eyes cast to the ground. Don't look, don't look, don't look. My neck screams with strain as I try to still its movement. My eyes burn with the effort to keep them from focusing. I can't look. I shouldn't look.

But I want to. *Need* to.

The man behind the voice sits on the toilet seat lid, his beautiful, ethereal face a mask of erotic delight. Hair dusted with burnish sunlight, his full, pouty mouth a sensual slash of a smirk. His eyes are neither blue or violet or hazel. Dusk. His irises shine with shades of dusk, shifting like the dozing sky.

He's naked, completely bare in his otherworldly perfection. Every bit of him is sculpted alabaster, hard and smooth and impenetrable. A woman kneels between his legs, wearing nothing but a corset and thong underwear, giving me a view of her supple, heart-shaped backside as she takes him in her mouth over and over and over. She moans around his length as if the taste of him is as delicious as he is hard. Her own petite hand creeps between her thighs to flick and knead through the wet strip of lace that covers her sex.

Another woman sits on the man's knee, riding him. I can hear the friction of skin-on-skin, can see the glistening dampness that glazes his thigh with every flex of her shapely hips. Her fingers are buried deep inside another girl who stands before her, kissing her lips and fondling her full breasts.

Their moans, their cries...his stare. I can't look away. I can't deny the gush of arousal beneath my scrap of satin. I've never seen anything so erotic in my life. And the more I watch—the more I scent their need heavy in the air, clinging to my skin like the mist of dawn—the more I want to feel what they feel.

They move together with such grace and fluidity, as if pleasure is second nature. The woman between the man's legs slides a hand over the grooves of his abs until she reaches a nipple. She pinches the small bud between black fingernails, causing his whole body to twitch. I find myself flinching as well.

"Come here," the man commands, his voice vibrating through me, embedding itself in my bones. He crooks a finger. "Come here."

I take a step closer, my legs not my own. My lips part reflexively and I suck in a breath of sex-scented air.

"Come to me," he croons, beckoning me. I imagine that finger grazing my nipples before trailing a slow path over my belly. I imagine it dipping inside me so deep that I scream. And with that *come hither* motion, he brings me to completion, knees shaking and eyes glazed.

I walk until the floor falls away and I am merely coasting on a cloud of my own devious desires. I walk until my shins touch the soft flesh of a pert ass. Until I can see devil-red lips sliding over his ridged hardness, swallowing him inch-by-maddeningly thick-inch. The girl riding this thigh reaches up to graze my goosefleshed arm with a feather's kiss, and I don't stop her. It feels good. Like I'm being licked. Like I'm being fucked.

I shiver where I stand as his eyes roam my body. Sin peeking through the white bars of my innocent imprisonment. I can feel his stare, stroking, prying. Seeing through to the wickedness festering inside me and relishing in the turmoil. He doesn't back down, doesn't recoil or shame me for my curiosity. It pleases him. Arouses him. And in that stare swirling with eroticism, it arouses me.

He brushes the hair of the girl between his legs, and she pulls away, releasing him with a resounding *pop*. I stagger back, letting her pass and watch her join the other women. As if it were choreographed, the woman on his thigh stands, and the three of them…the three of them…

"Don't be scared," the man coos. "I won't hurt you, and neither will they. They're very friendly."

At that, the girls begin to giggle between kisses and licks. They look so…fun. So free with their bodies. I've always dreamt about being a girl like that—obviously beautiful, carefree, unstoppable.

"You can be," the man remarks, reading my thoughts. "You can be like them and more. Just come to me."

I don't question how he heard my unspoken ramblings. I don't question the absurdity of his claims. I take a step forward, close enough that the sides of my legs brush his knees. He's still hard, still glistening with a mix of ruby lipstick and saliva. I could lean forward and feel it against my thigh. I could reach out and take it in my hand.

"Do it," he urges, flexing his hips forward slightly. "Do it. You know you want to."

I do want to. He would pulse wildly in my palm. I could almost feel that silkened skin against mine.

"Do it," he says again. "I want you to."

My fingers tremble with longing. I need to do this. My body is aching with the need to touch him.

So I do.

He moans loudly the second I brush the slickened tip of him. Spurred by his reaction, I drag my fingers over the veins and ridges, all the way to the root. He throbs for me. Wants me. His body becomes radioactive just by my touch.

"More," he rasps, eyes hooded.

I fist his length slowly at first, building momentum and pressure with every stroke. My mouth waters as I imagine him pumping in and out of me. I want his massive hardness deep inside me. I want to feel his heartbeat within my womb, coaxing the strongest orgasm of my life.

"Yes," he groans. "Turn around."

I don't even try to deny myself the feeling of pure exhilaration and craving as I do as I'm told. He grasps my hips from behind, pulling me closer to him. He spreads my legs so they fall on either side of him and positions me to hover right over him. Right over the part I want buried inside me to the hilt.

My skirt is shoved up over my ass. My lace thong is pushed to one side. And before I can object or breathe or think, we collide.

I cry out in a heat of ecstasy that I've never experienced. The sheer size and strength of him tears me apart, but the pleasure eclipses the pain. He touches all the ugly parts of me—all the deviousness and deceit—and makes them beautiful. I'm invincible, untouchable, as I sit on his throne built of sweat and sin. The queen of corruption. His empress of evil.

The woman reclaims her spot between his legs and begins licking…licking where he and I meet. Licking the wetness that pools with every deep thrust. Another comes to palm my breasts, bringing them together to lick and nibble. And the other kisses me, long, deep and sensually, swallowing my moans and replacing them with her own.

I've tasted contentment. I've eaten euphoria. The taste of paradise coats my tongue and slides down my throat, filling me until I am whole.

We move together, as if this was always meant to be. As if I was always meant to be his, and theirs, and ours.

I lean back and rest my head against his shoulder, reveling in this state of pure bliss. My hips move on their own accord, meeting him thrust for impossibly deep thrust. He knows my body so well—they all do. I would have been afraid with anyone else, but I'm not with them. This is where I belong.

"Eden," the man grunts in my ear as he pushes upward. He begins to swell within my quivering flesh, filling me to the brim. "Eden. Eden." He says my name over and over as he gets closer. Over and over as he brings me to the brink with him.

"Eden. Eden. Eden…"

My heart pounds in my ears, echoing with every resounding slap of skin against skin.

"Eden. Eden. Eden."

The banging becomes louder as I get so close I can taste the sweet and saltiness of release on my tongue. I gasp on lips made of sugared cherries. My hands grip strands of spun sunshine. I feel it…feel it pounding toward me, against me, inside me.

"Eden. Eden. Eden!"

Eyes shut tight, I throw my head my back and scream, releasing every drop of liquid need from my quaking frame. It's never ending, unrelenting, a force of nature within itself. Sensation sweeps through me like a hurricane, and I am the eye of the storm—weightless, still and deadly.

When I finally open my eyes, I'm alone and leaning up against the door. It rattles violently, surely from the aftermath of my orgasm.

"Eden! Eden, open this door before I rip it the fuck off the hinges."

Oh shit.

I blink, and look down. My skirt is up to my hips and my fingers are between my legs, completely drenched with my own warm stickiness.

Oh. *Shit.*

Legion bangs again before rattling the doorknob. I quickly fix my clothing and run to the sink to wash my hands.

"Um, uh, coming!" I stammer, hurriedly getting to the door before he makes good on his promise. That wouldn't bode well for any of us. I have no clue what the consequences would be for interrupting the party, and I don't want to find out.

I take a deep breath before turning the lock and opening

the door. Legion stands before me, fists clenched tight at his sides, and glowing silver eyes wild with rage. He takes one look at me and grimaces.

"Come on," he growls, grabbing my arm. He pulls me from the bathroom, and from the phantom that just fucked me on the toilet seat.

SEVENTEEN

"**W**HAT THE HELL WERE YOU DOING IN THERE?" Legion yanks me through the hallway, maneuvering through the groups of loiterers mingling and making out against the wall.

"What?" My brain is still foggy with the remnants of alcohol and orgasm.

"I said, what the hell were you doing in there? Dammit, Eden, you can't just run off by yourself. There are about a dozen creatures here that would love to sink their teeth into you."

I roll my eyes. "I was fine."

"Fine?" He whirls around to face me yet his feet keep moving. We've bypassed the ballroom, still in full swing with the sounds of *Thirty Seconds to Mars*. I wouldn't be surprised if they're actually on stage performing. "Eden, you are not fine. You left The Watcher's quarters so quickly I—"

"You *what?*" I snap, jerking out of his grasp. I fold my arms over my chest, refusing to take another step with him. "Didn't have time to wipe the drool off your lip? You really thought I'd stick around to watch you suck face with that sadist? Sorry, but live porn isn't my thing. I'm sure your friends provided enough moral support though. Geez, L. I expected you to last longer than that. But I guess for someone who hasn't fucked in a century, you couldn't hold back."

Nostrils flared and mouth curved in a vicious sneer, he takes one menacing step towards me. "What did you say?"

"It's ok. It happens to everyone. Even demons, apparently." I look away dismissively, too emboldened by pink sparkling liquor to have the good sense to be afraid.

One long stride, one heartbeat, one breath, and he's so close I can feel the blaze of his fury radiating from his massive frame. Those ancient eyes made of dying stars burns straight into my soul. I force myself to look up into his face, giving him a scowl of my own.

"You don't..." His jaw works as if the words refuse to come out, trapped between wrath and frustration. Instead, he snatches my hand back. "Come on."

"Where are you taking me?" I shout, trying to keep up on my ridiculously high heels. The floor has finally solidified underneath me; that's a relief. But it still sways and rocks like a funhouse platform. "Hey, slow down! Not everyone is a supernatural freak like you."

"Yeah? Well, maybe you should've thought about that before you ran off to play with monsters." He's moving unnaturally fast, yet no one seems to notice. Either that, or they don't care.

"I don't know what you're talking about. You're the one who practically threw me into the lion's den wearing prime rib panties. You think I want to be here? You think I liked watching you taste Goth Stripper Barbie's tonsils?"

He stiffly shakes his head, refusing to give me the satisfaction of a retort. I don't realize that we're headed for the exit until we're already outside.

"Where are you taking me?"

"Home," he deadpans.

"But what about…"

"Finishing up. They'll be fine."

"L, slow down," I urge as he heads for the line of cars stationed around the drive, bypassing valet. Gravel crunches under my shoes, making it impossible to walk without stumbling. When we reach the Jag, he nearly rips the passenger side door off the hinges before practically throwing me inside.

"What the hell!" I shriek as he climbs over me to buckle my body in. The heat of him smothers the fight right out of me. I refuse to breathe for fear that I'd inhale his scorching ire and fall victim to his scent. I can't quite pinpoint what it is exactly, but it's intoxicating. It reminds me of the beginning of a tumultuous storm, before lightning rips open the sky, quenching fire-blazed earth.

He's in the driver's seat and peeling out of the driveway before I can shake the feel of his hard body against mine.

"Seriously, dude, what is your problem?" I ask after several minutes of silence. It's pitch dark out, and he's racing around winding curves faster than I can see them.

"My problem?" he snorts. "You're my problem, Eden. Where the hell were you?"

"I told you. I didn't want to stick around for the main event, so I left." Bitterness drips from every word. Bitterness and…hurt. "Guess you aren't as noble as you wanted me to think."

"What are you talking about? You think I…" He shakes his head. "Never mind."

"What, Legion?" I angle my body around as much as I can in the confined space. "You don't want me to see you for what you are? I guess it's ok to unearth all my dirty, little secrets, and humiliate me, but you get a pass. I can be seen as a dirty, immoral bitch, but you…you get to maintain your pristine image. I get it."

"You're being ridiculous."

"Am I?" My voice comes out weaker than I intend. But with alcohol rousing my stupid human emotions, I can't just let it go. "Back at the apartment, you acted as if touching me repulsed you. You couldn't get away fast enough. But with Irin, or whatever her name is…" I suck in a flustered breath. "Look, if that's what you like, fine. But don't lie about it."

He looks straight ahead, that jaw ticking with irritation. "I wasn't lying, Eden. Nothing happened."

"That didn't look like nothing. But keep telling yourself that. Maybe it'll become true."

We don't speak another word as we drive back into the city. The sleek Jaguar rides like a dream, but I can't even enjoy it. I can't shake the image of him touching her, kissing her. As if he truly wanted her. And then the bathroom…none of it makes sense. But I felt them. I *still* feel them. My skin sizzles with the ghost of their hands, their tongues. Deep in my belly, my muscles clench as if he's still inside me, thrusting…

pulsing…

"We're here," Legion says, pulling off the main road into a side street, practically hidden from the public. He takes a sharp turn and enters what looks to be a narrow, old garage that can't possibly be large enough for us to fit. The garage stretches into an underground tunnel, and we drive another mile before I see bright floodlights. We're under the Se7en's building.

"When will the others be back?" I ask, as we pull into a space.

"Soon." He still doesn't look at me. A few days, maybe even hours, ago, I would have done anything to escape his vicious stare. But now…

I feel weak. And insecure. And still so damn aroused.

He exits the car and heads to the elevator without waiting for me. I follow after like a pitiful lost puppy, my body sagging with sudden exhaustion. Every step I take, something stirs inside me, sliding around like honey in my core. I stifle a gasp as I enter the elevator and stand beside him. He doesn't acknowledge my presence but I swear, I feel his knuckles whisper against mine.

The apartment seems cold when we enter. Eerily so. Without the presence of the Se7en and their stifling body heat, I can almost see my breath mist in front of me. I hurriedly make my way to the back bedroom—Legion's bedroom—for a shower and warm clothes. Just being here with him, after all that's happened tonight, I've never felt so naked.

"What are you doing?" he asks, as I rifle through my box of clothing.

"Getting out of these ridiculous clothes," I bite out. I

snatch up a pair of sweats and a long sleeve thermal and spin around, nearly colliding with his chest. When I try to step around him, he blocks my path.

"Eden." His voice is raw, stripped of its usual gruffness.

"Let me pass," I demand, again trying to get around him.

With surprisingly gentle fingers, he pulls the bundle of cotton from my grasp. "Wait. I need to explain something to you."

"Explain what? What else do I possibly need to know? You heard The Watcher: I'm evil. And you knew that, didn't you? You knew that it was me all along, not some satanic influence pulling the strings. Not even your precious Adriel. You didn't have to take me tonight and let some freak humiliate and taunt me with my *petty, human defects*. You *knew*."

"Yes."

My expression crumples with hurt. I rip out the censor in my top and throw it at his chest. He lets it tumble to the floor. "Then why?"

He gazes down at me, abandoning his usual scowl. "Because if I told you, you wouldn't believe me. And even if you did, you'd let it eat you alive." He takes a step forward. "I can help you. All those urges that push you towards immorality, I can help you overcome them."

"Thanks, but no thanks," I say, trying to sidestep him. "We can't all be born again like you. And maybe…maybe I don't want to."

Legion shakes his head. "You don't mean that."

"How do you know? Look at you," I trill, throwing my hands up in exasperation. "You've probably spent centuries alone and pissed off, wound tighter than a knot. You walk around here like the world is going to implode at any moment. Do you ever have any fun? Hell, do you even know what fun is?"

"Eden…"

"I saw you, Legion. I saw how you responded to that… to that woman. How you ran your hands all over her body as if the feel of her skin was made of silk. I saw how you reacted when you tasted her lips. You wanted more. And if we weren't all sitting there, you would have taken more." That slow-moving sensation begins to rouse again at the memory of Legion's fierce passion. I hated watching it. But only because I hated wanting it that much more.

His eyes widen with shock and he steps back, letting me pass. I've struck a nerve. And considering he's not denying it, I know that everything I'm saying is true. And that…that fact stings.

"If I'd known you only wanted to use me as an excuse to get what you wanted, I wouldn't have gone. You could have done your sordid little deed without using me as bait."

I snatch my clothes away from him and brush by him with a huff. Before I can pass, he grabs my elbow with enough pressure to force me to pause.

"Eden, wait." I don't fight out of his grip, but I also don't turn around. "I didn't want to kiss Irin. I didn't want anything to do with that egotistical, self-serving shrew."

"Could have fooled me."

"The Watcher thrives on information that can be seen as weakness. And she's in the business of trading such information to those who wish to use it against me when it serves her purpose."

"And what does this have to do with me?"

He pulls me to him, causing me to stumble back into the hard warmth of his chest. I inhale sharply at the contact, wishing I could stay, but knowing I can't. Still, he holds me there, his front pressed to my back, his fingers searing my skin with his grasp.

"Eden, if The Watcher knew who I really wanted to kiss, who I really was imagining as I gripped her ass through that flimsy little skirt; who I wanted it to be as I pressed her hardened nipples to my chest while I brushed my tongue against hers—she would not have hesitated to sell that secret to the highest bidder."

I shift on my feet nervously, causing me to rub up against his stiffening groin. I bite down on a gasp. "And who were you imagining?"

He doesn't pull away. Even as he thickens in his slacks, nudging the top of my backside, he doesn't pull away. He wants me to feel him. And God…he feels so fucking good.

"I think you know, Eden."

My breath escapes in heady pants as I fight the urge to crush against him even more. He feels hotter…stronger. As if his entire frame is thrumming with unrelenting power. He could break me in two as if I were no more than a delicate twig. And I would let him. Right now, I would let him do whatever he wanted.

"Legion…" I breathe, never loving the sound of his name on my lips more than in this moment. It scared me the first time he said it, rumbling the ground under my feet. But now…it's sensual, seductive. I want to whisper it as he kisses my neck. I want to scream it as he pushes inside me.

I feel him dip his head down to brush my hair with his lips. His abs flex with tension, causing those hard ripples to mold to my back. Like the very tip of a feathered caress, the backs of his fingers stroke my arm from elbow to shoulder, causing me to shudder.

The sound of a heavy steel door closing shatters the moment into a thousand pieces, and just like that, I'm swathed in the brittle chill of Legion's quick retreat. My chest heaves frantically as I try to regain my wits and I turn around to face him.

"They're home," he rumbles, his voice as thick as the obvious bulge in his pants. He looks down at me, a frown dimpling his forehead.

"Yeah," is all I can get out.

"We should…" His glassy gaze darts to the opened bedroom door.

"Yeah."

I watch him close his eyes for just a moment before he takes his scent and his fire and strides to the hallway. I'm so cold that I'm not sure that he ever really held it flush against me.

After a shower that does nothing to wash away the remembrance of his molten touch, I pad out to the common area to find everyone stationed around the dining room table, all still in their dark finery, all waiting for me expectantly. I look down at my heather gray sweats, purple thermal and rainbow socks. I couldn't be more out of place than I already was.

"Now that we're all here, we can begin," Legion announces, without looking at me. I take my seat to his right. "Phenex?"

The golden-eyed demon nods once at me then addresses the table. "Irin informed us that the only way we could potentially glimpse Lucifer's plan for Eden is to enlist the aid of a witch. But not just any witch. We would need a powerful one—one whose magic was not born of this world."

A witch? What the… Seriously, is anything I believed a week ago true? I know none of this should surprise me, but *shit*. What else is out there that humans have no clue about?

"So what you mean is, we're fucked," Cain groans from the other side of the table. Great. So all of this was for nothing.

"Well, yes, and no," Toyol chimes in. "The good news is, the wards around the building were cast with blood magic from a warlock I've had dealings with in the past."

"Can you contact him?" Legion questions, intertwining his fingers in front of his chin.

"That's the bad news." Toyol heaves a heavy sigh, his shoulders sagging a fraction. "He's dead."

"Great," Andras mutters. "So what now? I just spent the entire evening occupying Irin's favorite pets."

"Not like you were complaining," Lilith jibes, earning a crude gesture from her roommate. She retorts with a flash of a finger. "At least you didn't have to watch her get off on a kiss. I swear, L, she's so hard up for you it's embarrassing."

"That's enough," Legion scolds, redirecting his attention to Toyol. "Are there any others you know that can do it?"

Toyol twists his lips in contemplation. "Well…not exactly."

"Meaning?"

"Meaning he has a brother, but I'm not sure if he will help us. The warlock I knew was more mainstream and was known to…dabble in things that their kind deem offensive. Working with demons being one of those things."

Legion taps a finger on his chin, his brow furrowed in thought. "Can you give it a shot?"

"I can try," Toyol nods. "But I can't be certain he'll go for it. And there may be a price to pay."

"All magic has its price," Legion agrees.

"I'll reach out to my source," Toyol says, pulling out his cell phone. He begins to tap the keys so rapidly that his thumbs are a blur. He doesn't even look at the screen. "He's not a warlock anymore, but he's family. If anyone has an in, it's him."

"Good," Legion nods before looking to Cain. "Any activity tonight?"

The scarred demon shakes his head. "None. The sister is safe. We checked before we came here. I don't even think Big Bad's goons realize that she's gone."

My heart stutters in my chest. Blood roars in my ears, making my choked words sound distant and distorted. "What? My sister is…gone?"

"We moved her," Legion answers, without so much as turning in my direction.

"Where?" I question, the word sounding more like a demand.

"Lincoln Square."

"L bought her old building," Lilith explains, taking my hand in hers. She gives me an encouraging smile to diffuse the horror screaming on my face. "He paid off the all the residents, informing them the complex would be gutted for toxic mold and that they had to leave immediately. But she was also told that part of the package included a new apartment in a nicer neighborhood, complete with a doorman and security."

I turn back to Legion who finally meets my gaze, those silver eyes shimmering against the moonlight.

"You did that? For Sister?" I whisper through the lump in my throat.

"No, Eden," he replies, shaking his head. "I did that for you."

He doesn't look at me again while they continue their meeting, going over the information The Watcher provided them about the angel venom supplier. I don't even hear their words. Legion took care of my sister, the only family I have left in this cruel, lonely world. Not because I asked him to, or even expected this absurd kindness in exchange for my compliance. He just did it...for *me*.

I climb into bed not much later, exhausted and emotionally drained. I can't process it all at once, so I focus on one thing and one thing only: my complicated feelings for a monster whose true nature is to kill me. Even that seems too much to decipher, considering I don't even know what I feel. I know he scares me. I know he makes it impossible to breathe when he's around. But I also know that something within me craves him like I've never craved anything in my entire life. Maybe it's the angel-demon thing. Maybe the Jumper's seduction draws me to him for the same reason the Se7en are all on edge with me around.

But as he steps from the bathroom, fresh from the shower and dressed in nothing but low-slung sweatpants, I know it's more than that.

Tiny liquefied crystals dry on his bronzed skin, adorning

the swirls and lines of blue-black ink. I allow myself one small kindness: I look at him. Really look at him, unabashedly, unafraid. And what I see is…beautiful.

The lines of scripture that cover his arms speak of words of redemption and salvation. Revelations, Jude, Romans, Matthew, Luke. I know these words, and I can understand why he chose them. They're his life story—his fall from grace and the journey back to God's favor.

On his chest, an intricate design covers his entire left pec. I've seen the same one on Cain's massive bicep and noticed it on Lily's shoulder blade, peeking out from her jumpsuit earlier tonight. I sit up on my knees, hoping to get a better look. Legion follows my eyes and looks down.

"It's the symbol of the Se7en," he explains. "The number seven is self-explanatory. The feathers are for the wings that were lost."

"Wings? You had wings?"

He angles his body so I can view the two tribal-like bands that run from the tops of his shoulders to the middle of his back. They're marked with distinct whorls and characters that I can't translate, shaped into long, thin rectangles.

"They were taken when I fell. Most demons are given wings as well—bat-like, black, vicious things studded with talons—but I never accepted them. I refused. The wings of the Seraph are massive and regal, and would span the length of this entire room. Sometimes I think I still feel them…" He dips his head down and slightly shudders, casting the memory to his own dark corner. I wonder what other sadness still haunts that cold, dead space. I wonder if they feel anything like mine. "The others left their wings behind when we chose this life. However, they can be summoned if we go back."

I incline my torso a little more, moving closer to where he stands at the foot of the bed. The runes within those bars of ink look like twisting vines reaching for the heavens. But upon closer inspection, I realize it's so much more.

The top sections are cast in what appears to be rays of brilliant light streaming through clouds. Where the inked light starts to fade, a new section materializes. Growth and life and change. Humanity. Foliage sprouts from the shaded earth and birds fly between the strange characters. It's beautiful in its fragility but, just like my world, something dark and far scarier lurks below.

The very bottoms of the bands are veiled in black, rippled in what looks like angry fire. There's nothing there. No life. No light. No hope. Just the darkness of despair layered upon the deaths of countless lost souls. Lost souls like him…and me.

In the tribute to his stripped wings, Legion has etched his fall from God's favor. Maybe it's to remind him of what he once was and all that he lost. Maybe it's a reminder of how to get back.

I dare to touch the smooth, marked skin with the barest brush of my fingertips. He shivers, yet holds still, allowing me to trace the map of his origin. His skin burns, but so does mine. Cold doesn't exist when he's near.

"It's beautiful," I whisper, my voice filled with wonder. *You're beautiful.* "Can you get them back some day?"

He shakes his head before turning to look at me, his bare chest and abs just a whisper from my still outstretched hand. "No. It'd be impossible."

"Why didn't you want your demon wings?"

Silver pools of pain swirl in his eyes, hypnotizing me. I want to dive in and save him…save him from himself. "Because I didn't want to lose myself."

I remember what Lilith had said to me days ago. He feels so much, contains so much suffering, for he is Legion. He is not one, but many. And sometimes, it's hard for him to distinguish what's singularly him—and what's *them*. All this time he's spent searching for penance for each one of them. Yet, I can tell he hasn't forgiven himself.

Earlier this evening, we shared a moment borne of lust. But this…this is carved of something else entirely.

"It's late," he says, breaking the spell of silence. He steps back and strides to his side of the bed. "We should sleep."

"Yeah," I agree. It is late, but every cell in my body is practically humming with sensation. I don't know how I'll sleep a wink, especially with him beside me.

He slips into the sheets while I click off the lamp. When we're both settled beneath the covers, he heaves a heavy, exasperated sigh.

"I felt you tonight."

I turn to him in the dark. "Huh?"

"I felt you. Your heart rate was elevated. Your pulse was wild. Something was happening in that bathroom."

I swallow down the truth, feeling my cheeks heat with shame. "It was nothing."

"I *felt* you, Eden. It wasn't nothing. I felt your body trembling. I felt things I…I haven't felt in a very long time." He releases a heavy breath. "Look, you don't have to tell me, but I know. And I understand that you have human, carnal needs. So if you need to sate them—if you need relief—I won't stand in your way."

    I nod, even though he can't see me, and turn away from him.

    Some time in the night, my entire frame is gobbled up by comforting warmth. A nightmare never comes.

EIGHTEEN

It's barely dawn when I'm awaken by the ear-splitting crack of dresser drawers being slammed shut. My skull is hosting a miniature marching band, and my eyes feel like I've been staring at the sun. My tongue is sandpaper and my mouth feels like I've been gurgling with chalk dust. I've been drunk enough times to know that I'm hungover. And while champagne hangovers are already shitty enough, champagne *and* punch hangovers clearly take the whole shit-filled cake. I need at least another five hours before I feel human again.

"Rise and shine!" Lilith chirps, way too damn chipper after the night we just had. Hell, she was still up when I went to bed.

"What the hell," I croak, my throat so dry that I can actually feel my vocal cords rubbing against each other with every agonizing word. "What are you doing here so early?"

"Packing." She neatly folds a slouchy, off-the-shoulder sweater and places it in a suitcase propped up on the bed.

"Packing? For what?"

"You, Legion, Phenex, and Toyol are going on a little trip. Toyol got word from the warlock insider. He's willing to meet—but on his terms, and on his territory. So you have to go to him."

"Oh." A spike of fear pierces my nerves. Warlocks, witches…I have no idea what I'm getting myself into.

"You better get a move on. You're leaving in thirty minutes."

Thirty minutes? I muster what little strength I have left and lift myself out of bed. The room rocks and sways, and I nearly give up and flop back onto the bed. This is our chance, and I can't ruin it over a hangover. I *will* push through.

"Where are we even going?" I ask her, practically crawling my way to the bathroom. I feel like I'm going to need to brush my teeth for eight hours straight just to get the booze grit off of them.

Lilith pauses just long enough to shoot me a devilish smile, her eyebrows wriggling impishly. "Colorado Springs."

***

"Why couldn't we fly again?" I ask, fidgeting in the passenger seat of the Jag. Legion focuses on the long stretch of I-80 before us, but I don't doubt he's rolling his eyes behind his dark Ray-Bans.

"If a human is Called while airborne, it would end badly. And I don't think we'd be able to check an AR-15, six glocks, and ammo with our luggage."

My eyes bulge from their sockets. "You brought all those weapons?"

His mouth twitches with a would-be smirk. "Eden, that's just what I have in this car. Toyol and Phenex are carrying just as much in their vehicle, along with Toyol's Katanas."

"But why? Is this warlock a threat to us?"

"Everyone is a threat, Eden."

I take a moment to let that sink in. Everyone is a threat. For the rest of my life—however long that might be—I'll always be on guard, always looking over my shoulder. I can't hide out in the apartment all the time, and I don't want to rely on others for my safety. I've used my ability as a crutch since I discovered I could manipulate people with just a single, whispered word. But what if I can't use it? What if I'm up against something inhuman?

"I want to learn how to fight."

At that, Legion finally looks over at me. "What?"

"I want to learn how to fight. I can't expect you all to protect me while I just sit back and cower. I should do something—be an asset. And it's not like I can live with you forever."

He looks back at the road, this lips flattened into a grim line. "Are you sure?"

"I am," I nod, and meaning it. "Phenex almost died because of me. If I trained and learned to protect myself, I could help."

"If that's what you want," he responds flatly.

"But that's not what *you* want."

I watch him purse his lips in distaste before he answers, "I want whatever keeps you safe, Eden. If teaching you to fight gives you an added sense of security that I can't provide, then so be it."

He says the words but they're weighted with a deeper meaning. One rooted in past pain. "L, I didn't mean that I don't feel secure. I do. And while I don't understand why you're doing all this for me, I appreciate it—for my sake, and the safety of those around me. I just hate feeling helpless. And I don't want to be a burden."

"What makes you think you're a burden?" he practically barks at me.

I shake my head. "I just don't get it. You heard The Watcher—I'm not…I'm not a good person. Why save *me*? Why care whether *I* live or die? It doesn't make sense."

"It's my job."

"No, but it's more than that, isn't it? Do you take all your missions home with you to sleep in your bed?"

"No," he grits, nostrils flaring.

"Then why, L? Why risk all this for me? Why waste your time on a single weak, pathetic human who was meant to be a weapon of evil?"

I glare at his profile, watching the way he works his strong, angled jaw for agonizingly long seconds before he finally answers. "Adriel dies if you're killed. She's able to jump from viable host to host, but she has to be willing. Even if she was, the host has to be living."

I feel like I've just been slapped back to reality.

All this time, all these nights sleeping tucked against his chest, it wasn't me he was shielding from the world. It was

Adriel. It's not me he wants to protect. It's the angel who intruded into my life and my body when I was five years old.

The angel who stood by and watched me be beaten and starved. The angel who gave me the power to inflict my desperate rage on innocent people.

I feel like such a fucking fool.

Last night, something sparked between us. And maybe it was just the innate reaction from the Jumper, but I know Legion felt it too. Shit, I literally felt *him* against my ass. And then after his shower, I could have sworn that we shared something more than alcohol-induced lust. He was vulnerable in a way I had never expected him to be. He let me touch him…let me see him…if only for a moment. In return, I allowed myself to feel something other than fear or confusion, or even pain. I felt hope, understanding. I was empathetic towards that small kernel of truth—that small act of broken humanity.

And now, I see that it hadn't been me he was exposing himself to. It was Adriel. I was just the vessel, a mortal sack of flesh and bone that stood between him and who he truly wanted to connect with.

I don't speak again for many miles. When we stop at a rest stop to gas up, I can't escape the confines of the car fast enough.

"Wait," he says, before I can place both feet on the fuel-slickened pavement. The smell of gasoline is nauseating, but it's much better than being trapped beside him and his scent of midnight jasmine and kindled earth. "You shouldn't go in alone."

"I'm fine," I say flatly, making a move to stand.

"Let me go with you."

"No."

He removes his glasses and runs a hand through his hair, causing a wayward lock to shade those peculiar silver eyes, casting them in twilight. "Eden," he sighs.

"What?" I snap.

When he doesn't respond, I take it as my cue to exit, part of me wishing he had fought a little harder. I would have still insisted I go alone, but still…his irritation was better than nothing.

When I exit the rest stop bathroom, which was surprisingly tidy—all things considered—Legion is standing by the door. I fight the urge to grin up at him, remembering that it's not me he's looking after.

"Would you like anything to eat or drink?" he asks warily.

I shake my head. "I'm fine."

I turn to head back to the car, yet he doesn't follow. When he emerges minutes later, he's carrying a plastic shopping bag.

"I got you water and some sugary coffee crap," he grimaces, the expression amusing on his usually hardened face. "They didn't have anything fresh that looked appetizing so I got you turkey jerky, trail mix and something that is supposed to be veggie chips."

I take the processed contraband and offer a half-grin of thanks. "No candy or chips?"

"Hell no. You'd be better off eating fiberglass. I'm not busting my ass to keep you alive only to let you die at the hands of hydrogenated oils."

I want to laugh, but he's dead serious. Still, a small smile creeps onto my face.

"What?" he asks, starting up the car.

I shake my head. "You're pretty much an oxymoron, ya know."

He frowns. Not in the way that hardens his features, but in the way that makes him seem almost…human. "How so?"

We pull out of the rest stop with Toyol and Phenex trailing us closely in the black Range Rover.

"You're a freakin' immortal who's made it his life's work to kill people. Hell, you originally wanted to kill *me*. Yet you're worried about hydrogenated oils? What's next? A stash of chia seeds and quinoa in the glove compartment?"

Legion winces just slightly before doing something that completely unarms me.

He laughs.

"I guess you're right."

"I know I'm right. Life is short, L. At least for me it is. I might as well die happy covered in orange Cheetos dust than waste away eating air-crisped cardboard."

He laughs again, the sound like velvet to my ears. There's no hint of darkness or malice. There's no underlying condescension in his sultry baritone. He laughed because something I said was funny. And through all the murk and mud of my soiled soul, I found a reason to make a joke, even if it was corny as hell. It was *our* corny as hell, just for a moment.

"Next time, I pick the snacks," I say, watching the way his cheek dimples with his smile. It's like the gesture is so rare and so beautiful that his face wants to covet it forever, scribing the moment deep within his skin. "You have dimples," I find myself gasping at the discovery.

He gives me a quick glance, yet makes no move to hide them. "Yeah. I guess I do."

"Why haven't I ever noticed them?"

"I don't know, Eden," he shrugs. "You must not have looked hard enough."

I want to respond, but there's nothing left to say. Maybe I had been so busy looking for reasons to be repulsed by him that I failed to see the beauty.

No, that's not right either.

Maybe I had seen it. Maybe it scared me the way his stunning physical attributes completely unarmed me. Maybe my attraction to him had grown so strong that I wanted to hate him—needed to hate him—to give myself a chance at redemption. Because if I let it take over, I'd find myself…feeling for him. Falling for him. And that was absolutely ridiculous in every sense of the word.

"We need some music," I say, needing to shake the intimacy of silence. We'd been driving for hours with nothing more than the sounds of my anxious breaths replaying on a constant loop.

I turn the dial for the radio, and am met with a fuckcophany of banjos, guitars and fiddles. I quickly turn it off. "What the hell was that?"

Legion chuckles, low and sultry. "We're in Iowa, Eden. Rural Iowa at that. Here." He presses a button marked with a Bluetooth symbol. "Connect your phone."

Gladly, I fish it out of the pocket of my hoodie. "You sure?"

"Yeah. Why not?"

A flutter of nerves stirs in my belly for some odd reason. Music has always been sacred to me, my escape from the crumbling world outside my headphones. It drowned out the taunting voices in my head, and my own devious consciousness. Sharing it with him is like letting him into that slice of my soul that I had set aside just for me. Something that hadn't been ravaged by my shame.

I scroll to my favorite playlist, a mellow mix of hip-hop and alt rock, even a little pop. When a haunting bass line begins to vibrate through the speakers, Legion gives me a sideway glance.

"What?"

"Interesting choice," he shakes his head, the corner of his mouth twitching.

I bite down on my own smile. "I think it's fitting."

"*Monster?*"

"Too close to home?" I ask, my voice dipped in saccharine.

"No. Not at all. But, really? Kanye?"

"He's a Chicago treasure!"

"But he's Kanye West. And trust me, it's not an act. He sincerely believes his own bullshit."

I don't question how he knows that bit of info, but store it away for another time. Instead I scroll to another song. He barks out a laugh as soon as it sounds through the Bose speakers.

"You've got to be kidding me."

I bat my lashes dramatically. "What?"

"*Lucifer* by Jay-Z? Are you sure you didn't know anything about angels and demons before last week?"

"Positive. Should I change it?"

"No," he smirks. "You can let it play. I like being inside your twisted little head, firecracker."

"What did you call me?"

The barest hint of color touches his cheek. "Firecracker. That's how Cain described you that first night. I think it rather fits."

I suck in my lips to keep from grinning like a buffoon, and train my attention on the road stretched out before us. I'm on a road trip with one of the biggest, baddest demons in history and here I am, sincerely stressed about some silly pet name and impressing him with my taste in music.

Priorities, Eden.

"I like this," he says after a few more songs.

"Yeah?" My heart actually stutters. If I could side-eye myself, I would.

"Yeah. Who is it?"

"Logic. I can make you a playlist if you want."

He nods once before his lips tighten, causing them to turn white at the seams.

"Everything ok?" I ask, my voice meek.

He nods again, but even that gesture seems contrived. I open my mouth to push for more, but decide against it. The moment has passed. The easiness that had settled between us, the casual banter—it's gone now. Maybe I imagined it all.

After several miles, and even more minutes, he finally sighs. "I haven't listened to music in a long while."

I turn to look at him but don't say a thing, for fear that his admission was not meant for me.

"It reminded me too much of…home. There was always music there."

I hold my breath, picturing that foreign place in my mind. He's remembering home. Remembering Heaven.

"Tell me about it," I urge softly, truly meaning it.

His face seems to soften from its regularly tense state. His knuckles ease at the steering wheel. Even those broad shoulders seem to relax as he remembers a place so unlike the darkness and destruction of my world, and his.

"It was eternal sunshine cradled in the soft down of grace. No strife or poverty. No wars forged of envy or greed. We smiled and danced. We loved freely and endlessly and unabashedly. Because love wasn't just a feeling. It wasn't roses and candy or other material possessions. It was what we were. What *I* was."

I don't dare speak, or even breathe. I just watch him, wishing I could touch him in an act of comfort. Wishing some of that love that he speaks so ardently about would rub off on me.

"But that was a long time ago," he utters, his words weighed with emotion.

"How long ago?" I whisper.

"Long before creation. Long before the existence of humanity." His voice takes on an ancient timber, as if he witnessed the birth of this world with his very own eyes.

The realization that I'm currently sitting next to a man—no, angel-turned-demon—that walked this earth long before the creation of man, hits me like a ton of bricks. How? How can someone, or something, survive for so long yet remain youthful and vital? What kind of celestial magic runs through his veins?

"How old are you?"

He watches me from the corner of his eye and answers, "I am without age. I just am."

"So you have no idea when you were created?"

He shrugs a shoulder. "Earth was created some four and a half billion years ago. I believe what I once was—who I was once was—was birthed sometime before that."

My mouth dries, yet I soldier on. "So you've been alive for billions of years?"

He shakes his head, a smirk on his lips. "Time moves differently as an angel. Years pass like days. Weeks are mere blinks of an eye. I had no concept of time then. Not until I left."

"So when..." I know I shouldn't ask, but I can't help it. There's so much to know. It's as if I've been infirm my entire life, and now I'm seeing and hearing and feeling everything all at once. "When did you fall from Heaven?"

His jaw tenses and darkness veils his face, despite his casual tone. "That's a story for another time. How about another playlist?"

I do as he requests, but I don't ignore the gnawing feeling in my gut, urging me to dig deeper. Legion's fall from grace is one story he's resistant to tell. And it may be the most important one yet.

NINETEEN

"**A**BSOLUTELY NOT."

I dangle the cellophane bag of sugar dipped jellied corn syrup in front of Legion's face, and put on my best pout. "Aw, come on. Sour Patch Kids are an American staple! And look—they're fruit flavored. That has to be healthy."

"It's riddled with dyes, additives and processed sugar. Of all the things to put inside your body, why would you want that poison?"

I blink at the mention of putting anything in my body and turn around before he can see my flamed cheeks. "Toyol, please tell your friend that Sour Patch Kids are totally healthy, and he should stop being the old fart that he is and live a little."

Jaw practically on the dingy, germ-infested linoleum of the gas station, he looks to Legion then back to me, a mix of shock and amusement etched on his exotic face. "Um-mmmm..."

"I swear, it's bad enough that he challenges all my music choices. I have to be subjected to veggie chips and turkey jerky too? Turkey is already dry as hell. Why would you dry it out even more?"

"I mean, she has a point," Toyol shrugs.

With his arms crossed over his chest, making his black thermal shirt mold to every curve of his biceps and shoulders like body paint, Legion gives us his pointed look. "It's better than consuming this toxic crap. And I am *not* an old fart."

Just the words on his lips causes me to break into a fit of laughter, with Toyol taking my lead. "Seriously, L," he chuckles, clapping the larger man on the shoulder. "Live a little. Not like it's gonna kill us."

Legion rolls his eyes before throwing the bag of candy contraband in the basket. "Fine. What else do we need?"

"Ooooh! These!" I squeal, holding up a package of Honey Buns.

Legion sucks his teeth but doesn't fight me, for once. "Put it in the damn basket."

As I resume my search for sugar-laden sustenance, I catch Phenex approaching out the corner of my eye, his brows pinched in contemplation.

"Status update?" L asks, reading his demon brother's expression. He stiffly nods and tips his head to one side, signaling Legion to follow. L hands Toyol the basket and disappears with Phenex outside.

"Everything ok?" I ask, feigning nonchalance.

A glimmer of mischief sparks the black depths of his

slanted eyes. "Nothing we can't handle."

"Will they be ok back…" Home. I stop myself before I say it. "Back in Chicago? Without you guys?"

"Yeah. Probably breathing a little easier now that you're gone."

"And why's that?" I frown, a pang of offense piercing my chest.

Toyol laughs and shakes his head. "The Jumper attraction. It's a real bitch in confined spaces. Imagine your own personal live porn show going down everywhere you turn, for twenty-four hours a day for a week straight. Now maximize that overwhelming appeal by ten. That's how it's been living with you."

Warmth floods my face, and I quickly turn towards a display of honey roasted nuts. Unconsciously, I toss a bag in, needing something to preoccupy my hands. "Oh. Sorry."

"Not your fault. But it can be difficult for those that aren't as disciplined."

"Is that why you and Phenex came along, and not the others?" I turn toward him in time to see him shake his head.

"I have a personal connection within the coven. Phenex is more of a diplomat than any of us. And L…well, you know how he is. Doubtful he'll leave your side ever again."

My mouth dries and my tongue turns to lead. I swallow down the thought of being tied to Legion for…shit. A few months? A year? Life? I can't expect that of him, and I'm not sure I want to.

No, absolutely not.

How can I chain myself to a man—a demon—that despises what I am, and merely feels bound by some ancient feud to protect me?

"Hey, would it be cool to ride with you guys in the Range for this leg of the trip?" I find myself asking. Toyol's obligation to me may not be any different from Legion's, but at least he isn't playing nice to keep me complacent. Or maybe he is. Still…I didn't confess my sins to Toyol. I didn't sleep in the comfort of his strong arms while he whispered sweet words in the dark. And I didn't press myself against him, begging with labored breaths and frantic heartbeats to feel more of his hard body.

He looks at me suddenly, his eyes squinted in rumination. But before he can open his mouth to answer, a gruff voice does it for him.

"No. It wouldn't be."

I spin around and nearly collide with Legion's taut chest. "Why not?"

He simply shakes his head and takes the basket of junk food from Toyol before heading to the register. That's all the answer I'm going to get.

"What's his problem?" I sneer at his back.

"Problem?" Toyol chuckles. "This is him in a good mood."

It'll be several more hours until we're in Colorado, and we've already been traveling for a solid ten. The sun is slowly sinking over the horizon, and I feel sticky with road trip grime. Still, Legion refuses to stop at a hotel for the night.

"Aren't you tired?" I whine, shifting in my seat. Even though the Jag is top-of-the-line luxury inside and out, my butt fell asleep miles ago.

"No."

"Well, I am."

"Then sleep."

"How? My neck will be stiff for days, even if I recline all the way. I need a bed, and a pillow, and a shower. And something to eat other than gas station hot dogs and Icees."

"You picked that stuff."

"I know, but…" I'm being a child—I know. But getting through to Legion is like trying to blow down a brick wall. I admire his tenacity, honestly. But I just wish he would give a little.

"I can't risk you staying in a place that's unprotected," he says quietly. "Even if I stay up all night and watch you, we could be falling into a trap. And I refuse to take that chance where you're concerned."

I stare at him, watching the shadows caress his striking features. His deep set, silver eyes seem to glow with moonlight. "Why?"

"I told you, Eden."

"Yeah, and I heard you. But…why? Why do all this for a stranger? Am I really worth it? Would you do this for any sad charity case off the street?"

"Yes."

"So that's your angle. You have a superhero complex and you see me as a broken bird that needs to be fixed." I fail to keep the ache of reality from echoing in my voice.

"No," he answers, shaking his head. "You are really worth it."

A sour note of irrational anger taints my tongue and I look away, focusing my bleary eyes on the vast open fields shrouded in night's approach. "See," I huff, my voice quivering. "You have to stop saying things like that. You have to stop making me believe that I'm more than just a host or a weapon or a pawn. Because sometimes, I want to believe it. And when you say things like that, I'm able to forget—even if just for a second—that my fate is sealed in blood and tears. I forget that I have no future and no purpose in this life. And the moment I forget what I truly am is the moment I'll allow myself to dream again."

I don't turn back to face him, but I feel him. It's just a feather-light brush against the back of my hand, but it's enough to tell me that he's heard me.

"You shouldn't have to forget," he says quietly. "You shouldn't be afraid to dream."

I nod but still refuse to look his way. I don't want to him to see me cry.

It's midnight when Legion gently shakes me awake. I must've been lulled to sleep while watching twilight swallow the sun, casting a haunting gloom upon ochre fields dusted with late autumn. And just as I expected, my neck is stiff as a board.

I lift my head and squint against the golden glow of floodlights intensified by soft white twinkle lights strung across a driveway. I stretch my sore limbs with a yawn.

"Where are we?"

"Hotel. It's safe."

"Finally." With sluggish fingers, I fiddle with the car door handle, but before I can get it open, Legion is on the other side. He waves off valet and opens the door for me. "Thanks," I smile.

"You're welcome. I'll get our luggage."

I stand on the cobblestone walkway in front of the hotel entrance steps, lost in awe at the sheer splendor of what lies before me. Across the driveway, encircled by a charming flagstone road, is a neatly tended garden featuring a grand fountain. Its backlit waters seem to flow into the foliage from spigots on either side, effectively keeping the trees and shrubs a bright green. Odd. From Chicago, all we saw were rust-colored, dried leaves and browning grass touched by the first signs of winter. Here, everything seems to thrive and bloom.

"Ready?" Legion asks, sidling up beside me, although his gaze stays trained on Toyol who is talking to a giant wearing dark shades. The man is massive. Taller than Legion and broader than Cain. It's a wonder how he was able to fit his solid frame in his black designer suit. But I guess when you work at a place like this, image is everything. Still, the black-out sunglasses at night seem a bit ridiculous.

We follow the hulk-size concierge through the stunning lobby to the front desk. He says a few hushed words to Toyol before nodding once in my direction and disappearing behind a door several feet away. A chill creeps up my neck before crawling down my spine.

"Good evening, my name is Dawson," says the chipper host behind the marble counter. "I see Mr. Skotos has reserved four rooms to accommodate your party, Mr…"

"L. Call me L," Legion answers, his voice as smooth as satin. "And we'll only require two rooms, thank you."

Poor Dawson looks at each of us, his keen green eyes

filled with unasked questions. "As you wish."

He taps something into his computer before handing us each a card key and jumping into a diatribe about the resorts amenities, which I quickly block out. I know I shouldn't, but it's been so long. So long since I've stretched my mental limbs and crawled into another human mind. It's risky, considering he, too, could be supernatural, but the allure of that power calls to me, beckoning me to reach out and scrape my nails against the thin barrier surrounding his thoughts. It's pliable like putty or foam, and molds around me as I apply just a touch of pressure, sucking my intent into its welcoming arms. I slip in easily without resistance, as if he's fearless. Safe. Unthreatening.

Hints of serene, ocean blue and fresh cotton are the first notes to flood my senses. But there's a foreign darkness lurking within an abandoned corner, as if he's ignorant of its presence. Not an evil darkness, but an all-consuming one. One that obliterates light wherever it touches. It isn't dead, although a bit cold and detached. The darkness does not belong to him, yet it has attached itself to him, as if taking ownership.

I say the words before the unknown gloom realizes I'm there. I don't want it to claim me too. *"Upgrade our rooms."*

Dawson lifts his head and beams brightly. "I'm pleased to inform you that we have upgraded your rooms to our executive suites. Complimentary, of course."

"Send food and wine." My voice is wrapped in an unshakable timbre so unlike my own as of late. I barely recognize it. I swallow past the bitter taste of his blood on my tongue.

"And we'll be sending up a cheese board and wine from the kitchen." He slides four key cards across the counter. "I hope you enjoy your stay here at the Broadmoor Hotel."

The doors of the elevator leading up to the upper floors aren't even fully closed when Legion roughly grabs my arm at the elbow.

"Are you *insane*? This isn't our territory. The warlock could take what you did as a serious offense!"

I try to twist out of his grip but it's like cement. "I didn't hurt him! I just wanted to see if I could still do it."

He tears his fingers away, yet steps in so close that the heat of his fury singes my nose. "You don't get it, do you? This is about more than you and your petty, human desires. You can't play with people's free will, Eden."

"I'm not," I bite back, refusing to let him intimidate me, even if he is right. "I'm still learning, still trying to wrap my head around all this. Excuse me for not being a reformed sinner like you."

"It's not about being reformed. It's about having a conscience." He shakes his head and roughly rakes a hand through his mussed hair, backing into the other end of the elevator wall. "If you want me to save you, you need to start acting like someone that's worth saving."

I open my mouth to retort, but he's stolen my words, my voice. He's stolen the fight right out of me.

"I think what L is trying to say…" Phenex pipes up, stepping between Legion and me. It's one of the few times that he's spoken to me since he was nearly killed by the angel venom. Strange. I thought he'd be more gracious, maybe even a little grateful. If I didn't know any better, I would say that he's avoided me. "Eden, we understand that humans, by nature, are not perfect, and we don't expect you to be. But the more you lean on the dealings of the devil and willfully avoid the righteous path less traveled, the easier it will be for Lucifer's influence to worm its way into your head. Angels and demons cannot interfere with the free will of humans, but you can. It's what you do with that power that sets you apart."

Thankfully, the elevator dings and the doors slide open, revealing our floor, so I don't have a chance to answer. I wouldn't know what to say anyway.

I follow Legion, feeling like a scolded puppy, although I refuse to let him see it. Head held high, I enter the executive suite. Phenex and Toyol are staying in one adjacent to ours.

Like the driveway and the lobby, the room is decked out in opulence reminiscent of 1700s French nobility, bursting with rich bronze, crimson and lapis. It's a bit gaudy for my taste, and judging by Legion's sneer, it definitely isn't pleasing to his shrewd, gray eyes.

"Garish fuckers," he mutters under his breath.

"A bit ostentatious, but anything is better than sleeping in a car." I stretch my neck from side-to-side and roll my shoulders, cringing at the resounding pop the movement makes.

Legion steps forward, his hand outstretched, but stops himself. "Um, you take the bed. I'll be on the couch."

I glance over at the gold and powder blue Cabriole sofa with raised brows. It's barely big enough to fit two people, one if we're talking demons. "Are you sure about that?"

"I am. Go ahead and get cleaned up and settled. We have a big day tomorrow." He tosses me my duffle bag and turns toward the mini bar. I watch him eye the wooden cart as if he can see straight through to the tiny bottles of liquor resting inside. A one hundred year struggle wages war across his features before he turns away.

I drop my bag and walk over to the mini bar, fishing out the delicate bottles of vodka, whiskey and rum displayed over the fridge. I set them on top and turn towards Legion, my arms crossed over my chest.

"It doesn't make you a bad person if you want it. It doesn't undo all the good you've done—all the good you're still doing."

I pick up my bag and head straight to the bathroom, eager to wash the day off my body, and the taste of blood from my mouth. When I emerge from the sanctuary of steam and solace wearing one of the hotel's terry cloth robes, I find a cart containing a bottle of wine and a platter under a metal dome in the sitting room. Legion sits at a small, round breakfast table. And of all the things he could be doing after a fifteen-hour road trip, he's cleaning his guns.

"Shower's available," I comment. He doesn't even lift his head. "You should eat something."

"I'm fine," he murmurs, his deft fingers moving skillfully over the hardware.

I shrug to myself and pad over to the untouched cart. Under the platter's dome sits a spread of various cheeses, meats and fresh fruit, perfect for the bottle of red wine. My mouth watering, I help myself to all and plop down onto the sofa directly across from Legion. He doesn't even acknowledge me.

"If you're pissy about what happened downstairs, I'm sorry," I say with a heaved breath.

"I'm not pissy."

"Really? So you're not talking to me because you're being

your regular happy-go-lucky self, complete with sunshine and daffodils?"

He doesn't answer, but the corner of his mouth twitches.

"Seriously, L. I'm trying. You can't change me overnight."

He drops the clip in his hand, the sound of steel on wood reverberating harshly around the lavish space. When he lifts his head to look at me, his gaze is icy. "I don't want to change you, Eden. I want you to see that there is more to you than you've allowed your abilities to become. You can destroy with a single, uttered word. Imagine what you could create. Imagine what you could *be*."

I shake my head. He doesn't know me. He doesn't know anything about me. He's read a few case files and watched me through the eyes of an assassin stalking its prey. He doesn't know about all the years I tried to block out the voice in my head, or all the nights I've grieved for the people I'd hurt. He doesn't know how hard it was for me in my formidable years when I was still struggling with abandonment and PTSD. He's never felt the weight of loneliness crushing me in the midnight hours, making it impossible to breathe.

He sees a broken doll. A project. A mission.

He doesn't see *me*.

"And you know this, how?"

Legion stands, deserting his weapons, and comes to stand before me. His daunting frame wraps me in shadow, extinguishing the light streaming from the nearby Tiffany lamp. "I know this because I understand that pull to darkness. I've felt it. I feel it every day. And it's so much easier to submit to its allure."

"You could've fooled me. You don't seem to submit to

anything."

Suddenly, he's hovering over me, his hands braced on the couch in a move that traps me between his arms. "Eden, I submit to you daily. Every moment we're together, every time you sleep with your cheek pressed against my chest, I am submitting to a side of me that was lost a long time ago. And in those moments, I remember what I was, and what I have lost. And I hate myself for missing it." He pushes off the back of the sofa and strides over to where those wicked little bottles are lined up atop the mini fridge. He plucks up the whiskey and unscrews its delicate cap. "I am Hell on earth, Eden. But that doesn't mean I want to be."

I watch the way his throat bobs sensually as he downs the scorching liquor, his eyes turned up to the heavens. Funny how a simple, natural act can cause every bone in my body to turn to liquid.

"Is that why you want me to be better?" I ask breathlessly. "To make it easier for you?"

"No." He chucks the bottle in a nearby bin and grabs another. "I want you to be better for you."

I shake my head and take a hefty gulp of wine. "I don't believe that."

"Then what do you believe?"

I take another sip, craving the courage. "I believe the very thing you despise in me, is the very thing you want."

A sinuous half small crawls across his lips. "Are you saying I want you, firecracker?"

"I don't know, Legion. Do you?"

The silence that stretches between us becomes stifling as he stares at me, his expression blank, save for the lustrous fire blazing in his eyes. I shift uncomfortably.

"You should sleep," he finally says, looking away.

"So should you."

"I will. Later."

I know it's a lie. Yet, I'm not sure why I even care.

I quietly finish my wine and food and return to the bedroom. Like the sitting area, the space is decked out in rich colors and lush fabrics, but I'm much too exhausted to appreciate it. I crawl between the softest linens known to man, and almost before my head hits the pillow, I'm out like a light.

Some time during the night, the scent of midnight jasmine and the brush of callused fingers invade my dreams. Dreams about breathless sighs and searing kisses and frantic touches. Dreams about Legion.

TWENTY

MORNING COMES TOO SOON. AND IF I HAD KNOWN what a big deal it was to gain the audience of a warlock, I would have stayed in bed.

"How's this?" I ask Legion after finally settling on a plain black dress with a V neckline and flats studded with silver and gold grommets. Somehow, Lilith fit three extra outfits in my bag, and I'm grateful for every one. After Legion informed me of the rarity of a warlock-demon sit down over breakfast, alluding that the warlock in question was royalty in the underworld, I'd been racked with anxiety. Royalty? Shit. I was hardly respectable enough for Red Lobster.

"So?"

His molten gaze singes me from head to toe, taking in the way I'd pinned my silver locks up in a messy bun, allowing a few curled tendrils to escape around my face. The dress is fitted, showcasing my waist and bosom, before flaring out around my hips. It stops just before the knee. Sinful yet sweet. I took a few more minutes on my eye makeup than usual, focusing on a heavy lash to accentuate my dark eyeshadow. My lips are simply slicked with pinkish nude gloss.

"You look..." The word slides across his tongue and drips from his full bottom lip. "Lovely."

"Stop," I blush, trying to suck in the smile that keeps trying to emerge. "I feel ridiculous."

"Why?" he frowns.

"I don't know," I shrug. "I've been described as hot by some of the guys I've dated—if you can call messy hook-ups dating. Maybe even a few thought I was sexy. But never lovely."

"Maybe you've been dealing with the wrong guys." His face is stone, but his voice is as soft and yielding as the brush of a rose petal. I don't know what to think of it, so I quickly change the subject.

"So these witches...warlocks...whatever. What exactly are they?"

Legion leans back in the Bergère chair and sighs. "The Dark are a very old, very traditional race of original witches. Their magic is one of only two types that were actually designed by the Creator at your world's birth. According to the bible, it was the very first magic, the Light quickly following."

"Huh? How is that possible?"

A small smile quirks his lips. "*In the beginning God created the Heaven and the earth. And the earth was without form, and void; and darkness was upon the face of the deep. And the Spirit of God moved upon the face of the waters. And God said, Let there be light: and there was light. And God saw the light, that it was good: and God divided the light from the darkness. And God called the light Day, and the darkness he called Night.'"*

He takes in my stunned expression and his smile broadens. "The Dark are the wardens of night, while the Light are the keepers of day. Their history is complex and sacred, but they are very powerful, drawing their strength from the elements. They are wind, water, rain, snow. Their emotions are directly tethered to the earth and their abilities are immeasurable. However, their power only extends to this realm. They have no control of anything or anyone whose existence is not tied to this world."

I find the meaning in his words and nod. "They have no power over you."

"Precisely. The Creator made us all in His image. The Dark and Light were derived from that prototype."

"Are they more powerful than you?"

Legion shakes his head. "Not necessarily. I don't have full usage of my powers on earth—a portion of it was stripped from me when I rebelled against Lucifer. But under normal circumstances—"

"Wait. You have *powers*? What? Why didn't I know this?"

He shrugs, a light of amusement flickering in his eyes. "You never asked."

Holy hell.

The brute strength, the animal-like reflexes, his superhuman will…I knew Legion was a demon, but I never imagined he had actual power. I don't know if I should be terrified or intrigued. Terrified. Definitely terrified.

Reading the questions flashing across my features, Legion climbs to his feet and crosses the room in four long strides. I shiver on my metallic-studded shoes as he stops in front of me, his intimidating presence claiming the space between us. Then in a movement that rips a gasp from my tight throat, he cups my face gently. The pads of his thumbs graze the apples of my cheeks with feather-light grace.

"You don't have to be afraid of me, Eden. I would never hurt you."

I nod, just slightly, not knowing what to do or say. Do I believe him? I want to. But he's hurt me before. I've seen the hatred in his eyes. I've felt it radiate from his frame, and wash over me like sticky, black blood. What's to stop him from doing just as he promised? Snapping my neck without a second thought when he's grown tired of my stubborn weakness?

"Ok," I whisper.

"You have nothing to fear from me," he utters, his intense gaze urging me to believe him. To trust him despite what he is. "As long as I'm alive on this earth, I will always protect you."

I want to pull away, yet I want him to stay. Stay right here, touching me, coaxing me with his urgent words and burning touch. When my life is filled with so much uncertainty, I want him to be that one constant I can rely on.

And it scares me.

A knock on the door breaks the spell, causing Legion to hiss between his teeth before dropping his hands. My skin still flames with remembrance of him.

"It's time," he says.

I nod, battling the nerves churning in my gut. Legion pulls away from me completely to answer the door.

"Showtime," I hear Toyol say from behind me.

I take a deep, steeling breath to keep the anxious nausea at bay. I don't know what I'm walking into. Witches, warlocks…I have no idea what to expect. Will they wear pointed hats and black robes? Will they fly around on broomsticks and gather toad's eyes and chicken feet to add to a steaming cauldron? Shit, maybe this isn't a hotel at all. Maybe I've been duped and we're at Hogwarts.

Seriously, this shit just doesn't seem plausible.

I shake my head and turn around, spying Toyol and Phenex, both dressed in dark suits much like Legion's, filling up the doorframe. "Come on. Let's get this over with."

"Very nice," Toyol remarks, brows raised.

"Yeah? I'll probably have to change before the Quidditch match," I snort.

"He's a warlock, not a wizard, Eden." His face is serious, but mirth dances in those dark slanted eyes.

"Is there a difference?"

"Yes," Legion answers. "And you'd do well to remember that." His tone is cool, but not exactly cold. There's a message attached, an unspoken warning for me to keep my wits about me. Maybe I was right to be nervous, considering each of their stony expressions.

We start down the long hallway towards the elevator when Phenex falls behind to walk beside me. Surprisingly, Legion leaves my side.

"I'm sure you're wondering why I haven't spoken to you much since you saved my life."

I shake my head. "It was nothing."

"That's where you're wrong, Eden. What you did for me—for us—was nothing short of miraculous. After everything… you chose to be of aid. And for that, I am in your debt."

"Then why have you been avoiding me?" I resent the tinge of hurt in my voice. Phenex notices it too, and casts his honeyed eyes to the ground in shame.

"I pride myself on restraint, almost as much as Legion. Because of you, I was able to recover from my physical injuries, however, my resistance was left weakened. I assume the others have informed you of the effect your special circumstances has on our kind."

The Jumper's allure. It calls to their malevolence, seduces the beast within. It's what angels use to lure demons then, ultimately, kill them. They felt it in me on that first day I was brought to their high-rise apartment. And they've been fighting the urge to sate their carnal urges ever since.

"I'm not strong enough to fight it right now," Phenex admits quietly, refusing to meet my wide-eyed gaze. "And I'm ashamed. Please don't be afraid of me. I would never let it overpower me. And if it did..." He flicks his golden orbs to Legion's taut back just feet away. "He would take me out before I could touch you."

"Take you out?" I whisper.

"There's a reason he's known as the Demon Slayer. He is the Collector of Fallen Souls. It'd be quite easy for him actually."

At that, I see Legion turn his head just a fraction, giving me a quick view of his tight, ticking jaw. The Demon Slayer? Collector of Fallen Souls? How will I ever really know him when everything about him is so steeped in secrets and myth? And, honestly, do I want to?

We arrive at the elevator before I can ask for clarification. Legion doesn't meet my eyes. I know he's heard every word

Phenex and I have spoken, yet he hasn't denied it. And even if he did, what reason would Phenex have to lie to me?

We descend to the first floor of the hotel in silence, the tension filling the ornate steel box like smog. Toyol leads us towards a hallway off the lobby while Phenex and Legion stay situated at my sides as if to ward off any unwanted eyes. They're being beyond ridiculous. No one knows me here. No one cares. And even if there was some unseen threat, what could they possibly do to avoid it?

Unless I'm the unseen threat. Unless they're not protecting me from others. They're protecting others from *me*.

I shake off the thought, desperate to not let it deter me or define me. Legion said I was so much more than what I had allowed myself to become. I have to believe that. Because if I don't…

I might as well surrender to the Calling right here and now.

We come to a set of elaborately carved ivory doors with golden handles fashioned like crashing waves. They're odd, yet beautiful, much like everything at this hotel. Elegant, regal and unique. And I'm completely out of place.

We enter what appears to be a conference room, and find that it's empty. There's a spread of charcuterie, fruit, sweets and cheeses, as well as wine and tea in the middle of a long mahogany table. Toyol leads us to one side, the end farthest from the door. He's positioning us so that we'll have full view of anyone—and anything—that enters. A small advantage considering we're in the heart of the deadliest coven on earth, according to Legion. For them to even consider this meeting must mean that they're desperate. There has to be something they're not telling me, whether it's to keep me in the dark or protect my fragile human heart. I bite down on the taste of contempt on my tongue. I'm so tired of being weak. I don't want to be shielded like some damsel in distress. I've never been good at playing that role, and I don't plan on trying now.

I feel Legion stiffen in his chair beside mine, causing me to follow his gaze towards the entrance. The doors glide open smoothly, as if pushed by a gust of ocean-scented air.

And I gasp.

There are six of them, all finely dressed in expensive fabrics: two women, both young and gorgeous, and four men: the massive suit from last night, a svelte, stunning blonde that would give Andras a run for his money, an exceptionally handsome man the color of a caramel latte, and positively the most beautiful man I have ever laid eyes on.

He leads one of the women—the one with soft brown curls almost to her waist and the most unusual eyes I've ever seen—while keeping his impossibly icy blue irises trained on me and my assassin companions. The others follow, falling into step as if this procession was choreographed. When they take their seats across from us, the doors close on their own. At least I think they did.

Tiny, frozen daggers rake up and down my spine. We are in the presence of immense power. I can feel it.

"Welcome to my hotel. I hope you've found your accommodations...comfortable," the lead warlock says smoothly, the hint of a smirk on his face. It's as if he knows what I did to his desk clerk, and he wants me to *know* that he knows. And regret it.

Toyol pipes up with a slight bow of his head, "We appreciate your hospitality, your majesty."

Your *majesty?*

Legion told me we would be sitting down with Dark royalty, but he never said anything about the king. I squeeze the arm of the chair to force myself not to flee.

"Please," the king says, waving a dismissive hand. "Call me Dorian."

Dorian. The Dark king's name is Dorian. That just doesn't seem fair. He's the most powerful Dark force in the world, he's impossibly gorgeous, and his name is *Dorian?*

"This is my Queen, Gabriella," he adds, looking at the young woman at his side. He squeezes her hand and brings it up to his lips to brush a kiss across her knuckles. It's several seconds before he turns his loving gaze from her to the man to his right, the one whose skin is the color of butter toffee. His eyes are also a shade of radiant blue. "My advisor and father-in-law, Alexander. And Light ambassador, Lars," he says nodding towards the tall blonde male before waving towards the other confidantes sitting beside the queen. "I believe you've met Cyrus, my cousin. And this lovely lady is Morgan."

I meet the eyes of each and nod, just as a chocolate pastry lifts itself from the platter between us. I yelp before I can stop myself, causing Legion to roughly grip my thigh in alarm. A child's giggle sounds right after, causing me to yelp again.

"Nikolai Christopher, that's enough," Gabriella admonishes gently. And right before my eyes, a little boy no older than three appears in the middle of the table, holding the chocolate confection.

"Aw, mama. Can't I have it?" The toddler scoots his pudgy body to the edge of the table where his mother sits, his glossy black curls bouncing around his adorable face. He has his father's eyes, but his mother's milky complexion. Rosy, chubby cheeks, thick, dark lashes, and a permanent pout. He has to be the cutest little thing I've ever seen.

"Not until after dinner, Niko," the peculiar-eyed queen coos, scooping her son up to deposit him on her lap. She smiles fondly at the little cherub, her gaze filled with so much love and adoration that I can literally feel it radiating from her petite frame, painting them in colors of rose and lavender.

Something inside of me twists uncomfortably. I've never been on the receiving end of a look like that. And I know I could never be in the queen's position—as a mother. To love and be loved so unguardedly, so completely…I wouldn't even know where to start.

"Please excuse my son," Dorian remarks. He reaches over to lightly pinch the boy's chubby cheeks, eliciting a peal of giggles.

"I want to sit with Gampy, Papa!" Little Niko squeaks, squirming on his mother's lap. Dorian picks him up with ease and passes him to his father-in-law, Alexander after kissing his forehead. The proud grandfather ruffles the boy's curls before bouncing him on his knee.

"Apologies," Dorian says with a bow of his head. "Please…" He waves a hand in our direction, as to give us the floor. "What brings you to Colorado Springs?"

Toyol clears his throat, taking point. "Your majesty—Dorian—as your cousin, Cyrus explained, we represent the Se7en."

"Ah, yes. The Se7en," Dorian muses, the blue in his eyes appearing almost opaque against the shocking backdrop of black hair. He leans forward, intertwining graceful fingers below his chin. "Demon assassins of redemption. Sinners of salvation. I've heard of you—all brute strength and merciless killing. They say you hunt humans that your master has...infected."

"More or less, yes," Toyol nods.

"And you feel no...remorse? For murdering innocents? For failing to preserve human life?"

Toyol opens his mouth to answer, but looks to Phenex who quickly pipes up. "Our goal is to preserve countless human lives by intercepting an imminent threat to their survival. Their world is constantly wrought with destruction—terrorist bombings, mass shootings. Incidents we can avoid by taking out a solitary perpetrator."

"Before they actually become the perpetrator. Before they've committed any actual crimes against humanity." The warlock king lifts a single, speculative brow, challenging him. I feel a fiery blast of heat from beside me where Legion sits, his knuckles white from gripping the arms of the chair, his jaw ticking frantically. *Don't say a word.* I mentally beg. *Just let Phenex handle this.*

"It's much more complex than that. Over weeks—months—of recon and research, we track signs of the Calling. Nothing is done without cause. We don't act unless necessary."

"And this girl," Dorian nods to me, "is your next victim?"

I swallow thickly as that penetrating, ice-filled gaze lands on me. *Victim.* It sounds like an act of violence on his lips.

"Eden is destined for the Calling, yes. But our intent is to spare her, and ultimately, spare the angel inhabiting her body." That seems to get the king's attention, and he leans forward just a bit more. Phenex continues. "When Eden was very young, she suffered a horrible incident that nearly claimed her life. A fallen angel seeking redemption was able to jump into her body, but could not fully control her soul."

"Because she had already been infected," the queen says, equally as interested in the account.

"Precisely. Because of the angel's gifts, Eden has the unique ability to bend the will of humans. And if she is Called, she could very easily become the most deadliest of all of Lucifer's weapons."

"Is that so?" Dorian replies thoughtfully. "How?"

Phenex spares me a glance before answering, "If Eden is Called, she could simply tell every human in her vicinity to walk off a bridge. Or tell a pilot to crash an airplane. If Eden is Called before we can stop her, she could instruct anyone to go home and murder their entire family before killing themselves."

I don't dare utter a word in protest even though my chest is caving in with the need to scream. It's like they're talking about someone else. Someone vicious and calculating. Someone who hasn't spent most of her life longing for just one person to love her, despite her scars, inside and out.

The king looks at his bride, an unspoken communication passing between them. Then he turns his unforgiving gaze on me. "Show me."

"It only works on humans," I manage to say, barely above a whisper.

"Morgan is human. Perhaps she would allow a demonstration?"

I turn to the mocha-skinned woman sitting beside the

queen. She appears just as reluctant as I, her brown eyes widened in skepticism. Could this be a trap? Is the Dark king dangling a carrot in front of my nose, only to catch me in his snare?

"I ask that you not hurt her. I'm afraid my wife and son would not take it well, not to mention Lars. Something simple—a show of this great power your friend speaks so chillingly about. You don't mind, do you?"

He words it as a challenge. As if he can't believe any measure of my mortal power could be a threat. I take the dare, allowing his condescension to only spur me on.

I take a deep breath, sucking in her scent of cinnamon, cardamom and herbs. It's not the perfume of her skin, it's the fragrance her thoughts emit, as if they are attached to a memory. I dig a little deeper, tasting the remembrance as I slide over the frontal lobe like slow moving oil. She stares back at me, perplexed by the intrusion but unable to fight it. She can feel me in her private space, stealing her thoughts, her feelings, her free will. She attempts to push me out, but it's futile. I latch myself to her mind.

"*Stand up.*"

She rises without preamble, her face marred in disbelief.

"*Pick up the chocolate donut.*"

She does as I command, and bends toward the platter of sweets, swiping the pastry.

"*Now give it to Nikolai.*"

Her limbs move as if disjointed from her body—jerky and uncoordinated—as she tries to fight each step. She's helpless to my compulsion, despite her iron will. Despite the flavor of magic that runs through her blood and now tinges my tongue.

Morgan offers the squirming toddler the donut, who squeals and claps at both the show and his treat. I pull back my invisible claws, dislodging them from her mind. She exhales loudly when she feels my exit.

"What did you do to me?" she frowns, quickly making her way back to her seat.

"I'm sorry." It seems like the right thing to say, although I had about as much control of this charade as she did.

"What did you *do?*" she demands.

I wrap my arms around myself, feeling exposed and dirty. I don't know what I've done and how I've done it. I've never understood how it worked. I just knew that I could make people do as I said, no matter how self-serving or depraved the request.

"You have an interesting gift, young one," the king remarks. *Young one?* He can't be more than a few years older than I am. None of them can. Which is really creepy considering Gabriella's father doesn't look a day over thirty.

"Thank you." It doesn't seem appropriate, but I don't know what else to say.

"However, this is angel-demon business. Why should my kind get involved in something we have no stake in?" He leans back in his chair with an air of finality.

"With all due respect, your majesty," I stupidly pipe up, refusing to accept no for an answer. It's out of character for me—the girl who's tried to go unnoticed for most of her life—but if there was ever a time to step out of line and fall back on courage, it's now. "You probably have more stake in this than any of us. You live in the human world. You sit beside them, work with them, build friendships with them. If humanity ceased to exist, wouldn't it mean that you'd failed? That you'd failed at being a just and worthy ruler?"

He silently contemplates my words, sitting so still that I'm certain he can't be breathing. It's like that moment right before a waiting predator strikes. Quiet viciousness seems to gravitate toward him as fury builds in waves of violence.

I hold my breath waiting for the onslaught, and when he leans forward once more, Legion does the same. But before he can open that perfect mouth, the queen raises one hand and it all…

Stops.

No more restless shifting or anxious breaths.

No more sounds of exuberant chomping and licking from little Niko as he devours his donut.

Everyone is encased in glass—living statues captured between heartbeats.

Everyone except me. And her.

"Don't be afraid," she says gently. "I was just getting bored with all the back and forth. I swear, I am so sick of politics. Dorian promised no business during family time, but…" She shrugs, looking more and more like a regular girl. "Duty calls. However, he has his methods, and I have mine."

"How did you…?" I swallow, trying to collect my thoughts and line them up with my words. "How did you do that? Freeze everyone?"

"It's simple. Although, it took me a little while to control it after my ascension. At first, it would only happen during high stress moments when I'd panic. Then the true test was getting them to remobilize." She chuckles as if she's talking to an old friend. I stare at her, wide-eyed, wondering if I missed something. "You'll have to excuse my husband. He's usually not so much of a prick. Not on purpose. Are you married? Boyfriend?"

"No," I answer truthfully.

"Oh. Well, I guess that's a good thing—all things considering."

I spare a glance at Legion's frozen form, still teetering on the verge of impatience and rage. If I were to ever have that option, in another life, in another time, maybe he'd be something I'd choose, or someone I'd hope would choose me. Someone strong and protective. Someone warm to the touch, and that just the sound of his voice would turn my insides to lava. Selfless, yet demanding. Beautiful, but brutal. In a perfect world, I wouldn't be a weapon of evil, and he wouldn't be a demon assassin seeking penance. I wouldn't be his mission or obligation. And he wouldn't be my captor or bodyguard. He would just be…mine.

Maybe.

In my next breath, I nearly fall out of my chair. The queen, Gabriella, is standing right beside me, somehow clearing a good six feet in a blink of an eye. But, I never saw her move an inch. It's as if she was one place then another, dissipating and taking form right before my eyes. I clamp my lips together, forcing the rising panic to ease.

"Sorry. It's just faster and easier for me," Gabriella grins sheepishly. "Come. Let's go for a walk. I want to talk to you."

I look to the demons at my sides, completely immovable and oblivious. Or maybe they aren't. Maybe they can hear everything that's going on right now and are incapable of breaking out of her spell.

"I thought your kind held no power over demons."

"We don't," she shrugs. "Well, in most cases." She holds out a hand for me. "I'll tell you all about it."

With a silent prayer on my lips, I extend my shaky palm and grasp the queen's hand. She could force me, but she's giving me a choice. She wants me to trust her. And as stupid as it sounds, I kinda do.

I follow her out of the conference room, despite the niggling feeling that I should stay put. But I'm curious about her and her powers. And if spending some time with her will get us the information we need, and shed some light on how she can control demons, then I'll do what she asks. This is me being an asset, not a victim.

"I was a lot like you a few years ago," she remarks, leading us towards a glass door. The moment we leave the lavish confines of the hotel and step onto the cobblestone walkway, springtime comes alive with bursts of emerald and honeysuckle. The air is brisk, yet somehow the cold isn't overwhelming—nothing like I'd expect for late fall. Considering the snow-capped mountains looming to my right, it's safe to say that magic is responsible for the climate control.

"Like you? How so?"

"I was human once. At least I thought I was. Brash, careless, sometimes reckless. No…always reckless," she replies, her voice tinged with amusement. She lifts her face to the sky, allowing the sun to cast a golden shimmer on her delicate features. "I had to learn and grow a lot faster than most. Not just for me, but for them—my family."

"Is that why you're able to control them?" I don't have to specify whom I'm talking about.

An elderly couple strolls along the slate stone path, hand in hand, basking in the splendor of the resort's lush grounds. Gabriella smiles and greets them by name as they pass before she answers me. "What I am…is different from my husband. I am a hybrid, so my magic manifests differently."

"And…your eyes?" I remark sheepishly. She may look my age, but I know better than to trust what I see.

She turns and smiles, and those peculiar irises—plucked from the sun and the moon—glitter with diamond luminosity. "I am both Light and Dark equally, so my magic is not only unique, it's an enigma for most of the supernatural realm. Some believe it is the most powerful magic on Earth."

"And is it?"

Her lips twist into a half smile, giving me all the answer I need. "You're here to see me, you know. Not my husband. What your friends seek is something only I can give. Which is why my husband was acting like a royal ass. But my question is, Eden…what is it that *you're* seeking?"

"What do you mean?"

"What do you want? All of this must be a huge change for you, and your friends don't seem like the compromising type. Is this what you've chosen for yourself? To be under their safeguard until the time comes when they must kill you? To be a pet, a novelty? Or to be the strong, confident woman that I know you're capable of becoming?"

Her words seem to echo in my befuddled mind as we follow the stone walkway edging a lake, so clear and vibrant that the surface looks like ripples of smooth sea glass. Many passersby offer warm smiles and waves, which Gabriella cheerfully returns. Not too exuberant, as if she's trying to put on a show. But in a way that says that she's happy to be alive. That every day, every breath, is a gift.

To have that sense of inner peace, to feel safe and assured in her skin… I envy her. Not because of the seemingly perfect husband and child. Not because of her expensive, stylish clothing or immeasurable power. I envy her because she knows exactly who she is, and she's not afraid of it.

"When I was younger, I wanted normalcy. I wanted what you would expect from a mother—love, comfort, security. She didn't even have to be good at it. I just wanted her to try. I think, in many ways, I've always searched for those things, even when I knew I was setting myself up for failure. Even when I knew all of that was completely unobtainable for me. The Se7en have given me a comfort I never knew before. And security—as frustrating as that can be at times. I think I am the most secure future serial killer in history."

"And love?"

I shake my head and muster a manufactured smile. "You know the saying, *"a face only a mother could love"*? Well…I have a soul only a mother could love. And even she couldn't. I wouldn't expect anyone else to take on that burden."

She stops, turning to me so quickly that I don't even register the movement. "You don't actually mean that, do you?"

"Why wouldn't I?" I shrug.

"What about the rest of your family?"

I look away, not willing to let her see the pain of remembering staining my eyes. "I have a sister—had a sister. From foster care."

"And what happened to her?"

"I told her I needed space and not to contact me. Then I

blocked her number."

"Why?" Her quiet, raspy voice is like the scrape of a fallen leaf against the ground.

"Because it's what I do—I push people away before they can figure out what a mess I am. Before they see the *true* me. She's used to my disappearing acts, and she's good about giving me time to stop feeling sorry for myself. But honestly, it's all because I don't feel worthy of her. I never have. She was the one good thing in my life since I was just a kid. And I hate myself for not being the same for her. She doesn't need me—she never did. Now she can stop worrying, and stop feeling obligated to care about me. Now she can get married and have kids without wondering if I'll ever get my shit together or meet a nice guy. Cutting her off was my last gift to her."

She stares at me with unabashed perplexity, the frown between those dual-hued eyes carved from disbelief, maybe a little bit of pity.

"You feel guilt."

I nod, not truly wanting to, but unable to stop myself.

"You don't think you're worthy of forgiveness…worthy of love."

I nod again, tears welling in my eyes.

The young queen reaches out to touch a hand to the base of my neck. Her hand is warm, but a burst of soothing cold radiates from her fingertips, seeping deep down into my chest. I don't dare move, not that I would want to. It's like an ice pack for my shattered, rusted heart. It won't fix what's broken, but it doesn't hurt as much.

"Eden, you are not beyond saving. I see that in you, right now. I see it in those demons that have vowed to protect you with their lives. And I see it in the way..." She stops herself and shakes her head. "All will be revealed soon enough. You just need to believe that you're worthy of salvation, despite what you've done. Despite the piece of your past that still grips you in your darkest days and haunts your nightmares."

"How can you be so sure?" I whisper through the emotion in my throat.

"Because I've been there." A small, tight smile curves her full lips. "I know what it's like to be lost and afraid. Right now, you're probably thinking that you're powerless to stop the inevitable. And maybe you are—maybe there's nothing you can do to change your destiny. But that's the beauty of humanity. You can change—evolve. You can be more than what you were bred for." She steps back, taking her cool, healing touch with her. The feel of her power echoes in my veins. "Come on. They'll be getting restless."

She reaches out to take my hand, and the moment my skin brushes hers, space folds into itself and unravels to reveal four walls and nine frozen faces, locked in time. We're back in the meeting room.

With a casual wave of her hand, activity resumes seamlessly, as if there hadn't been a twenty-minute gap between me challenging the king in his own home and reemerging out of thin air with the queen.

Upon realizing that I'm no longer at his side, Legion jumps out of his seat as if it's on fire, his towering frame nearly trembling with unspent rage. Phenex stands as well, if only to act as a buffer.

"I'm fine," I insist, before anything is said that could compromise our stay here. "Gabriella and I were just talking."

"Oh?" Dorian remarks, much calmer than the demon standing across from him. "And what did my lovely wife have to say?"

"Girl talk," she winks playfully in response. However, a look passes between them—an unspoken communication—that prompts the king to nod. It's intimate in a way that makes me shuffle on my feet, so I take the opportunity to return to my seat. Somewhat satisfied, Legion sits. Gabriella takes her spot beside her husband as well.

"Very well. So, shall we address the terms?"

"The terms?" Legion gruffs. It's the first time he's spoken since we stepped into this room. I couldn't imagine him going toe-to-toe with the Dark king anyway. They'd probably level the entire resort.

"You are here because my cousin vouches for you. Apparently, you all had worked with my brother before his untimely passing, and were hoping I could lend similar assistance, correct? And if I knew my brother—and I did—I am sure he didn't provide his services without some type of reciprocity."

"Yes," Toyol answers before looking over to Legion with a pointed look. "And please accept my deepest condolences. Nikolai was a good man. He is missed."

"Yes." Dorian's voice is sharper than it had been, as if his tongue is tipped in venom. Even his eyes seem brighter, icier. The memory of his brother not only saddens him…it angers him. "That's why you're going to help me find him so I can bring him back."

"What?" Toyol looks to Phenex before flicking his gaze to Legion.

"I want you to find him. From there, we will do the rest.

That is, if you want us to help the girl."

"But that can't be done," Phenex pipes up, shaking his head. "We don't have that authority."

"No. You don't. But he does." The king's glacial stare falls on Legion with unrelenting certainty. "Legion, Collector of Fallen Souls. I knew exactly who you were the moment you stepped into my city. It's been a long time, hasn't it?"

"Indeed it has," Legion's voice is just as chilling, those silver eyes swirling with their own mystic fire.

"If memory serves, you have the authority to find any slain soul that may not have attained the Divine's favor. I want you to locate my brother."

"And how do you know I can even do that? How are you so certain that he didn't receive His favor?"

The king smirks wickedly and steeples his fingers under his chin. "My brother was good at being Dark. I'm not deluded to believe he was a saint. These are my terms—agree to find him, and our magic is at your disposal."

Legion eases back into his seat, that tight jaw jumping with contained tension. At the break in the conversation, Phenex jumps in.

"Your majesty, I'm sorry, but Legion can't do as you request. The only way he has access to that power is to return to the underworld. And to do that, he must die on earth. And once we die… You understand how that would be difficult—"

"I'll do it."

"What?" I yelp in disbelief. "You can't! No! I won't let you."

"We have a deal," he reiterates, ignoring my pleas, along with objections from his friends. He stands to his feet and extends a hand to Dorian. "I'll find your brother. As long as you help Eden."

The Dark king stands, his movements as fluid as water, and joins hands with the demon assassin. "It's settled. Tonight. Dinner. We'll send word."

Then within a single, ragged beat of my shattered human heart, they're gone.

TWENTY-ONE

When Dorian said he'd send word, I should have known it would be more complicated than that.

The four of us are in the sitting room of our suite, arguing with the brick wall known as Legion over his senseless agreement to go on a suicide mission to locate the king's deceased brother, Nikolai Skotos. Of course, he won't hear anything other than the sound of his own voice, his stupid reasoning replaying on a constant loop. His life is too steep of a price to pay for me, regardless of the consequences. I'm not worth it, and every time I try to tell him so, he shuts me down.

"We'll find another way," I plead. "You don't even know if the information they'll give us will be of use. You could be sacrificing your life for nothing."

"Listen to her," Toyol urges. "How do we know we can

even stop the Calling? It's never been done before."

Legion doesn't bother meeting our eyes. He just continues to clean his guns, although they're still immaculate from the night before. "Then it's time we find out. I didn't commit my life to the Se7en only to cower from the first sign of adversity. I said I would protect you, and I will. Or I'll die trying."

The frustration leeches from my voice, and I step forward, so close that I can feel the heat wafting from his powerful frame. "But there's no guarantee that you can, L. And I don't want you to give up everything you've worked for—fought for—over a shot in the dark. Please." I risk a step closer and gently let my palm rest on his shoulder. He flinches at the intrusion at first, but before I can pull away, he reaches up to lay his hand over mine, holding it in place.

I don't know what it is—maybe the feel of skin or just the emotion of the day—but I find myself confessing, "I'm not afraid, L. I'm not afraid to die."

His voice is thick and tinged with a secret sadness. "Are you so ready to give up on yourself?"

"If it comes to that—yes. If it means you get to live—yes."

"Well, I'm not." He rescinds his blistering touch and looks back to the pieces of hardware on the table.

I gaze over my shoulder and meet eyes with Phenex, my expression pleading. He has to get through to him. He can't let his friend—his brother—risk everything just for me. He's too important to the Se7en. He's too important to…

The voice echoes in my head, but its tone is unlike the one that whispers devious commands that inflict pain and cruelty. This isn't the sound of my conscience. It's the voice of a petite queen with eyes the colors of night and day.

"*Dinner in the private dining room in the restaurant at seven. All will be revealed then. Have faith, Eden.*"

Then she's gone before I even realized she had slipped in.

"Dinner is at seven. Downstairs in the restaurant," I relay, my eyes wide and my face pale.

"How do you know that?" Toyol questions.

"Gabriella just told me. She…pulled a me on *me.*" But better, I should add. Her connection to my mind was seamless. I didn't even feel it. It didn't seem intrusive, as if she was sifting through my thoughts or memories. And her voice was so clear, as if she was standing right beside me, whispering in my ear.

If Gabriella could march right into my head without me detecting it…what else could she do? How easy would it be for her crawl into those dusty, dark corners of my psyche and unearth all my secrets? How incredibly simple would it be for her to expose me for what I truly am and reveal what I've done?

Panic squeezes my neck, choking all rationale. I don't know if I can go through with this. I can't allow her, or anyone else for that matter, to get into my head. It'll not only cost Legion his life. It'll cost me…everything.

We agree to put our conversation on ice, and I'm grateful to have a few moments alone to get ready for dinner. I hate to admit it but I'm afraid. Legion said that he would protect me or die trying. But how far will that mercy extend when he finds out what I've done? Would I even be worthy of saving?

I shake it off, tired of torturing myself with questions that I'm too chicken-shit to answer. Things are already in motion, and if I interfere, I could be making things worse…for all of us.

Still, I have to try. Not for me or my selfish reasons. But for Legion. For once, I have to do what's right.

Since I packed light, I keep on the dress, and just pair it with a pair of nude heels Lilith snuck in the bag. I retouch my hair and makeup, giving myself a bolder, more glamorous look with red lips and loose curls. I remember Legion's words earlier, and smile to myself, touching my fingertips to the hollow of my throat. He said I was lovely. I can't help but wonder if he'll still feel the same after tonight.

We travel down to the restaurant in silence, each wondering what the evening holds for us. Gabriella said that all would be revealed, and while that terrifies me, I'm anxious to see what she meant by that. What is it that they hope to find, and how will they find it? I must admit, the world of Dark and Light fascinates me. To know that such limitless power exists here on earth, walking amongst humans for centuries undetected, seems unreal to me.

Just days ago, I was a lost girl, ruled by pain and anger. Today, I am about to dine with demon assassins and supernatural royalty. Oh, and I'm a sleeper cell for the devil.

The hotel's fine dining restaurant is everything that I expect it to be. Prime cuts of meat and lush wines appear to be plentiful, and the atmosphere is chic without being stuffy. However, when we approach the hostess station, we're swiftly led to a private area without having to utter a word.

Unlike this afternoon, the Skotos family is already there, minus Alexander and young Nikolai. They chat casually over glasses of rich red wine and charcuterie.

"Welcome," Dorian greets us, an almost warm smile on

his face—if you could call it a smile. His mouth can make the movement, but there's something too sinister…too sensual…about it to be carved from merriment. I don't believe he's being deceptive. I just think he's incapable of being anything less than wickedly seductive, even when he's not trying.

We're greeted with kind, relaxed offers to sit and enjoy, another difference from this afternoon. I look to Legion, who observes the welcome with a tight, calculating stare, yet takes a seat across from the warlock. I follow his lead, taking the space to his right. Toyol sits beside me, with Phenex on Legion's left.

"Now that we've all gotten comfortable…" Dorian begins, swirling the blood red wine in his glass. "I hope you enjoyed the rest of your afternoon. Eden, is this your first time to the Springs?"

Small talk? Really?

I feel like I'm missing something—like some underlying meaning in his words. Or maybe he's just trying to be nice. Life and circumstance has made me a skeptic.

"It is," I answer.

"And are you enjoying your stay?"

A server comes around to our side of the table, presenting two bottles of wine. Before I can think about choosing, Legion signals for him to pour the red one.

"Considering that I haven't left the hotel, what I've seen thus far is beautiful. A far cry from the south side of Chicago."

"Ah, Chicago. It's been ages since I've been. Maybe we're due a visit. Gabriella?"

The queen nods. "I've never been. The only things I know about Chicago are deep dish pizza, the Cubs and Kanye West."

"See!" I squeal, forgetting myself and nudging Legion in the ribs. "He's a Chicago treasure!"

He flinches from shock, those silver eyes wide with bewilderment, no doubt wondering if I've lost my ever-loving mind. Then, he equally stuns me by shaking his head and— *could it be*— grinning.

"I swear on this life, you all have no idea what music is."

"Agreed," Dorian cosigns, holding up his glass in salute. "Half the drivel Gabriella and Morgan play makes my ears bleed. I refuse to let little Niko grow up without knowing what *real* music is."

"Hey! Don't put me in this!" Morgan laughs, pretending to flick an olive at Dorian. "I have great taste in music. Right, Lars?"

The tall blonde god with golden eyes strokes her hair lovingly, a keen smile on his face. "You're so pretty. I love you."

"Liar!" she trills, playfully brushing his hand away. "Why didn't you ever tell me you hated my music?"

"Because you were so happy listening to it. And I was so happy to watch you."

The look of adoration on his face…his soft words falling from sensual lips…Morgan nearly melts into a puddle on the polished wood floor, and I don't blame her.

"You have to admit," Gabriella chimes in, seeing that her friend is too busy making googly eyes at her beau, "not all modern music is bad."

"I'd have to agree," Toyol nods. "I'm a fan of the 21st century myself. Actually, Eden has some great playlists. Aside from Kanye, of course."

They all have a chuckle at my expense, and I don't fault

them for it. Legion seems to be loosening up, and I have to admit, the Skotos family isn't half bad. They almost seem… normal. Human, even.

Dinner is superb, as expected. The juiciest, most tender cuts of steak, buttery lobster, crisp vegetables, and fluffy, whipped potatoes are served on huge platters family style, over bottles and bottles of the best wine I've ever tasted. A far cry from the cheap, fruity libations Sister and I would down on Friday nights. I miss her terribly, but I don't let myself think about it. She's safe now, content and secure. I couldn't give her those things in all the years she's been by my side, even though she's been the one person in my life that deserved these comforts. But Legion did. And according to him, he did it for me.

I don't know what to think about that fact, but I'm grateful.

And here I am, dining and laughing and chatting with royalty. Eating food I'd only seen while watching Food Network, and drinking wine that probably cost more than my weekly paycheck.

I hate why I'm here and why I've been thrust into this world of myth and fantasy. But part of me is so damn amazed by it all. It's as if my eyes are seeing color for the very first time, and tastes and sounds are no longer muted by poverty and crime. And if I don't have much time left on this earth—as a human girl or otherwise—I'm going to appreciate this gift, even if it was packaged in a curse.

"Oh, Eden, I hope you left room for dessert," Gabriella says after we polish off dinner. I can't remember if I've ever eaten that much…ever. Meals at the Se7en high rise were delicious, yet I was always too nervous or too afraid to actually eat my fill. A tiny piece of me stirs as I think of how Jinn had spent so much time and care cooking for me. He can't even eat half the food he prepared, yet he enjoyed having someone else—someone human—to cook for.

I look down at my stomach. I'm about eight weeks along with a food baby. "Dessert? Are you trying to make me burst?"

Right on cue, a line of servers enter with trays of every type of confection one could ever dream of. Cakes of all flavors and fillings, fresh baked cookies, beautiful pies and tarts, and delicate custards replace the platters of remaining meat and shellfish. My wide eyes bulge from my sockets as I spy a sheepish grin from across the table.

"I like dessert," Dorian says with a half shrug. There he goes. There he goes appearing almost human and seemingly harmless and thoroughly flawless.

I understand what Gabriella sees in him. A blind woman could see it. But there's something about him that makes me unable to trust the effortless charm and alarming good looks. Like, it just doesn't seem real. It's more of a mirage.

"No one could possibly still be hungry," I scoff.

"Speak for yourself," Toyol snorts, stacking a fresh plate with sweets. I look to Legion who is doing the same, while the ever-so-civilized Phenex settles for a modest serving of crème brûlée and fresh raspberries dusted with sugar.

"I think I'll slip into a food coma if I eat another bite." I rub my tight stomach and try to take a deep breath.

"Not until you try this."

I hear the words, but I don't understand them until there is a fruit tart just inches from my lips, hoisted by the very tips of Legion's fingers. I flick my gaze into pools of sparkling silver, swirling with expectation.

Is this part of it? This game that he's playing to appease the king and persuade him to help us?

I look up to find that everyone is staring, although they're much too polite to make it obvious. They're waiting to see if I'll play nice, if I'm content with being the Se7en's consort or with them under duress. Or maybe they want to see if there's more to the Demon Slayer than what legend has boasted.

So slowly that I can count my every breath, I lean in and part my lips. The tart is flaky and buttery on my tongue as Legion gently slides it between my teeth, his hooded eyes watching and waiting for my reaction. I give him what he craves, failing to bite back the low hum of approval that rumbles my throat.

"Good, huh?" His voice slides over me like warm honey.

"Very."

"More?"

"Yes." The word is nothing more than a breathless sigh.

He feeds me again, until I taste only crumbs on his fingertips. His skin is sweet from the sugar and burning hot, just like the rest of him. A manufactured memory invades my head, something I couldn't have possibly known. I've tasted him before. I don't know how, but the feel of his fingers on my lips, tracing my cupid's bow…I know it like I know my own name.

"I guess this would be a bad time to discuss business," Dorian remarks, his tone laced with a sinister edge.

His words bring me back to reality, and I turn away, shifting my body as far away from Legion as it will go without making it noticeable. "Of course not," I answer, schooling my voice.

"Since we can agree on the terms, I believe it's pertinent to your cause to get started, yes? Are you ready, Eden?"

"Yes. But I'd like to renegotiate the terms." I feel Legion go rigid beside me but I soldier on. "Finding your brother would lead him on a suicide mission. That's unreasonable, and I think you know that. Legion is the Se7en's leader. Without him, having the information about my Calling could be made pointless."

Dorian dips his head from side to side as he contemplates my statement. "Maybe so. But that doesn't change our demands. However, there may be something that can be done to avoid death."

"And what's that?"

"Only time will tell—time we don't have. And I don't suppose I can turn him."

"Turn him?" I grimace.

"There are…alternatives." I don't miss the quick glance he flicks to Cyrus, who has been lurking by the doorway. He stands inhumanely still, his massive body blending into the wall like a life-like statue. The effect is one of a deadly predator; how easy it would be to eliminate unsuspecting prey as they pass by him, unaware of the danger that waits in the shadows.

"In any case, this is what we want, and we wouldn't be requesting such a steep price for our services if it weren't of great importance. We recognize that the ramifications are dire, but I'm sure you can understand. You, too, have someone that you care for—that you would do anything for—even if it went against your more delicate, human instincts."

He doesn't have to worm his way into my head to know

that he's struck a chord. Sister. He knows about Sister. Meaning, he could use her against me if it came down to it.

"I'm sorry—is that a threat?"

"Absolutely not," he responds coolly. "But family is everything to me. To us. It's all we have. And when you are the head of a coven as strong as ours, it is pertinent to know your friends just as well as your enemies. I'd like to think of you as friends. Otherwise, you wouldn't be sitting here."

"What my husband is trying to say," Gabriella chimes in before cutting her eyes at the king. "We want to help you—and we plan to. But in return, we need the Se7en's help. Specifically, Legion's. We wouldn't be asking if there was any other way."

"Wait," I frown. "So you knew we would need your gifts? You knew we'd come asking?" It's all so evident now. If Legion is the only one who could find the king's brother, why didn't *they* come to *him*? Unless they already know…

"Your future keeps shifting," Gabriella says, confirming my suspicions. "I'm not clairvoyant, but I can feel it. When I took your hand earlier…I connected to your life force. I saw a room underground. There's cement under my bare feet—your feet. And I'm—you're—naked."

My mouth instantly dries and blood rushes my face, roaring in my ears. My heart rate spikes with panic as I listen to Gabriella relay my worst fears.

It's the dream. The reoccurring nightmare I've had almost every night since the day I spotted the first gray strand of hair. It was my eighteenth birthday when I first experienced it. It was just a flicker then—a flash of pale, quivering skin, the bite of a cold blade, a dribble of warm blood.

The nightmare eventually became more defined over

time, until it was a snuff film played on a constant, horrifying loop night after night. No matter how many times I had to feel his hands on me and smell the overwhelming stench of blood in the air, I could never grow used to it. It still frightened me to tears and left me choking through sobs in its aftermath. No matter what I did to alleviate the terror—sleeping pills, tea, alcohol, even drugs—I still couldn't fight the dread behind my eyelids.

Until Legion.

The nightmares still plagued me, but for once in four, torturous years, I saw something else when I closed my eyes. I saw light and heard laughter. I felt warmth and goodness and safety. And an intense desire that I never knew existed.

"There's someone there with you—watching you," Gabriella says, bringing me back to the here and now.

"Yes," I whisper, my voice quivering. I shift uncomfortably in my seat, feeling several sets of eyes on me. They're all listening as the darkest, goriest parts of my psyche are splayed upon the dinner table.

"You kill them. You kill them all."

"Yes." The knot in my throat is so large that I doubt the word is even discernable.

"And he…he takes you. And you want him to. You beg him to." Her face is stricken as if she is in pain. As if she can feel the agony of my victims as I instruct them to mutilate and torture each other before sinking my blade deep inside their mangled bodies.

I should have known. The answer was right in front of me all along. It wasn't just a nightmare. It was a prophecy.

"You resisted him at first, didn't you?" the young queen

asks, her piercing stare seeing right through to my tattered soul. "You didn't want to like it. You didn't want to want him. But you couldn't help it."

"Who?" Legion asks, speaking for the first time since Gabriella began to unravel my biggest fears. I feel those eyes of quicksilver rage burning into me.

"Lucifer." My voice is no more than a broken whisper. I utter the words on autopilot, not truly feeling their weight on my tongue. If I registered their meaning, it would make it too real. "I kill them all. Sister. Logan. My mother. Everyone I've ever known. I watch and I laugh as they rip each other to shreds before I spill what's left of their blood on my naked skin. Almost every night…I dream it almost every night."

"But you know it changes. You have the power to alter your future." Gabriella's gaze shifts to Legion just a fraction, but I know he sees it. Nothing gets past him.

"Is there nothing we can do to stop it?" he asks.

Gabriella looses a breath before leaning back in her seat. "The next sign of her Calling is coming soon. At the end of the signs, he'll come for her. Unless…"

"Unless what?" Legion nearly growls.

"Unless she longs for something more than she craves the evil that calls to her. Whatever impulse will draw her to him… it's strong. Stronger than any magic we can wield to stop it. In the same way that she can bend the will of humans, he will bend hers. She has to fight it. She has to live for something more than she'll want to kill for him."

"When will it happen?"

"I can't say for sure. There's a chill in the air, but no snow. I'm sorry, but that's all I see."

Great. We traded Legion's life for something I, for the most part, already knew. However, there's a way to fight against it. And considering the perplexity on Legion's brow, he didn't know it was even possible.

"But there's something else..." Gabriella says, her voice weary. "Back when I was...just a girl...Dorian told me about a story he'd heard. It was about a child that would reign in the underworld, conjuring up all the evils within and unleashing them on the earth. Wars would wage for thousands of years, bringing endless death and disease. All that is devious and malevolent would be celebrated while mercy would be extinct. The child would be evil incarnate, bearing the mark of the beast. The antichrist."

I open my mouth but not a sound escapes. I clutch my throat, choking on the unspoken words. I know this story. Revelation. The end of days.

"Are you saying that Eden is the antichrist?"

Gracefully, the queen shakes her head. "No. The child will be the direct offspring of the one you call Master. Lucifer."

"We don't call him shit," Legion grits. "So he'll produce an heir."

"He will," she nods. Then she presses that intense gaze into me, digging those irises into me with all the power of the sun and the moon. "And I believe she will be its mother."

Its mother. My fate is to birth the antichrist. To bear the seed of hate and destruction in my womb.

Intense nausea churns my gut, causing cold sweat to bead on my chest and neck. I'm going to lose it, right here on this table. Right here in front of supernatural royalty and demon assassins. I was afraid of them, when in reality, I'm destined to be the most deadly of them all.

I don't know what I'm doing until I'm on my feet and making my way to the door. I have no clue where I'm going, but I have to get out of here. I have to flee these walls and their looks of sympathy and their speculative stares. I'm so sick of being the topic of discussion. Tired of being a wounded lamb amongst monsters. When *I'm* the monster. I'm the nightmare I had been trying to escape.

I don't know if Legion follows me, and I don't look back to check. I just know that I can't sit there a moment longer and be their freak show. I've been playing that role my entire life. And just like my nightmares, it never gets easier.

I don't stop until I'm at the door of our suite, realizing I don't have a key to get in. Releasing the sob that had been caught in my throat since I ran from the dining room, I slide to the floor, a defeated, crumpled mess of a lost girl. I don't know if I'll ever find my way.

The first tear slides down my cheek just as the carved wood against my spine is jerked away, sending me tumbling backward. Alarm bells sound in my skull as I scramble to face the intruder in the doorframe.

I don't even have a chance to scream before he yanks me inside.

TWENTY-TWO

"WHAT THE HELL?" I shriek, scrambling to my feet. "How did you get in here?"

Legion crosses his arms in front of his chest, causing his dress shirt to stretch around his biceps in the most appealing way. "What the *hell?*" he bites out incredulously. "What do you think you're doing running off by yourself in a place you're not familiar with? Shit, Eden, how am I supposed to protect you when you insist on making my job harder? It's bad enough the witch queen stole you away from me earlier…"

My cheeks flame at not only his words, but the possession in his tone. "I was fine, L. I just needed…" Air. Space. Time to think about my impending doom.

"You're not fine, Eden. How could you be?" His voice softens, taking on that raspy, emotion-drenched timbre that

I've only had the pleasure of hearing during his most private confessions. "We'll find a way—I promise you that. We'll find out how we can stop the Calling. Even if I have to fight until my dying breath, I won't let him take you. I won't let this happen to you."

He stalks toward me as if to hold me or slap me or shake some sense into me, but I quickly turn away. "There's nothing you can do."

"Fuck if there isn't. I told you—I will protect you or die trying. I mean what I say."

"Did you listen to anything that was said? Or do you just hear what you want to hear?" I screech, suddenly furious. "I'll *like* killing those people. I'll crave to feel their blood on my hands. And if you weren't listening, get this—I'll beg Lucifer to fuck me on their stiffening corpses."

He drops his hands, tightening them into fists at his sides. "It was just a bad dream, Eden."

"A dream I've had for four years straight. And you know what? I don't wake up screaming all the time. No. Sometimes I'm so wet between my thighs that my panties are soaked. Sometimes I wake myself up with my own moans of pleasure. And sometimes I'm so horny that I finger myself and get off on the carnage. Don't you see, L? You're wasting your time with me. It'd be better if I were dead!"

He sees the light bulb flicker on in my wild eyes at the same time the thought pops into my head. He shakes his head. "No."

"Please. Please, Legion. It's the only way I can ensure everyone's safety. It's the only way we can stop the Calling." I'm moving towards him with pleading hands as he backs away, refusing to listen to desperate reason.

"No."

"There's nothing we can do. This is what needs to be done for the greater good. Isn't that what the Se7en are all about? *Kill one to save a million?* Kill me. Don't let me be the cause of even more pain and strife."

"I said no, Eden!" he roars.

With tears welling at my red-rimmed eyes, I look up at him, begging for the mercy of death. Not my mercy. Theirs. No matter which way this goes, it won't end well for me. And you know what? It's not supposed to. I don't want to take anyone else down in flames with me.

"You'll have to do it…eventually. You'll have to kill me. And it's ok. Just please…don't let me become a monster."

His back hits the wall, cornered by my trembling frame. "I can't, Eden. I can't hurt you."

I nod with solemn understanding, breathing through the hurt. It's not me he wants to save. It never was. "The Jumper."

"No." He shakes his head. "It's more than that. I think you know that. I think you've known that all along."

"How could I? I only know what you tell me, which isn't much of anything. Tell me, Legion. Why do you even care? Why are you even wasting your time on a lost cause?"

"You're not a lost cause."

"Really?" I throw my hands up in hysterical frustration. "Because from where I'm standing, my future looks pretty damn bleak. And my present isn't so great either. Tell me: what else do I have to live for? What reason do I have to fight against the inevitable?"

"You have your sister."

"Hmph," I snort, turning my back to him. "You taking me is the best thing that has ever happened to her. She has a new place to live; she has comfort and security. Now she doesn't have to feel guilty about spending time with her boyfriend and actually *living* her life for a change."

"You have your mother," I hear him say from behind me. He's closer now, but I don't turn around.

"My mother? My *mother?!* I've never had a mother. Just some psychotic Jesus freak who thought she was doing God's Will by trying to kill me. She'd be first in line to spit on my grave."

"You have…"

"Pretty pathetic, right?" I laugh sardonically. "I've spent my whole life avoiding any permanent attachments. Never caring, never getting too close. Never letting someone in to see what I really am for fear that I would hurt them. You know I've never had a boyfriend? Hell, I don't even think I've ever been on a proper date before. Now you tell me—why is that someone worth saving? The girl that no one would miss?"

Silence stretches between us like a frayed rubber band.

"Eden…"

I shake my head at the sound of my name. Warm hands lightly grip my shoulders, holding me in place. "Face it. It's easier this way. It's…better for everyone." I swallow down the thick emotion in my throat and try to shrug out of his grasp, but I'm too weak. Nothing but a frail, broken doll that should've been discarded long ago. "I have nothing and no one left to live for anyway."

"You do." His voice is just a hoarse whisper. "You have me, Eden. Live for me. Hold on for me."

I turn to face him, his hands still braced on my trembling shoulders. "Why?"

Silver eyes glow in the dim evening light. "Because from the first moment I saw you—through the dingy window of that store, your headphones on, oblivious to the dangers right outside the door—I knew that I would die for you. So please… live for me. Just for a little while longer."

His words embed themselves in the hollow space in my chest, radiating with light and heat. They slither through me like liquid fire, singeing the dead, cold remains of my past pains, turning the hurt and abandonment to ash. I don't want to believe him. I don't want him to give me hope only to rip it away. But I have so little left to hold onto these days. So maybe…maybe I can believe in him, this beast of a man that makes my heart pound with fear and exhilaration whenever he's near.

I fix my lips to tell him just that, but before I can, a knock sounds at the door. My first thought is Toyol and Phenex, coming to check up on me, but just as I take a step towards the soft rapping, Legion swiftly whirls my body around, stationing it behind his.

"What is it?" I whisper, peering around his hard frame as if the door will implode at any moment.

"Warlock," he grimaces, as if he can taste whomever stands just yards away. "And vampire. Stay here."

With a huff, he goes to open it, one hand positioned at his back where his 9 millimeter is tucked at his waist. I hold my breath. Vampire? Shit, do I really want to know?

I contemplate escaping to the back bedroom, but before I can, Legion opens the door, an annoyed sneer on his lips.

"Oh, apologies. Am I interrupting?" the Dark king smugly says, that permanent smirk perfectly in place. Cyrus stands behind him, ever so silent and lethal, as a vampire would be. So that's what Dorian must have meant about turning Legion. He meant turn him into a vampire. But how?

Don't ask, I tell myself. I've had one too many revelations for the day. I'm pretty sure one more would tip me over the edge.

"Is there something you need?" Legion's voice is sharp with annoyance. Of the three men, he's better matched with Cyrus in the size and strength department, but there's something about Dorian—something dark and menacing that tells me that he has no need for bulging muscles and towering height. He could kill with just a wink of his pale blue eye.

But that's not to say that Legion isn't capable of the same. He's so shrouded in secrets and unspoken myth that I can't be sure. I know he's a killer, but in how many ways could he rip someone apart? I have a feeling the possibilities are endless.

"I've come with a bit of a peace offering. From my family to yours." He flicks his hand and the door bursts completely open, allowing him to stride in casually. Cyrus silently follows.

"What's the catch?" Legion asks. His tone is almost polite, but the frantic ticking of his jaw says otherwise.

"No catch," Dorian responds, his expression sober. He's not even smirking with condescension. "My wife has grown fond of the girl. It would hurt her to see her harmed. I'm here to try to remedy that."

"You can stop the Calling?" I ask. I fail to keep the blind hope from reaching my voice.

"Unfortunately, no. The signs of the Calling are a natural

progression triggered by stress and time. I can't stop them, just as I can't stop you from aging, but I can slow them down. I can give you more time."

More time? For what? What are they waiting for?

"Again, what's the catch?" Legion interjects, stepping in front of me. He's risked everything for me. What else could we possibly bargain with?

"And again, there's no catch. I'm not what you think I am, Legion. I never was. There once was a time when you saw that."

From around Legion's bicep, I watch the two men share a weighted glance, as if communicating telepathically. Legion *knew* Dorian before this? How? And when? Shit, if Legion is billions of years old, how old is the Dark king? And do the others know? It seemed like Toyol had the inside connection through Cyrus. Obviously, he wasn't privy to the fact that Legion knew more about the Dark monarchy than he let on.

"Fine," Legion says, nodding once. "Do whatever you have to do, as long as you can ensure she will be unharmed."

"You have my word." Dorian flicks his gaze to the bedroom. "In there. And we'll need privacy." Legion's whole frame twitches, no doubt about to object with vehemence, when the king shakes his head. "She will be safe. However, you'll need to stay close. She'll need you afterward." The king extends his hand to me, not at all dissuaded by the hulking mass of demon standing between us. "Come."

I look at his outstretched palm and gaze up at Legion. His silver eyes swirl with uncertainty, however he gives me a single nod. He's reluctant to leave me alone with Dorian, but he knows it's safe. He wouldn't be breathing if he posed a threat.

I take the king's hand, not even bothering to still the subtle shaking. He gives it a gentle squeeze of reassurance and leads me to the bedroom. I'm not foolish enough to believe that anything remotely sexual would be going down. Gabriella doesn't seem like the sharing type, and considering her power far exceeds anything the world had ever seen, I doubt he'd be stupid enough to test the limits of her tolerance. Plus, he's here for her.

"Lie down," he instructs, his voice a tender caress. So different from the haughty tone he used during our first sit down earlier today.

I do as instructed, my body stiff as a board above the satin duvet. I don't even bother to remove my shoes.

"What I will do to you won't hurt, however it may seem disorienting. Your mind—and essentially—your heart will be open, allowing all your fears and fantasies to completely rule your emotions. Do you understand?"

I nod through my fear.

"Good. Now take a deep breath. Think of something that brought you happiness. Something that made you feel loved and alive. Focus on that; hold onto that."

His earnest words pierce right through my skull, reverberating with a sense of authority. I find myself flipping through my mind's Rolodex without even meaning to. I don't fight the impulse. I can't.

"You are so beautiful." He strokes my cheek with the back of his hand. It's the only part of him that I'd ever consider soft, other than his full lips. "You know that, right?"

"You say it all the time, but with a reverence I'll never comprehend."

"That's because you can't see what I see. You can't feel what I feel when I kiss your lips. You don't smell the sunshine in your hair. You can't taste the milk and honey between your thighs. But I can. And everything about you—your entire being—is absolutely beautiful."

I have no response, so I simply reach up to slide my fingers in his hair, and bring his lips to mine. He kisses me deeply, drinking me in. His tongue firm and thick, just like the rest of him, yet, his kisses are soft and pliant. I gasp in his mouth, and pull him closer, longing to feel his rock solid frame pressed against mine. He laughs as I gently claw at his back.

"Easy, baby. I don't want to hurt you."

"You can't hurt me," I giggle into his throat, licking a trail from his chin over his pronounced Adam's apple to his collarbone. "Unless I let you."

"And under what circumstances would you let me?" He nestles his body between my legs, and slides a palm up my bare thigh, parting me wider.

"When you scrape your teeth along my ribcage and nibble down to my hipbone," I moan.

"Like this?" He descends until I feel his mouth—hot and wet—under my breast bone. Then he lightly scratches the thin skin, traveling down to my arching pelvis.

"Yes," I reply breathlessly, the sensation somewhere between tickling and stinging. "And when you take my nipples between your fingers and squeeze. I'd let you do that."

On cue, he reaches up to roll the already pebbled flesh between his thumb and index finger before pinching it with enough pressure to make me inhale sharply at the prick of pain. So good…so good that I can't help but grasp my other breast and *knead, mimicking his assault.*

"You're doing great, Eden," Dorian coos from far away. His voice is a balm, soothing and healing. It coaxes the manufactured memory.

"Tell me more," he growls against my skin. He pulses against my leg, hard and ready. His body begs for relief but he likes his games. He loves to tease me until we're both beyond denying ourselves for another second. And when our bodies collide, when he buries himself inside of me with enough force to make the heavens tremble, we both break apart from impact. Loving him is a lesson in restraint. I restrain myself daily from mounting him whenever I see him. I restrain my heart from revealing how much I truly love him.

"I let you hurt me…" my voice cracks under the strain of trying to hold back from him. "…when I let you leave me. Every day, when you have to go and pretend for them…pretend like we're not lovers, it hurts me deeply. But I let it happen, because I know it has to be this way. It's not safe for us otherwise."

He halts his playful biting and lifts his head, his expression sober. His sensual mouth parts, but I shake my head, not wanting to hear it.

"I know, I know," I say, tears gleaming in my eyes. "I know there's nothing we can do."

His pensive, silver gaze studies my face. "Let me go to Him. Explain. Maybe if we show Him this is real—that our love is true and pure—we will gain His mercy."

"No. You know that is not possible. If he finds out…"

"It won't matter if the Creator bestows his blessing."

I shake my head once more and pull him to me, aligning his stunning face with mine. He is and always will be the most dazzling being I've ever seen. "I don't need anyone to tell me what I already know. What we have is real and good and beautiful. No one can take that away from us. No matter what anyone says, I know that within my heart of hearts. I love you, and I always will. Even when I'm just an echo in the wind and my bones are specks of dust amongst the stars, I will love you with every inch of my body and soul."

He kisses me like he's trying to taste my aching heart and lick its bleeding wounds. I kiss him like I'm trying to rewrite our fate with the tip of my tongue.

He enters me swiftly with a desperation that I feel in my spine. I cry out, but I beg him to keep going. Hurt me. Hurt me so good. Maybe it'll eclipse the pain gathering in my chest.

"Just a little while longer, Eden," Dorian's distant voice sounds. He chants quietly, the words melding into a low hum.

Ecstasy washes over me in violent waves, emitting a white glow from our sweat-slickened skin. He matches my moans with his groans. He meets my cries with his hisses.

I clutch his strong shoulders as he empties his passion into me, creating slick friction at my swollen flesh still quivering around him. He doesn't stop flexing his hips until I feel that tidal wave building again, this time stronger and more devastating than before. I can't catch my breath. I feel like I'm dying, drowning in his deep sea of delicious agony over and over again.

"Hold on to me," he grits through clenched teeth. "Hold on and never let go…"

"It's done," I hear Dorian say. My eyes are still closed but I feel his presence—his magic—coursing over me.

"What did you do to her?" Legion growls. There's heat at my side, sweltering intensity that makes tiny beads of sweat gather across my chest.

"She's fine. The spell was effective, but has left her vulnerable. Her emotions are completely exposed. Be gentle with her. She'll need you, and she won't be able to understand why."

There's a beat of silence, then Dorian asks, "Does she know?"

"No."

"Do the others?"

"Phenex."

"And how do you expect to explain this to her when it's revealed? Do you really think he'll let this go?"

"It's none of your concern, warlock. You've helped her, and for that I am grateful. However, this is above your pay grade."

A low chuckle. "Whatever you say, *demon*. Just remember our bargain."

Soft footfalls trail away from my position on the bed and halt. "Be careful with her," Dorian warns. "Her heart is…cold, but fragile. Hurt her, and it'll shatter like ice. Then you'll have to answer to Gabriella."

The click of the door is the last thing I hear before falling into a deep, dreamless sleep.

TWENTY-THREE

MY SKIN IS ON FIRE.

I'm so hot I can feel the blood boiling in my arteries. I thrash, seeking relief, but I only end up colliding with more overwhelming warmth. So hard, yet smooth and inviting. I wrap my arms around it, trying to contain it against my tender breasts. I maul and scratch, wanting to ink myself with its molten fire.

"Easy, firecracker," a harsh whisper tickles my ear. His lips stroke the delicate patch of skin where it meets my jaw.

"Mmmmm," I purr. "More."

"Yeah?" He runs the blunt of his fingertips across my shoulder, easing my pale hair to one side. I feel him trace a line down my neck with the tip of his nose, scenting my burning skin.

"That feels so good," I gasp as pinpricks scatter down my

arm. *More, more, more,* I mentally beg. He rewards my unspoken plea by sliding his hands down my arm and intertwining our fingers. His touch is like heroine glitter in my veins. I'm wild and addicted to this garish beauty, sparkling like splintered diamonds in the sun.

We lay in the dark, face to face, our legs tangled like twisted vines underneath the sheets. Mine are naked, much like the rest of me, save for my panties and bra. Legion's chest is bare, but slacks cover the lower part of his body. I look down at my lace-covered breasts, wondering where my clothes went, but grateful for their absence from my scorching skin.

"You ripped them off," Legion says, answering the slight frown dimpling my brow. "And mine too. You would've shredded the pants had I not stopped you."

"Why did you?" I coo, snuggling closer to his bare chest.

"Because you only think you want what's underneath."

"I don't think I want it. I know I do." I slip my hand between us, tugging at the belt buckle. He grips my hands in one of his, stilling my advance.

"No, you don't, Eden. It's the effects of the magic. It can make humans insatiable, irrational. It'll wear off soon. Just try to rest."

"Please," I beg, struggling to free my hands. "I want you so bad. It hurts." I squeeze my thighs together, trying to extinguish the fire simmering in my core. It only rages hotter, brighter.

"I don't want to hurt you." His voice is gentle, his breath stirring the hair grazing my forehead.

I don't even recognize my own voice. It's too eager, too raw with need. "Then don't. Make it stop. Please. Make the burning stop."

"I can't." His own gruff tone is laced with a touch of desperation. "Not how you need me to."

"Please. Just do something. *Anything*."

He sucks in a breath, steeling his resolve. "Okay. But… hands to yourself."

"How?" My palms are scorched with the need to touch him. He's hot, but somehow, it squelches the flame roaring under my skin.

"Just try. If you want me to help you, you have to do as I say."

"Okay," I whine, near tears. "Just take it away. Put out the fire in me."

He gently pushes me until I'm flat on my back, and rips the sheet away. Reflexively, I part my legs wider, welcoming him into my melting core.

"Careful," he warns, kneeling between my opened thighs. I want to wrap them around him, and pull him closer, but he stops me by gripping me at the knees. "I'm serious, firecracker. Try to stay still."

"But what if I can't?"

"Then I can't touch you. And you want me to touch you, right?"

"Yes," I answer too quickly. "I'll be still."

Moonlight slices a silver shadow across his face and chest as he gazes down at me, a thousand dazzling supernovas in his eyes. They seem to glow as he slowly slides his palms from my knees up to my outer thighs. I moan, tipping my head back. Those callused fingers tremble over lace. I silently beg for it to disintegrate into ash just from the friction of his searing touch.

He touches my ribs, stroking each one, before he caresses his way to the middle of my belly. Pressure builds at my navel, a hard, throbbing knot that knocks the breath from my lungs. It glows within my womb, pounding with its own hedonistic heartbeat. Faster, harder, deeper inside me until I gasp for air. Its weight anchors me to the bed as I drown in a torrential downpour of pleasure. Then all at once, the knot bursts into a million jagged fragments of orgasm, each shard stabbing my hypersensitive nerve endings until they ache with ecstasy. I buckle off the bed, my movements no longer my own, and cry out. His hands grip my waist, pressing the knot inside me until it's expelled every drop of agonizing bliss.

"Breathe deep," Legion instructs. "Let it flow through you."

My spine is a rigid beam, but my limbs are jelly. Only his hands hold me up, my sex aligned with his belt buckle. The cool metal bites into my swollen mound, adding another layer of sensation.

"Wha-what did you do to me?" I stammer, my words slurred.

"I took care of you. A little too well, I see. Shit, you're soaking," he grumbles, looking down at the strip of black lace between my thighs, no doubt drenched with my release. Even in the dim lighting, I see him lick his lips.

"Taste it," I whisper, through panting breaths.

Glowing eyes flicker to mine. "Stop it."

"Do it. I won't touch you. You don't even have to take off my panties."

"You don't know what you're asking for."

"I know exactly what I'm asking for. I want this. *You* want this."

A war wages in his menacing stare for what seems like eternity. Then, too swiftly for my human eyes, he leans down to meet my elevated lower half, and rests the backs of my knees on his shoulders.

Had I known that I would break apart a second time merely from the scrape of his hot tongue against my skin, I would have braced myself. But before I can even take a deep breath, I'm moaning to the moon, howling his name, as he laves the tender skin between my swollen sex and the most sensitive part of my thigh. A low growl rumbles his throat as he tastes the other one, savoring every drop that's escaped my panties. I want to plead for him to tear them off, but I can't. The sound of him indulging in the taste of me, the feel of that thick, firm tongue licking and sucking and—oh, *shit*—nibbling…coherent words fail me completely. I only know wet. And hot. I only know this all-consuming pleasure that makes my blood shimmer with silver starlight and golden fire.

He eases my sated body to the bed. His mouth still gleams with the remnants of my release. We stare at the other, each of us needing more to quell the craving roaring in our veins.

"Kiss me." My voice is hoarse from moaning, screaming.

"Eden…"

"Please. If you won't let me taste any other part of you, at least let me taste your lips."

He closes his eyes, letting his chin touch his chest. "You'll forget this. You'll forget wanting me as badly as I want you—shit, as badly as I've wanted you for longer than you've been alive. You'll forget what you felt tonight while the taste of you will be forever embedded on my tongue. You'll wake up tomorrow without an inkling of how I made you shake from just my touch, while I'll still smell you on my skin." When he lifts his head, pearlescent sorrow swirls within his brilliant depths. "So if you have to forget—and I know you do—I don't want to kiss you. Not tonight. I want to save that piece of us for a time when you'll remember, for a time when you'll *want* to remember. And I want you to touch your lips days afterward and smile at the memory. I won't take away your free will. I can't steal that away from you, even if that moment never comes."

"Legion…" I don't know what I can say to ensure him that this is all I've wanted for so, so long. Even when I didn't know him. Even when I didn't think there was anyone out there in this vast, lonely universe for me.

He shushes me by brushing his thumb over my bottom lip. "I wish I didn't have to do this."

When he brings that thumb to caress his own lips, I plummet into a sea of darkness, speckled with flecks of silver stardust.

I jerk awake under a blanket of warm sunshine streaming through the heavy, gilt curtains. Panic fills my lungs, and I stifle a yelp when I realize two major things:

One: I'm nearly naked, with only my bra and panties on.

Two: Legion is sleeping soundly beside me.

My body feels…different. Not bad—not at all—but different. There's a tenderness below, the kind that echoes with the remnants of a deep throb. I squeeze my thighs together, igniting a manufactured memory of wetness and warmth, and sigh, reveling in a whisper of phantom pleasure. I know we didn't sleep together—that much is evident. The last thing I remember is the Dark king casting a spell to slow the progression of the Calling then…nothing. Still, I don't believe Legion would rape me in my sleep, not when he's had more than enough space and opportunity to do so in my captivity. And considering that he's celibate, why jeopardize his vows for a lost cause with skewed morals and a dark destiny? He could have his pick of any female in the world—supernatural or no. I'm nothing. Not compared to everything I've been made aware of in the past week.

I swallow down a knot of illogical sorrow, and roll over to face his sleeping form. His face seems so peaceful in slumber. Vulnerable, calm. So different from his usual scowl. Even with his itchy disposition and aloofness, he'd be the kind of guy I could fall for. Like calls to like, and maybe my demons could find solace in those lost souls that seem to swirl in the depth of his eyes. But that would never happen, even if I wasn't doomed. Even if I was just a regular girl and he was just a regular guy. I'm a little too lost at this point to ever be found. Even by him.

Without thinking about the consequences, without understanding my motives behind them, I reach out to stroke his jaw. It feels as strong and hard under my fingertips as it looks, and the short scruff that shades his face from cheek to chin is as soft as down. I fleetingly imagine what the hair would feel like brushing my face, my breasts, my inner thighs. Then I shake them from my skull completely. My thoughts are dangerous. Even the ones that don't inflict harm.

With the need to relieve my bladder, I pad to bathroom on legs made of rubber. My limbs feel languid as if they'd been stretched taut. The effects of the magic, I tell myself. That's the only explanation. A hot shower is indeed in order, and after yesterday, I may use every drop of hot water in this entire hotel.

With our plans to head back to Chicago today, I dress in a pair of jeans, a flannel and my white Chucks. Legion is still sleeping, so I take the liberty of ordering breakfast from room service. Oddly enough, there's a knock at the door a mere ten minutes later. I don't know if magic has anything to do with the prompt service, but I go to the door—

I'm two yards away from the entrance of the suite when Legion's giant form is looms over me, blocking me from the door.

"What the…"

"What do you think you're doing?" His voice is gruff from sleep and fury, and his eyes are as wild as his tousled hair.

"Opening the door for room service."

My gaze widens when he takes a menacing step toward me. Gone is the man who just slept peacefully beside me. "That isn't room service, Eden."

I look at the door as if I have X-ray vision. "Then who is it?"

Without a word, he stalks over and yanks open the carved wood door, revealing Phenex and Toyol, both dressed in black leather. Fighting gear. They'd traded the garb for tailored shirts and slacks since we arrived. This must be serious.

"News from Chicago," Toyol says by way of greeting, entering the room with Phenex on his trail. "There's been some heavy angel activity."

"Angel activity?" I frown. "What would angels be doing in Chicago?"

He nods. "We need to get back asap. Cain says they're keeping an eye on it, but if things turn aggressive…"

"Any indication who? And what they're seeking?" Legion asks, any signs of wariness gone.

"No, but they think we could be dealing with the Seraph."

The Seraph? According to bits and pieces of history lessons from Legion and Phenex, the Seraph were the most powerful, most deadly of all the angels. Phenex was not one before he fell. But Legion had mentioned the word more than once when referring to his past. If he was one of the seraphim… then he was once an archangel.

My mind is saying *holy shit*, but it just feels wrong. Sacrilegious.

A deep scowl carves itself into Legion's face as he considers Toyol's words. Even as he stands there, arms crossed over his chest, I can see the ominous power vibrating his frame. "Pack up. We leave in ten minutes."

"What of the Dark king?" Phenex asks. "We have unfinished business pertaining to the deal you made."

"Later. We need to get home."

His declaration is final, and the two turn and leave without further question, leaving me alone to face a demon with uncontained rage brewing in his eyes.

"Be ready," is all he commands before turning around to stride to the bedroom.

No mention of last night. Not that I would expect one. Not that anything could have happened.

I take a deep breath, releasing the uncertainty, and follow him to the bedroom to pack my things.

TWENTY-FOUR

The ride back to Chicago seems like racing towards an impending death.

I'm glad to get back...*home?*...but I can't deny that I enjoyed living it up at The Broadmoor in Colorado Springs. The room service, the lavish digs, the break from Cain's constant scowls. Plus, I liked meeting people that sorta knew who I was. I didn't have to hide that I was different. I didn't have to pretend that I was normal for fear of being deemed some troubled weirdo. Gabriella didn't balk at my appearance or try to give me some backhanded compliment by calling my look "edgy." Shit, she probably has more ink than I do. And for a queen—*the* queen of the Dark—I think that's pretty fucking awesome.

I fidget in my seat, trying to get comfortable after riding for the past three hours. While I *think* Legion and I had fun while listening to my (amazing) playlists on the way to Colorado, going back to that easiness just doesn't seem right. Not with so much anxiety over the Seraph showing up in our city. Not with his aggravation so palpable that it chokes me. Not with my insides still pulsing to a foreign, riotous drumbeat.

"You did well these past few days," he says suddenly, offering seven of the ten words he's spoken to me since we started our journey home.

"Did I?"

"You did. You handled yourself with the queen when I was left incapacitated and couldn't protect you. You didn't back down from the king. I think they appreciated your courage. Admired it, even. I wouldn't be surprised to find that that's why they agreed to help us."

"For an extremely steep price. I honestly don't think it was worth it, either."

"It's not your price to pay. I made a vow to you, and I intend to keep it."

I turn in my seat, staring daggers at the side of his head. "Not my price to pay? L, you're choosing to die for me. Don't you think I should have a say in it? Considering that *I* wanted to make that choice, and you shot *me* down?"

"I'm not just dying for you, Eden. I'm dying for a cause much greater than any of us. I'm dying for mankind. I'm choosing to trade my life so that you, and people like you, may have a chance to actually have one for a change." One hand on the steering wheel, he scrubs a hand behind his head. "I've roamed this earth for longer than your eldest ancestors have been alive. If this is what will send me back to Hell, I can't imagine a more noble cause."

"Fuck nobility." The words are spit from my lips before I even have a chance to stop them.

"What?"

"You heard me. You're going to give up for one human life? One selfish, insecure girl who can't control her emotions? That's disappointing. I thought you were stronger than that—smarter than that. How stupid would it be for you to waste all you've done for your cause, all you've done for the Se7en, for someone who twists souls for the fuck of it. I'm not worth it, L. You know that, I know that, and so does everyone else. Yet, it's ok for you to play martyr, not me. Right? That's bullshit."

His voice is level, calm, despite my brash tirade. "Your life isn't bullshit. Not to me."

"Well, you'd be the first," I reply flippantly. "If you knew what I've done, the pain I've caused, you'd think otherwise."

"We're all sinners, Eden. Some of us just sin differently than others."

I let his words go unchecked and resort to staring out the window, as flat, brown earth and deadened grass whiz by—such a contrast to the rich emerald greens of the Broadmoor grounds. Gray clouds hang low above us, threatening the frostbitten, barren land with icy sustenance. The car's silence is deafening, so I flick on the stereo system and scroll down to a playlist labeled, "Dark Days." It's the one I listen to when I'm feeling particularly emo.

"Why did you block her number?"

I don't need to ask him whom he's talking about. *Sister*. Just the name echoing in my skull clouds my eyes with unwanted emotion.

"She would have never let go. She would have never given up on me. I would have had to lie to her every day, and shit…I'm so tired of lying. To her. To myself. She would have felt responsible for me, as if she did something wrong, and I can't handle her guilt. My guilt is one thing, but hers…"

"You love her."

I glance at him, wondering if he can hear my heart breaking. "Yes."

"I wouldn't have faulted you, you know…if you spoke with her."

I shake my head. "It would have given her false hope."

"There's nothing false about hope, Eden," he says, his voice trembling with a nostalgic timbre, as if he once had felt, tasted, and held hope in his palms. "It can be blind—foolish, even—but it's never false. Not if you truly feel it in your heart."

"And your heart?" I ask, remembering the cold void in his chest when my cheek lay against it under the shroud of night.

"Sometimes it feels too much. Other times it feels nothing at all."

His words are empty, a ghost that sweeps through the small space between us. It taunts me, daring me to challenge it with my own human fragility. I don't believe that he is devoid of feeling, considering all that he has made me feel in the span of mere days. But the trivial, overly sensitive side of me worries that those feelings may have nothing to do with me. And that…hurts.

A quiet settles within the car, and I fill it with my own torturous thoughts. What has become of us? I don't hate him. I don't particularly like him either. He's broody, reticent, and stubborn as hell. And if I'm really being honest, downright frightening. But there's also a side of him that's compassionate and—dare I say—kind. And he's fiercely protective and loyal. All those times when I was broken and vulnerable, he could have taken advantage. But no. He's been maddeningly, annoyingly virtuous.

To my relief, we turn into a gas station to fill up. I've had to use the restroom for miles, but I couldn't stand for my mortal needs to be yet another burden.

"Where are you going?" Legion questions when I hop out the car behind him.

"Bathroom."

He opens his mouth to protest, but I wave him off. "It's either going to happen in there or on your leather seats. Your choice." When he closes his mouth, I assure him with, "I'll be quick. Promise."

Keeping my word, I hurriedly relieve myself and make my way back into the mini mart, deciding to grab a couple of drinks and snacks for the road. I spot the Arizona Ice Tea and smile. Maybe this'll smooth things over. I can't stand for us to spend the next thirteen and a half hours in silence. I'd rather him bitch and moan at me than have to ride beside him, pretending not to notice every time those silver eyes shift to me behind his dark shades.

I spy Legion's broad back, dressed in a worn leather jacket, at the front of the store. He must've come in to pay while I was in the bathroom, probably just itching to give me the side eye for leaving his sight. Tough. He can't play bodyguard and babysitter forever.

"Well, if you're done being Mr. Doom-and-Gloom," I tease, coming down the potato chip aisle, "I have a little surprise for—"

"Eden, don't move."

The dark tone of his voice stops me in my tracks. That's when I notice his hands raised at his sides and the eerie quiet of the mini mart. I look to my left to see a man with a gun trained on Legion's head. To the right, there's another man, also holding a rifle as long as my arm.

Ice tea and soda slips from my fingertips, spraying sickly sweet liquid at my feet.

"The girl comes with us," the man to my right says. "So much as flinch, and my associate will splatter your insides all over the lotto tickets."

Demons? No. *Shit*—humans.

"I can't let you do that," Legion retorts, his voice deadly calm.

"Oh yeah?" the asshole with the assault rifle says. He's nearly as big as Legion—a trained fighter. I can't see much of his face but a shock of blonde hair peeks out from underneath a black skull cap. "Well, considering that I have guns trained on your associates outside, as well as surrounding this building, it'd be wise of you to reevaluate your priorities. Your job is done, demon. She's our concern now."

"See, that's where you're mistaken, *human*," Legion spits. "If she had been your concern from the beginning, we wouldn't have had to step in to protect her. So…if you'd like to see another day of your miserable, pathetic existence, you'll lower those guns, and walk the fuck the away."

The man barks out a laugh, maybe from fear, or hysteria, or both. "Immortality has made you arrogant. Let's see how cocky you'll be when I send you back to your maker with a hole in your head."

There's a shout in the distance, from outside, and then… all Hell breaks loose.

With one swift movement, faster than any of us can see, Legion is behind the gunman on his left, his hand pressed on his trigger finger. With his human shield, he trains the weapon of the guy with the rifle as he dives and rolls behind the hot dog counter. Legion lets off at least half a dozen rounds before whirling the gunman around and snapping his neck like a twig with a sickening *crack*.

"Come on!" he roars, plunging for me, as the guy with the rifle returns fire.

It's all too familiar. All too close to that scene just a little over a week ago. But this time, I won't scream. I won't cry. I won't vomit from fright.

Two more human gunmen enter the store, spraying wild bullets in our direction. Legion swiftly whirls me behind him, shielding my body with his as he unsheathes twin 9 mills from behind his back and squeezes off round after round with only an Icee machine as cover. He hits them both in the head with precise aim. More file in, armed to the teeth. We're outnumbered…by a lot. And after putting down five more, we hear the *click-click-click* that seals our fate. We're out of ammo.

"Stay behind me," he whispers harshly, holding me at his back. We're crouched down, half crawling our way through broken glass and shell casings. My knees and hands are bleeding, but I don't feel the pain. Cocaine-like adrenaline races through my veins, stilling all urges to scream or cry. We have to get out of here, and the prospect of doing that alive is looking pretty grim.

We round a corner and nearly collide with a human

strapped with what looks like a machine gun. Legion knocks his arm to one side before he can squeeze the trigger, and pummels his face with a fist, causing blood to spray from his nose. It happens in a split second, but it's enough time for him to swipe the man's gun and put a few bullets in his friend just a few feet away. Without even pausing to look, he turns and aims right over my shoulder, popping six more into the chest of an approaching assailant without even blinking.

He moves with the quickness of a viper and the stealth of a panther. If I didn't know any better, I would think he's part animal. A man this tall and this broad should not be as agile and graceful as he, but he's not a man. Not even a little bit.

Our path littered with dead bodies, Legion scoops me into his arms and runs out of the mini mart. There are more corpses out front, thanks to Phenex and Toyol. It's a mystery how no bullets hit the gas pumps and blew us all to bits.

"The Alliance," Toyol shouts at our approach. His Katanas gleam with bright red blood, dripping from the blades like warm strawberry syrup.

"More will be on their way," Phenex adds. He looks as poised and elegant as he always does. I can't imagine him in combat.

"Let's get the fuck outta here," Legion barks, setting me down to toss me into the car.

"Is she hurt?" Phenex questions, spying the blood on my hands and legs.

"I'm fine," I assure him. The cuts are superficial. I can clean up with just a First Aid kit. Plus, most of the blood isn't even mine.

Legion jumps in the driver's seat, and speeds off, loose

gravel kicking up behind us. He doesn't even look at me until we're miles away.

"Are you okay?" That voice again…tinged with dread and ice.

"I'm fine," I repeat, unable to find any other words. The kit in the glove compartment did the trick.

"Shit. Shit!" he shouts, punching the steering wheel. "I should have been more careful. I should have swept the store. If anything would have happened to you…"

"L…" I place my hand on his, the knuckles white with tension. He twitches, still jumpy from the fight, but I don't let go. I can feel the power flowing through him—fire and violence in blood form. "I'm okay. It's not your fault. Honestly, I should be thanking you. I would be dead if it weren't for you."

He spares me a quick glance, scanning my entire frame. "I swear, on everything that I am, I will never take risks with your life again. Forgive me."

"There's nothing to forgive." I finally remove my hand from his and ball it in my lap, capturing the feeling of his immense power in my palm. "If anything, I should be apologizing to you. They were *human*. I could have stopped them. But I just…froze. I should have done something to help."

Legion shakes his head. "Not your fault. You're untrained, unfocused. I don't expect you to do what I should have done."

"Then teach me," I urge, turning toward him in my seat. "Train me. Show me how to harness my gift and use it to fight."

Nearly a minute passes before he answers. "It's not your job, Eden. I don't expect you to put your life on the line any more than you have."

"So…who were they?"

He heaves out a heavy sigh. "The Alliance of the Ordained. A very old secret society that unifies every religion in the world for one purpose: eradicating evil."

What the…? "So they want to eradicate *me*?"

"No. Just the opposite actually. They think they can *save your soul*." He laughs sardonically, the sound chilling my bones. "Really that's just PC code for wrapping you in a straight jacket and locking you away for the rest of your days. Among other things."

"But how…how do they know about me?"

"Probably much like we know about you. The Alliance's minions span the globe. They've probably got moles inside every hospital, school and mental institution in the world."

Shit.

Shit shit shit.

What else have I been completely blind to? Who else could possibly be looking for me?

And who can I truly trust?

"Why aren't the Se7en and the Alliance working together? Since you both are hunting the Called?"

"Because they're pious sycophants that wouldn't know the Word if it bit them in their self-righteous asses," he growls. "The Alliance don't believe in taking human life. However, they think they can exorcise the Called and save their mortal souls, when in actuality, they are dooming them to a far more grave existence. Shock treatments. Beatings." He flicks his angry glance my way. "Lobotomies. Since they don't actually kill their victims, they feel as if they are doing God's Will. Death would be much kinder considering what they inflict on their victims."

"Death. Exactly what the Se7en exacts."

"It's not something we take lightly, Eden. If there was truly another way, we'd—"

"I know, I know. *Save one to save a million*. But why save *me*? Why not go through all this trouble for anyone else?"

I think he has resolved to ignore me until he answers several seconds later. "You are very valuable. To us." His throat bobs as he swallows. "To me."

"Why?"

At that, he really does ignore me, focusing on speeding towards our war torn city. We've taken a different route, avoiding the priority roads in order to stay out of sight. It also makes it easier to tell whether or not we've been followed. When we stop to fill up, Phenex and Toyol sweep the entire perimeter, the bathrooms included. I don't protest when Legion insists he stand outside the door.

"Thank you," I wince, not really understanding why the hell I'm thanking him. He saved my life—yes. More times than I can count on one hand. But I don't *get* it. And I don't buy the whole Jumper explanation. Not when there's really nothing in it for them. Hell, they're demons, for crying out loud. What do they care?

Shit, why does *he* care?

A short lifetime of shitty people and shitty foster homes has left me jaded and guarded, but for good reason. No one has shown me anything else. No one but Sister.

And now even she is just a shadow of my past.

Legion hurriedly leads me to the car under the cover of night, his hand on the small of my back. Even with doubt digging a hole in my brain, his touch never fails to disarm me.

When he settles onto his side and revs the car to life just seconds later, he turns his silver gaze on me, its brilliance even brighter in the dark.

"Every human life I've ever taken stays with me. Haunts me. I see them in my dreams. I see them whenever I look in the mirror. I hear their screams overpowering my own thoughts. Eden, if there were another way, I'd do it. And maybe we can't save you. Maybe we're just prolonging the inevitable. But I can't do it. My soul is too heavy to bear one more unwarranted death."

He doesn't speak the rest of the journey back to Chicago, but I keep the music on. Hopefully, it'll drown out the screams in his head.

TWENTY-FIVE

"SO WHAT THE FUCK ARE YOU SAYING?" Cain's scarred face is screwed up in a scowl, his pitch black eyes darting from me to his leader. We hardly had time to get cleaned up before Legion called a mandatory briefing, despite the late hour.

"I'm saying that when the time comes, I'll have to uphold my end of the bargain and find the warlock."

"You're saying that you've resolved to lay down and fucking die!" The chair behind him screeches and falls with a loud crash as Cain jumps to his feet. "For her! She isn't fucking worth it, L. She's *human*." The last word is bile on his tongue.

"A human that we have vowed to help. A human that *you* will continue to protect, unless you'd like to challenge my authority," Legion retorts, climbing to his feet. The two demons stare each other down for long moments before Cain finally looks away and trains his malicious glare on me.

"This isn't over." The slamming of the heavy, steel front door is the proverbial period on the threat in his words.

"He's right, you know," Andras says quietly, sitting beside Lilith.

"Andras," she scolds.

"I'm sorry. L, you've been our leader…our brother. Our friend. What does it say about us if we just sit idly by and let you give your life for a girl you hardly know? There has to be another way. We'll fight the warlocks. Their coven will be no match for the Se7en, regardless of their magic."

"We will not defy the Dark." Legion sags back into his chair, his face weary. He drove all day without stopping for food or water. And after taking on the Alliance, he has to be exhausted.

"L is right," Phenex adds. "Waging war on them would divide the underworld. It would also mean more casualties—potentially human casualties. Earth cannot be collateral damage."

"And what will we do without a leader?" Toyol asks. He looks at Legion, his expression pleading. "Together we are strong. But without L, what will keep us together? Who will reel in Cain when he goes on one of his tirades?"

"Phenex," Legion answers.

"What?" the rest of the table—save for Jinn—shrieks.

"He's a scholar, a diplomat. He'll be able to talk Cain down, and lead you all down the path of the righteous. Plus, he's fallen. He knows His word. Maybe even better than I do."

Phenex shakes his head. "But I was never one of the Seraph, L. My relations with them are fragile, at best."

"But they know you. And they know I trust you."

"And speaking of the Seraph..." Lilith begins. "There has to be some special reason they've decided to convene here. It's as if they know Eden is here, under our protection. I know they like to check in every once in a while, but something about this visit is different."

"Irin?" Toyol questions.

Legion answers with a shake of his head. "The Seraph despise the ways of The Watcher. They'd never be so humble as to ask. And they definitely don't associate with the Dark. That would be seen as blasphemous in their eyes."

"Then who? Or *what?*"

"I do not know." There's a touch of defeat in Legion's voice, as if admitting that fact pains him. "But whatever it is, the Seraph's involvement isn't good."

"Maybe I..." Every eye turns to me at the sound of my voice, a meek whisper compared to theirs. I swallow down trepidation. I'd been invited to their meetings as a mere courtesy. But I have to speak up. I have to do something—anything—other than sit around and be a victim. "Maybe I can talk to them—the Seraph. Maybe if they see that I am safe and cared for, they'll back down. Maybe they'll even help."

"No!" Legion growls, his face morphing into something fierce and carnal. It's enough to make me flinch, but I'm not afraid. Not of him. Not anymore.

"Well, what about the Alliance? One less enemy on our trail would help. Maybe they were the ones to tip off the Seraph. I could go to them—tell them that I have not been harmed and that my life will be spared."

"I said, no!" The harsh tone of his voice rumbles the

ground beneath our feet.

"But it's not right!" I counter, ignoring his edict. "I have to do something! I refuse to cower and hide for the rest of my life!"

"You won't have a life if you go anywhere near the Seraph *or* the Alliance!"

I jump to my feet, slamming my palms on the marble tabletop. "So what the hell am I supposed to do?"

Legion stands as well, dwarfing my frame with his. Power gleams from his eyes like flares. "You're supposed to listen for once in your damn life! You're supposed to stay with *me!*"

I look up at him, my mouth suspended in a stunned O. The silence around the table is deafening, eerily so. Not even the sound of my panting breaths fills the space.

Unable to shoulder the weight of his words and the intensity of his stare, I back away from the table, away from him. *Stay with him?* Nothing has ever seemed so tempting, yet so insanely impossible.

Like a coward, I run to the back room, the very space I have been his prisoner and his enemy. His confidant. I know I can't escape him, and something in me—something irrational and ruled by pure emotion—doesn't want to. I don't understand it enough to fight it. And if I did, I can't be sure that I would.

I keep my back turned to him as I hear his approaching footsteps. I don't even breathe until I hear the door shut. But as his overwhelming heat grazes my back, my body gives over to instinct, and I spin around and press my chest to his, pulling his face down to meet mine. And I kiss him.

I kiss him with everything in me, all the fear, all the rage, all the hopelessness. I kiss him like he can take them all away, surrendering to his lips and the feel of the fire raging within his chest. I kiss him and pray that he will save me once more, and kiss me back.

Taut bands of muscle snake around my back as he lifts me off my feet, giving me access to more of his mouth—as hot and sweet and commanding as the rest of him. His tongue, so thick and unyielding, delves between my trembling lips and collides with mine. In a frenzy to taste more, I wrap my arms around his neck, fisting the long layers of hair that graze his nape. I pull hard enough to hurt, ignoring the bite of pain from the cuts on my hands. He answers my violent eroticism by palming my ass, digging his fingers into my pliant flesh, until he supports my entire weight. I lock my legs around his waist, the sting at my backside exciting me.

I've never been that girl.

The one confident enough to take what she wants. The one who could make men wither under her charms. The one who wouldn't let fear keep her from sating her body's desires.

But now that I'm in his arms, absorbing his stifling heat with mine, I can't remember a time when I felt more beautiful, more carefree. Because as he lays me flat on the bed and traps my body with his, none of that matters. I'll never be that girl. But in the span of just a few minutes, or maybe since the day he brought me here, I became his, just as Lilith said. Just as sure as the ink etched in our skin. Just as sure as the blood pumping in our veins.

He pulls away, just slightly, but I still tighten my legs around his waist, skinned knees be damned. Those silver eyes scan my face, searching for any signs of doubt. When he finds none, he frowns.

"What is it?" I whisper, holding his cheek.

"Eden…" A flash of torment passes his gaze and he closes his eyes. "You make me want to sin."

I cup his other cheek, hoping he can feel every ounce of my conviction. "Then do it."

Those star-flecked eyes find mine for just a second, before his lips join mine again. He kisses me urgently, as if my breath sustains him. My tongue meets his, stroke for stroke, lick for lick, mimicking all the ways I need him. I ache in the space between my legs as I flex against the hardness in his jeans. His erection is so full and pronounced that it pulses under the rough fabric down his thigh, burning, begging to be adored by my mouth and hands and body.

He is need. He is passion. He is fire. And he can only be extinguished inside me.

I tear at his pants at the same time that he rips my shirt, shredding the cotton into scraps. The tops of my heavy breasts feel the chilled air for only a second before they are covered with the heat of his mouth. He pushes them up, freeing them from the lace of my bodice to reveal my peaked nipples. Wet lips graze the tips, one at a time, before he draws one into his mouth, sucking hungrily, greedily. I moan loudly as he nibbles and licks before laving the other, eliciting even more erotic sounds.

I could come from this alone. Shit, I'm close to it already. But I have to feel him. I want his fury, I want his aggression. I want him to fill me with the fire that rages underneath his golden skin.

I tear open his fly and paw ravenously at the massive

thickness that throbs between us. It's too long and rigid for me to maneuver so I unhook my legs and use my knees to push down his jeans. My mouth salivates with the anticipation of holding it in my palms and tracing each vein. I imagine etching them with my tongue, those ridges pumping with life between my lips. I've never actually been intimate enough with a man to explore that carnal side of me, but for some reason, I can't wait to taste him. It's as if I already have, and the memory of his flavor is embedded on my mouth.

Legion releases my sensitive nipples and sits up on his knees. With that penetrating stare trained on my writhing flesh, he hooks his fingers into his jeans and slowly, torturously eases them down. A sharp V flows into the hard root of him, smattered with fine, dark hair. I lick my lips. He's thicker than I could have imagined, but the thought of him ripping me apart in erotic rage only causes the trickle of wetness between my thighs to soak my panties even more.

He pushes the jeans down to his thighs, and I shiver. I haven't even seen the tip of him yet, but I know every long inch of him is beautiful. I extend my hand towards him, hoping to feel that silken skin on my fingertips. The heat that radiates from him promises to melt my walls and turn my insides to liquid. His sheer size would probably penetrate every part of me until I choke on my moans.

A little bit further down, and I see the beginning of a generous, swollen head that will lick at my quivering womb. A little bit further down and—

There's a knock on the door.

"L," Toyol calls out. "Cain is back. We need to do the Blood Oath."

"Shit," he spits, pulling his jeans back over the cut of his hips. "Shit!"

The moment's magic dissipates like dust particles in the air. I suck in a ragged breath. The tingling in my limbs begins to recede, replacing the fire with icy cold. I look away from Legion, ashamed of my nakedness, and pull the shreds of my shirt over my breasts.

"Hey." His voice is soft, apologetic. "I have to…"

"I know," I nod, still unable to meet his gaze. Just seconds ago, I lay before him, baring myself, begging to taste him, feel him. Now I can't even look him in the eye.

I listen to the rustle of his clothes as he rights himself. When I hear his footfalls towards the door, I finally sit up.

"You should be there."

I shake my head, giving him my naked back. "No. You go."

"I want you to be there. The Blood Oath is sacred, but… I just want you there."

I dare a look over my shoulder. "I don't think that's a good idea."

"It's up to you. But, if you want…if you would let me share this piece of me with you, it would mean something. To me. I want you to see *me*."

And I understand exactly what he means.

He's carried the weight of thousands of lost souls for centuries, hoping to atone for their sins. That's what people see when they look at those swirling silver eyes. That's what they think when they hear his name. But that's not who he is. That's not *all* he is. He's just never let anyone see it.

"I am Hell on earth, Eden. But that doesn't mean I want

to be."

Maybe this is his way of opening up and showing me exactly who and what he wants to be. Maybe this is the first step.

"Okay."

He nods once, placing his hand on the doorknob. "Okay. I'll meet you in the hallway."

I have no idea what a Blood Oath is, but it sounds daunting as hell. I probably should have asked what I would be getting myself into, but I was too shaken up by the almost-sex we just had. Still am, if I'm being honest. One minute we're fighting for our lives, then the next, we're tearing off each other's clothes. I don't *get* him. Most days, he acts like he doesn't even like me. But then there are the times when he's gentle and kind. Like when he holds me during my nightmares. And after The Watcher's party…how he pressed himself against my ass and told me that it was someone else he was thinking about as he kissed Irin. And how he shared the story of his tattoos, specifically the one in tribute of his lost wings.

Bit by bit, he's been showing me who he truly is, and I've been too occupied with fighting against him to see it. So whatever this Blood Oath is to him, I'll stand beside him. It's the very least I can do, considering all he's done for me.

Considering all that he means to me.

I dress quickly and step into the hallway. Legion rests against the door across from the infirmary—the door Phenex said was storage.

"Ready?"

I muster up a nervous smile and shrug. "As I'll ever be."

He opens the door, and the first thing that hits me is the smell. Scorched earth, burning wood and some kind of incense. The only things that light the vast space are a multitude of tall candles, casting a golden glow from different points in the room. At the center of the room, the other members of the Se7en stand in a semi-circle where they await their leader. Legion gives me a nod, leaving me near the entrance before striding over to complete the loop around a large star etched into the floor. A pentagram. Holy shit, this is a satanic ritual.

"It's not what you think," Legion says, reading the trepidation on my face.

I nod but don't dare take a step closer. Now that my eyes have had a chance to adjust to the dim light, I take a beat to look around the room. High tech workout equipment stands on one side, complete with heavy bags suspended from the ceiling. On the other side, there's what appears to be targets, some pelted with holes. They have their own gun range in here.

How? I mean, yeah, the room is huge, at least twice the size of the shared bedrooms. But how can people not hear the shooting from the street?

The same reason why screaming was futile when I first arrived.

Everything is soundproof. Hell, I wouldn't be surprised if there is some type of spell that binds the noise.

"Let's begin," Legion calls out. I feel the others' eyes on me, questioning my presence. I don't doubt Cain is seething. But Legion ignores them, instead walking over to a small pillar off to the side. A red, ornate pillow rests upon it, and on top of that, a dagger.

Legion picks up the dagger, cradling it carefully in his palms with a sense of reverence. Its hilt is adorned with gleaming red jewels that seem to glow with his touch. He walks over to his spot between Phenex and Cain.

"The Blood Oath signifies the unity of the Se7en," Legion says, his voice adopting an ancient tone. "In this, we are one, for our purpose is singular. Our blood sacrifice represents the lives we must take in order to save those who cannot save themselves from iniquity. It strengthens our bond and our resolve. Within this circle, we are of one entity."

With that, he takes the blade in one hand and slices his palm open, causing thick blood to drop onto the floor. He hands the dagger to Phenex who does same, then the two join bloody hands. Beside Phenex stands Lilith. She takes the knife and not only slashes her hand, but Phenex's too, before placing their severed palms together.

It goes on like that until the dagger makes its way around the circle. When it reaches Legion again, Cain does the honors and cuts both their palms before returning it to the pillow. He returns to take his leader's hand, blood trailing at his feet.

And then shit gets really weird.

Their blood…moves. To the center of the star. It literally slithers together, creating a large pool of deep red. The Se7en begin to chant—a language unlike any I've ever known to exist—all in unison. It starts as a low murmur at first before their timbres increase in volume and speed. Shouted words of myth and magic conjure a violent, cold wind that stirs my hair and creates goosebumps to prick my skin. I back up as far as I can go, until I hit the brick wall. The chanting reaches its apex, and with a wild, animalistic screech—maybe from me or some other unknown source—the candles blow out.

It's quiet. The kind of quiet that only exists in death.

Suddenly, fire roars around the room, the candles exploding with vicious flames. And what their light reveals terrifies the fuck out of me. I no longer see the Se7en. I see evil. Standing in their places are the heads of beasts. Monsters. Horned, red-skinned creatures with glowing eyes that scratch their way into nightmares and haunt your waking hours. They flicker in and out, as if the scenes are mere flashes of ghosts, trying to gain a foothold onto this plane. Still, nothing I've ever seen is more horrifying, ripping screams from my lungs that are foreign even to my ears.

My cries go unheard as the chants begin again, this time in gravely, inhuman voices. The monster heads continue to flicker, giving me glimpses of terrifying evil. I can't quite take it all in or blink them away, so I crouch into a ball, hiding my face in my knees. My jeans are wet with tears, my body seized in fright. I couldn't run even if I tried.

I thought I had known fear before as a poor, troubled kid born and raised in the wrong part of Chicago.

I was wrong.

Minutes, maybe hours, later, I think it stops, but I can't be sure. I'm too afraid to lift my head. What if they're still there, standing solid in their true forms, looking for a human to feast on?

A warm hand touches my shoulder, and I scream, arms flailing wildly. Legion easily captures my hands and pulls me into his chest.

"Shhh. It's me, firecracker. It's me."

I don't stop fighting him, because I know it's him. And what he is…is really Hell on earth. But he doesn't stop holding me, doesn't stop soothing me with his words. He has shown me who he truly is, and I can't handle it. I can't see that strong, stoic, beautiful warrior in him anymore. I can accept the killer wrapped in legend and secrecy. But I don't know if I'm strong enough to accept *this*. And that is the real reason for my tears.

He holds me to his chest until my cries turn to whimpers and I sag into his body, no longer pushing him away but pulling him closer.

"I'm so sorry," he whispers into my hair, kissing the wind-whipped strands. "I didn't mean to frighten you."

"Then why?" My voice is hoarse from screaming.

Legion lifts my chin to meet his gaze. His eyes churn with contained power that I never could imagine in my darkest nightmares. I force myself not to look away.

"I wanted you to see me and all my demons. Just as I see yours. You want the man, but can you want the monster inside too?"

I don't answer him.

I don't have an answer to give.

TWENTY-SIX

EXHAUSTION IS THE FIRST COUSIN OF FEAR, AND AS SOON as my tears dry, it seems like I can't keep my eyelids open. Legion still has Se7en business to attend to, and while I find it impossible to imagine sleeping after the night I've had, I manage to drift off as soon as I hit the bed.

However, exhaustion does nothing to stave off the nightmares. And considering what I've just seen—what I've just felt—the scene that manifests seems to be more vivid than ever.

"Sweet Sister," I purr, raking my bloodied fingers through her tight ringlets. "It will all be over soon, you know. Just say the words and it all goes away."

"Why are you doing this?" she cries. "Why are you hurting all these innocent people?"

"Hurting them?" I bark out a laugh. "I'm not hurting anyone, Sister. You are. You all are."

"No," she shakes her head furiously, tears streaming down her blood-streaked cheeks. "You know what you're doing. How could you be so evil?"

"Evil?" Again, a sinister laugh erupts from my throat. I tighten my hand into a fist around the hair at her scalp and pull sharply, bringing my face close to hers. She struggles in my grip, but she's at the full mercy of my wrath. I bear my teeth as I seethe with contempt, just centimeters from her ear, "You haven't even seen fucking evil. Not yet."

On cue, I hear his footsteps enter the room, causing a pool of wetness to collect between my naked thighs. I let a soiled hand slide down my belly to tease myself.

"Mmmmm. Just in time for the finale."

I climb to my feet, giving him full view of my backside. I burn for him, my breath escaping in excited, short pants. When he presses against me, a small whimper vibrates my heavy swollen breasts.

"Are we having fun yet?" he croons, grazing my shoulder with the barest tips of his fingers. I shiver, feeling his touch all over my body like a thousand, spindly spiders.

"Yes, Master," I respond breathlessly.

"Good. Continue." He strides across the dank room and leans against the gray cement wall.

I train my vicious gaze on the lovely woman with skin the color of toasted marshmallow and dark, corkscrew curls. Sister. "Bite her."

Sister looks at the bleeding girl beside her. The girl I've forced her to beat and cut and burn and sodomize for the past hour. It's a wonder she's still conscious, although she is...just barely.

The human will is such a beautiful thing. Strong, yet extremely pliant. Especially when it's been broken.

"Please," she begs, sobbing uncontrollably. "Please don't make me."

"Bite her breast until you taste blood," I command. "Then do the same to the other. And while you're biting her, finger her. She'll like that. Use your entire hand."

Like a sad, blubbering puppet, Sister leans forward and attaches her mouth to the girl's left breast. She can't be older than eighteen, but she has a spectacular body. A body I've enjoyed maiming.

The young girl cries out in excruciating pain as Sister's teeth tear through skin and tissue at the same time that she rams her fingers into her brutalized vagina. She should be thanking me. It's better than the splintered broomstick I had Sister use on her earlier.

They both cry and scream in agony, but I don't hear them over the sounds of my own maniacal laughter. And when my master approaches and pushes me to my knees, I can do nothing more than moan as he unsheathes his thick cock and roughly shoves it down my throat…

There's a siren going off in the dark bedroom, and I'm afraid.

Blackness and heat encompass my trembling frame, smearing the fright of my dream into my disjointed reality. The siren sounds like my hoarse voice, and the moment I take a ragged breath, it stops. I paw at my damp face, trying to scrub off all the blood, but there isn't any. Tears. I'm crying.

And the heat that cradles me is *him*.

"I've got you, Eden. It's just a dream, baby. You're alright."

Legion.

His arms are like anchors, tethering me to the safety and security of his bed. His words are like a balm, soothing my ravaged psyche. I crush my body to his, hoping he can absorb my trepidation. In response, he rolls me over so I am draped over his chest, my legs on either side of his torso beneath the sheets. I feel so small, so frail, on top of his massive frame. Yet, the way those silver eyes gleam for me under the veil of moonlight, he seems vulnerable and timid. So I lower my face to his and covet his kiss in an act of lust-filled madness.

He kisses me back as if the world will shatter against my lips, soft and gentle and urgent. Strong hands grip my backside, my long sleep tee covering hardly anything in this position. I'm glad for it. I need to feel his unshakable strength. I need to know that he won't slip between my fingers like everything else. Like everyone else.

My fingertips caress the hard, chiseled planes of his bare chest and abs before trailing a path down to his thin pajama bottoms. I don't stop this time. I keep going, grazing the patch of downy hair at his thick base. A tremor racks his entire frame, but he keeps kissing me, his tongue delving even deeper.

The heat of his body, and the need to feel more of his is too much to bear, so I pull away, only to whip off my shirt. His hands go to my breasts, and the memory of them in his mouth causes a small whimper to pass my lips. He remembers too, and sits up just far enough to suck a pert nipple into his wet mouth. I moan loudly, longing to feel that mouth all over my quivering skin.

I can't wait another second. I need his ache inside me. I

need to tremble with something other than fear and anger. I need to erase those dreadful nightmares with the fullness of him.

I yank down his pants to his knees, unsheathing his proud, thick hardness. The sheer size of him is daunting, but I crave it. I want him to tear me apart, bit-by-bit. Maybe it's exactly what will make me better. Maybe I need the strings of my fragile sanity to be pulled, unraveled and be laid bare for him. Maybe he'll see the beauty behind my chaos.

I told myself I needed to taste him, but right now, with him hot and pulsing in my palm, I can't imagine not taking him inside the part of me that burns for him. I lift up just enough to place him at my entrance, not wanting to lose the connection of his tongue and teeth on my nipples. Those starlit eyes meet mine.

"Are you certain?"

I nod. "More certain than I've been about anything for a very long time. Are you?"

A flash of emotion darkens his gaze for just a half a second before he nods. "Yes. I've waited so long—too long—for you."

And with that, he sucks in a harsh breath and rips my panties to shreds, then flexes his hips upwards. And with his hands on my waist to push me down, he slides inside me.

We both gasp at the sensation, the feeling unlike anything I've ever felt before. My body hungrily sucks at the scorching intrusion, begging to swallow him whole. It takes a few shallow thrusts before he's fully fitted inside me. I could just sit right here and find release. I wouldn't even need to move. Just the sheer euphoria of his body connected to mine in the most intimately intense way would be enough.

But where Legion was hesitant—almost reluctant—before, he makes up for in exuberance. His hands gripping my hips, he pumps inside me, slow and deep and sinuous, in time to a hedonistic beat. His movements are fluid and erotic, positioning each thrust to hit every sensitive spot inside me. It's as if he's dancing, rotating his hips, flexing his ass, creating delicious friction against my swollen mound. And just as the first prickle of orgasm begins to snake up my spine, he flips me over onto my back in one swift move without breaking his rhythm.

He hoists my leg over his shoulder, allowing him to dig deeper into my core. I break apart in a thousand jagged pieces, the pressure in my womb releasing in a flash flood that seeps between us. It had been a long time for me, but shit…he's been abstaining for a century. Yet, he's still going. Still pumping towards an orgasm that will surely move Heaven and Earth. And when the base of his spine finally tightens and he throbs and swells inside me, heated little daggers stabbing his flexed thighs, he roars unto the moon, and fills me to the brim with every ounce of his violent beauty.

"Oh. My. *God*," I pant, staring up at him in wonder.

A sinister smile snakes onto his lips. "Even He can't save you now."

I'm flipped onto my stomach faster than I can catch my breath, and Legion is thrusting inside me. His fingers roughly dig into the flesh of my ass, kneading the skin with every hard stroke. I feel his chest against my sweat-slickened back as he lies on top of me, holding me hostage with his body.

"This is what you wanted, right?" he grits, his lips on my

ear. "To see my darkness. To feel it spreading inside you, violating you. You want my sin, Eden? Now you have it."

I can't breathe through my muffled cries, let alone respond. I bite the pillow to keep from screaming out.

"What's wrong?" he purrs like a deadly jungle cat. Teeth graze the nape of my neck, my jawline, my neck. I squirm underneath him. "Don't you like my brand of evil? I told you, firecracker. I've waited a long time for you. I have no intention of letting you go."

And while I should be afraid at his dark tone, like any rational thinking woman would be, it only encourages my body to wrap tighter around him, clasping onto his wickedness and begging for more.

"Yes, that's it," he groans for me. "Hold me. *Feel* me. I want to live and die deep inside you."

I hold on as long as I can, relishing in the sensation of his fire burning bright between my thighs. But every stroke is like a kiss of death, and the harder I fight against it, the closer I come to completion. His weight, his size…it crushes me, yet makes me whole. I've never felt so solid in his arms, so strong. Even though I know he's destroying me from the inside out.

"Legion," I beg, feeling an orgasm crawling up my legs. He speeds up his rhythm, coaxing it from my body like a snake charmer.

"Don't fight me," he whispers. "The chase only makes me want it more."

His taunting words are like an erotic elixir. I feel drunk, lightheaded with lust, yet there's something more that lies between our damp, panting bodies. Something deeper than anything I've ever felt. And every time he pushes inside of me, that feeling digs deeper, tying itself to my flesh and tainting my blood. Attaching itself to my heart.

I don't want to feel it, but the more I buck against him, the deeper I feel him infecting my soul. I quiver from head to toe, calling out for mercy. Legion hears my cries and raises me up to my knees, parting my legs to spread me even wider. When he thrusts to the hilt with enough force to split me in two, I cry out, shaking uncontrollably. His hand snakes between my thighs to prolong my orgasm, sending me soaring through a storm of sinuous pleasure. I am wetness and warmth. I am bliss and pain. I am Heaven. I am Hell.

He comes again soon after I do, purging his sweet sin while his fingers tangle in my hair. We both collapse onto the bed of twisted sheets and strewn pillows, our breaths ragged. Silence falls on us like morning dew.

Legion turns to me just as I roll onto my side to face him. And in the shade of afterglow, we smile.

"What is it?" he asks, his voice husky, yet amused.

"Nothing. Is it so hard to believe that I'm smiling because I might be happy?"

"It is, actually. Not that I'm complaining."

"Mmmm. My body might be later, but right now, I'm just…amazed."

"By what?"

I watch a bead of sweat slide down his bicep before catching it with my finger. "That you're here with me. That after more than 100 years, you let someone in. You let *me* in."

"I guess I could say the same thing about you." He brushes a wayward lock of hair from my forehead. "Aside from the hundred years part."

I turn my face into his touch and kiss his palm. "Some days, it feels like longer." I meet his questioning gaze. "Intimacy was never easy for me. Knowing how someone feels about you—feeling their vile thoughts when you're at your most vulnerable—it can kinda be a cock block."

"So how did you combat it?"

I shrug. "Get really drunk so I either don't care or can't make the connection. I need concentration. Anytime my emotions are frazzled or my head is cloudy, it's damn near impossible."

"Hmmm." He nods. "Maybe I can help with that?"

"Really?"

"Yeah. The mind is like a muscle. We just need to work it out."

"And the rest of me?" I raise a wicked brow.

"I can work that out too."

Teasing kisses and light touches lead to him on his back with me straddling him again. He's hard, but I want to prolong this moment. It's rare to see him so buoyant and generous with his smiles.

"Tell me something. Why me? After all this time, why break your vow for me?"

He furrows his brow, his mouth pressed into a thin line. Oh shit. I shouldn't have gone there. Just as we were breaking serious ground, I had to open my big mouth and remind him of what he's just sacrificed. I take his silence as my cue to go, but he holds me in place just as I try to roll off him.

"I've roamed this earth for a long time, and Hell for longer than that. I've basked in the pain of others and thrived in debauchery, just as I've known immeasurable grace. Yet, in all those years, I could never be who I am—what I am—without the preconceived notions and preambles. People are drawn to the allure of darkness, but they're afraid of it. They want to dip their toe into it, but not let it consume them. But you… you were born into sin. You were made for this darkness. And even though I know you are so much more than that, I feel at…home. With you, inside you, it makes me remember what it feels like to belong somewhere."

I gaze down at this man—this demon…this angel—with tears shining in my eyes. "You can be you. Just you. And nothing else." The gentleness in the middle of the night. The fierce protectiveness. The glimmers of playful flirtation. That was all him. Not what everyone expects Legion to be. Yet, I haven't even scratched the surface.

"Yes."

He carries the burden of lost souls. I carry the weight of my own vicious demons. We are different, yet kindred in so many ways. As if the universe or God or some other force greater than the both of us had been waiting for us to find each other.

I don't need to ask him any more questions. I lift myself up onto my knees and position him at my entrance. And then I let my body do the talking. It's a slow, deliberate exchange full of raspy whispers and melodic sighs. And when there's finally nothing else to say, we come together, our fingers and tongues intertwined. Spent and sore, I fall asleep right there on his chest, lulled by the hummed lullaby of his heartbeat. It's the only place on earth that I ever want to be.

When I wake up after too little sleep, I look up to find him watching me, a small smile on his face. It looks different in the daylight—more vulnerable. It's easily the most beautiful sight I've ever seen.

"When you look at me like that, I can see why you were an angel," I whisper, my voice hoarse with sleep and sex.

"Can you?"

"Yes. I can also see that you're very, very bad."

He chuckles, causing his chest to vibrate and tickle my bare chest. "Only when provoked."

"Well, considering that I can feel you stabbing me from behind, I think I must've done something to provoke you."

His fingers rake through my hair before traveling to my back, igniting tingles up and down my spine. "You do every day. Just by breathing. Just by being who you are."

My arms, stiff and sore, wobble as I lift up onto my elbows. "I should've known. I seem to have a thing for bad boys."

"That's good to hear."

"Is it?" I purr and nudge my ass against him.

"Mmmm," he groans. "You better stop that or we'll never leave this bed."

"Sounds good to me." Another nudge, and a roll of my hips.

"Me too. I'd love nothing more than to spend the entire day inside you. But…" He gives me an apologetic look that makes him seem almost human. "The Seraph are in the city. Meaning they want something."

"I understand," I reply, stifling a tiny twinge of disappointment.

"But I want to take you somewhere. Tonight. Will you wait for me?" His earnest question seems odd, as if it is wrapped around a hidden meaning that I can't quite decipher.

"Of course," I reply, meaning it. "When do you have to leave?"

"In an hour. I was just waiting for you to wake up."

"An hour, huh?" I bite my bottom lip seductively. "What ever shall we do to pass the time?"

A wicked gleam shines in Legion's silver eyes. "I don't know. What do you have in mind?"

"I've got a few ideas."

And with that, I crawl down his body and brace my hands on his powerful thighs before taking as much as I can of him into my mouth. He groans loudly, unabashedly, twitching against my tongue and gathering my mussed hair into his tight fist.

He tastes even better than I'd dreamed.

TWENTY-SEVEN

Everyone goes with Legion to meet with the Seraph except for Lilith, who opts to stay behind to keep me company. I can't deny that I'm glad for it, especially after last night. And this morning. And the shower fifteen minutes ago. I know that I can't share anything with her—not that I would—but it feels good to have some female camaraderie, even if it is a lie. Even if she was deliberately planted to befriend me. Still, I miss her friendship, and just connecting with another girl. And I miss Sister.

Lilith seems just as exuberant to have a girl's day, and nearly pushes the guys out the front door. I hardly even get a chance to wish Legion good luck. I want to say more—do more—but I know that wouldn't be a good idea. I've built my life on a foundation of secrets. Now is not the time to open the vault.

"So I have tons planned for us to do today!" she beams. "Mani/pedis, movies, ice cream—the whole nine!"

"Really?" I fail to hide my cringe. "You don't have to do all that for me. Besides, your nails are perfect." It's hard to believe this girl fights for a living.

"But yours aren't."

I know she doesn't mean it maliciously, and she's totally right, but...ouch.

"Ok, fine. Where do you want me?" I sigh. Resisting her would be futile.

Lilith claps her hands with glee. "Follow me!"

We spend most of the day in her bedroom, which she has pretty much transformed into a full service luxury salon. I've gotten my nails and toes done, my hair deep conditioned and color touched up (which was much needed) and my brows waxed, all while sipping champagne. Girl Power classics such as *Legally Blonde* and *Mean Girls* play in the background while she plays life-size Barbie with me. The fact that she's enjoying every second of it definitely helps to thaw my attitude. I can see why she was excited. She's surrounded by men all day every day with no real connection to the outside world. Maybe she misses what we had just like I do. Maybe it wasn't all a lie.

"Can I ask you a question?"

Lilith refills our glasses with fizzy pink bubbles and nods. "Of course."

"Don't you ever get...I don't know. Do you ever date?"

"You mean, have I hooked up with any of the Se7en?"

My face heats with guilt, and I take a sip.

"No. We're all too close for that. You saw the Oath. The sharing of blood is sacred. In their eyes, I'm their sister. Closer, even."

That makes sense. "And other guys?"

"I've had lovers," she shrugs. "Many of them. But no attachments. It's not feasible in my profession, and I don't like the lying. That was the hardest part when I met you. I knew you were someone I could genuinely care for, and I hated the thought of deceiving you."

I nod, understanding. She did what she had to do, and I can't fault her for that. I can't hold it against her considering that I've forgiven Legion for his part in all this.

"I get it," I tell her.

"Do you?"

"I do. I've had to pretend my entire life. Not because I wanted to deceive people, but because I wanted to protect them. And honestly, that's all you've done. You and the Se7en. Even Cain, even though he hates me. It would probably be a thousand times worse if those Russians had snatched me that first night, or even the Alliance. So…thank you."

Lilith smiles and looks away, but not before I see the tears in her eyes. I'm not good with that type of emotion, so I just let her have her moment, silently praying that it passes quickly.

"So, how was Colorado Springs?" she says after a few minutes of silence. She swipes under her eyes, careful not to smear her eyeliner.

"It was good. Weird, but good." I frown slightly. Even with all the crazy hocus-pocus, I actually enjoyed meeting the Skotos family. The prophecy shit I could've done without, but I won't tell her that. Not when I'm still trying to wrap my head around it.

I tell her about the splendor of the Broadmoor, and its

lush, green grounds and mild temperatures.

"Elemental magic," she explains. "Not surprising, especially since they have a Light Enchanter on their payroll."

"It was amazing, either way. I've never been out of Illinois. Seeing the Rocky Mountains and all that open land was like being on another planet."

"You've never been out of the state?" She looks stunned, as if I've just told her that I sniff powdered sugar recreationally.

I shrug, ignoring the embarrassed flush of my cheeks. "No money for travel. I've always wanted to, but you know how it is."

"Well…hopefully, we can change that soon." She offers me a hopeful smile, followed an arm squeeze.

We spend the rest of the day gorging on her hidden stash of junk food and pints of gourmet gelato. I have to admit, between the movies and the makeover, I'm having fun. No talk of nightmares or impending doom. We don't even mention her demon form during the Blood Oath. And oddly enough, I don't see her that way, just as I don't see Legion as some fanged, horned, red-skinned beast. And it's so damn refreshing to just pretend, even for an afternoon, that we're just regular girls for a change.

The rest of the Se7en don't return until after nightfall, their expressions grim. No one speaks, resolving to retreat to their rooms and private corners of the house. Cain and Toyol take up in the living to play video games, murmuring something about blowing shit up. Phenex disappears to read. Andras, Lilith and Jinn prepare to go out for patrol. And Legion… Legion doesn't say much of anything.

"Hey," I say to his back. He goes straight to the bedroom without a word and heads for the locked closet I noticed when I first arrived. He doesn't answer, so I keep talking, just to fill the awkward silence. "How did the meeting with the Seraph go?"

"Fine."

He fishes a key from his pants packet and unlocks the door, revealing—not a closet—but an armory. Illuminated with florescent lights, guns of every size and make are proudly displayed on each wall. There are also other weapons: knives, swords, crossbows, and a plethora of deadly gadgets. A small section is reserved for his fighting leathers and utility boots. No wonder he kept it locked. Even untrained, I could have done some serious damage if I had gotten in here. Still could, but he's trusting me. He's letting me in, and that fact makes his aloofness sting a tiny bit less.

"Is there something wrong?" I finally ask, shifting uncomfortably on my feet. I hate that I feel insecure. I hate that I spent the entire day getting pretty in hopes he'd like it. I hate that I even care.

"No. Just..." He sighs heavily, scrubbing a hand on the back of his neck before whipping off his beanie. The same beanie he would wear when he would come into my store. An ache of nostalgia echoes in my chest.

"Come on, L. I don't want there to be secrets between us. If it has something to do with me, then I deserve to know."

He releases another breath before training his gaze on me. "The Seraph not only know that we have you, they also know about the Jumper."

Adriel. This is about Adriel.

"And what does that mean?"

"It means that they want you too. How badly? I don't know. Maybe enough to supply demons with angel venom, although an offense that severe would result in banishment. So naturally, they're denying all knowledge of it."

"You think they could be lying? I mean, they're *angels*."

"That means nothing, Eden. The greatest evil that has ever existed was once an angel. *I* was once an angel. And you see where that got me. Trapped between two worlds, shamed and discarded."

I take a step closer, placing a tentative hand on his arm. When he doesn't move away or shrug out of my touch, I step in closer. "None of that matters, because who you are—what you are—is not defined by a name or a title or some centuries old legend. You have the capacity for goodness, integrity and fairness. And you've shown me all those things—someone who doesn't deserve that type of mercy. Give yourself some credit."

He looks away before nodding once. When he doesn't turn to look at me again, I say, "Hey, we don't have to go out tonight if you don't want to."

"No, I want to." He moves away, replacing the weapons on his person with fresh ones. "There's a full moon tonight, and I don't want to miss it. Besides, you just endured Lil for an entire afternoon. I don't envy you, but I must admit, I'm not mad at the results."

Legion gives me a look that makes my knees wobble, his ire erased and replaced with something much more carnal. I nervously touch my hair.

"You noticed?"

He mimics my gesture and his hand comes up to touch the strands of hair tangled in my fingers. "I notice everything about you, Eden. When are you going to start believing that?"

I blush and divert my eyes to the floor like a foolish schoolgirl. His searing touch vanishes, and I feel him take a step away.

"So tonight then."

I nod. "Tonight."

"Good. Let's see if I can still shock you."

And as if he hasn't already shocked me enough in the last twenty-four hours, he gives me wink before exiting the space.

Most girls would expect dinner, maybe a movie. But I get the feeling that Legion isn't the type to date. Lucky for him, neither am I.

We ride through the city under the cover of night, zipping through cars and pedestrians like a slithering black snake. We've spent more than our fair share of time together inside the Jag, but now being here with him just seems different after last night. More intimate. Like there's an electric current that constantly flows between our bodies, spiking our blood with neon sparks.

I silently wonder if he can feel it too. And as if answering my unspoken question, he releases a slow hiss between his teeth, that tick in his jaw on overtime. Either he's pissed or as turned on as I am. I'm hoping for the latter.

"We're here," he announces, pulling up to a ramshackle

building. I had been so engrossed in his presence that I didn't even notice that we had traveled to the Southside. Not just the Southside. My neighborhood. My building. Shit, this is where I used to live with Sister.

An ache radiates from gut to throat as I remember all the laughs and tears we shared within those peeling walls. I remember the way Sister's light and love had once filled the tiny space and made it a home. It was all we could afford while she was in nursing school, and even though she made enough to move afterward, she didn't want to leave me. I wouldn't let her take care of me financially, and she let me have my pride. Even though I could barely make my half of the rent and expenses, she never resented me.

I don't even notice that Legion has exited the car until he's opening my door.

"Why did you bring me here?" I whisper, my words drowned out by sirens and gangster rap pulsating from passing cars.

"Because I want to show you something. It won't take long, promise."

I nod and take his outstretched hand, letting him pull me from the vehicle. He doesn't let go when I stand, and neither do I. Not during the trek through the ramshackle lobby. Not as we take the elevator to the rooftop. Not until we step outside, feeling the crisp, cold air whipping our cheeks. He holds my hand, offering me warmth and comfort, as if he knows how difficult it is for me to be here. It hasn't been long, but already this place seems like a distant memory.

"It's empty. Abandoned," I mutter.

"I bought the building and paid off the residents. Handsomely." He shrugs sheepishly. "It really is unfit to live in. The offer to leave was received exuberantly."

"I bet. This place was a Hell hole," I remark, the irony not lost on either of us. We share a small chuckle.

"But it was your home."

"It was. But without Sister, it just seems like any other shitty dump in the city."

He nods before striding over to the ledge and looking out over the twinkling lights of Chicago. I follow him, spying the drug dealers and prostitutes that I had grown familiar with at their usual posts. The crack house across the street still has a steady stream of consumers. And Willie, the resident drunk, is staggering around in a dirty trench coat with a half empty bottle of cheap rum in his dingy palm.

This once was my home. But now it just seems like someone else's life being played out in some cliché movie about the slums of Any City, USA.

"I spent many days on this roof as you slept in your bed." His gaze is still trained on the scene stretched before us, but he's speaking to me. "I watched over you, listening to your screams through the paper-thin walls, wishing I could save you from the terrors of your nightmares. No one ever tried to help, even if they could hear you, and it sickened me."

I don't have the words to tell him that that was the norm around here. People didn't get involved with matters that didn't concern them. For all they knew, I was just that crazy girl that kept to herself. Drugs, alcohol, mental illness, domestic abuse…they were all dealing with their own problems.

"We couldn't interfere—not just yet. Not until we were certain that you were the one."

The one. Lucifer's little pet. The girl that would unleash Hell on earth.

"You said you wanted to show me something," I say, eager to shift the conversation away from me or anything remotely prophecy related. I can't stomach it, not yet.

"I told you I had certain abilities that are nullified here on earth. What is left of me is just a small fraction of what I am capable of. But still…it can be effective."

"What *can* you do?"

Legion finally looks at me, his eyes glowing brighter than the moon and the stars combined. "Let me show you."

He lifts a single palm and…nothing happens.

I expected a glow or sparks or fire, but nothing.

Seconds later, I hear the distinct sound of flapping wings approach. I can't see them all but I can hear them. It's hard not to. Dozens, maybe hundreds, of birds fill the sky, flying in formation towards us. They eclipse the full moon for several long seconds, painting it in shimmering blackness. My first instinct is to cower but Legion reassures me, telling me it's ok.

"They won't hurt you. They are my eyes and ears, my tiny, winged ambassadors."

"You speak to them?" I ask in wonder as feathered creatures of all shapes and sizes begin to rain from the sky. He's right—they don't bother me. It's as if they are all under his control.

"Yes, but not in the way that you think. I don't chirp or sing, although I've been told I can belt out a mean rendition of *Highway to Hell*."

I laugh out loud, covering my mouth with my chilled hands. "Well, I'll be damned. Legion, did you just crack a joke?"

He shrugs a single shoulder and dons an amused half grin. "Maybe I did. You didn't think I was just fire and brimstone all the time, did you?"

"No. Not at all. It's just nice to see you like this." I smile at the brute that had watched me sleep on top of his chest. The man that had laughed with me about music and junk food and comforted me in my darkest hours. I have never felt so special, so revered, than when I was in his arms.

Legion juts out a finger, allowing a small yellow and black bird to land on it. Such a fragile little thing in comparison to his size and strength. He could crush it in his palm in a heartbeat. The tiny creature cheeps and chirps as if speaking to him.

"He said it's good to see you, Eden."

My eyes grow twice in size. "What?" I swallow thickly. "He told you that? He's *seen* me?"

"They simply watched you when I couldn't. They never interfered."

"Aren't birds supposed to be south for the winter?"

"They'll leave soon," he nods. "Then other animals will be summoned to do my bidding."

I shiver. "Please tell me a bunch of rats aren't about to convene up here."

"No," he chuckles, shaking his head. "Although, I am able to control most small beings. They can come in handy when I'm called away or occupied with other missions. Larger animals are harder, more strong willed. I don't have any need for them inside the city, anyway."

"Is that all you can control?" I ask, my niggling suspicions causing the question to come out much icier than I intend.

A smug smile. "For now." He turns his attention to the little bird on his finger, his expression softening, and whispers, "Fly, little friend."

The tiny bird spreads its ombré wings and shoots into the star-speckled sky, taking the flock of feathered guardians with him. It seems as if they're all careful to avoid brushing against me, although their sheer strength and volume sends a fierce wind to stir my hair and clothing. For long moments, I'm wrapped in a cocoon of soft feathers and down, looking up in wonder at the sheer splendor of God's creatures. Legion included.

We spend the rest of the evening talking, purposely avoiding the war-torn reality below us. It's cold up here, but when Legion reaches out for me after seeing me shiver and pulls me into the warmth of his body, I can no longer feel the chill. I know I shouldn't be surprised by his affection. He doesn't seem like the type to give it freely, but he has, even when I didn't know it. That person—that monster—that threatened and assaulted me after snatching me from carnage, I don't recognize anymore. And while there are things about him that frighten me, I'm not afraid of him. To be honest, I'm more afraid of myself.

"Can I ask you a question?"

"Anything." His hot breath fans over me, warming my insides.

"What Dorian, the Dark king said to you…" I feel him stiffen at my side, but I soldier on. "What did he mean when he said, *it's been a long time*? Did you know him before?"

He shifts on his feet but doesn't let me go. "You caught

that, huh? The Dorian I met was much different from the polished royal that we sat down with. Long ago, I stumbled upon Dorian Skotos at a time when there was dissention amongst the Dark and the Light. He was cold, ruthless and power hungry, but he was also very young and unchecked. We received word about a small coven that had been siphoning humans recklessly. Since we were all at risk of exposure, and neither the Light nor the Dark could tame him, the Se7en stepped in to handle it. That was nearly two hundred years ago. He was spiraling, so filled with rage and pain. But I saw something in him—something that gave me hope for his future. I made it a point to check in with him from time to time, maybe even tried to mentor him. I liked him; I still do. And I'm glad to see he turned things around, especially for his people. It seems like his is a reign of peace."

"Wow. So he's over two hundred years old?" The gorgeous warlock couldn't be pushing thirty on his worst day. But then again, Gabriella's father, Alexander, didn't look much older.

"Older actually, but not by much. He's still fairly young, by their standards. His brother, the one I am to locate, is even younger. For him to die after merely two centuries is rare for their kind. I can understand why they'd do anything to get him back."

I lift my head to peer into his face, an obvious frown carved between my brows. "But at the expense of your life? Look, I like Gabriella, and I even like Dorian, but to ask you to die for their cause…it's selfish. It's outlandish. What kind of person would even request that?"

He gazes down at me and gently cups my cheek, gently stroking it with the callused pad of his thumb. His hot skin on mine causes a zing of electricity to surge in my gut.

"When you find something worth living for, you won't hesitate to die for it." A small, sad smile rests upon his lips. "We're all dead, firecracker, yet no one really dies. Don't worry. I'll make my way back to you."

"You promise?" I whisper.

"Even if I have to crawl my way out from the depths of Hell, I'll never leave you. Not again."

Before I can ask what he means by his heartfelt words, his mouth is on mine, and I'm drinking his scorching elixir, drunk off the taste of him. We kiss fervently, wildly, until the closeness is just not close enough.

"Come on," he pants against my lips. "Let's go home."

"Already?" I tease. I was ready to go the moment his arms wrapped around me, desperate for more of his body.

"I may not have been able to spend the day inside you, but I intend to spend the night."

Legion takes my hand and leads me to the elevator. The moment we're inside, he pushes me up against the dingy aluminum and claims my mouth, his large hands kneading my breasts through my sweater. I moan at his strength, at the palpable frenzy that seems to course through his fingertips. I want this man so much that I don't care what he is. I don't care what I am. I just need him, every bit of him, inside my body, my soul. My heart. And it doesn't make sense, but in a world full of monsters, both human and other, nothing seems more solid than the charged chemistry between us. In that, I believe.

We make it to the floor level and nearly sprint for the car, both of us laughing with lust-filled bliss. The moment we slide into the butter-soft leather seats, Legion revs the engine and takes off into the night, one hand grasping my thigh. I lay my own on top of it and intertwine my fingers with his, craving the contact.

I don't hear the sirens anymore. I don't see the criminals shuffling into the shadows, slinking further away from their humanity. I don't even feel their malice and disgust. No blood taints my tongue, for all I taste is *him*. And my city—the very same streets that chewed me up and spit me out covered in filth and blood—has never looked more beautiful.

I rest my head against the seat and smile, letting myself feel pure, unpolluted happiness for the first time since…since forever. After all that's happened, after all that will happen, I'm going to be selfish with it. I'm going to relish the feeling of Legion's hand joined with mine, and his scent of fire-spliced earth and smoke embedded in my skin. Resplendent. In this very moment, I feel resplendent beside him.

"Why don't you play us some music," he suggests, his voice husky.

I reach over and turn the dials, settling on a smooth R&B station. No hardcore hip-hop to drown out my rage and sorrow. I want music that speaks to the song in my soul.

"I like this song," Legion remarks, nodding his head. His hand on my thigh squeezes before slowly inching upwards.

"Yeah?"

"I do. It reminds me of—"

An explosion rips open the entire left side of the car, twisting the metal into ribbons of silver and glittering sparks. Glass erupts around us and rains jagged droplets onto our heads, slicing us open with tiny daggers. The barrier of sound collapses and everything around me becomes muted screeches of steel against the pavement. I gnash my teeth against it, struggling to just hang on to something, but I'm weightless, the gravity stripped from the atmosphere. I'm flying through clouds of blood and burning rubber, and I can't see ground. Not until I'm tumbling back down to Earth.

All becomes silent and still around me, despite the screams echoing in the distance. I blink against the pressure in my skull, my eyes burning with tears and blood. I smell gas and charred plastic, the noxious fumes intensifying the sick feeling in the pit of my stomach. I'm so tired. So, so tired. I just want to sleep until it doesn't hurt anymore. Until this nightmare erupts into a beautiful dream, its blinding light blotting out the ugliness surrounding me. And in that dream, Legion will be there, smiling, holding me, filling me with his brilliant heat. Soothing my ravaged body with the hardness of his.

But I don't feel his fire beside me. There's only the soiled pavement under my raw cheek and broken glass under my palms. There's only the bone-chilling emptiness of death.

TWENTY-EIGHT

I KNOW THIS ROOM.
I've felt the damp, cold cement floor under my bare feet. I've breathed the dank air, tinged with the taste of blood. I've smelled the sickening stench of rotting flesh.

My arms are bound, tied behind my back, and my legs are trapped as well. I sag in the chair I'm tethered to, the metal biting into my back. I'm covered in cuts and scrapes, some of them oozing, but at least I'm dressed. That's the only thing that's keeping me from crumbling in two. That and the fact that Legion is tied to another chair on the other side of the room. Hurt, unconscious, but breathing.

I knew all signs would lead me here, but I thought I had more time. *We* thought we had more time. *I'm not ready.* I push the words out, hoping they will reach that piece of me that's not really mine. *Adriel, if you can hear me, I'm not ready.*

No voices. No whispered commands. Just the silence of a lonely death.

"Legion," I whisper harshly, the hushed words rattling in my aching skull. "Legion, wake up!"

He groans, giving me just a flicker of hope. Clearly, whoever took us from the wreckage is an amateur. Nothing will be able to bind him once he's fully awake.

"Legion, please! Listen to me. I need you to wake up."

He groans again, and his head lolls from side to side as if he's trying to fight his way to the surface. There's a steady stream of blood trickling from a gash on his head, and his sweater is soaked with the thick, sticky substance. I have to get to him. I have to get him out of here before my nightmares come to fruition.

I pull at the rope around my wrists, but the more I struggle, the weaker I feel. Plus, it seems to be coated in some type of solution that burns my skin whenever I try to pull. I grit my teeth, take a deep breath and pull—hard. I can hear my skin sizzling, and it feels as if my arms are being dipped in battery acid, but I bite down on the scream. But despite all my struggling, the rope just won't give.

"It's coated in a very special silver mixed with angel venom. Uncomfortable for you. A little more debilitating for our friend," a sinuous voice croons. A voice that's haunted me for the past four years.

I jerk in overwhelming fright and scan the room, searching for the source. It's still empty, save for Legion and me. *It's just in my head*, I tell myself. There was an accident. I hurt myself and lost a lot of blood. I'm just hallucinating.

"You don't truly believe that, do you, Eden?"

I swallow my terror at the sound of my name on his lips. No, no, no. This isn't happening. Not yet. I shake my head as if to shake the voice from my ears.

"You're not here. This isn't happening."

"After all the time we've spent together, how can you say that? I've been with you all along, waiting for you to come to me. And here you are. All you have to do is say the words."

"No!" I shout. The word echoes and dies in the darkness.

"No?" Footsteps from behind me, although no one has passed through the entrance since I've been awake. And if he's been here the entire time…

It's him. The man from my nightmares. The stranger from the bathroom who I fucked while being licked and sucked by his female companions.

Lucifer.

Every depiction of him plastered in books or shown in movies are false. Merely scary stories to detract from the truth that stands before me, clothed in a dark, tailored suit that fits his body like a glove. He's much younger than one would expect, tall and lean like a swimmer. And his face…

I always wondered why he was said to have been God's favorite, the most beautiful and talented of all the angels. Now, I undeniably understand why.

Handsome doesn't quite seem to do it. Gorgeous seems contrite. His beauty transcends any word in any language that could possibly begin to describe it.

His eyes are just as I remembered from The Watcher's home—dark and stormy, flecked with the shades of dusk. They remind me of aurora borealis, the eerie colors ever changing. Not human. Those haunting irises rival only his extraordinarily sensual mouth that appears almost too full yet just the sight of it makes me crave the taste of his lips. His gold-dusted brown hair is perfectly styled and falls just slightly over his proud forehead. Thin nose, distinct cheekbones. His face is a work of art.

"I can make this all go away, you know. Just say the word."

I squeeze my eyes closed and turn away, refusing to look at him. "What do you want from me?"

"Oh, precious Eden. Do you really have to ask?" I suck in a terrified breath as I hear him step towards me. "You. I want you. Haven't I made that clear? You certainly understood that when we met in Irin's bathroom."

"No." I shake my head furiously, my eyes still shut tight. "It wasn't real. It wasn't real."

"But wasn't it? The way I made you feel, the way I made you moan. It felt real to me."

Another step closer, and his warm hand brushes my cheek. I jerk violently, refusing to be seduced by his touch. But the feel of his skin propels me back to that mansion, back to that bathroom. Back to me bouncing up and down on his cock with a strange woman between our thighs.

"You can still feel me, can't you?" I glare up at him through angry tears just in time to see a smug smile grace those pouty lips. "Yes, you do. You were on fire that night, Eden. You were radiant, unbound by your human inhibitions. Freedom looks so gorgeous on you. And that's just the beginning. Imagine how you could look—how you could feel—if you just surrendered yourself to me fully. You'd be unstoppable."

"Fuck you," I spit.

He laughs heartily. "You have. And you will again. It's

fate, darling. And you don't fuck with fate."

"If you think for one second that I will do anything with you, you are fucking deranged. So you might as well kill me now, because I will never, *ever* be your toy."

"My toy?" He has the nerve to look affronted, and even *that* makes me quiver. "I don't want you to be my toy, Eden. I want you to be my bride. Can't you see? All those dreams, all those thoughts I implanted in your mind to make every worthless, pathetic fuck suffer for disrespecting you…they're my gifts to you. To show you how much I care."

A slight wave of relief sweeps through me as I digest his words. It was him. *Him.* He made me do all those things. He told me to hurt, to steal, to fight. Irin was wrong about my skewed conscience. It wasn't me. The Devil made me do it.

It doesn't make me feel any better, considering I was weak enough to listen, but maybe I'm not beyond salvation. If the Se7en can seek it, why can't I? I just need to hold on long enough to find a way out of here and get Legion to safety.

"What do you want?" I ask for the second time. Keep him talking. Surely the Se7en are aware of the accident, considering there are cameras all over the city. Maybe there was some alarm system in the Jag that alerted them to distress. They *have* to be on their way.

"I told you—I want you. Your fealty. Your body. Your heart. Come with me and you can shed the filth and feebleness of this world. You will be a goddess—a queen. You will rule beside me as my equal, respected and feared by all. You will want for nothing. You will never have to spend a second on useless human emotions such as guilt or doubt. I will take care of you, Eden, the way you should've been taken care of all these years. Let me be your true family."

The temptation of his offer is undeniable, but I know that's just the evil talking. He calls to me, piercing that seed of malice down inside me that he implanted when I was just a fetus. I have to fight it. I *will* fight it.

I school the panic in my features, donning an icy mask. He's a prick that likes to hear the sound of his own voice. All I have to do is play to his narcissism long enough to give Legion a chance to come to. Hopefully, he's already awake and just faking, waiting for his chance to strike.

"And if I refuse?" I ask flatly.

A devious smirk. "Mary, dear. Can you come here?"

The blood in my ears roars so loudly that I can't even hear her shuffling towards me from some unseen part of the room. Red clouds my vision, casting her tear-streaked face in blood. Sister. Sister stands before me, naked and shivering, her arms and mouth bound. Her dark, corkscrew curls are matted and wild, and her legs are covered in dirt as if she's been imprisoned in filth. Other than that, she appears unharmed. But I know that stroke of luck will expire soon if I don't play Lucifer's game.

"If you refuse, your Legion will die, sending him back to Hell where he will spend eternity in everlasting agony. And your precious *Sister*… You'll have a little fun with her and her new friends. I may not be able to force you to come with me willingly, but I will make you wish you had. And when you realize what you've done, you'll see that Hell would have been a kindness."

I swallow down the rising bile in my throat and try to focus. Speaking out of rage and terror won't save us. If he sees how this affects me—if he knows that I am literally crumbling inside—he'll use it against me.

"Not good enough. If you want me, you have to free everyone. Release humans from the Calling and never use them again, myself included. You can never, ever infect another person."

He cocks an amused brow. "And you're in the position to negotiate?" he questions, sweeping a hand towards me. My glare is as rock solid as my resolve.

"You want me for a reason, and it isn't to be your evil bride or some other bullshit. You want an heir, and you know I can give it to you."

I flash of surprise passes his features for half a blink. "Ah, I see the warlocks have been busy. I may have to pay them a visit and remind them of their place."

"You will not. You will leave them be, just as you will leave the Se7en be."

"The Se7en?" Again, he laughs, tipping his head back. "Oh, darling Eden. Why do you think you're here? How do you think I was able to take you and their mighty leader so easily?"

Is he…is he alluding that the Se7en had something to do with this? They would never betray Legion. They love him. They respect him. And me… Well, they mostly tolerate me. Everyone except…

Cain.

The demon of murder. The villain in the story of Cain and Abel.

"Bullshit," I say, denying the thought of Cain betraying his brother. But it wouldn't be the first time.

"Oh, I'm afraid so. I guess there's been some dissention in the ranks. Seems like they're tired of Legion's little distraction." He shrugs.

"You're bluffing. They'd never go against him. They are a family, something you would know nothing about. And even if someone did want me out, they could have killed me a long time ago. So fuck you, and your mind games. I'm not falling for it."

"You don't get it, do you?" Lucifer grits, showing the first signs of frustration, and causing Sister to flinch beside him. "You don't understand just how unimportant you are to them. Truly. Even to your beloved Legion. I know him. I've loved him as my own flesh and blood, I've fought and killed and *fucked* beside him. You mean nothing to him. You are a distraction—that is all. You are one of *thousands*."

"You're lying."

"Am I? Did he tell you why he's really infatuated with you? And it has nothing to do with that pretty face or those perfect tits."

Stay strong, Eden. He's just trying to mess with your head. "I know what you're trying to do, and it won't work.

"He hasn't told you!" He claps with glee, almost giddy with the prospect of spreading more vitriol. "Let's invite him to this little party, so you can ask him for yourself. Shall we?"

He looks across the room to where Legion still slumps in his metal chair, unconscious. Then as if he's trying to lure a frightened cat, he coos, "Legion."

With a violent intake of breath, Legion jerks awake, thrashing wildly. The scents and sounds of sizzling flesh fill the atmosphere as he tries to break free from the silver-coated rope. But he's *alive*, and he's awake. Grateful tears fill my eyes.

"Nice of you to join us, old friend," Lucifer taunts.

"What the fuck did you do?" Legion rasps, baring his blood-stained teeth. I know the bindings are hurting him, but he doesn't cry out. A quick glance my way to assess my injuries, and then his murderous glare is on the beautiful beast standing before me.

"I was just getting to know our darling Eden and her sister, Mary. And you know me…we just got to talking and your name came up. You see, Eden seems to think that you may actually care about her. Ha! Yet, you haven't shared why you seem so overly interested in her, have you? You didn't tell her the best part."

"Eden has nothing to do with this. Let her go." Legion's voice is hoarse, yet the force behind his words are fierce enough make grown men wet their pants. "You have an issue with me, then stop being a fucking coward, and let's handle it. Or are you still too much of a pussy to fight your own battles?"

Lucifer chuckles as if Legion's threat is a tickle on his ribs. "Oh, I've missed you. Truly I have. Eden, did you know Legion played an intricate role in our fall from grace? It's an interesting story, actually. Now brother, shall I tell her, or you?"

"Shut your fucking mouth, you pompous dick."

Lucifer turns his attention on me, ignoring the seething demon glaring daggers at him. Yet, all I can see is Legion. Trapped, helpless. I refuse to let the people I love die like this.

"It all started when Legion and I led the Seraph…" Lucifer speaks as if all eyes are on him, refusing to give up the spotlight. He begins to pace the floor thoughtfully. "As you know, I was the favorite, but Legion was just as beloved. There was one that was particularly smitten by him. So smitten, that she defied her mate and gave herself to him. Very, very scandalous for us celestial beings, as you can imagine. But he was convinced that he was in love and nothing could keep him from her. And maybe he was, but, unfortunately, that love was not enough to save him from God's wrath.

"This was right around the time when I had become, quite frankly, bored with the politics and ass kissing, and I wasn't the only one. So when the news spread of Legion's deceit and shame, we concocted a plan—revolution. I would be the brains and the face of it, yes—because honestly, look at me—and Legion would be the muscle. We would make our own paradise, live by our own rules. We would do whatever the fuck we wanted without fear of judgment or persecution. However, poor, poor Legion's beloved did not feel the same. And he was painted as not only an adulterer, but a rapist. She said he forced himself on her."

"No, she did not!" Legion roars. "It was *you!* You lying sack of spineless shit."

"Oh, semantics. My version is much more salacious." Lucifer comes to stand in front of me again, his eyes filled with glee. I don't look away this time. I don't want to listen, but I can't help it. All the secrets, all the lies…it makes sense now. "Anyway, ever since then, he's been drowning in self-loathing and sorrow, pining after his long lost love, yada, yada, yada. What was her name again, dear brother? Was it…"

"Adriel," I whisper, the name strangling me.

"Yes!" Lucifer exclaims, feigning surprise. "Adriel. The very same angel that is now inhabiting your soul. You see, she would have taken over completely had it not been for my influence. You're welcome, by the way. But I guess a little bit of his true love is better than none."

"Don't listen to him, Eden. He's insane. Eden, look at me. Look at me, baby."

I can't. I can't look at him. I can't see the regret in his eyes. Not regret for letting me believe that it was me he desired. Regret that I found out that I am merely a body—a host—for the one he truly loves.

My tears flow freely now, but I don't make a sound. My sister is bound and naked in front of me. Her life has been ripped apart. My broken heart doesn't get to matter right now.

"I thought it was best you knew," Lucifer says quietly, almost seemingly…compassionate. Remorseful, even. He takes a step closer. "No one should be treated that way. I haven't lied to you, and I never will. He doesn't love you; he can't."

"I know." The knot in my throat throbs with every syllable.

"They're all wretched creatures, Eden. The Se7en only used you for their own selfish gain. And as soon as they were done with you, they threw you away. Just like your mother, your father. Just like everyone in your life. Left to be forgotten forever."

I don't have the strength to disagree with him. And even if I could, I don't. I know what he's saying is true.

Rapid, heavy footsteps approach, and before I can look towards the door, it bursts open, shading the room in night.

"What the fuck! You promised he wouldn't be harmed."

"Well, *I* didn't hurt him. The armored car I drove into him did." Lucifer merely shrugs at the demon that rushes to Legion's aide. It's just blow after blow after blow. I'm not sure I can take much more.

It wasn't Cain that betrayed us. He wasn't the one that set this up, handing me over to Lucifer on a silver platter coated in angel venom.

It was Lilith.

"This wasn't part of the plan," she mutters, unsheathing a blade to slice through Legion's rope. He grunts and thrashes in response.

"Get the fuck away from me, you traitor," he roars. There's rage on his face. But more than that, there's pain. Something I know all too well.

"L, I'm sorry, but…" Lilith has the fucking nerve to look hurt at his outburst. "She was tearing us apart. We can't fight the Calling, the Alliance *and* the Seraph. Lucifer promised to protect her, to respect her wishes. He vowed not to hurt her."

"True," Lucifer agrees. "And let's not leave out the little part about our sweet, little Lilith being in love with you. I swear, I don't get the appeal…"

"You did this because you're in *love* with him?" I shout. Rage and violence rush through my veins, and smother all feelings of shock and hurt. I'm nothing but a pawn—a bargaining chip. "What kind of sick, twisted bitch are you? You said he was like your brother! And you risk my life—my sister's life—over a crush? You stupid fucking cunt. I swear to God, you better be glad I'm tied up right now."

"Isn't she delightful?" Lucifer beams, only deepening Lilith's vicious snarl. I don't care what the fuck she is. Hell hath no fury like a woman scorned. She should know.

"I have spent centuries by his side, and some ugly little twit comes along, shaking her ass and tits, and suddenly, nothing else matters. Not the Se7en. Not the mission. Not me. I've been there for him! I've done everything right! And I'm supposed to stand aside and let some *human* steal his attention? I've worked too damn hard for this cause. I will not let you bury us with your sad-ass existence."

"Shut your fucking mouth, Lilith," Legion commands.

"It's true!" she shouts back. "You would risk the lives of your brothers, the future of the Se7en, for her? After all we've been through together? Tell me you love her, and I'll accept whatever punishment you demand. Tell me that you choose her over us."

Those silver eyes find mine, churning with moonlit lies and his lips part. Even with his face bloodied and etched with regret, he's still as handsome as he was the first night he walked into that corner store. I smile through the painful memory, wishing I had never seen him, wishing I had never laid eyes on such wicked beauty. Then I would never know the agony of never seeing it again.

"Let my sister go. Let all the innocent humans go. Never Call another human again. And I'll go with you. I'll do whatever you want."

"No!" Legion roars. "Don't listen to them! Eden, look at me, please!"

A slow grin spreads on Lucifer's face, and the rope at my hands and feet suddenly disintegrates. I jump from the chair, ignoring my protesting body, and wrap my arms around Sister's trembling frame.

"I'm sorry. I'm so sorry," I cry, removing her gag and the rope around her wrists. Luckily, there's no silver, but not even that could keep me from freeing her. I strip off my torn, bloodied coat and wrap it around her shoulders. "I never meant for this to happen. Are you hurt?"

"I'm ok. But Eden, you can't. Please, don't do this." But even as the words pass her cracked lips, she knows it's too late. Now she understands why I tried to keep this from her. But it wasn't enough to spare her.

I turn to Lucifer, refusing to let go of Sister. "Let her go. Make sure she's safe. Give me your word."

He nods. "As soon as you take my hand, she will be in her apartment, clothed, warm and comfortable. She won't even remember being here."

I swallow thickly, mimicking his gesture. "And them?"

"The binds will slip away. He'll be free to go." He extends a hand towards me, and offers a reassuring smile. "It will be ok. I promise, Eden. I promise to never hurt you."

I nod again and bury my face in Sister's wild mane, silently praying for strength. I'm not surprised when, once again, my pleas have fallen on deaf ears.

"I love you, Sister. Even if you don't remember this, remember that I love you."

I kiss both of her tear-stained cheeks then close my eyes, pushing my mind out to hers one last time. Fear has made the infiltration easy, and I slip in within seconds, tasting the goodness and sincerity of her sweet soul.

"Let me go."

Her arms drop to her sides immediately, allowing me to back away. *Let me go.* That's what I wanted her to do per Legion's request. He wanted me to alienate my own sister just so he could use and manipulate me for his own selfish needs. And I let him. I was all too happy to be his little pet, simply a placeholder for who he truly wanted. And now I don't have either one of them.

"Would you like to say goodbye?" Lucifer asks. I know whom he's referring to.

I look across the room to wear Legion sits, Lilith standing beside him. I trusted them. I cared for them. After all they had already done to me, I actually believed they could be redeemed. I really thought they were capable of kindness and grace and love. And now, as I look at them, I see them for the vile, disgusting creatures that they truly are.

"No."

"Eden, no! Don't do it! Please, just listen to—"

With my next breath, I exhale the crippling fear and pain that had covered me like a second skin. I let go of the human life that I had been stumbling through for twenty-two years like a ghost. I exorcise the dark, demented demons of my past, and I take Lucifer's outstretched hand.

And usher in the End of Eden.

TWENTY-NINE

"DON'T FUCKING TOUCH ME. YOU WILL NOT EVER touch me again. Do you understand?"

Legion tears his arm from Lilith's grasp, her nails scraping his already ravaged skin, and flings open the front door, nearly tearing it off the hinges. He doesn't feel the sting. He hasn't felt shit since he woke up and found Eden tied to a chair with silver on her wrists, her naked sister shivering in front of her, and him—Lucifer—smiling smugly. Fucking sadistic prick. He was going to tear his fucking throat out the very moment he had a chance.

"What happened?" Phenex leaps from his place on the couch and bounds over to the entranceway within seconds, the others on his heels.

"*She* is what happened," Legion snarls, pointing a bloodied finger at Lilith, who stands by the door, tears shining in her eyes. "She is a fucking traitor and has betrayed the Se7en."

"Please, L. Just listen to me. It was for the best. For the greater good—the very thing that we're fighting for."

"Where's Eden?" Phenex questions. Yet, the scene before him is answer enough.

Legion brushes past his brothers, each of them painted in varying shades of shock. "She set us up. She gave him exactly what he needed to make his plan work. He has her now. Fuck! That spineless fuck has her." He tears at his blood-matted hair and bounds down the long hallway, stopping at the first door to the left. The rest of the Se7en—Lilith included—are right behind him.

"Are you fucking kidding me?" Cain shrieks. "Lil, please tell me this is a mistake and you would not be stupid enough to betray us."

The teary-eyed blonde sobs silently, unable to refute the allegations.

"Holy fuck," the scarred demon remarks, shaking his head. He looks at his brother, his leader. "What are we going to do?"

The band of demons enter the room, watching as Legion stalks to the pillar showcasing their sacred dagger, The Redeemer. He picks it up, and hands it to Phenex.

"Use it."

"What?" Phenex shakes his head, shoving it back into Legion's palms. "That's ludicrous. L—brother—please be reasonable."

Refusing to hear his words, he offers it to Cain. "Don't be a fucking coward. Do it. Kill me. It's the only way I can get to her."

"L, I hear you. But this isn't the way. If you're gone, the Se7en are done. Then what?"

"Then you'll lead them. Or Phenex. I don't give a fuck. I have to get to her. Now!"

"Please, Legion. I'm so sorry," Lilith cries in the corner. "Don't do this! Please!"

"Someone get her the fuck out of here! I never want to see her traitorous face again. Get the fuck out before I rip you apart with my bare fucking hands!" Desperate rage coats his venomous tongue, causing Lilith to sob harder.

"Come on, Lil," Andras whispers, ushering her from the room. He spares a sorrowful glance towards Legion before disappearing to the room next door.

"Maybe there's another way…some loophole we're not seeing," Toyol offers. He looks to Jinn, who wears the same grim mask as everyone else. "There has to be something we're missing, right? Another way to anchor him to earth and bring him back."

Jinn releases a heavy breath and shakes his head, casting his glance to the ritual circle etched into the floor.

"Shit. I'm sorry, L." Toyol scrubs the back of his neck, just as panic seizes his features. He snatches a small, black device attached to his waistband and curses. "Dammit. An alarm was tripped, but…" He looks at the tiny monitor, switching through screen after screen of surveillance. "There's no one… wait. Is that…? I'll be back."

Toyol slips out of the room to grab his Katanas with Jinn on his trail. To be honest, they're grateful for the intrusion; neither one of them could do what Legion was requesting, and they couldn't stand the look of dejection in his eyes. Their brother was hurting, and they could feel it. His pain was their pain, and they had never felt anything quite like the intensity of his suffering. Losing Eden was bad enough, but Legion too? After centuries of camaraderie and companionship? They'd have no part in their friend's death wish.

"L, let's calm down for a second and think about this," Phenex suggests, his palms raised. "Say you do go back. You find her. Then what? How will you bring her back here when you can no longer enter this realm? Then what good would you be to her? We need a plan. One that ensures that you both come back safely."

"And if she's there, then she chose to go," Cain adds, pacing the circle. "She chose him, L. Maybe you should accept that."

A visceral growl rips from Legion's throat as he trains his murderous glare on his closest friend. "She didn't choose him. We were set up. It was either me and her sister, or her. And *fuck*…she submitted to him in exchange for our release. And I'll be damned if I sit around and let her sacrifice herself for nothing. That should have been me. Don't you all see that? I should have been the one to sacrifice for her." Again, he holds out the dagger to Phenex. He's the logical one, the even-tempered one. He'll understand how important Eden is to him. Only he knows of the love he once had, and lost. And finding Eden—not Adriel—gave him hope again. He finally knew what it felt like to be alive.

Reluctantly, Phenex takes The Redeemer into his hands, running his thumb over the rubies embedded in the hilt. "And you're absolutely sure? You are irrevocably certain that this is what you want to do?"

"No, it's not," Cain interjects behind his two brothers, cursing furiously. "He's being a fucking fool."

Ignoring his brother, Legion rips off his bloody, tattered sweater, revealing the dark ink etched in his tanned skin. His cuts and bruises have already healed, although the welts around his wrists are still red and angry. It doesn't matter. The second he steps foot back into Hell, he'll be able to walk in any form of his choosing.

"I made a vow, Phenex. To her…to all of you. I gave my life to this cause because I was lost and searching for redemption. But in reality, I was searching for her. I have been since the day I was cast out of Heaven. Not Adriel. But *her*—Eden. I told you all before…I will protect her or die trying." He lifts his chin, offering the column of his throat. His chest heaves with the last of his jagged breaths on Earth. "Well, I'm not dead. Yet."

Want more?
Dive into the Dark Light series, and get to know
Dorian Skotos…intimately.

Other works by S.L. Jennings:
Ink & Lies
Taint
Tryst
Fear of Falling
Afraid to Fly

ACKNOWLEDGEMENTS

I am incredibly fortunate to have had so many amazing people in my corner during the creation of this book. I honestly could not have done this alone, and it's comforting to know that they believed in me enough to keep pushing me…keep inspiring me. I am extremely blessed to have them in my life.

Maureen Sytsma: Woman, you are my rock. No disrespect to my husband, but you are definitely my better half in all things bookish. I can't thank you enough for all you do day-to-day to keep me on track, and ensuring the S.L. Jennings brand continues to grow. Thank you, Mo, for having my back. You are a great friend, as well as a kick ass personal assistant.

My betas, Sunny Borek, Kristina Lowe, Andrea Kelleher, and Lauren Bille: Thank you, ladies, for your honesty and encouragement. It's been a pleasure working with you, and I hope we can continue to create magic together. Not many people would put up with my nagging and demands, and I am lucky to be able to rely on you for feedback, as well as lean on you with my concerns. Thanks for your friendship, your listening ears, and your help in making Born Sinner the best it can be.

My squad…the SLJ Unicorns: Thank you so much for all the pimping, sharing and enthusiasm! You women are killer, and it is because of YOU that people know about this story. Let's continue to spread the sparkly rainbow love. We got this!

The Jonesin' for S.L. Jennings reader group: As always, I am blown away by your love and support for my stories, and I hope that I can continue to entertain you. Thank you so much for sticking by me over these past few years. I appreciate every one of you!

BBFT: What an amazing group of reader bishes! You all are incredible, and I hope our little bookish haven continues to grow. Thanks for all the laughs and support!

The author friends that continue to push me, inspire me and encourage me—Mia Asher, Claire Contreras, Corinne Michaels, Tillie Cole, Leylah Attar, Mandi Beck, K.A. Linde, Amelia Hutchins, Mary Elizabeth, CD Reiss, Tijan, Brittainy C. Cherry, Karina Halle, SL Scott, Tarryn Fisher, Tee Tate, Colleen Hoover, Jessica Prince, RK Lilley and Cynthia Rodriguez: I love you. I appreciate you. This book world is a better place because of you.

The bloggers that consistently show their support and love: Black Heart Reviews, The Rock Stars of Romance, The Scarlet Siren, Kindle Crack, Totally Booked, Angie and Jessica's Dreamy Reads, Schmexy Girl Book Blog, Two Book Pushers, Shh Mom's Reading, SBC, Garden of REden, Erotica Book Club, Blushing Babes are Up All Night, Ana's Attic, Beauty & Heartbreak, and so many more (sorry if I missed anyone!): You all are the best! And I am forever grateful for everything you have done for me and my career. Thank you!

The chicks that make my heart smile with their killer teaser pics—The Reading Ruth, Bookish Life, Bossy Book Pusher, Book Whores and Crazy Book Lovers: Thank you for making my words beautiful. You all are so incredibly talented, and I am so honored by your support.

The folks that rocked the hell out of the Born Sinner Cover:
Hang Le- You did it again, girl! Working with you is a dream, and I am so excited for what the future holds with this series. Your talent and creativity continue to amaze me.
Tess Farnsworth Photography- Thank you so, so much for capturing my vision and helping to create something phenomenal. I am so honored to have worked with you!
Maud Artistry- I only see amazing things for you ladies, and I am so proud to be able to witness it. Thank you so much for believing in me, and devoting your time and effort into crafting something incredible!
Tyson Holley- Working with you was perfect! Thank you so much for being so personable and professional, and bringing L to life. Wishing you much success!
Durkin's Liquor Bar- Thank you so much for allowing us to use your gorgeous space. It was truly inspiring!

The folks that rocked the hell out of the words:
My editor, Tracey Buckalew- We did it again, babe! Thank you for all you've done for me and my words. This makes book seven… Let's do it again!
My proofreader, Kara Hildebrand- You are amazing, woman. I appreciate your kindness, professionalism and friendship. Thank you!
My formatter, Champagne Formats- Stacey, you continue to

blow my freakin' mind. Born Sinner has to be my favorite format of all time. I am so proud to have worked with you, and can't wait to create more magic!

My amazing readers: Without you, there is no S.L. Jennings. There's just a girl with crazy ideas that rambles on about fictional worlds steeped in magic and myth. Thank you for giving me a voice and a platform. Thank you for believing in my words and purchasing my books. Thank you reading, reviewing and shouting your enthusiasm from the rooftops. Thank you for helping to make my dreams come true.

My family: Tim, Tzion, Tzuriel and Tzachai… Everything I do is for you. None of this would mean a thing without you all in my corner. Thank you for allowing me to chase my dreams, and keeping me grounded with your love. I hope to continue to make you proud.

If I managed to forget anyone, please chalk it up to my head and not my heart. I am so grateful for what I have achieved, and know that I could not do it alone. So if you're reading this… Thank you.

Always,
Syreeta

ABOUT THE AUTHOR

Most known for her starring role in a popular sitcom as a child, S.L. Jennings went on to earn her law degree from Harvard at the young age of 16. While studying for the bar exam and recording her debut hit album, she also won the Nobel Prize for her groundbreaking invention of calorie-free wine. When she isn't conquering the seas in her yacht or flying her Gulfstream, she likes to spin elaborate webs of lies and has even documented a few of these said falsehoods.

Some of S.L.'s devious lies:

Ink & Lies

FEARLESS SERIES
Fear of Falling
Afraid to Fly

SEXUAL EDUCATION SERIES
Taint
Tryst

THE DARK LIGHT SERIES
Dark Light
The Dark Prince
Nikolai (a Dark Light novella)
Light Shadows

Printed in Great Britain
by Amazon